PRAISE FOR THE NOVELS OF
Penny McCall

Packing Heat

"A great story, nonstop action, snappy dialogue, witty humor, and chemistry between the hero and heroine that is white-hot. I'm very happy to give *Packing Heat* the highest possible recommendation." —*Romance Junkies*

"This action-filled novel will knock your socks off with intense chemistry and intrigue that holds your attention from the first page. An awesome read!" —*Fresh Fiction*

"[A] fast-paced thriller . . . Action-packed romantic suspense." —*Midwest Book Review*

Ace Is Wild

"Humor and witty repartee are sure signs that you are reading a McCall romance." —*Romantic Times* (4 stars)

"This story is a keeper . . . Don't walk but run to the nearest bookstore and pick up *Ace Is Wild*." —*Night Owl Romance*

Tag, You're It!

"The characters are smart and witty, and the chemistry between them is crackling, making the happy ending well worth the wait. I can hardly wait now for her next book." —*BellaOnline*

S0-ADH-392

All Jacked Up

Titles by Penny McCall

ALL JACKED UP
TAG, YOU'RE IT!
ACE IS WILD
PACKING HEAT
THE BLISS FACTOR

Anthologies

DOUBLE THE PLEASURE
(with Lori Foster, Deirdre Martin, and Jacquie D'Alessandro)

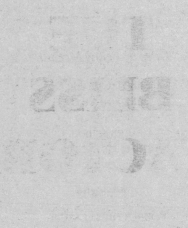

THE BLISS FACTOR

Penny McCall

BERKLEY SENSATION, NEW YORK

THE BERKLEY PUBLISHING GROUP
Published by the Penguin Group
Penguin Group (USA) Inc.
375 Hudson Street, New York, New York 10014, USA
Penguin Group (Canada), 90 Eglinton Avenue East, Suite 700, Toronto, Ontario M4P 2Y3, Canada
(a division of Pearson Penguin Canada Inc.)
Penguin Books Ltd., 80 Strand, London WC2R 0RL, England
Penguin Group Ireland, 25 St. Stephen's Green, Dublin 2, Ireland (a division of Penguin Books Ltd.)
Penguin Group (Australia), 250 Camberwell Road, Camberwell, Victoria 3124, Australia
(a division of Pearson Australia Group Pty. Ltd.)
Penguin Books India Pvt. Ltd., 11 Community Centre, Panchsheel Park, New Delhi—110 017, India
Penguin Group (NZ), 67 Apollo Drive, Rosedale, North Shore 0632, New Zealand
(a division of Pearson New Zealand Ltd.)
Penguin Books (South Africa) (Pty.) Ltd., 24 Sturdee Avenue, Rosebank, Johannesburg 2196,
South Africa

Penguin Books Ltd., Registered Offices: 80 Strand, London WC2R 0RL, England

This is a work of fiction. Names, characters, places, and incidents either are the product of the author's imagination or are used fictitiously, and any resemblance to actual persons, living or dead, business establishments, events, or locales is entirely coincidental. The publisher does not have any control over and does not assume any responsibility for author or third-party websites or their content.

THE BLISS FACTOR

A Berkley Sensation Book / published by arrangement with the author

PRINTING HISTORY
Berkley Sensation mass-market edition / February 2010

Copyright © 2010 by Penny McCusker
Cover design by Rita Frangie
Cover art by Tony Mauro
Interior text design by Laura K. Corless

ISBN: 978-0-425-23307-8

BERKLEY® SENSATION
Berkley Sensation Books are published by The Berkley Publishing Group,
a division of Penguin Group (USA) Inc.,
375 Hudson Street, New York, New York 10014.
BERKLEY® SENSATION and the "B" design are trademarks of Penguin Group (USA) Inc.

PRINTED IN THE UNITED STATES OF AMERICA

10 9 8 7 6 5 4 3 2 1

To all the Renaissance faire
re-enactors, vendors, and volunteers:
You are crazy and wonderful people!
Thank you for the hours of enjoyment you've given me.
I'll see you in September!

chapter
1

"STEP LOIVLEY THERE, DARLIN'."

"Yeah, c'mon, milady, move yer arse."

Rae Blissfield gave the loudmouth behind her a baleful look. Not surprisingly he sported full facial hair and Robin Hood tights. Thankfully he had a big enough belly to hide what his tunic didn't. She stepped forward, handed the buxom wench her admission ticket and walked through the stone entry arch of the Michigan Renaissance festival in Holly Grove, knowing it was going to get worse than grown adults sporting mock homespun and bad British accents. A lot worse.

And boy was she right.

Quasimodo, hump, gimlet eye, rags, and all, handed her a booklet and a map, but she couldn't go anywhere because she had to wait for the Queen of England, waving regally to her lowly subjects, to parade by. Her Majesty was followed by her ladies-in-waiting, court jesters, bagpipers, tradespeople with signs hawking their wares, and an assortment of kooks wearing costumes from four different centuries and every socioeconomic group imaginable, including leprous beggars.

It wasn't all bad, Rae told herself, taking a mental stab at optimism. It was early October, Indian summer, and the sun was shining in a cloudless blue sky. The air was the kind of crisp that followed a week of rain, and although she should have been thrilled to be outside in a wooded grove instead of stranded in an office staring at a computer screen, really she was in hell.

Hell was populated by crowds of tourists gnawing on roasted turkey legs, and otherwise sane artisans wearing medieval dress in a desperate attempt to unload wooden swords and plastic Celtic crosses on consumers caught up in medieval fever. Hell was women who thought it was attractive to have their breasts cinched up to their clavicles, and men who hadn't thought through all the ramifications of an outfit that included a short tunic and tights.

Rae had on a cream linen suit, the skirt a perfect inch above her knee, and bone-colored pumps with a sensible heel, and she was the one getting the weird looks. But then she'd always felt out of place at these things, even as a kid wearing whatever getup her mother had dredged up out of her imagination—which could have been anything from a fairy costume, complete with gossamer wings, to the rags of a fourteenth-century beggar. The woman could have been a successful costume designer, but instead she chose to live in hell.

As always this thought made Rae roll her eyes and smile indulgently at the same time. Despite her residual childhood resentments she loved her parents. Why else would she take an afternoon off with quarter-end rapidly approaching? Now if she could only figure out where they were.

The place was a maze of food stands, small stages where comedians or dancers performed, and booths with vendors selling everything under the sun. Annie Bliss would be painting faces or braiding flowers into wreaths. Nelson Bliss would be selling the beautiful hand-screened textiles her mother designed and he made. Rae did their taxes every year, and only because she ignored her father's tirades about the demon government. Amazingly they did all right, very little overhead, traveling around in a camper, more often than not parking in some friend's yard between shows. It wasn't right for her, but it suited her parents.

She pulled out Quasimodo's map and unfolded it, working her way through the place in an efficient, methodical manner, until she came to a crowd that stretched from one side of the wide dirt path to the other. And it was all women. That didn't pique her interest; she was a goal-oriented kind of girl, and her goal was finding the Blisses and getting back to work. It barely registered that most of the women were in advanced stages of hormonal upheaval, staring slack-jawed, fanning themselves, sighing. One glimpse of sweaty, flexing muscles, and Rae made the fervor unanimous. She was focused, not undersexed.

She lifted onto her toes and managed to spy a carefully banked fire within a shedlike opening, decorated with intricate metalwork pieces and medieval weaponry, and filled with a half-naked man. A tall, bare-chested, rugged-looking man with dark, shoulder-length hair and arresting blue eyes. Of course, it took her a minute to get to the eyes. No sense rushing things, she thought, dropping her gaze to the dirt floor of the shed and working her way up over knee-high boots with homespun britches tucked into them. He wore a leather apron over the britches—disappointingly—but the scenery improved from there. Six-pack abs, pecs the size of dinner plates, and biceps she couldn't have spanned with both hands. His neck was corded, his face was square-jawed, and then there were his eyes, bright blue and laser sharp against his black hair and tanned skin.

He looked up, their gazes met, and Rae felt it all the way to her toes, where it boomeranged back up and clamored for notice in body parts she ought not to be thinking about. Those body parts would only get her in trouble, and anyway, her feet seemed to be in charge at the moment because she found herself standing between the front of the crowd and a wooden railing with no idea how

she'd gotten there except that raw impulse had had something to do with it. She didn't usually let impulse anywhere near her. But she wasn't moving. She'd look up her
parents, she told herself, just as soon as she found her way
out of those impossibly blue eyes.

He gave her directions by smiling. Her eyes dropped to
his mouth, white teeth behind a smug grin, and she began
to feel something besides lust. She felt foolish. She felt
her feet again, too, but unfortunately she was surrounded
by a solid wall of women, most of whom were just a hor-
mone surge away from jumping the railing and trampling
her in the process.

The object of everyone's attention wasn't helping the
situation any. He turned to face the fire, the back view just
as impressive as the front, consisting as it did of wide
shoulders, tapering down to a narrow waist and hips, his
lower half clothed in buff-colored pants so tight they appeared to be painted over a really, *really* nice butt. He
started working the bellows, the muscles in his back and
arms flexing impressively.

The fire wasn't the only thing whipped into a frenzy.

The crowd lunged forward, shoving the front row, including Rae, into the railing. The entire enclosure shuddered; the man spun around and scowled. The onlookers
froze, then took one step back. In unison.

Rae rolled her eyes. Sure, he was drop-dead gorgeous
in a medieval, man-is-the-master-race kind of way. The
attitude could probably be overlooked, or at least ignored
if she chose to concentrate on the form-fitting pants and
bare everything else. But he was counting on that.

"Whatever he's selling," a woman behind Rae said, "I'm
buying."

Tall, dark, and sweaty met Rae's eyes, just the hint of a
smirk lifting the corners of his mouth.

She popped up one eyebrow and shook her head
slightly, unimpressed. It was a bit more work not to get
swept up in the silent conversation they seemed to be having. He saved her again by turning back to the fire. He
took a red-hot piece of steel out of the flames with a set of

pincers, and carried it to a crude-looking table facing the audience. Rae managed to ignore his raw sexual magnetism long enough to see that he was making something intricate, a gauntlet or maybe a chain mail hood.

He might have the body of a blacksmith, but he used the careful touch of a watchmaker, bending over a small anvil and working the steel into something that resembled a wafer-thin leaf. He quenched the leaf in water then straddled a bench, legs spread wide, apron hiking up. Everyone but Rae let out a sigh. There was so much air moving it was a wonder he wasn't blown onto his ass in the dirt. But then, that would have ruined the show.

Two men burst through the back of the booth and added the only other ingredient that could have made the situation more irresistible to a bunch of lust-stricken women. Danger.

The men were dressed like Disney's idea of pirates, scruffy beards, pantaloons, bad teeth and all, and they were brandishing swords. They split, coming at the blacksmith from either side. He jumped onto the bench, balancing on the thin plank of wood while both his attackers raised their swords and rushed him. They nearly chopped each other's heads off when their target spun out from between them, tore the red-hot poker from the fire, and turned in time to face off against them.

He parried one pirate with the poker, slashing at the other with a two-foot blade he plucked from the wall, then changing up to thrust with the poker and block with the sword. The pirates traded a look and then attacked simultaneously. The blacksmith's arms were a flurry of motion almost too fast to follow as he danced around to keep either one of the men from getting behind him.

The fight was staged, but the peril seemed so real the crowd's reaction might as well have been choreographed, too. They swayed and flinched on cue, gasped and sighed in chorus, clutching at each other when one of the combatants made a particularly good attack or defense.

Rae had the urge for a tub of buttered popcorn and a box of Jujubes. It was just like an action flick, complete

with the cut hero facing off against superior forces . . .
Okay, it was only two to one, and they couldn't compare
with the armorer's skills, but there didn't really seem to
be any contest. Yet, just when she was sure he was going
to fight them off with no trouble, he faltered. His legs
went wobbly, and he shook his head a couple of times,
like he was trying to clear it. One of the attackers took
advantage of the seeming weakness, his slashing stroke
leaving a thin line of red along the armorer's biceps.

Fake blood. Or was it? Rae leaned close. Hard to get a
good look at the wound, what with the guy snapping back
to full alertness, and dancing around the other two men.
But she could have sworn the wound was dripping,
slowly, and fake blood didn't drip. She lifted her eyes to
the armorer's face, but there was no pain there. He didn't
acknowledge the wound in any way. If possible he moved
even faster, beating the two men back by sheer force. And
when he managed to return the favor by singeing the man
who'd pinked him, the pirates apparently had enough.
The wounded man took off, his partner hot on his heels.

The armorer stood there for a moment, his impressive
chest heaving as he watched his attackers disappear into
the crowd. Then he turned, and his eyes met Rae's again,
piercing blue, primed for violence. Or maybe sex because
he vaulted over the low rail directly in front of her,
slipped one arm around her waist, and took her mouth.

She should have protested, her brain was instructing
her to take issue with this . . . assault. She even raised her
hands, intending to shove him off. Instead, her fingers
flexed into rock-hard muscle, and she sank into the kiss.
Her breath oozed out with a little sigh, her tongue tangled
with his, and she lost track of her body aside from the fact
that it was pressed tightly to his and tingling from head to
toe. Then he let her go, so quickly she stumbled before
she found her feet again.

He bowed to the audience and stalked off, leaving the
fire to tend itself—the one inside the enclosure and the
one outside, most of which seemed to have moved up into
Rae's face.

Shutting out the giggles and whispers of the crowd, Rae turned on the heel of one Italian leather pump and strode off in the opposite direction, to find her parents. She needed to solve whatever problem they were having and get back to work, in that order. But it was going to be hell concentrating on numbers.

chapter
2

IT TOOK ANOTHER HOUR AND A LOT OF AIMLESS
wandering, but Rae finally spied her father working at his
loom in the shade of a huge, spreading oak next to a small
wooden building crammed with wench dresses and jester
tights.

"That's different," she said, bending to take a closer
look at the cloth on his loom, so finely woven she couldn't
see the individual threads.

Nelson Bliss shot to his feet and gathered her close,
laughing slightly as he rocked her from side to side, so
happy to see her it brought tears to her eyes. She'd never
intended to leave her parents behind when she'd run away
from the lifestyle. She had, though, and it was moments
like this when she understood the price she'd paid for her
so-called normalcy.

They broke the hug, Nelson looking down while Rae
blinked furiously, both of them avoiding the emotion. Rae
might have inherited her mother's looks, but she'd ended
up with her father's reserve. The nomad gene had by-
passed her completely.

"The color's amazing, Dad," she said, using the stiff

cloth as a tension breaker, then taking a closer look when it really caught her eye, the off-white covered in places by shimmering copper swirls that transformed to a pretty spring green depending on the angle. The colors had been applied more than dyed, she saw before Nelson flipped a piece of rough linen over the loom. "What are you going to make out of it?" she asked him.

"Um . . . It's a surprise for your mother. Don't say anything, you know how these people love to gossip."

"Sure. Is everything okay? You look tired." He looked more than tired. He looked . . . sick, was her first reaction, followed by a thumping heart and an urge to dial 9-1-1.

He waved her off and turned away. "I'm fine."

He clearly wasn't, but when she got past that instant of panic that her father, one of the pillars of her life no matter how far apart they were, was ill, she could tell it wasn't physical. Something was preying on him, though. New lines of stress wrinkled his forehead and bracketed his mouth, and he looked unhappy and closed off—more than usual.

"Something's wrong," Rae said.

Nelson took a deep breath and let it out slowly, his way of calming his nerves. Those nerves wouldn't have anything to do with her mother. Rae had never known two people so like-minded and so devoted to one another that nothing short of death . . .

Her heart thumped again. "Mom—"

"Your mother's fine, too. C'mon." He nipped next door and asked the woman at the dragon candle shop to watch his place, then led Rae a little way down a narrow path running behind the maze of stalls, to a small gate leading back to the twenty-first century, or as close as it got for the hard-core re-enacters and craftspeople who followed the faires from one town to another.

Civilization consisted of a labyrinth of potholed dirt lanes along which RVs, pop-up trailers, campers towed by an assortment of aging vehicles, and various other so-called living quarters rubbed shoulders with each other in an amicable mishmash of a mobile neighborhood. Rae

followed her father along the road, picking her way carefully around puddles and large rocks, finally giving up
any attempt to spare herself when he went cross-country,
taking her through knee-high weeds between a state-of-
the-art RV and something resembling a wigwam.

"Here we are," he said, turning in time to see her holding up the sides of her skirt, surveying the wet, muddy
mess of her own bare legs and once pristine shoes.

"I'm sorry," he said, reaching into his pocket, she thought
for a handkerchief. He pulled out a phone instead and flipped
it open.

"You have an iPhone? And you know how to text?"

"Things have changed," he said, looking sheepish. "I'll
give you my number. And your mother's."

Too late to keep her from wasting a couple of hours
looking for them, not to mention the embarrassment of
being accosted by a complete stranger. Except embarrassment wasn't exactly the residual impression, Rae
thought, remembering those warm, hard muscles, and that
hot, talented mouth and how strong and broad he'd felt
under her hands, how she'd lost her breath and grown
dizzy as she fell into him, the sexual spell he cast so
overwhelming she forgot where she was, what she was
doing, and what kind of kook she was doing it with . . .
And then he'd let her go and walked away like she'd been
just another woman in the crowd. Which was exactly
what she'd been. Her brain got it, flashing back to the
snickers and the whispers and the humiliation. Her body
held out hope.

She fell into step with her father as he started down the
road, trying to eject the armorer from her mind—and any
other body parts that were currently re-experiencing that
kiss, not to mention all that . . . manhood plastered against
her.

She was grateful when her parents' familiar old Airstream travel trailer, with its lifetime of distracting memories, came into sight. To some it would be vintage, with
its shiny aluminum skin and the rounded corners that
came straight off a sixties' drawing board. To her parents

it was home, as lovingly cared for as any brick or frame house on a square of suburban lawn. To Rae, it represented the past, okay to visit as long as she didn't have to stay too long.

"Air-conditioning?" she asked when her father opened the door and coolness flooded out.

"Your mother insisted," Nelson said. "Something about power surges. I tried to ask her how using more electricity, which only adds to global warming, could possibly be a remedy for power surges. I mean, we only live in this little trailer, but driving it from place to place, using all that fossil fuel, is a big enough carbon footprint, if you ask me, and we use just as much water as anyone else so—"

"Dad."

The tirade cut off abruptly, Nelson Bliss blinked owlishly at his daughter for a second or two before he remembered where the conversation had started. "You don't know what she meant, do you?"

Rae almost chuckled, her father was so endearingly clueless. "She was probably talking about hot flashes."

"Oh," he said looking relieved. And then the mysterious-female-drama angle hit him, not to mention the fact that he was discussing it with his daughter, and his face turned red. "Ahh . . ."

"The air-conditioning feels good," she said, putting the conversation back on comfortable ground for them both.

"Just between you and me, it's kind of nice to come into all this cool after a long day in the heat and the crowds and the dust. Speaking of which, why don't you clean up while we're waiting."

Rae did just that, but she left the bathroom door open. "What's with all the mystery?" she called out over the sound of running water. Her skirt could be dry-cleaned, but her shoes were a dead loss, waterlogged and mud-stained. She gave up on them and settled for washing the dirt off her legs. "Is Mom okay? Aside from the wonky internal thermostat?"

"Mom is fine, wonky thermostat and all" came an unmistakable voice, the one from all her worst memories. And her best.

Rae poked her head out the bathroom door and there was Annie Bliss, a circlet of flowers on her head, her hair falling in wild curls to her waist, the copper mixed liberally with white strands so shiny it looked more like highlights than gray. She wore a cream-colored peasant blouse under a bright green, ankle-length tunic dress, the hem wet almost to her knees, her bare feet muddy in hemp shoes.

Rae's suit and leather pumps cost more than her parents made in a week. And she would have given a year's salary to carry herself with the same confidence, the same disinterest in anyone else's opinion, as her slim, beautiful mother.

"Sunshine!" Annie Bliss exclaimed, arms out, crowding into the tiny bathroom to hug her only child.

The embrace was just as tight and just as long as her father's, and Rae felt just as nostalgic, but there was a different dynamic with her mother, a history of conflict that had Rae pulling away sooner.

"I've missed you, Sunny."

"It's Rae, remember?" she said, avoiding the hand that lifted, not to smooth her hair, but to pull at the clip holding it in the sleek bun.

Some children would find it refreshing to have a mother who pushed them to be a free spirit, but Rae had always craved structure. And so she'd rebelled, if you could call it rebellion to refuse to picket and protest. She'd changed her name, for starters. Sunshine Bliss just didn't suit her. Rae Blissfield was steady and dependable, some might add closed off to that list, maybe even a little repressed and straitlaced. But if other people wanted to label her that was their problem. Rae knew who she was. She'd *chosen* who she was. How many people could say that?

"I like my hair up," she said.

"You have such beautiful hair."

Rae made a face and changed the subject. "Why did you call, Mom?"

Her mother sighed, backing out of the bathroom. Rae followed her down the hallway into the kitchen, even more cramped with three adults crowded into it. Annie stopped by the door, Rae perched on the edge of the bench seat curving round three sides of the table, and her father leaned back against the tiny galley sink, smiling at the two of them falling into the same old routine. And since routine was her thing, how could Rae be angry about it?

"You would have come to visit anyway," Annie said.

"Yes, but you wanted me here *today*."

"Just tell her," Nelson said.

Rae frowned when Annie stayed uncharacteristically silent. "You know you can tell me anything," she said. "I mean, we have our moments, but . . . you're my mom."

"I'm glad to hear you say that because I have a pretty big favor to ask."

"That's an understatement," Nelson muttered.

The look Annie shot in his direction had him doing an I'm-staying-out-of-it routine—one-shouldered shrug, hands and eyebrows raised, little take-it-away gesture. Annie might be wearing a dress but her status in the marriage was undisputed.

"I was wondering if a friend of ours could stay with you for a little while," she said to Rae.

"Why?"

"Because we asked for your help."

"For whom?"

"A friend," her mother repeated with a bit of an edge to her voice.

"How long?"

"All these questions," Annie said huffily. "I thought you were an accountant, not a journalist."

"I'm being asked to take in a complete stranger. It would be nice to have a little information before I make a decision."

"You know *us*," Annie said, sounding and looking hurt.

Rae refused to be manipulated. "I know you, Mom, but I'm not you. I can't jump first and ask questions later."

Annie threw up her hands. "Here we go. First you insult me, and next I'll have to hear how horrible your childhood was."

Rae looked to her father, staying carefully neutral, then back to her mother. Her first impulse was to defend herself, but that would only take her somewhere she didn't want to go. Her mother might be unconventional, but she used guilt as well as any churchgoing Catholic. One minute Rae would be giving reassurances and professing her love, the next she'd be agreeing to take in this *friend* of theirs, no questions asked.

"Who is it?" she asked again. "Why do I need to take him or her in, and for how long?"

Annie dropped the theatrics, pressing her lips together for a second before smiling slightly. "You're determined to ruin my fun, aren't you?"

"Fun?"

"I only get to mother you once a year. I was trying to fit it all in."

Rae had to smile over that. "I'll consider myself mothered."

Annie kissed her on the forehead. "Now you can consider yourself mothered."

Even though Rae was savoring that moment of accord she knew there was some misdirection and manipulation involved, too. "Why can't this friend of yours stay with you?"

"The trailer isn't that big, and three's a crowd," her father said, winking at her mother.

Rae grimaced, as much for the heat rushing into her cheeks as the *ewwwww* factor. She ought to be past the my-parents-have-sex revulsion. Or maybe a child never got past it, no matter how old they were. "It's just not a good time," she said, getting back to the real problem. "I'm up for partner."

"You're always up for partner," Annie said, "and that putz of a boss of yours will never give it to you until you stand up for yourself."

"I can handle Mr. Putz—Mr. Putnam," she amended

before she started to think of him as Mr. Putz and stood a chance of slipping and actually calling him Mr. Putz to his face because she became pretty absentminded when she was deep into someone else's finances. "You take care of your stray."

"It's life or death—"

"Mom," she said, making it a three-syllable verbal eye roll.

Annie toned down the drama, but she made up for it with sincerity. Very intense sincerity. She took both her daughter's hands, squeezing them for emphasis. "He's special, Sunny."

A man then, that made things a bit uncomfortable. "I'm not sure—"

"He's perfectly safe. We've known him for . . ."

"What?" she asked when her mother stopped to calculate the time. "A few weeks? You're probably lucky he hasn't killed you in your sleep."

"Three, no four months. And he's not the first young man we've taken under our wings."

"No, he's not. You took in strays my whole life, and you were lucky you never got tied up with a bad one."

"Do you think it was just luck?" Annie demanded "That we would have let anyone near you we weren't sure of?"

"No," Rae mumbled, eyes dropping to her lap.

Her mother cupped her cheek. "If I'd had any idea you were frightened, that you didn't feel safe . . ."

It was worse than that, Rae thought. She'd felt she wasn't enough for them, that she was a disappointment or they wouldn't have needed someone else to look after.

"We didn't need luck," Nelson said, his calm voice giving more weight to that reassurance than all her mother's impassioned pleas. "Good and bad, there's nothing more basic, Sunny, and we learned early on to tell the one from the other, even through camouflage. Life on the road teaches you that quickly or you don't survive it."

Rae knew that, and looking back she could see they'd known, somehow, who to trust and who not to. Annie and

Nelson Bliss had always been willing to lend a hand to someone deserving, but there'd been times when she was a child when they'd run across someone who'd asked for their help, and help wasn't given. "I really wish I could give you a hand, but it's such a bad time . . ."

"It's only for a few days," Annie said, "maybe a week, tops."

A week, she thought, just any week for her parents, but the end of the quarter for her, culminating with the partnership meeting at her firm.

"His name is Connor Larkin," Nelson said. "He's a perfect gentleman. Very chivalrous, as a matter of fact."

Her parents both laughed.

"Care to let me in on the joke?"

Annie opened the door. "Come in, Conn."

And in he walked, all six and a half feet of him, dark hair waving back from that rugged, almost-handsome face, still wearing leather accessorized by a bandage with a slight seep of blood showing through. Instead of setting off alarm bells, it just seemed to add to the . . . okay, dashing figure he cut.

He stopped just inside the door, as surprised as she was. He recovered in seconds, though, giving her a bow and a flourish while she sat there staring, open-mouthed, heart pounding, nerves throbbing in places that hadn't throbbed since . . . an hour ago, when he'd kissed her. Before that it had been a long time. A really long time. Too long, if she was throbbing over a man who chose to live his life as an historical anachronism.

"Milady," he said as he straightened, returning her stare with an irreverent grin. "A pleasure to . . . see you again."

Those sparkling blue eyes dropped to her mouth, her face heated to roughly the temperature of the sun, and she was on her feet, even before she'd formed the intent and despite her suddenly wobbly knees.

"You have got to be kidding," she said to her mother, but her eyes stayed on the man Annie Bliss had called Conn, which was a pretty apt name for him since Rae felt like she'd been had.

And there stood her parents, acting like it was an everyday occurrence to send a man like that to stay with her. Rae tried to work herself around to the door, hands out to ward them all off before they dragged her into their delusion.

"He looks like he can take care of himself," she said. He looked like he could take care of her, too. And she had no business thinking about that kiss, not to mention any other surprises he might come up with if she were stupid enough to let him get that close to her again. "He didn't have any trouble with those two guys earlier. Wait . . ." Her eyes went to the bandage. "That was real, wasn't it? They actually wanted to kill him?"

"They only had swords," her father said.

"They only had . . ." She threw up her hands, wondering why it surprised her that she was the only one who found that comment ridiculous. "What if they come after him with guns next time?"

"Guns?" Conn asked. "What is *guns*?"

Rae didn't move, but her eyes shifted to her mother's face.

"Oh, by the way," Annie said with an infuriatingly calm smile. "Conn has amnesia."

chapter
3

"AMNESIA?" RAE STAGGERED BACK TWO STEPS and dropped onto the hard bench seat. Her gaze went to Conn again, still smirking at her but with no sign of prevarication on his face, then to her father, smiling reassuringly.

Annie just looked smug. Rae hated smug. It was the expression she'd seen every time she lost a fight with her mother, which was every time they'd fought. Except that last time, when she'd walked away for good.

Annie's smile faltered, as if she, too, were remembering where being right all the time had gotten her. "It's the way between mothers and daughters," she said.

"Still reading my mind?"

"Reliving my own childhood," Annie said.

Rae smiled faintly. "So, let me get this straight, that fight wasn't staged."

"No."

The answer came from Conn, but she kept her eyes on her mother's face, which, *surprise*, was the safer way to go. "And you want me to take him home with me, so the bad guys will come after me, too?"

"We wouldn't ask you to take him in if it wasn't safe."

True, but her mother's version of safe and her version of safe were two different things. Annie might choose to think the best of Connor Larkin, but Rae wasn't getting the warm fuzzies from him. *Volcanic eruption* was too mild a description for what she felt when she looked at Connor Larkin. And then there were the Captain Jack Sparrow wannabes to worry about.

"He really does need your help," Annie insisted. "He's not safe here."

"What makes you think he'll be safe at my house? Not to mention me?"

"For one thing they weren't actually trying to kill him," her father said. "They had plenty of time to finish him off and they didn't. Second, they won't know he's at your house. Or where your house is. Or even who you are."

"How do you arrive at that conclusion?"

"Because you changed your name, and lived at college for four years before relocating here to get your CPA. Because there's no way to connect Rae Blissfield with Annie and Nelson Bliss. Your birth certificate isn't a part of your college record, and I doubt the tiny town where it was registered has converted to electronic record-keeping."

"It sounds like you've thought all this through." To back her into a corner. "But the people you travel with—"

"None of them will talk."

She knew her father was right. "But—"

"They'll just think he took off."

"They who?"

Annie shrugged. So did Nelson.

Rae steeled herself and turned to Conn. "I don't suppose you know who's after you?"

"Brigands," he said with a perfectly straight face. "Lawless mercenaries."

"Why do they want to harm you?"

"'Tis a mystery, milady." But he grinned. "Perhaps my skill with the gentler sex annoys them."

She rolled her eyes. "Cut the Knights of the Roundtable act."

He drew himself up, as far as he could with a low ceiling cramping his style. "I am not a knight, I am an armorer, and far superior as my skill with a hammer and forge protects their very lives."

"O-kay." Rae got to her feet, her father headed her off before she could try for the door again.

He shooed her down the narrow hallway, crowding her back so she had nowhere to go but into the bedroom at the end of the RV. Rae managed to completely ignore the rumpled double bed.

"You told me he had amnesia," she said, keeping her voice down and shooting King Arthur's tailor a quick glance over her father's shoulder to make sure he couldn't hear them. "This guy is delusional. He thinks he's actually from the Middle Ages."

"Rae—"

"Either he's crazy or he's doing it to tick me off, which, since he wants my help, is not very smart."

"It's not an act," Nelson insisted in a harsh whisper. "Somebody whacked him over the head about a week ago, hard. The blow would have killed anyone else."

"I'm not surprised. He strikes me as a guy with a hard head." But she stopped trying to get by her father, and he relaxed, too.

"When he woke up, he thought he actually was an armorer."

"As in sixteenth-century England, indentured-to-the-lord-of-the-castle armorer?"

"Yep."

"He doesn't have an English accent."

"Neither does anyone else."

Right, so he thought he didn't have an accent at all. That actually made sense. In an alternate universe sort of way. "There aren't any castles, let alone lords," Rae said, "and people don't ride horses or wear period dress—well, normal people."

"He hasn't left the faire grounds since he lost his memory. It's odd, really. He sees the tourists dressed in modern clothing but it doesn't seem to shatter his belief in who he thinks he is. The doctor said—"

"Wait a minute." Rae put her hand on Nelson's arm. "You took him to a doctor?"

"No, but we called Mutch the Court Jester's cousin. She's a doctor in Philadelphia."

"What did Mutch the Court Jester's cousin say?" Rae asked, shaking her head a little because she didn't find any part of that question strange.

"That it's probably a defense mechanism."

"A defense mechanism that's likely to get him killed. Or at least hurt again."

"It's not about his physical safety," Nelson said. "There might have been some emotional stress in his life before the injury that caused him to . . . check out for a little while. Or it could be a result of the blow, short-circuiting his long-term memory so that all he knows is the re-enacting but he doesn't remember it's a pretense. That would explain why the throngs of tourists don't seem incongruous to him."

"But his memory will come back, right?"

"A blow to the head can cause memory loss of indeterminate severity and indefinite duration," he said, clearly repeating word for word what he'd been told. "That didn't sound very hopeful, so we looked it up on the Internet— iPhone, remember?"

That Rae found strange.

"There's no specific set of symptoms for amnesia," Nelson continued. "Conn could've lost short-term or long-term memory, or a combination of both, and there's no telling how long it will be before it comes back. But it will come back. It's just a matter of time, and the doctor didn't think it would take very long. When it does come back, and he can remember who's after him, he won't need our help anymore."

Rae let it all sink in, glancing over her shoulder at Conn, who was staring at her. And looking harmless, for all his bulging muscles and oozing sexuality.

"He seems to be okay with the amnesia," Nelson said. "Curious about everything, but very laid back and accepting."

"What was he like before?"

"Less laid back, but still very nice. He's a good guy."

"He's a nutcase." And if she was crazy enough to get involved they might as well put her in the rubber room next to his.

Her parents might choose to believe everything would work out for the best, and she figured Conn's memory would come back, too. But all you had to do was read the newspaper to know that he might not get it all back, especially the part where he was attacked. "Why don't you call the police?"

"No!"

"I know you object to authority, Dad, but—"

"It's not that. I . . . I can't explain. Just promise me you won't call the police. Please, Sunny," he pressed when she didn't immediately agree. "We wouldn't ask you if it wasn't important, and we wouldn't send him to stay with you if it meant putting you in danger."

There were all kinds of danger, she thought, glancing back again to find Conn staring at her backside. And the worst kind was the danger you wanted to throw yourself into. Without any regard for the consequences.

"OH MY GOD, YOU'RE DRIVING A HUMMER?" ANNIE Bliss said when Rae parked the tank of a vehicle next to her parents' old Airstream trailer, which didn't look much larger. "Do you know how much fossil fuel these things burn? Do you realize what this is doing to the ice caps?"

"No idea," Rae said, listening to the Hummer suck up enough gas, even at idle, to light a third-world country, and refusing to deplore the waste of energy. Not that she subscribed to rampant, thoughtless consumerism, but it would be nice, for once, to feel like she was exercising her own opinion rather than doing a watered-down imitation of Annie Bliss, Crusader for all Worthy Causes. "Just be grateful my Jaguar was in the shop this week and they chose to saddle me with this thing."

"Jaguar," her mother said, sounding only slightly less disgusted than she'd been when confronted with the Hummer. "Why couldn't you buy a nice hybrid car?"

Right, like tall, dark, and forgetful would have fit into one of those any better than he would the Jag. And why was she suddenly making automotive judgments based on an overgrown fairy-tale character? "I have a sudden urge to go hybrid shopping right now," she said.

Annie frowned at her, but there might have been a smile tugging at the corners of her mouth. "It's best if Conn isn't seen getting into your gas-guzzling monstrosity. Just be ready to go," she finished and, when Nelson all but shoved Larkin out of the trailer, she wrenched the passenger door open and propelled him toward it, using his own momentum.

Rae made the mistake of looking over right when his big body filled the door. He'd changed into a dark blue T-shirt and jeans, and not the saggy, baggy kind of jeans, either. These weren't unfashionably tight, but they were well-worn and molded to his long legs and lean hips. Her knees went weak just at the idea of having that big, hard body, not to mention that mouth, barely inches away. Her foot slipped off the brake pedal, the Hummer lurched forward just as Larkin was ducking inside, and the door frame impacted his skull with an audible crack.

He fell on his butt, one large hand cradling the side of his head. Rae shot the Hummer into park, her heart so high in her throat she could barely breathe.

"Are you all right?" Annie asked, looking around nervously and pulling at his arm as if she had even a remote chance of heaving his bulk out of the dirt.

"I'm so sorry," Rae said, bracing her hands on the passenger seat so she could look down at him, while genuine concern and impossible hope chased each other around her brain. Hope won. Fueled by desperation. "Maybe he got his memory back," she said to her mother. "You know, a second blow—"

"That only works in the movies," Annie said.

"What day is it?" Rae asked him anyway.

"The same day it was a moment ago," he said with a slight, one-shouldered shrug. "What matter if it be today or tomorrow or yestere'en?"

"Today somebody tried to kill you," Rae reminded him. "*Yestere'en,* too, as a matter of fact. I'm hoping tomorrow you'll get your memory back and figure out who so you can deal with it, and I can get on with my life."

He grinned full out. Rae's already weak knees started to tremble, along with several other strategic regions of her body, and she began to think Connor Larkin should worry less about the aggression of strangers and more about her.

"I look forward to seeing your castle," Larkin said. "I will strive to be of service to you."

And that was the point where Rae knew she was doomed because her brain understood what he was saying but her body gave the word *service* a whole other interpretation. And then her imagination supplied pictures. If she got that hot just thinking about having sex with him, Larkin wouldn't make it one night in her house before she asked him to demonstrate just how handy he could be. Considering the fact that he'd kissed her when she was a complete stranger, she doubted he'd turn her away.

She looked at her mother.

"You promised," Annie said before Rae could even form the word "no," let alone draw the breath to say it. Annie tossed a canvas duffel into the backseat, adding, "And it wouldn't be the worst thing for you."

"Mom!"

"Take some of the starch out of your spine."

If he did for her spine what he'd done for her knees, she'd be flat on her back for the next week, and at some point she'd invite him to join her. And then the inconvenience of having him around would be notched up to serious potential for disaster. She wasn't a casual-sex kind of woman, and no way was she falling for someone who lived his kind of gypsy lifestyle.

"Dad," she said, feeling like her whole world was hanging on this one decision.

"We wouldn't ask you if there was another way," Nelson said.

Rae took a deep breath—and caught a big whiff of Connor Larkin. Soap, man, a touch of sweat, and just enough wood smoke from his forge, like a hint of danger that made the combination irresistible. If they bottled his scent and made it available to normal men, the women of the world would be in real trouble. She exhaled through her mouth, shutting her eyes for good measure.

Her parents rarely asked her for favors. Most of the time she was trying to get them to follow enough rules so the IRS or local law enforcement didn't come after them. They really didn't want more than a little of her time, and when it was her father appealing to her . . . If this guy, Larkin, was the cause of his distress then she'd damn well get him out of there. And take him straight to the police, because she didn't for a second believe his cockamamie story.

"Fine," she said to Larkin. "Come on."

He grinned again. This time she had the presence of mind to look away. It was harder to ignore the way his deep voice made her shiver. His words didn't help, either.

"I look forward to our time together," he said.

"Just get in," she said with a heavy sigh.

But he only stood there, staring at the Hummer, having the typical male reaction to a piece of monstrous equipment that would have been complete overkill for a mountain trail in Nepal, let alone a paved road in Michigan. He circled the shiny black vehicle, pausing to study the chrome grille with a slightly dazed look on his face.

"Come on, Hercules, let's go," Rae yelled out her window before he asked her to pop the hood—or whatever the sixteenth-century equivalent of that phrase might be.

He climbed into the Hummer with an ease she envied, and said, "Hercules is a Greek myth."

"And it doesn't strike you as odd that a medieval armorer would know who and what Hercules is?"

"I must have heard the tale as a child," he said without missing a beat. "I'm looking forward to our journey. I have never been away from the gathering place."

Rae shook her head, put the Hummer in gear, and motored away from the Airstream, waving good-bye to her parents and trying not to notice Connor Larkin sitting next to her, so big his shoulder was practically brushing hers. And he kept looking over at her. She didn't have to see him to know he was doing it because every time his eyes landed on her it felt like his hands did, too. And his mouth, and . . . "Stop it," she said.

"Stop what?"

"Looking at me."

"I assumed you desired my regard."

"Why would you assume that?"

"You dress in provocative clothing, you paint your face. If you let your hair down . . ." He caught a loose tendril, his fingers brushing the side of her neck.

She almost drove the Hummer off the side of the dirt road leading out of Holly Grove, and she missed most of the rest of his comment. She got his drift, though. "Let's get a couple things straight," she said, muscling the vehicle back into the slow-moving stream of departing revelers. "First, keep your hands to yourself. And second, I'm not going to be saddled with you long enough for hairstyle to be an issue."

"Saddled," he said, his voice dropping another impossible octave. "An interesting turn of phrase. It brings to mind riding."

"It brings to mind an unwelcome burden." But she reached over and cranked up the air conditioning.

She made the turn onto Dixie Highway, four lanes of road winding through fields and small towns, heading toward I-75 and normalcy. Except for six-odd feet of crazy sitting in the passenger seat. "It would help if you'd tell me what's really going on so I know my parents aren't in any trouble," she said.

"Annie and Nelson are perfectly safe, as are you."

"Not as long as you're keeping secrets."

"I would reveal the blackguards if I could but remember their names," he said, sounding solemn and earnest, and completely serious about not only the answer he gave, but the way he gave it.

"So you're sticking with the amnesia story."

"'Tis a choice I make most unwillingly."

Rae wanted to roll her eyes, but she didn't. Connor Larkin used the ridiculous and hackneyed Renaissance faire jargon, but he did it without the overdone English accent. From the people in Holly Grove it was just plain cheesy. He managed to make it sound completely natural. Either he was a really good actor or he believed his own improbable story. And what rational adult would choose to live the part of a bad re-enactor?

A man who had something to hide, that's who. So what if he did a good job of selling his shtick, that didn't mean she had to buy it. Even if he seemed harmless, the guys who'd attacked him weren't. And she wasn't safe as long as she stayed with him. She didn't know how she wanted her epitaph to read, but *innocent bystander* wasn't anywhere on the list.

"None of us are safe until we find out who's after you."

He didn't say anything, and really, what could he say? She'd made it clear that she didn't believe he had amnesia, and he'd made it clear that he wasn't going to feel a sudden urge to come clean.

"So," she said, indicating the small town they were driving through, "none of this looks odd to you? I mean, this could resemble some parts of England, but there aren't any castles around, and these homes are probably palatial compared to the mud-and-stick huts country folk called home in feudal times."

"Perhaps the Druids worked some magic on me."

"The Druids were gone by the sixteenth century."

"Tell that to Merlin the Conjurer."

This time she did roll her eyes. And shake her head. And sigh heavily. Then again, he was living in a cross-cultural crazy farm, and if he had lost his memory, it actually might make sense of a situation that didn't make any.

In fact, once she suspended disbelief the idea got some legs. Maybe Larkin really *had* lost his memory. He probably hadn't been attacked at all. It was more likely he'd simply fallen over and hit his head. Probably drunk, she thought, giving him a judgmental sidelong glance. He looked like he could be a drinker. Okay, that wasn't exactly true. He didn't strike her as a guy who indulged, at least not on a habitual basis. But everyone took a drink now and then, and some of the Renaissance regulars made homemade hooch that packed a real punch if you weren't used to it.

Okay, so he'd fallen and hit his head, that had to be it, and since he didn't remember his real identity, he'd bought the pretend one. Probably all those goofballs, with their ridiculous outfits and stupid accents, stopping by to ask him how he fared, or if he wanted to be bled, or offering to bring by some leeches. And thinking he was from a culture that waged war with regrettable regularity, he'd concluded someone had tried to kill him.

Really, she thought, wasn't it just like her parents to overdramatize the situation? Those two guys in the forge could have killed Larkin any time they wanted. There'd been dozens of opportunities she'd overlooked at the time because her hormones had been busy noticing bulging, sweat-sheened muscles. The muscles were under cover now, and more important, she wasn't looking at them, and thinking back now, the fight seemed so well choreographed. Larkin could simply have forgotten it was all a performance, maybe missed his timing enough to earn himself a scratch in the process. Which meant the danger was all in his head, and she just had to humor everyone for—

Crash. The Hummer gave a shimmy, and Rae's gaze flew to the rearview mirror. It felt like they'd been hit, and sure enough she caught a glimpse of light blue car roof close on their rear bumper. And then she looked over at Connor Larkin, and she was sure. She started to pull over, but he curled his big hand around her wrist. That didn't stop her. One look at his face did. He'd gone from laid back to high-alert, blue eyes almost laser intense as he looked out the rear window.

"It's just a fender bender," Rae said, "no reason to break out the big knives."

"Keep driving."

"Why?" she asked, just as there was a second, louder thump from the rear, one that made her put her foot back on the gas pedal. "That wasn't the car hitting us," she said.

"What do you suspect it was?" he asked her.

"Remember when you asked me what a gun was? I think you're about to find out."

chapter
4

RAE PUT HER FOOT TO THE FLOOR, TELLING herself with every beat of her pounding heart they hadn't just been shot at. And not believing it. "Friends of yours?" she said to Larkin.

"Why would friends try to harm me?"

"That was sarcasm."

Nothing. Not because he didn't get the concept, because he was busy staring out the back window. Rae blew out a breath, glad he wasn't looking at her like that.

"What manner of coward strikes from hiding?"

"The kind who means business," Rae said, splitting her attention between the road and the mirrors.

A powder blue Honda Civic, circa 1990 and stuffed with three men—at least one of them dressed like a pirate—zipped into the next lane and pulled up alongside the Hummer. The roof of the car didn't reach the bottom of the driver's-side window. Rae thought she saw the Honda's window go down—hand-cranked by the guy in the passenger seat. Not that it did him much good since what he got was a face full of shiny black paint, and anything he did would be the automotive equivalent of David and Goliath. Then again, David had won that fight.

She stepped on the gas. The Honda kept up and closed in. Rae fought instinct and held her position in the lane. No way was a Civic going to force a Hummer off the road. "Score one for Detroit," she said, not so freaked out by the gunshot anymore since the Hummer had been impervious to that, too.

"Detroit?"

"Made in the U.S.A.? Domestic versus foreign?"

Larkin shrugged that off, so Rae did, too. Besides, the Honda wasn't gone, just staying on their back bumper. She ought to be more alarmed, but it was like being threatened by a car full of circus clowns. "Larry, Moe, and Curly Soprano," she muttered.

Connor Larkin laughed.

"You got that?"

"Got what?"

"Oy," Rae said, which wasn't a word but seemed to sum up the whole situation nonetheless. If he was trying to drive her crazy it was working. "There's a state police post not much farther along this road."

"Police?"

"Law enforcement."

He still looked puzzled.

"Constable? Scotland Yard, cops, deputy, sheriff—"

His hand closed around her arm again, long fingers overlapping in a grip that was firm without being tight. But she could feel the power he was holding back. He could snap her wrist without a second thought. "No sheriff."

"I don't want them following me home, and it's probably the only way we can lose them."

He kept his hand where it was, his eyes intent on her face but with none of the threat she'd seen when he looked at the assault vehicle. He might believe he was a guy who solved his problems with three feet of cold steel, but at least he knew who his enemies were.

"As soon as they see the police station they'll take off," she said. "Trust me, we won't even have to go inside."

"Your word?"

"Um, sure."

"Then we are in accord." And he let her go.

"Taking the word of a woman? That's something a sixteenth-century armorer would never do," she said as she hooked a right into the state police entrance, trying to do it without slowing down too much so it would be a surprise to the guys in the Honda. She didn't quite pull it off. A stunt driver she wasn't. Not to mention the Hummer cornered like a parade float.

The Honda kept going, though, just as she'd predicted. She parked at the far edge of the mostly empty lot and turned to him. He stared back, brow furrowed over guileless blue eyes.

"How much do you remember?"

He shrugged.

"You do that a lot, and it's getting very annoying. Do you even want to remember your real life?"

"Aye, but what would be gained by haste?"

"How about getting rid of the three guys in the Honda?"

"They have fled like the curs they are, nor will they know where to find us again."

"Fine, but you could have a wife somewhere, maybe some kids."

He looked troubled for a second, then his expression turned . . . sunny again. There was no other way to describe it. "If that be the case, I must have left them already. I was with the faire for many months, and Annie says I never spoke of a family."

Not so unusual, Rae thought. More than a few of the people in her parents' traveling group were keeping secrets. Connor Larkin could be one of them, and what better way to keep a secret than to claim you couldn't remember it?

They sat there for a minute more, Rae's eyes on the building, willing someone to come out and ask them what they were doing there. No such luck.

"We should be on our way," Larkin finally said.

"Are you sure?"

"You promised your father."

"Yeah," she said on an outrush of breath, her eyes still on the door to the police station but her body making no attempt to take her there. "If you agree to talk to the police, I'm sure my father would understand."

It only took one glance at Connor Larkin to make her feel ashamed.

She fired up the Hummer and guided it out of the parking lot, her shame turning to anger, and since anger was preferable she let herself get good and ticked off. How did her parents do this to her? she fumed as she made the turn back out onto Dixie Highway. She'd reasoned with them. All her objections had been perfectly logical and rational, too, yet here she was, doing exactly what they wanted.

She slid Connor Larkin a sidelong glance and found him staring at her. *Jerk.* Jerk with muscles, and a great butt, and killer eyes, and a face that appealed to her, not because it was handsome, but because it showed character, from the small scar along his jaw to the smile lines around his eyes and mouth. Problem was, what kind of character?

Sure, she could tell he'd seen some things, been through some hard times. A man who shifted from hapless Renaissance kook into Rambo's slightly saner cousin between one heartbeat and the next probably couldn't include *choirboy* on his resume. That didn't mean he was a good guy. And okay, it didn't take a genius to know the cartoon characters in the Honda weren't the good guys here, either. Cops usually didn't cork their suspects over the head or try to run them off the road, definitely not with an innocent bystander in the vehicle.

So what kind of trouble had Connor Larkin brought on himself, and now her? And why didn't he want the police involved? Rae had an answer for those questions. In fact, there were several possible answers. None of them was comforting.

* * *

CONN SAT BACK IN THE HUGE CONVEYANCE THAT
at once felt familiar but also completely foreign. Nearly
everything was like that. He knew he should recognize
things, knew he wasn't as simple a man with as simple a
life as the Connor Larkin he saw in the mirror every
morning. But it was like having something on the tip of
your tongue. The harder he tried to remember it the further it seemed to slip away.

Every now and then he got a flash of something, a
lightning strike of memory that was there and gone so fast
he couldn't quite wrap his brain around it and hold on.
And he didn't want to. For the most part they were unpleasant scenes, full of violence and dark emotion. Whoever he'd been, Conn had a feeling he would dislike that
man, so he saw no need to pursue those memories or his
true identity. He was content being simple. He enjoyed
moving easily through the world with no specific destination and no urgency to get there even if he'd had one.

Then again, he could think of one destination that
seemed to carry with it a great urgency. He glanced over
at Rae, the taste of her still lingering on his tongue, her
scent, her warmth, the feel of her in his arms. That split
second when she'd melted against him was unforgettable.
He wanted that again. Need weighted his blood and
blurred his mind, heat rising up inside him, making him
blind for a minute while he simply accepted that it was,
without concerning himself over the why of it, or where it
might go. He was a man who lived in the moment, and in
that moment nothing mattered except getting her into his
arms again, taking her mouth as he laid her down on any
flat surface—or against any horizontal one, for that matter. If she hadn't been busy driving . . .

He'd still keep his hands—and his mouth—to himself.
He'd kissed Rae when she'd been a complete stranger,
attracted to her beauty and the knowing expression on her
face. It was as though she understood him—who he was
inside and what he was thinking, including his slightly
odd view of life and humanity. Especially his odd view.

He knew it was ridiculous. He didn't know her at all. But he'd bowed to instinct and allowed himself to capture one kiss regardless. Problem was, memory or no memory, now that he knew who she was the man he was inside wouldn't trespass on his friendship with her parents by kissing their daughter.

Unless he was invited. Judging by the cold reception she'd given him, an invitation—that kind of invitation— would not be forthcoming. She'd let him stay in her dwelling, but not in her bed.

"Hey, you awake over there?" Rae said.

Conn turned to look at her, saw her eyes glued to the rearview mirror, and kept turning. "Our pursuers are very persistent," he said, his mind already making the leap before his eyes spied that damned light blue vehicle, coming after them like a fly chasing an elephant. Not really threatening at first glance, but if a fly stung at the right moment, real damage could be done.

The sense of peace and well-being inside him lifted like a shroud, revealing the ugliness beneath. For that alone he might have hated the men in the Honda, but the ugliness was as wintry as it was black, and he embraced it because his own safety was not his only concern. Or even the most important. He would not see Rae hurt because of him.

The driver of the vehicle stayed behind them, however, following them to their destination. Conn had no desire to live with the demon inside himself for that long, nor would he give his enemies the choice of where and when to strike.

"Can you bring us even with them?" he asked Rae.

"They shot at us, remember?"

"And it gained them nothing."

She met his eyes, her own widening at what she must have found there, before she looked right and left, and behind them before they began to slow measurably.

They moved along on the extreme right, the dirt and stone edge of the road a blur outside Conn's window, even at the slower speed. The other vehicle moved over

into the next section of roadway, coming even with them
as Rae dropped back.

Conn waited until the smaller vehicle was beside theirs,
put his hand over Rae's on the steering wheel, and jerked it
to the left.

"Hey!" Rae stomped on the gas and the Hummer
swooped over in front of the other car. "What do you think
you're doing?"

"'Tis clear, is it not?" Conn said. "The principle is not
unlike jousting. You are the knight, this is your steed, and
size can be as devastating a weapon as steel."

She glared at him.

"I learned it from them," Conn said in his own defense,
watching the blue car slow as the Hummer sped up, opening a safe distance between the two.

"People die jousting," Rae reminded him, needlessly
as that would not have been an unwelcome fate for three
men who sought to harm them.

"We are perfectly safe."

"The other drivers, the innocent drivers, aren't."

He took that in, recognized his oversight, and put it
away, not in the least insulted at being corrected by a
woman, especially as she had failed to consider all angles
of her own actions. "The blackguards are following us to
our destination."

"Yeah," she said, sounding grim, "I get that."

"It cannot be allowed."

Rae didn't respond, but Conn could see her thinking,
working the problem over in her mind. For a minute, a
split second really, he warred within himself, wanting to
take charge of the situation and thwart their enemies himself. Then she looked at him, smiling coldly, and he let
the ugliness slide back under its shroud and the world
become a simple, sunny place again.

"I fail to understand your intention," he said to her, "but
I rejoice that it will be inflicted on someone else."

Rae pushed some buttons on a small device on the panel
to one side of the steering wheel, her smile turning yet
more devilish as a tiny picture popped into colorful life.

Conn stared at the little picture, again feeling that sense of vague familiarity without definitive recognition. He reached for the buttons, but Rae slapped his hand away.

"It's GPS—Global Positioning System." She shook her head, apparently deciding it was too much to try to explain. "It provides a map to anyplace you want."

"How is a map going to help us?" Conn asked, letting the rest of it go.

"It's not the map," Rae said, a glint in her eye that would have gotten her hanged as a witch had she lived in Conn's time, "it's the destination."

When she was in college at the University of Michigan, Rae had interned one summer for the United Auto Workers union. Part of her job had been to travel around to the different Locals and audit their books. She'd managed not to find any irregularities. She might not have been born and raised in Michigan, but everyone had heard of Jimmy Hoffa, and she had no desire to solve the mystery of where he was buried by joining him there.

Probably not the kind of education intended by the internship program, but knowledge was knowledge, and sometimes it came in handy when you least expected it.

She stayed on Dixie Highway, heading into the city of Pontiac, Michigan, following the Hummer's GPS directions to Woodward Avenue and then Martin Luther King Jr. Boulevard. UAW Local 594, proud representatives of large truck and SUV makers, sat along Martin Luther King Jr. Boulevard.

Rae guided the Hummer into the entrance of the local union hall, the Honda following right along. Until, she assumed, the driver got a good look at the building, with its large lettering and distinctive logo. The Honda made a wide circle around the parking lot. Rae floored it, the Hummer's tires squealing as it lumbered toward the single driveway, just barely beating out the smaller, more agile car. Rae angled the Hummer across the exit, completely blocking in the Honda.

Even on a Sunday there were men in the union hall.

They came spilling out the door, alerted by the shriek of rubber on pavement and the roar of engines. And then they spied the Honda. The driver backed away, circling the parking lot again, looking for a way out.

A couple of guys disappeared into the union hall, the rest scattered into the parking lot, coming back with tire irons, baseball bats, and a whole lot of anger directed at anyone misguided enough to drive a foreign vehicle onto union property during the current automotive meltdown.

"Are those men angry?" Conn wanted to know.

"Yes, but it's too complicated to explain."

Like the GPS, the ins and outs of the world market, bankruptcy, and the domestic workforce's disgust with foreign-built vehicles were a lot for someone from twenty-first century Detroit to comprehend, so Rae chose to forego explanations.

The Honda rolled to a stop, the three guys inside radiating fear. Even the car seemed to brace itself for what it knew was coming.

A tire iron smashed into the Honda's windshield, and the driver's panicked face disappeared behind a maze of shattered safety glass as the rest of the blue-collar assault team got into the act.

"Gives the term *beater* a whole new meaning," she said instead, earning another of those chuckles that seemed to be reflexive for Connor Larkin, amusement without complete understanding.

They looked on for a moment or two, as the Honda took a fair beating, although its passengers were still intact, shouting and swearing from inside the increasingly damaged vehicle. They weren't foolish enough to get out of the car.

"How long do you plan to sit here and watch?" Larkin finally asked her.

"Until I'm sure they can't follow us."

"I hope never to anger you to this great a degree."

"It's not anger, it's self-preservation."

chapter
5

"IT'S ME," HARRY MOSCONI SAID GRUFFLY WHEN the party he'd dialed came on the line.

"Well? I don't have all day. Give me a progress report."

"There's no progress to report. We tried to snatch Larkin again, but he fought us off. With a red-hot poker and a sword." Harry studied the scorched and puckered skin on the back of his hand. He chose not to look at his ear.

"He still thinks he's Lancelot?"

"Yeah."

There was a heavy sigh from the other end of the conversation, the kind of sigh that told Harry he'd fucked up again. Like he needed a two-bit criminal in a five-hundred-dollar suit to tell him that.

"What was we supposed to do, let him turn us in to whatever agency he works for?" he said, hating the whiny note of defense in his voice.

"You should have called me before you did *anything*."

He should have had his head examined a year ago, before he'd gotten involved in this stupidity. Not that he'd known what he was getting into at first.

It had started out as a courier job, picking up boxes at various Renaissance faires around the Midwest and bringing them back to Detroit. Why one of the established shipping companies wasn't used Harry hadn't understood, but he hadn't asked any questions, either. Getting laid off from the auto plant where you'd worked for twenty years, and facing the loss of everything you'd worked for, did that to a guy. Jobs had been few and far between, especially for a man with a lot of debt and not a lot of education. Just making his mortgage payment each month had felt like a major accomplishment.

The new job had involved a lot of driving and nights away from his family, but it had paid well, and the work was easy. He and Joe Salerno had shared the driving in the beginning, spending a lot of time together and getting to be friends. Six months ago Joe had brought in his cousin, Kemper Salerno. Kemp was dumb as a box of rocks, and he wasn't up to anything much physical—unless it involved consumption—but he could follow instructions, he didn't ask questions, and he liked to drive, which allowed them to keep up with the ever-increasing workload.

Harry was the one who'd fucked up a good thing. He hadn't done it on purpose, but that didn't make it any less fucked up. Accidentally getting a glimpse of the printing press, putting that together with the size and shape of the packages, and coming up with counterfeit bills had been bad enough. Confronting the guy behind the crime had been downright stupid. True, he'd wanted to be sure he wasn't getting screwed over, not to mention duped into passing bogus bills because he'd been paid in them.

His peace of mind had come at a high cost, though. He was getting paid in real bills, but he knew about the crime, and he hadn't gone to the police. That made him part of it, and it was too late to back out, even when the boss started asking him to do other things. Like hurt people.

"Hello, are you there?"

"We tried to call you," Harry said, checking back into the conversation. "You was busy, and we couldn't wait."

"And look how things turned out. If you'd finished him off—"

"You told us not to hurt anybody, just keep an eye on them. We was gonna question him, find out how much he knew and who sent him."

"So you knocked him out and then left him for the first Renaissance kooks who wandered by. Which just happened to be the Blisses."

"Yeah, well, you ain't seen this guy," Harry grumbled. "He's practically seven feet tall and he ain't no featherweight. Me and Joe went to find something to haul him in, and when we got back he was gone. Didn't take long for us to figure out where he was. We shoulda just gone to that stupid trailer and—"

"*No!* We need the Blisses. This thing goes south, they're on the hook, just like the rest of their goofball friends. If you'd told me who you thought Larkin really was, I would have shut down the operation."

Harry breathed a sigh of relief, and then the *would have* part of that comment sank in. "Why don't you shut it down now?"

"As long as Larkin's in fantasyland there's no reason to. Besides, if he'd had any concrete evidence he'd have called in whatever agency he works for by now. One more big score, that's all it will take, and then we won't need him anymore. We won't need any of them."

"What are you saying?"

"Don't be an imbecile—that means *stupid.*"

"I know what it means. And I don't appreciate being talked to like I am one."

"Or what? You're as deep into this as I am. If Larkin gets his memory back and calls in reinforcements it will only be a matter of time before we all go to jail."

"Why can't we just snatch him, like I wanted, and find out who he works for? Maybe he's just a nosy SOB, not a fed or DEA. Could be you're just paranoid—that means *jumping at shadows.*"

"Don't be smart. It doesn't work for you." The voice turned colder, but with an undercurrent of weary fatalism.

"You'll do what's necessary. We all will. And after we make an example of Larkin we won't have to worry about the others staying in line."

What's necessary. Translation: He wanted Larkin dead. He just didn't want to say it in so many words. That way if anything went wrong he could put it on them.

Like hell, Harry thought. He hadn't gone to college, but that didn't mean he was stupid. "He don't even remember what's going on."

"He will."

"I didn't sign up for this. I just wanted to save my house from being foreclosed, make sure my kids have a roof over their heads."

"Just do it or we all get new living arrangements. I don't know about you, but I don't want to wake up one day and find out my new roommate thinks orange is my color."

Harry heaved a sigh. "Good point. But this is it."

"Yes, I agree. Just one more big push and then we shut it down."

"Whatever," Harry said, accepting the fact that he was well and truly stuck. Forward wasn't the direction he wanted to go, but there was no turning back now. "I need an advance."

"Another advance, you mean."

"If you want me to deal with Larkin I'm gonna need my car fixed. It ain't in the best shape right now."

There was another heavy sigh, this one long-suffering. "Very well."

Harry disconnected before the urge to smash something got too big to resist. The only thing handy was his cell and they cost.

Joe stood a couple feet away, chewing on a thumbnail and looking anxious, like always. Kemp was in the Honda, parked a little way off, looking like it belonged in a salvage yard, thanks to the fine members of UAW Local 594. And Connor Larkin. The Honda idled rough enough to make the whole car shimmy, the motor coughing every now and then, a little curl of smoke seeping out from under the hood each time. Things couldn't get much worse, Harry thought, and then the sideview mirror fell off. He turned to Joe, who jerked back a couple of steps.

"I look that pissed off, huh?" Harry asked him.

"Scary is more like it," Joe said, but he relaxed back to his perpetual case of low-grade anxiety. He gestured at the phone fisted in Harry's hand. "You didn't tell him Larkin left the nutfest."

"He don't want to know where Larkin is," Harry said, putting that particular humiliation away. For the moment. "He just wants us to take care of him." *Kill him*, Harry qualified in his own mind, because saying it out loud would put Joe into a full-blown panic attack, and he didn't have the time—or the paper bag—for that.

Besides, if the guy calling the shots wanted to keep his instructions vague in order to protect himself, well, that left Harry free to interpret those instructions any way he saw fit, right? "He doesn't want any of the details, and it's not like he's keeping us in the loop," Harry said to Joe. "And what he don't know won't hurt him."

"Yeah." Joe exhaled heavily, running a hand back through his graying mullet. "But—"

"That Hummer had dealer plates. We won't have no trouble finding them."

"Then what?"

"I don't know," Harry said. "I'm making it up as I go along."

RAE CONSULTED THE GPS AGAIN, LETTING IT NAVI-gate her out of Pontiac, heading toward Grosse Pointe. She drove silently, embarrassed. Sure, she'd needed to keep the guys in the Honda from following them home, but she shouldn't have enjoyed their comeuppance quite so much. Conn chuckling every now and then didn't help matters.

"Men always get off on violence," she grumbled.

"Get off?"

"Uh . . ." She stalled, the true meaning of that phrase

popping into her head, not to mention a mental picture
that made her cheeks burn. "It means you find pleasure in
it." Orgasmic pleasure, but he didn't need to know that.

"Violence is often necessary," he said with a shrug,
"and sometimes entertaining. That was both."

Rae smiled, reluctantly. "It was kind of funny."

Conn laughed outright, long and deep and full of a joy
that warmed the cold, empty places inside her. She'd always been a loner, but it suddenly occurred to her that she
was lonely, too.

Connor Larkin was a remedy she could not afford.
Even if he was the remedy she wanted to try.

"They screamed like helpless women," he said, shoving her back to her center, even if she couldn't quite believe it was the well-adjusted place she'd once thought.

"That's insulting."

"You, Rae Bliss, are not helpless."

She wasn't delusional, either. A man like Connor Larkin
would be company, sure, but only for as long as he chose.
She needed stability, permanence, or at least the faith that
she wouldn't wake up to find him gone one day because his
own wanderlust was more important than what he might
feel for her.

"You're going to find that most women aren't," she
said firmly, "but thank you. And it's not Bliss."

"It could be."

Bliss. If he kept looking at her like that . . . A horn
blared, she dragged her eyes back to the road, and let it
go, at least outwardly. Inwardly it was World War III,
reality fighting with fantasy. Reality had gunshots and
vehicular assault on its side, but Connor Larkin was right
there, and his physical impact was more than enough to
make her body forget that kind of visceral fear. Even
more frightening, it could make her forget herself. "It's
Blissfield," she said, her barriers going back up. "I changed
my name."

"Why?"

Good question, she thought, her reasons not as clear-cut
as they'd once been. "It made perfect sense at the time."

"To deny your heritage?"

"That's not why I did it."

"Was it not?" he asked, the same question sneaking in around the cracks in her own certainty. "Your parents are good people."

"Of course they are, but I hated that name." She shuddered. "Sunshine Bliss. It's just not me. And that life . . . It's no way to raise a kid."

"So they should have sacrificed everything for their child, settled somewhere and been miserable by denying their own desires?"

"Yes—no—I don't know. And it's really none of your business."

He nodded, but Rae couldn't stop thinking about it. She'd changed her name as a way to distance herself from her parents' life and all the unhappiness of her childhood. But had she done it to distance herself from her parents, as well? And had it been more than teenage rebellion? Had she wanted to hurt them, to make them understand how much she'd hated being dragged along on their gypsy travels?

"You're supposed to be from the sixteenth century," she said, annoyed that he kept putting her off balance.

He looked at her, one eyebrow cocked.

"It wasn't a time period known for turning out sensitive men."

He shrugged, and this time she was only too happy to let him blow off the subject. She whipped off the highway at the first exit she came to, made a couple of quick lefts, and got back on going the opposite direction.

Conn twisted around, peering out the back window.

"There's no one following us," Rae said. "That's the whole point. This is the best time to go back to the Renaissance festival and try to figure out why you're a target."

And okay, the closer they got to her house the more nervous she became. The Hummer was a whole lot smaller, but there was an intimacy to having him in her home, where she ate and lived. And slept. If she could wrap this thing up today, without the cops' and her parents' interference, she could go back to her life and pretend none of this had happened.

Right, and the IRS would suddenly take an understanding approach to delinquent taxpayers. There was no way she'd forget Conn, and that kiss, in her lifetime. The man left an indelible impression. Like a lobotomy.

"DID YOU SAY SOMETHING?"

Conn smiled a little. "That was my stomach growling."

"Missed lunch in all the excitement, huh?"

"I rarely eat when there are crowds."

Rae glanced over at him. "Why not?"

"Women," Conn said, "then men, then trouble."

"Come again?"

He frowned. "When was the first time, and how did I miss it?"

Rae's face flushed, and she glared at him, clearly not comfortable with her sexuality, which was a shame for any woman but especially for one Conn was so attracted to.

"Stop it," she said. "Whatever's going on in your mind, cut it out."

"My mind is not the problem. Yours is. You should spend less time thinking and more time enjoying."

She chose to ignore his remark. "The phrase 'come again' means I didn't understand what you said, so please repeat it."

"Oh, uh," Conn said, scrambling to remember his place in the conversation, which meant getting his mind out of his breeches, "women, then men, then trouble. When I go into the crowds—"

"The women get all worked up, their husbands or boyfriends get jealous, and you get in a fight?"

"Not me, them. Marital strife is an ugly business."

"So you going hungry is a public service," Rae said.

"Aye."

Rae shook her head, smiling at him. "I'm sure my mother would bring you lunch."

"Annie and Nelson have their own concerns. I attempted to hire one of the food purveyors to deliver my midday meal, but that created other problems." Even when he'd paid a young man, the duty had been usurped by a woman, which invariably became sticky, so he chose not to even give the appearance he was favoring one of the young women over another.

"Women can be like that," Rae said, seeming to understand.

She eased the Hummer into the center of the road, bounded by yellow lines, turning when traffic cleared into a narrow parking lot surrounding a building made mostly of glass. The sign proclaimed it a Scottish establishment.

"I will take the eggs," Conn said to Rae.

"They stop serving breakfast at ten thirty."

Hmmm, Conn mused, no Scotch eggs. "Perhaps an oatcake would be good, then, but not haggis. I like the Scottish—"

"They're very bloodthirsty," Rae put in.

"Precisely. But their common nourishment leaves something to be desired."

"The only thing this place leaves to be desired is nutritional value."

She pulled around the building, stopping next to a large sign displaying their options and rolled her window down. Conn leaned across her so he could see all the pictures on the board, but then looked at Rae instead, his eyes meeting hers, their mouths a whisper away, before he said, "You choose."

Neither of them believed he was talking about the menu.

Rae's lips parted, her breath slipping out on a soft moan. Conn leaned in, slowly, savoring the beat of his heart thudding against his ribs, the feel of his blood rushing through his veins, slow and hot, those seconds of anticipation, remembering the taste and feel of her mouth, and already knowing this kiss would put that first one to shame—

"AnIakeoror-er?"

Rae jerked back and sucked in her breath.

Conn stayed where he was, in front of Rae, searching for the source of that garbled voice, yet finding no one.

"It's the speaker," Rae said, a bit breathless but her voice even enough that Conn fought harder to compose himself.

He managed it, barely. "Aye, someone is speaking," he said, "but where is he?"

Rae sighed. "What do you want?"

Conn searched her face, not as composed as he'd thought he was.

"To eat."

He grinned.

"Never mind," she said, brushing him back with her hand so he had no choice but to flop into his seat.

The voice blared out again, still garbled, still disembodied, but he caught something about orders. The place must be run by soldiers, which made sense since the Scottish were perpetually at war with one another when there was no other enemy to be found.

"We'll take a Big Mac," Rae said, talking to the sign, "a fish filet, a chicken sandwich, a chocolate shake, fries, and nuggets."

"How many?" asked the invisible solder

She slid a glance in Conn's direction. "Do they come by the gross?"

Ten minutes later, money had exchanged hands and Rae had plopped two paper sacks into Conn's lap, placed a drink in the cunning holder built into the vehicle, and pulled onto the road again. Conn knew he should be paying attention to their journey, but their attackers weren't coming after them anytime soon, so his stomach took precedence.

Conn mowed through the sandwiches and fries, slurped down the shake, then paused to study one of the small brown lumps of food in the last container. "What is it?"

"A Chicken McNugget."

He shrugged, popped one in his mouth, then devoured the rest and searched for more. To his disappointment the bags were empty, but by then they were back at Holly Grove. Rae parked the Hummer in the public lot, and they walked in, bypassing the tourist entrance for the participants' camp.

She eased the door to her parents' trailer open, and when she was sure they weren't inside she went in. When she came back out, she was wearing her own blouse and jacket, along with a pair of Annie's walking shoes and blue jeans. Her body was pretty amazing when she was wearing a skirt. She looked even more incredible out of it, long legs, slender curves, and the kind of unconscious grace she'd clearly inherited from her mother in a package that made him feel a thousand degrees hotter than friendly.

"So," she said into the awkward silence, "where do you live?"

The last thing he needed was to take her to a place that included a bed—or what passed for a bed—but he walked by her, circled around the end of the Airstream her parents called home, and stopped at the lot next to it.

"This is where you live?"

"Aye."

"In a tent."

"As you see."

"It's smaller than my bathroom. Shorter, too."

"But I can carry it on my back."

The look she sent him over her shoulder told him she didn't consider that much of a recommendation. She dropped to her knees and crawled between the front flaps of the tent, Conn following her denim-clad bottom—a little too closely for her preference, because when she looked over her shoulder and saw him right behind her, she flipped around and tried to scoot backward. She came up short against the far side of the tent. Conn kept going and ended up with his hands braced on either side of her, his knees between her thighs—all of him between her thighs, and his face already lowering toward hers. His lips brushed hers, once, twice, settled, but before he could sink in, before Rae could do more than begin to respond, she scrambled out from beneath him.

She distanced herself from him as much as possible, and her eyes were wide and a little panicked when they met his. He watched, fascinated, as she regained control of herself. Conn did the same, one jangling nerve at a time, but he did it—even though he wanted to take over for her when she lifted one cheek and rubbed.

"I think I sat on a boulder. How do you sleep on this thing?" She poked at the thin pad lying over a waterproof ground sheet, a sleeping bag laid out on top.

"It's not sleep on my mind at the moment."

"Right, we're supposed to be hunting for clues," she said, deliberately misunderstanding him.

It was close quarters when he was in there alone, so Conn chose not to tempt fate, watching Rae through the front opening. There was just his bedroll, a lantern, and a small chest that held his clothing and personal items, most of which he assumed Annie had packed into his duffel. Rae opened it unapologetically and dug through. She found nothing.

She moved to the bedroll, searching it systematically, although she was careful to put everything back the way it was, just as she'd done with his chest.

"You're very orderly," he said. "You would make a good chatelaine."

"I have a career, thank you very much, and it doesn't involve cooking or cleaning."

"Taking care of a home is dignified work."

That took her off guard. "I'm not saying it isn't. I just prefer not to be dependent on a man."

"Any man who thinks his woman is at his mercy, or underestimates her strength, is a fool."

"That's a nice little fantasy," Rae muttered. She sighed heavily and plopped onto his bedroll. "Most men aren't that evolved. Most women, either," she added, but absently, her eyes fixed on the ceiling of the tent. She got to her knees again, reaching up to tug at one of the seams. When she ducked back into view, she had a big smile on her face and a map of the faire grounds in her hand.

"Mean anything to you?" she asked.

It looked vaguely familiar, but then, he'd seen hundreds of those just since he'd lost his memory.

Rae unfolded it. Most of the merchant booths were X'ed out, but a couple dozen had circles around them. Jewelry designers and purveyors, metal workers, silk screeners, places that sold prints and posters. "How about now?"

"I don't recall making the marks."

"They have nothing in common, so I'll need to check them out, ask some questions."

"I?"

"Me. Alone. You stay put. And make sure my parents don't see you."

"They sent us away for a reason."

"Yes, and that reason is stranded in Pontiac." And hopefully they were still alive. "This is the best opportunity we're going to get to find out what's really going on."

"How will you do that? You don't know what questions to ask."

"I'll snoop. I have the advantage of being able to see what's out of place because I know the shtick."

"Shtick?"

"The con . . ."

He popped up an eyebrow.

"It means confidence game. That's where someone gets you to trust them but they're really lying to get something from you." Yeah, that made her feel better. "The point is, I grew up in places like this."

"I don't think it's a good idea for you to go by yourself."

"I'll avoid the people who know me, and I don't need to ask questions, so they won't know I'm looking for something. I'll be perfectly safe." As long as she could avoid her parents, too.

chapter
6

ESPIONAGE DEFINITELY WASN'T FOR HER, RAE decided, fighting the almost constant urge to look over her shoulder. She felt like she was being watched, which was ridiculous since the bad guys were carless, her parents were manning their shop, and she was careful to steer clear of any re-enactors who might remember her.

She opened the map, found the closest circled booth, and headed for it, clamping down on the little surge of excitement—and dread—that made her heart pound. She wasn't in danger, she reminded herself. It was probably just a misunderstanding between Larkin and someone in his group. And yeah, hitting him over the head was a bit extreme. So was the gun, but some of these people were a turkey leg short of a feast, and he wasn't the kind of guy you took on face-to-face. She could even understand how one of these kooks might think it took a gun to put a good scare into him.

All she had to do was discover who'd sent the clowns in the Honda, figure out what their beef was, and get them to talk it through. Child's play, right? Except she'd lived with a group of these people the first eighteen years of her life. They were a hell of a lot harder to handle than children. But if there was even a remote chance of solving this thing and getting Larkin off her hands, she had to take the shot.

She kept her eyes open, making sure she didn't run into anyone who knew her. She checked behind her at fairly regular intervals to quiet the buzz between her shoulder blades. Since she failed to spot anyone threatening, she wrote it off to the general feeling of menace that had dogged her since the guys in the Honda had used her car for target practice.

The first circled booth she came to was called Earth Enchanted, proprietor Onyx Chalcedony. Yeah, slight possibility that wasn't her real name.

Rae wandered the booth, sifting her fingers through the bins of semi-precious stones, looking at the mystical and Celtic symbols strung on chains as pendants or fixed to hoops for earrings. She worked her way around the small enclosure, moving steadily toward the back room.

"Can I help you?"

"Jeez." Rae jumped, slapping a hand over her heart as she spun around.

A small woman wearing a deep red wench dress stood close behind her, eyes darting around so quickly they looked like screen-saver balls bouncing off the sides of her eye sockets.

"I'm just browsing," Rae said, turning to look at the next section of goods.

Onyx jumped in front of her. The dozens of stones at her wrists, neck, waist, and ears rattled, and her fingers worried at the cords twisted around her neck. "The designs are mystical," she said of the silver pendants on the counter in front of Rae. "I create them right here in my shop—" She lowered her voice. "—according to ancient Celtic rituals that imbue them with special protective powers. Are you from the police?"

She ought to be more worried about the men in the white coats, Rae thought.

"The Secret Service? The IRS?"

"I'm from Grosse Pointe."

"You look like an accountant."

Rae looked down at herself. She had a point. "Maybe it's the jacket."

"No." Onyx narrowed her eyes, gave Rae another lightning-fast once-over. "You're wearing turquoise earrings. Turquoise is for money, success—love, too, but you're not wearing a ring, so that's not it."

"They're just earrings," Rae said, trying not to be insulted. She wasn't entirely successful.

"Your eyes are squinty, like you spend all day staring at numbers."

"What's wrong with numbers?"

"People use them to hang you."

"Rope works better."

"Not kill, hang. You know, out to dry, twisting in the wind. Taxes, social security, license plates." Her eyes darted around, and she dropped her voice to the scratchy whisper that had freaked Rae before. "It's all a way for the man to keep track of you, keep you under his thumb."

"Uh-huh, sure." Rae reached for a pair of earrings, managed to get a look into the tiny back room, and didn't see anything suspicious. Heck, there wasn't much of anything to see at all, just a cardboard box with plastic bags sticking out of it, and a small table with what appeared to be a tackle box, probably where Onyx made her paranoia talismans. "If I see the *man*—" She used finger quotes. "—I promise not to mention your name."

Onyx narrowed her eyes.

"Speaking of men, do you know the guy who makes the armor?"

"Why, did he say something about me? Is he a cop, too?"

Rae rolled her eyes at the idea of a floater like Connor Larkin being in law enforcement. "It just seems like he might be cutting into your business, you know, the smaller pieces he makes."

Onyx snorted. "He's just a technician. And anyway, mostly what he sells is sex."

She had that right. And from what Rae had seen, there was no overlap between Onyx's goods and Larkin's—not that Onyx would have anything approaching a logical motivation for attacking him. Paranoia pretty much ran her life, and paranoia wasn't logical.

Paranoia didn't like contemplative silences, either. Onyx made a sound in the back of her throat and nipped behind the counter. Rae didn't stick around to find out why; she'd been thinking the woman wasn't the violent type, but she could have been hasty there.

The minute she'd put Earth Enchanted behind her— and assured herself it wasn't Onyx causing the familiar itch between her shoulder blades—she felt better, foolish but better.

Her next stop was a shop called Paper Moon. A lot of the booths in Holly Grove were built in rows. Dozens of them followed the curving contour of the grove, with common walls, boardwalks in front, and small back rooms that were used as workshops for those who personalized items or made them on-site, and where most proprietors kept back-stock and bags.

Paper Moon was a little way off by itself, along one of the stone paths that wound through the center of the grove in a haphazard maze. Rae had a bad feeling as soon as she entered the place, but it had nothing to do with Conn or his troubles. The small wooden building was lined with prints. Prints of ladies in medieval gowns besieged by dragons, prints of ladies being stolen away on horseback by knights in black armor, prints of ladies locked in towers, in glass coffins, tied to stakes with fire inching toward their skirts.

It was a disturbing pattern, even before she met the proprietor. The sign behind the counter identified him as Hans Lockner. The way he looked her up and down told her the prints were more a personal statement than mere decoration.

"Say the word, and you can see more than a paper moon," he said.

Rae felt her lip curl and tried to hide it with a smile she knew was sickly at best. "Do you print these here?"

"I don't just print them, I do the artwork."

"Gee, I never would have guessed."

"I don't look much like an artist. That's what you're thinking, right?"

She was thinking he looked like a pervert, and it wasn't just the perpetual leer on his face. He wore the costume of an Elizabethan courtier, complete with a codpiece that would have been ridiculous on a giant, let alone someone who barely topped five and a half feet and who, presumably, wasn't riding high on Viagra. That codpiece probably wasn't regulation, either, since Hans wore a cape over his ensemble, only letting it flap open when he chose.

Unfortunately, he chose to flap for her, and despite the disgust she was sure showed on her face, he sidled a step closer. Rae scoped out his hands to make sure he wasn't a grabber, backpedaling as far as she could without completely putting him off. That it took her closer to the back room was a bonus. Until Hans caught her looking toward the curtain covering the doorway.

"You wanna see the wizard?"

Rae froze, too revolted for even sarcasm to rescue her.

"It's from the movie, you know, with Judy Garland."

"I know." Only in his version it would be called *Dorothy Does Oz*. "I . . . have to meet someone."

"A guy, right? Women like you always have a guy."

"Sort of. I'm meeting my friends at an armor-making demonstration. Supposedly it's going to be the high point of my day."

Hans's face went through a range of emotions, from *Damn it* to *Oh well* to *Lots of fish in the sea*. No resentment, no surprise. If Hans had sent the Honda after them, he'd know Larkin had left Holly Grove, and as Rae had just noted, the man didn't exactly have a poker face. He did seem like the kind of guy who'd get others to do his dirty work—and be cheap enough to hire cartoon characters. He did not strike her as someone who would bother, though, not unless he was jealous of Larkin, because what Hans Lockner cared about was between his legs.

"You sure you don't want a print?" Hans said. "I'm willing to give you a discount."

Rae took another visual tour of Hans's salute to female degradation. "Thanks, no."

This time, as she walked away, she knew she was being watched, but she didn't have to fight off the urge to look over her shoulder. The need for a shower, now, that was another matter.

Mettle Works, owned and operated by Cornelia Ferdic, wasn't far away. Cornelia was tall and gangly, wearing a plain, dark-colored wool dress with a paisley scarf wrapped around her head in a sort of turban, the ends of which were loosely nestled around her neck. She was wearing too much perfume, and she must've had really bad skin, because foundation was caked on her face.

"Can I help you with something?" she asked Rae in a two-pack-a-day voice.

"These pieces are gorgeous," Rae said, bending to take a closer look at the earrings and pendants in the glass display, and not because she was using it as a ruse to get a look behind the sales counter.

The earrings were metal hoops filled with tiny gears and cogs that shifted like clockworks as they were moved. The pendants were flat glass disks, also filled with intricate workings in three dimensions. Rae lifted one, smiling as the colorful miniature gears rolled around inside their clear case, the patterns beautiful and mesmerizing.

"Do you make these yourself? There's another booth with amazing metalwork."

"You mean the armorer? The guy with the bare chest and the completely female audience? I hear he planted a hot one on a woman in the audience this morning, and now every female between the ages of twelve and ninety is hanging out at his place."

Rae felt her cheeks heat again, not to mention the heat blooming in some other body parts that were reliving that kiss.

"He actually does some pretty intricate work," Cornelia said with grudging admiration. "Nothing like this,

though. I make all my own creations, right down to the
gears and glass."

"They're very clever, and beautiful." So clever and
beautiful Rae pointed to a pendant. "I'll take that one."

It turned out to be a pretty good deal. For fifty dollars
she got a unique piece of jewelry and a look at Cornelia's
back room, which consisted of nothing more than a tiny
space at the back of the booth where she ran credit cards
and bagged purchases.

She must have hit an odd lull, because just after she
made her purchase the place was jammed with customers,
and they weren't just admiring the goods—they were
buying. Cornelia Ferdic had nothing to worry about com-
petition-wise from Connor Larkin. And of the three re-
enactors Rae had met so far, she seemed the most normal.

She stepped out of Mettle Works and started working
her way down the row of booths, visiting four more of
Conn's circled artisans with no more luck than she'd had
with the first three. Probably it had something to do with
the fact that she had no idea what she was looking for.

She came to one of the crowds that periodically
blocked the path, as people gathered around some per-
former hawking a show or a demonstration like Connor
Larkin making armor. She was working her way around
the edge of the crowd when she was grabbed, spun
around, and lifted into the air, leaving her dizzy and dis-
oriented, struggling to make sense. Hard hands locked
around her legs and arms. She fought, knowing it was
useless but determined to inflict some damage. Rae didn't
know what her abductors had in mind for her, but she was
damn well going to make them sorry they'd ever laid eyes
on her, let alone hands.

"Relax. Stop struggling and you'll be fine."

Relaxing was out of the question, but she gave up the
fight, and when she did the sound of bagpipes registered,
along with the laughter and cheers of the crowd. She was
facing up, the treetops and sky all she could see until she
tipped her head back and realized she'd been hijacked by
a bunch of men wearing kilts, and not much else. They

were bare-chested but for a swatch of folded plaid slung over their shoulders. They all had bushy beards and big smiles—and really strong arms, she hoped, since they were passing her from one to another overhead. She'd never been a fan of crowd surfing. It was oddly invigorating, more than a little scary, and some of them weren't very careful where they put their hands.

"Put me down," she said, then screamed it over the din of the crowd.

"We're not going to hurt you," one of the muscle-bound idiots told her, "unless you keep squirming. We might just drop you then."

"I'll be sure to tell my lawyer I was threatened as well as accosted. And if one more of you guys cops a feel—" Her tirade ended on a shriek as she was grabbed again.

There was that moment of disorientation, of trying to find some frame of reference with the world—and her brain and stomach—spinning, and then she was plunked onto her feet. She stumbled a little, coming up hard against something solid, warm, and comforting. And very male.

Conn. Her body recognized him first, warming, weakening so all she could do was lean into him, lose herself in the feel of him hard and strong at her back. His hands came to her waist, flexed once before inching up her rib-cage, the breath that she had sighed out coming in fast and catching in the back of her throat.

"Bliss," he said, his voice low and deep and close to her ear. She shuddered, but even as the need inside her notched up another impossible degree, her mind was already getting in the way. Or saving her, depending on how she looked at it. She chose the latter, stepping forward and turning to face him, though it wasn't easy.

"Don't call me that again."

He nodded once, tightly.

"You've been following me the whole time, right? That's why I felt like I was being watched."

"Aye."

She checked out the Highlanders, but they'd moved on

to abusing telephone poles and tossing rocks that probably weighed more than she did.

She started walking, maintaining enough distance to see his face—and keep her thoughts clear. "One of those people might want you dead, or at least seriously hurt, and they weren't going to talk or give anything away with you skulking around."

"They didn't see me any more than you did. And I was trying to make sure you didn't blunder into trouble."

"Blunder?"

"Blunder."

Rae huffed out a breath since, yet again, he'd left her searching for a suitable comeback. "Men," she said, settling for the generic complaint of women everywhere.

"This is not about gender. You came back here, hoping to solve the unsolvable."

"It's not unsolvable."

"It is at the moment, but here you are trying, because you don't want to take me home with you."

Rae snorted softly. "You're overestimating your appeal."

"'Tis not my appeal I'm thinking of, but your fear."

Her mouth dropped open, it took a second for anything to come out. "Wow," she finally said, "you don't hold anything back."

"If it troubles you this much, I will stay—"

"No," she said, although she was thinking *yes*. Connor Larkin was a double threat, physically appealing and philosophically evolved. "We should go. You're right about me not knowing what questions to ask."

And he was right about her level of fear. Taking him home was definitely freaking her out. But she'd made a promise to her parents, and stalling wasn't going to get her off the hook.

chapter
7

"THESE CASTLES ARE TOO CLOSE TOGETHER, NOT defensible," Larkin said, staring out at the modest neighborhood they were driving through on their way to Grosse Pointe.

"We don't have a lot of warfare in Michigan," Rae said. *Union halls and Renaissance festivals notwithstanding.* "And if you want to see castles, I'll show you castles."

She shut off the GPS, detouring from the route that led directly to her house to veer north and pick up Lakeshore Drive. Grosse Pointe actually consisted of five separate cities, each with its own identity and wealth strata, the most prestigious of which was Grosse Pointe Shores. And the top of the real estate food chain boasted a Lakeshore Drive address.

Lakeshore Drive ran along the shore of Lake St. Clair, smaller than the Great Lakes and not considered one of them, but vast in its own right, and definitely prime real estate. Many of the houses overlooking the lake had been built during the Gilded Age by people like the Dodges and the Fords. Those houses were impressive, to say the least, huge and sprawling, some of them on lots so big the driveways had to be marked as private so the riffraff didn't mistake them for actual roads.

"These are castles, indeed," Connor Larkin said as Rae eased the Hummer down to a crawl so he could get a good look at the rambling homes, each more incredible than the last. "But they are still too near one another. Miscreants can sneak up with ease."

"The miscreants aren't as big a problem as the neighbors." Rae nudged her speed back up to the limit and continued on as Lakeshore Drive turned into Jefferson Avenue, leading to the more realistically priced areas of the Pointes.

She lived in one of the older neighborhoods, and she wasn't just talking about the median age of the homes. Most of her immediate neighbors were elderly, and most of them considered her an upstart because she hadn't sprung from five generations of Grosse Pointers.

Blue blood might come along with big piles of money, but there were side effects. Rich people called themselves eccentric. Some of them, as far as Rae was concerned, were downright crazy.

All of them were nosy.

Rae swung the Hummer into her driveway, which widened out behind the house to a paved courtyard with a detached three-car garage at the far back corner of her lot. Only one of the three bays had been converted to an automatic overhead door. She hit the button on the opener before she remembered that the Hummer didn't fit inside the narrow opening.

"This is a . . . surprise," Conn said, peering into the gloomy interior with its century-old wood floor and pretty much nothing else. "Why is the inside not as welcoming as the outside?"

"It's the garage," Rae said dryly.

"Garage?"

"Carriage house. At least it used to be."

"Ah, the stable."

Not for the kind of horses he was thinking about, but she nodded anyway.

Conn angled out of the Hummer, Rae did the same, then almost climbed back in when a voice bellowed, "Blissfield!"

Rae closed her eyes, striving for patience—which was in short supply considering how often she'd dipped into that well in the last few hours. Apparently exhaustion was setting in, too, because she turned with a polite smile and said, "Mrs. Vander Snooty," which was what she called the woman with the imperious and obnoxious voice. Behind her back. "I mean Mrs. Vander Horn," she corrected herself, wincing in anticipation of the tongue lashing she was about to get.

Fortunately, Mrs. Vander Horn's tongue was busy hanging out. The woman had to be close to eighty, but she was having the predictable female reaction to Connor Larkin, including, apparently, the urge to loosen various articles of clothing, since one hand rose to toy with the fussy bow at the collar of her lavender silk blouse.

"Mrs. Vander Horn, Connor Larkin," Rae said. She should have known even a simple introduction would be trouble.

"Well met, madam," Conn said.

"Is that a crack about my age?"

"It's a crack about his age," Rae said, and while Mrs. Vander Horn didn't get it, Conn did because Rae looked over and he was smiling slightly, just one corner of his mouth quirked up enough to tell her he understood her play on words.

Even that meager a smile was enough to have Mrs. Vander Horn forget her indignation. She sidled over to Rae and said, "If I were ten years younger, I'd give you a run for your money."

If she'd been ten years younger she'd have jumped him already, bad hip and all. "Is there something I can help you with, Mrs. Vander Horn?"

"You can tell me who the stud is."

"He's not a stud, he's a friend of my . . . friend. He's in town for a few days, and I said he could stay here. As a favor."

"I'll bet you did." Mrs. Vander Horn put an ancient tarnished brass opera glass, which she wore on a chain pinned to her heather plaid suit jacket, up to her eye and walked around him, taking a good long look. "Wait until Hildebrandt gets a look at him."

"Mrs. Hildebrandt lives next door," Rae explained for Conn's benefit. "Mrs. Vander Horn lives directly across the street from her."

"Best you keep your distance from her," Mrs. Vander Horn put in. "She'll have you for dinner. And breakfast. If she has any appetite left after she gets done with the lawn boys."

"Lawn boys?" Rae asked, curiosity getting the better of her common sense.

"Do you know she hired my lawn service?" Mrs. Vander Horn said, dropping her opera glass to squint at Rae. "And I'll be damned if they don't do her yard first, every time. She says it's because they like her more than me, but I'll bet you my granddaddy's fortune she bribed them. And now every week she comes out on her front porch and sits in that damn white wicker fruitcake chair, swigging lemonade with a vodka kicker and watching the young men mow and trim with their shirts off . . ."

She turned to Conn. "Would you be interested in making a little spending cash?" she said, her gaze locked on his chest, definitely picturing him shirtless. And probably sweaty. "Hildebrandt will be so jealous she'll pop an artery."

"It is unseemly for mature women to feud," Conn said, a sparkle in his eye—which only Rae caught since Mrs. Vander Horn had drawn herself up to exclaim, "Mature!" her dignity affronted.

"Elderly."

"Elderly!" Her hand came up.

Rae stepped in front of him. It didn't seem to deter Mrs. Vander Horn. Conn did.

"If you strike Lady Blissfield," he said, his hands settling warmly on her shoulders, "I will have to invade you."

"Lady Blissfield?"

"He means me," Rae said, trying not to think about the way his fingers were kneading the back of her neck. It felt so good she wanted to collapse against him so she could feel that warmth all over, lean into that strength again, just for a moment or two—

Mrs. Vander Horn snorted. "You can't talk to me like that, young man. Nobody talks to me like that. And don't think I didn't miss the threat. I should call the police."

"Okay," Rae said, feeling utterly calm and relaxed, which was amazing, even better that she could handle this officious old bat the way she'd always wanted to. At some point she'd regret this, probably the second she didn't have Conn's warmth and strength to borrow from anymore. But for the moment she was letting old Vander Snooty have it with both barrels. "When the police come out I can tell them all about how I watched from my kitchen window while you vandalized Mrs. Hildebrandt's prize roses. Right before the flower show."

Mrs. Vander Horn Hoovered in a breath, her mouth going wide before she pressed her lips so tightly together they all but disappeared. "I did no such thing. And if I did it was an accident."

"Tell it to the cops. I'm sure they'll understand. I don't imagine I could say the same of Mrs. Hildebrandt."

The old woman narrowed her eyes at Rae. "Fine, but you're on my list." And she took herself off in a huff.

"List?" Conn said, his voice a deep, quiet, soothing rumble. "I presume this list is not a good thing. I can still invade her."

"She would probably enjoy that," Rae said.

AFTER THEIR RUN-IN WITH THE OLD DRAGON ACROSS the street, Rae had shooed Conn inside the house, "Before any of my other half-baked neighbors can escape their keepers and ask questions," she'd told him.

Baking people? And who was keeping them prisoner? Conn didn't follow most of that so he stopped paying attention. At least to what she was saying. He'd been doing that a lot since he met Rae Blissfield. But then, that could be due less to her confusing conversational style and more to other distractions. And he wasn't just talking about the physical. To be sure he could have spent hours exploring the nape of her neck, the ripe fullness of her lips, the small of her back where it nipped in at her waist then curved out below. Her skin was warm and perfumed and so sensitive he could all but feel her shudder, hear the way her breath sighed out as he touched her. She was a woman a man should take his time pleasuring. A woman who would return that pleasure a thousandfold.

But she would not give in easily. Rae Blissfield had already proven her strength, keeping her head during the kind of peril she should never have had occasion to experience. She'd shown herself to be intelligent, finding a solution to that peril that neither risked their lives nor caused her to go against her own dislike of violence. Even her insistence on going back to the faire, of trying to find a solution to his problem, showed a dogged determination that was to be admired and respected, as was the grace with which she'd accepted failure.

And there was an accord between them, an unspoken meeting of the minds that appealed to him more than he'd have believed possible. No, Rae Blissfield would not surrender willingly, but he would not find himself bored in the pursuit. And, although he understood it to be a weakness for any number of reasons, there would be a pursuit.

But not tonight.

Rae had been through enough that day. She was only trying to help him, after all, so he followed her from room to room in her house, knowing she wanted to race through the task and get away from him, but unable to do anything except take his time. There was so much to see and experience, and hurrying just wasn't in his nature.

"How about we move it along," Rae said, "if you're done getting up close and personal with the walls."

"Why the urgency?" Conn asked, running his finger-tips over the faded green cloth covering the walls in what Rae called the spare bedroom.

"It's been a long, eventful day. I'm tired."

Without doubt, Conn thought, being wound so tightly must be exhausting.

"Flocked," she said, sighing eloquently, giving up the attempt to impose her timetable on him. "The wallpaper."

"Then this is wool?" he asked, curiosity getting the better of chivalry.

"No."

His gaze shifted to her face, and he forgot about sheep and why anyone would dye their wool such an ungodly color and fasten it to walls.

Rae's expression went even more tense, her eyes dropped to his hands, slowly brushing across the textured bits of the wall covering, and her teeth sank into her full bottom lip.

Interesting. And arousing.

"Will you stop that already?" she snapped, wiping surreptitiously at her upper lip.

He could have—he *should* have—if only because she'd requested it of him, and he owed her a great debt. He could not. In his defense, there was just too much to experience. He'd seen a lot at the faire—automobiles, tiny devices for communicating or making music—but he'd never seen a house like this stuffed with so many wonders, both seen and felt. The way the little box of moving pictures raised the hair on his arms when he passed his palm in front of it, the shapes and textures of her furniture, the fine carpets and quarried stone covering her floors.

"What manner of craftsman made this?" he asked, brushing his fingertips across the incredibly smooth, impossibly thin sheet of what she called aluminum covering her refrigerator.

She didn't respond—not with words, but when he turned to look at her he found in her eyes the answer to a different question. *Touch me*, her eyes said, *take me. Right here, right now.*

She covered her weakness with animosity. "I know this is your first time away from Holly Grove, but you must have seen a television before, and there's a refrigerator in my parents' Airstream."

"Not like this one." He opened the door. "Your parents had food in theirs."

"Some things," Rae said, "are timeless."

"Aye," he replied, knowing she meant his stomach, and thinking of an entirely different hunger, "but I think we should dine instead. I would enjoy some Scottish chicken."

She sighed. "I'll get my purse."

"YOU MOWED THROUGH EVERYTHING EDIBLE IN THE house, listened to music, and watched television," Rae said several hours later—once she'd exhausted her repertoire of heavy sighs, eye rolls, and polite hints that it was getting late. Conn had ignored all the histrionics so he could avoid the inevitable reality that he was going to be sleeping alone—likely somewhere uncomfortable, but alone was the real problem.

He wasn't sure what it was about Rae Blissfield, but he wanted her. Bad. It was that simple. His memory loss, coupled with his friendship with her parents, made it very complicated. And made her untouchable—at least in most of the ways he wanted to touch her.

It made no sense at all. She could have taught a bowstring lessons, she was strung so tight. She had never opened up to herself, let alone anyone else, and she kept him at arm's length, except when he'd rubbed her shoulders. He'd only wanted to relieve some of the tension there, but for a moment, just a second really, he'd felt her begin to relax against him. And what had been a gesture of aid and warmth had turned hot and selfish, just wild enough to scare him, and very little scared him. If she'd give him the least encouragement . . . And if he kept thinking like that he would surely test the waters again, which he had no business doing. A man who didn't even know himself had no right becoming involved with someone else.

"And my water bill is going to be astronomical," she was saying, "because you flushed the toilet about a hundred times . . . Yeah, I know, Porta-Johns. I'm exhausted. Can we go to bed? And by bed I mean me. You're sleeping on the couch."

"My second choice," Conn said, but he kept his eyes off her.

The couch turned out to be comfortable enough, if a little solitary. It was too short, as well. He tossed and turned all night. And dreamt, although he had a pretty good idea they hadn't been dreams at all, but flashes of memory. Each had been more disturbing than the last, and each one was stronger, longer, harder to step away from.

He rose just as the first flush of dawn pearled the eastern horizon, cat-footing it to the doorway of Rae's bower, which she'd insisted on leaving open. In case there was a problem, she'd said with a meaningful look at him, as if he were a two-year-old who needed watching. He figured it was really all those years of sleeping in a tiny trailer. She probably couldn't stand being closed in.

She certainly slept like a woman who treasured her space, sprawled across the bed, her skin rosy with sleep, her rich red hair tousled. She looked so relaxed Conn almost wished she could stay asleep. Waking her meant watching that pinched look settle around her mouth and eyes. She only thought she was happy, but then, he could say the same of himself. Why else would he lose his memory and not want to get it back?

And that, he thought as he eased quietly away from her doorway, was a question for another time. The sun would soon shine in what promised to be a cloudless sky, the birds already sang in the trees, and the neighbors had yet to emerge.

He went out the back door, stepping barefoot onto the well-clipped ground covering behind her house. Gardens surrounded the lawn, and the Hummer sat on the paved area to his left where Rae had parked it, everything enclosed by a tall wooden fence with stone posts. It was all peace and perfection. And then the sounds of an intruder came from Rae's carriage house.

Between heartbeats Conn snapped from relaxed to ready, slipping across the grass, his footfalls silent as he rounded the yard. He approached the small building from an angle that wouldn't expose him to either the door or the windows, creeping up to the side of the carriage house, the wall chilly against his shoulders as he eased around the front corner, far enough to spy the intruder. Which turned out to be an old man clad in a robe decorated with swirls of burgundy and midnight blue and gold down to his spindly bare ankles, his feet shod in deep red velvet slippers with fur lining.

"Do you require assistance?" Conn asked him.

The old man spun around and whacked him over the head with a clear sack filled with metal, glass, and plastic containers, cocking back for another blow.

"'Swounds!" Conn caught the arm holding the sack and the collar of the conjurer's robe, then quickstepped him into the house, the old guy sputtering objections and digging his heels in the entire way to Rae's bedroom door. Even without factoring in the age difference, it was no contest since Conn had at least a foot and fifty pounds of muscle on the other man.

Rae must have heard the commotion because she sat up, clutching the bedclothes to her chest, blinking and rubbing her eyes. "I know, you're hungry," she said around a yawn, clearly not entirely awake. "I'll scare up something for breakfast if you give me a minute to wake up."

"Breakfast?" the old man said before Conn shook him and he decided it might be a good idea to hold his tongue, even though it was too late because Rae went still, just her head swiveling to land on Conn, shift to the old man for a beat or two, then move back to Conn. She didn't look happy about the situation. Conn got the distinct impression she was blaming him.

"Mr. Pennworthy?"

He drew himself up, as much as he could with a relative giant clutching the collar of his robe. "Your house-guest has accosted me. I'd like to borrow your phone to call the police."

"It looks like you've already borrowed a few things from me," Rae said. She tossed the covers back, long, bare legs swinging over the side of the bed, distracting Conn enough that he almost let the thief go. "I thought we agreed you could steal my returnables, but the paper is off limits."

"Alchemy must not provide a decent livelihood in this time," Conn put in.

"Alchemy?"

"Aye, and magic."

Rae looked Mr. Pennworthy over from head to toe, grinning. "He's not a magician, well, not the kind you mean. He's a CEO—he runs a big company. Considering his track record with my newspaper, I don't doubt he's familiar with creative accounting, but I'd bet he's been honest since Sarbanes-Oxley weighed in after Enron."

Conn caught about every other word.

Mr. Pennworthy apparently understood it all—and took offense to it. "I will not stand here and be discussed by the likes of you as though I were a common criminal."

Conn smiled politely. "Some cultures cut off a man's hand for stealing. The Moors, the Infidels we battled in the Crusades, even some of the titled lords where I come from."

Mr. Pennworthy took one look at Conn's face and gave a little bleat of fright.

Rae rolled her eyes. "We're not going to cut anything off." But she took her newspaper away from him. "Go home, Mr. Pennworthy."

He squared his shoulders when Conn let him go, straightened his robe and, the bag of returnables cradled tightly in his arms, sidled away from Conn, picking up speed as he got out of arms' reach.

"I will retrieve the containers, if you like," Conn offered.

"What I'd like is a cup of coffee," Rae said. She pulled on a robe and went into the kitchen.

Coffee Conn understood, although preparing it seemed to belong to his area of lost memory. He followed her, watching carefully while she measured aromatic grounds into a small white paper bowl and placed it into a machine sitting on her counter. Water followed, and in seconds steaming hot coffee spilled out into the glass pot below.

He closed his eyes and inhaled, and when he opened them again, she'd replaced the large pot with a mug, switching back again when the mug was full and holding it out to him.

"It's going to be strong," she said.

He wrapped his hands around hers on the mug and met her eyes. "I like strong."

Watching her react to his touch was fascinating. Color flooded her face and she seemed to soften. Her eyelids fluttered as her breath sighed out. She never broke eye contact, though, even as she pulled her hand from beneath his and covered her desire with irritation.

"You also like to eat," she said, and turned her back to get another mug as if nothing had happened.

Conn took it as a challenge, and he had never backed down from a challenge. He couldn't say how he knew that; it probably had something to do with all the fighting in his memory flashes, along with the way he'd reacted to the two altercations the day before. Or maybe it was the feeling building inside of him, the urge to *win* that had him saying, "You feel attraction toward me. Why do you deny it?"

"Because I've known you less than twenty-four hours, for starters." She turned, a package of bread in her hands. "You live the kind of life I couldn't wait to leave behind, and then there's the memory loss, which is a pretty big problem by itself, but you don't seem to care if you ever get it back, which is the bigger problem if you ask me. If I accept your memory loss is real I have to wonder what happened in your past that you don't want to revisit."

He thought about that, a muscle working in his jaw.

Rae felt bad for pushing him. But he wasn't meeting her eyes, either.

"Is anything familiar to you?" she asked, opening the bread and popping two slices into the toaster.

"Yes and no. Things seem familiar, but when I attempt to build on a shred of recognition it only slips away."

"Don't try to remember, just answer without thinking about it. How old are you?"

"I cannot say."

"Where do you come from, do you have family somewhere?"

He shrugged.

"Wife, kids, parents, siblings?" God forbid he had a brother. One of him was almost too much to imagine. "You must at least have a feeling when you hear these questions, a gut reac—"

"I do not," he ground out, scrubbing his hands back through his hair. "Why do you seek to tally and measure?"

It felt pretty damn important that he didn't have a wife. But the toast popped up just then, saving her from blurting that out. He might be struggling with his memory, but he had a very agile mind otherwise. He wouldn't miss the implications. And take advantage of her for them.

"It's what I do," she said instead, turning away from him to butter the toast. "I'm a CPA—Certified Public Accountant."

"And what does a . . . certified public accountant," he repeated carefully, "do?"

"Tally." She put the toast on a paper towel and carried it to the small table in her breakfast nook. "Measure."

He sat, picked up a slice of toast and studied it. Not a lot of toast at the Renaissance festival, she thought.

"You ate everything else in the house last night, so this will have to do for breakfast. We can go to the market later."

He took a tentative taste, then ate the rest of the toast in three bites. Rae sighed, putting two more slices in the toaster.

"Tell me more about your work," he said. "What do you tally and measure?"

"Money. Profit and loss for businesses, income for people. I keep track of that income, calculate what taxes a person or business owes so they don't get in trouble with the government."

"The king must have his share. That, at least, has not changed."

"We don't have a king, contrary to the opinions some of our elected officials hold of themselves, but I guess it amounts to the same thing."

"Then you are a steward."

"In a way." She ferried more toast to the table.

"Do you have a man?"

"No."

"For someone who wants roots, you have not established any. You have a home, but no husband, no family."

Rae went back to her toast production line, dropping two more slices into the toaster and buttering the ones she'd just removed. "I've been busy," she said, "and we're supposed to be talking about you."

"I have precious little to report of myself."

"Then I suggest you spend some quality time with your brain, see if you can tap into your memory banks," she said, dropping the last two pieces of toast in front of him. "I'm going to take a shower."

Conn looked toward the bathroom, back at her. "And you expect me to concentrate on a task I already know cannot be accomplished? I have always been a man of action."

"Typical," she said. Not that she should be surprised that he was a man who thought he could muscle his way through a problem; he had all the right equipment for that particular mindset.

"I could be of service to you. In my time it was common to have an attendant when you bathe. To wash your back."

"*This* is your time," she reminded him. "Come anywhere near that bathroom and you'll be getting conked on the head again, whether it helps your amnesia or not."

"I would not impose myself on you."

"Of course not." Rae was worried she'd impose herself on him, and then where would she be? *Satisfied*, a traitorous little voice whispered. *Probably several times*. "But it wasn't my back you were thinking of."

He grinned. "Perhaps not only your back."

chapter 8

RAE THOUGHT OF HER BACK THE ENTIRE TIME she was in the shower. It was better than the other body parts she wanted to think about, most of them belonging to Connor Larkin. And it was better than not thinking. Not thinking left her with feeling. Feeling might lead to acting, and acting wasn't a good idea. Acting was the furthest thing from a good idea she could imagine, no matter how incredible acting was in her imagination.

The steaming shower didn't help, so she washed and rinsed in record time, then dressed in jeans and a cotton sweater. A low-cut, vee-neck, cleavage-baring sweater . . . Right, like that wasn't a blatant invitation, and issuing an invitation to a man who invaded people would probably be a bad idea. Not that being invaded by him didn't have its attractions. But it also had its repercussions, and a few moments of pleasure— Okay, she thought, picturing Conn and his . . . attributes, an entire night of pleasure wasn't worth a moment of the hell she'd put herself through for getting dragged into her mother's odd little world.

She whipped the sweater off, pulled on a square-necked camisole and replaced the sweater, checking to make sure there wasn't even a hint of cleavage. She almost never left her hair down to air dry, but this situation definitely called for it, since primping seemed to fall under the heading of *actions with seriously misguided ulterior motives*.

"The bathroom's all yours," she said when she came out, careful not to look at him—or offer him help. If he didn't know how the shower worked she wasn't about to show him, not when the water wasn't the only thing that might get turned on.

And then she had to get her mind off what he was doing in there. The only thing more dangerous than thinking of Conn was thinking of him naked and wet, soap suds rinsing down the long, lean lines of his body, muscles flexing as he bent—

She snatched up the portable phone, just the thought of calling her boss enough to drag her back from fantasy to reality.

"Hello, Mr. Putnam," she said, not surprised to find him in the office, even though it was barely six A.M. She should have been there, too. Everyone worked twelve-hour days at quarter's end.

Mr. Putnam's silence told her he was thinking the same thing.

They can't live without me, she reminded herself. At least not in the short term. "I won't be in today," she said, flying high on self-delusion.

"Not ill, I hope," he said with the same amount of sympathy he'd show a client past due on their bill.

"I'm fine, but something has come up."

"What?"

"Well . . . it's personal."

"Then perhaps I should ask who?"

"Uh . . ."

"It must be something very important to take you from your work at one of our busiest times."

She took a deep breath, blurting the rest of it out in a ripping-off-the-bandage kind of way. "I'll need to work at home for the next week. Or so."

Silence. Heat flooded her face, stress spiking her blood pressure high enough to blast the top of her head off.

"Problem?"

She swung around, coming face to chest with Conn, which took the heat out of her face—and sent it rushing elsewhere. Thankfully, Mr. Putnam had traded in the cold, disapproving silence for a cold, disapproving lecture, droning on about responsibility and accountability, not just to her clients but to her employers, since, *surprise*, her special request gave him another excuse to send the not-making-partner message.

And it all sank in. It just couldn't compete with Connor Larkin's bare, damp muscles. It took every ounce of willpower she possessed not to let her gaze wander down. She was pretty sure only a waterlogged towel stood between Conn and full frontal nudity, which would lead to complete carnal knowledge, and while that would be good—heck it would probably be mind-blowing—it wasn't what she needed to learn about Connor Larkin. And who gave a damn, she thought, her willpower no match for her curiosity, not to mention the hot, melting desire to—

"Ms. Blissfield, are you still there?"

She whipped around, pried her tongue off the roof of her mouth, and said, "Yes, Mr. Putnam. I'm sorry, I understand this is a problem, but—"

"Is it one of your parents?"

"Um, no. Not directly."

"Because I received your message that your mother called. Something about an emergency."

Rae looked over her shoulder, then lowered her voice. "It's, uh, my plumbing. In the basement." And now she could never invite her boss to her house, because she didn't have a basement. But she'd realized too late that he'd wonder how she could work from home with no plumbing. That was the problem with lies. They tended to multiply. "It's a mess, Mr. Putnam, and I can't let it go or it will just get worse. And I have to be here for the plumber. I know it's a bad time, but I promise my work won't suffer." And she was rambling because her eyes had dropped to Conn's chest again. She lifted her gaze to his mouth, found him smirking at her, and it took the wobble right out of her knees. "I'll be in later to get my files."

"Very well," Putnam said and then hung up.

She disconnected as well, stifling a sigh of relief.

Unfortunately, Connor Larkin was way too observant, and way too in touch with his inner Freud to miss her reaction.

"This man you spoke with has made you unhappy," he said.

"Not in the way you think. I work for him. It's our busy time. Under normal circumstances he wouldn't let me take any time off."

"So you lied to him."

"I made up an excuse."

"To keep me entertained."

And out of trouble.

"Can I make a suggestion?" Conn asked her. "About the entertainment?"

Rae let her eyes drift down to the towel. "No," she said, pretty sure what his suggestion would be, and not all that sure she'd turn him down if he made it.

RAE SENT CONN OFF TO GET DRESSED. HE FOLLOWED instructions. Unfortunately, he chose to come back as a sixteenth-century armorer, complete with buff-colored suede pants and knee-high boots. And no shirt.

"Why are you wearing *that*?"

"You told me to put my clothes on, but I will gladly take them off—"

Rae brushed past him, stomping into the spare room. There, on the chair, were the jeans and T-shirt he'd worn the day before. She picked up the duffel from the floor. It was empty. "Mom," she snapped out.

"Annie said there was no need to thank her."

"I'll bet." Rae dropped the duffel and gathered up the jeans and T-shirt, tossing them to him. "Put these on."

"But—"

"In case you hadn't noticed, all the people who went to Holly Grove had shirts on."

"Some of them just barely," he said with a leer she didn't find charming, or even amusing, probably, in part, because she knew he was thinking of the teens and twenty-somethings with their belly-baring, strappy, low-cut tops. Typical man, being led around by the codpiece.

"Get. Dressed. And make it snappy. I'll be waiting in the car."

He was barely thirty seconds behind her, and when he came out he was wearing the T-shirt and jeans, which wasn't much of an improvement, considering the denim fit him almost as snugly as the leather. No relaxed fit for Connor Larkin. But then, he was going to get attention no matter what he wore. No way to avoid that. And she couldn't leave him home alone. There was no telling what he'd get up to.

He opened the passenger door, but he didn't get in. "Can I drive?" he asked her.

"No." Then she turned to look at him. "Can you drive?"

"I think so."

"That's a no." She fired up the Hummer. Conn climbed in, and she backed it down her narrow, curved driveway, inch by careful inch. It already had a bullet hole in it; no point in doing it any more damage. Or her house, for that matter. She didn't have to look at Conn to know he was grinning. "I suppose you think you could do better."

"I could try."

"Still no."

Conn flopped back in his seat, the grin morphing into a sulk.

"And buckle your seatbelt," she added, giving in to a smile of her own as she headed the Hummer toward Troy, the second largest city in Michigan—based on property value. It was also home to the Detroit Red Wings' training facility and a thriving center of business, including Putnam, Ibold and Greenblatt, LLP, Certified Public Accountants and Personal Financial Consulting.

Conn spent the trip gawking at the scenery. Rae spent it trying not to have a panic attack. She managed to talk herself out of turning back a dozen times, only to get to the parking structure of her firm's building and find herself faced with a new dilemma.

She hadn't wanted to leave Conn alone at her house, but she certainly couldn't take him into her place of business. If she walked in with a man like him, her plumbing excuse would fly right out the window, taking her reputation—and her future—along with it. There was no way she'd ever make partner if Putnam felt he couldn't trust her.

It was just past seven thirty in the morning, but the structure was pretty full. Rae took the first parking spot she found, luckily one that was around the corner from the other cars where it wouldn't be easily seen from the elevator doors, muttering, "anal," which was completely hypocritical since she'd have been at her desk if not for Conn.

"Anal?" Conn repeated.

She opened her mouth, but there just didn't seem to be a frame of reference to bridge the gap between her century and his, at least not one she was willing to say out loud. The look on her face must have said it all.

He held up a hand. "That one I don't want to know."

"Stay here," she ordered Conn. "Do not look at anyone, do not talk to anyone, do not get out of the vehicle for any reason." She hit the door locks, walked a couple steps off, and stopped, letting her head fall forward as she gave in to the guilt. He wasn't a child, and he wasn't a puppy— a child she would have taken with her, and she'd at least have cracked the windows for a dog.

Then again, Conn already had the door unlocked and open before she turned around.

"I'm sorry," she said to him. "I have to go all the way up to the top floor, but I promise I won't be long, and then we'll have lunch—the midday meal."

"Bribery?"

"Is it working?"

He studied her face, long enough to let her know it
wasn't the promise of a meal that got to him, even though
he said, "What kind of lunch?"

"No Scottish chicken, but I can promise there'll be
meat involved."

"As long as there are no turkey legs," he said. "I've had
enough of them to last a lifetime."

She knew exactly how he felt. Renaissance faires did
big business in turkey legs, and the tourists didn't seem to
mind the smell of roasting fowl. But it was sickening
when you spent day after day with it. On a whim, she
handed him the keys. "You put it in the . . . right, like
that," she said when he slipped the key into the ignition,
telling herself she was grateful he'd figured it out and she
didn't have to reach across him. "You know how to work
the radio, right?"

He nodded, already reaching for the buttons, so she
made her escape, trekking through the structure, then taking the elevator to the top floor. It was a shame she couldn't
bring Conn. He'd have loved the view.

He'd probably get a kick out of the lobby, too. Even a
guy who thought he was a sixteenth-century armorer
would take one look at the Putnam, Ibold and Greenblatt
sign, the capital letters big and gold, and have a good
laugh.

The joke had lost its luster for Rae, but she stifled an
urge, as always, to shake her head. They could solve their
unfortunate acronym problem if Mr. Putnam would stop
being stubborn about having his name first. And since
Putnam was being a putz, Ibold, the cofounder, refused to
be named last. So they were P.I.G.

The G in P.I.G., Morris Greenblatt, met her at the door,
opening it and ushering her in with a big, welcoming
smile on his face. Mr. Greenblatt was the one and only
partner who'd ever been added to the firm, and that had
been twenty years ago. Probably that should have been
Rae's first clue that her hopes were doomed, but Putnam
and Ibold were getting up there in age, and since neither

of them had children to fill their shoes Rae had decided Italian leather pumps would do the job nicely.

It had seemed, at first, that they felt the same way. After all, she'd been chosen from hundreds of applicants, at the behest of the partners, she'd been told. Unfortunately, the two senior partners showed absolutely no inclination to either retire or expand the business, so what had sounded like the opportunity of a lifetime had instead turned into a treadmill workout. No matter how fast she ran she got nowhere.

"Mr. Putnam asked me to help you gather your files," Mr. Greenblatt said, looking sheepish because he knew *help* was really *watch*.

"I don't need anything from the vault," she said.

Most of the accounting work was done on the computer, but the paper printouts were kept in a locked room called the vault, where files had to be checked in and out. Those files belonged to the big corporate clients of Putnam, Ibold, and Greenblatt, and while Rae had worked on every one of them from time to time, they weren't her regulars. And even if they were, there was no way she'd be allowed to take them off site.

Mr. Greenblatt fell into step with her anyway, accompanying her into her office, which officially put it over the fire marshall's maximum occupancy. The narrow window kept it from feeling completely claustrophobic.

"I'm sure I can be helpful," Greenblatt said. Translation: He'd been instructed not to let her out of his sight. Just in case she'd turned into a raving criminal overnight.

Greenblatt took a step back, eyes on her face, sounding tentative when he said, "I hope everything at home is all right."

"The plumber assured me it will be fine but, well, it's an old house, you know?"

"Of course, of course." He waved it all away with a couple nervous flutters of his hands. "Perhaps this time next year you won't have to clear your work schedule with Putnam, or anyone else for that matter. Not if I have my way."

"Thank you, Mr. Greenblatt," she said, and meant it. "You know how much it means to me to make partner."

"Oh, now, it's nothing," he said, looking over his shoulder in case, she assumed, Ebenezer Scrooge poked his head out of his cave. Or Jacob Marley, for that matter, because if Putnam was Scrooge, Ibold would be Marley—before Marley had died and gotten a clue. Not that she saw herself as Bob Cratchit. The pay was better, but mostly it was because she had goals, and she was only going to hang around there as long as she stood a chance of meeting them.

"Well," she said to Mr. Greenblatt, "I have to go." She stuffed the entire contents of her two-drawer file cabinet into a box and hefted it. "Thank you."

"Let me help you with that."

"No! It's not heavy. Really. And I'm sure you have other things to do."

"Nothing impor—"

"Mr. Greenblatt!" One of the assistants stuck her head in the door, "You have a visitor. Mr. Putnam said to make sure you tell him the rates because he doesn't look like he can afford our services."

Greenblatt scurried out. How he'd made partner when he was so clearly scared of Putnam and Ibold was beyond Rae. Not that Putnam didn't take pains to be intimidating. Hell, two days ago Putnam's disapproval would have been absolutely mortifying. Now . . . What she wanted to do was shrug her shoulders.

She hitched the box up and walked out, running into Mr. Putnam in the hallway.

"Please check in at regular intervals," he said to her.

"I will, Mr. Putnam."

As she passed him, he gave a dry, disapproving little sniff. Rae stopped and looked back at him; he was doing the same, the expression on his face speculative at first, then warning.

She drew in a breath and let it out slowly, realizing she stood at a crossroads, and she couldn't take the fork she always chose, the one marked CAUTION. And sure, it was because her parents had unintentionally put her in the position of jeopardizing her job, but she refused to feel guilty about it. She'd worked thousands of hours of overtime for this firm, and if they decided to fire her over one special request, she'd survive it. She'd struck out on her own at eighteen, no money, no friends, no safety net, and she'd managed to make a life for herself. She could do it again. If she had to.

chapter
9

RAE KEPT HER HEAD UP AND HER SPINE STIFF. She didn't look back until she was in the elevator and the doors had closed. Her last glimpse of Mr. Putnam had not been reassuring. By the time the elevator hit the garage level all her bravado had evaporated, and her heart was pounding.

She didn't waste time wondering what the hell had gotten into her. It was a useless question because she knew exactly what had gotten into her. Connor Larkin, and not in a good way. She'd been with him—she consulted her watch—less than twenty hours, and she was willing to throw her job down the tubes? In this economy?

She was good and steamed by the time the Hummer came into sight—or rather hearing, since she caught the thump of the bass from the radio well before she turned the last corner. And found the passenger door open and Conn gone.

"Shit," she said under her breath, "shit, shit, shit," as she climbed into the driver's seat, started the Hummer, and screeched out of the parking space, the passenger door flinging itself closed from the acceleration.

How in the world had the bad guys found them? she

wondered frantically. They didn't know where she lived or worked, and the Hummer wasn't registered to her so they couldn't have found her that way.

She took the first turn practically on two wheels and hit the brakes when she saw an unmistakable form in the gloom by the exit. He was peering in the window of a Chevy Impala.

She pulled up next to him, shot the Hummer into park, and jumped out. "I thought you were going to stay in the car," she said, hands on hips, toe to toe with him.

He gestured to the car he'd been examining. "I thought maybe one of these vehicles would strike a chord."

"You don't strike me as the family sedan kind of guy."

He shrugged, which ticked her off even more, especially in light of her recent behavioral readjustment. "What's that?" she demanded, lifting her shoulders to her earlobes. "This," she did it again, "is not a response. *No* is a response. *Yes* is a response. *This*," she mocked his shrug one more time, "just means you don't care."

"That is not my intention," he said solemnly. "I simply mean that I feel no urgency—"

"No urgency? Two pirate wannabes with swords tried to carve you up like a Thanksgiving turkey. Three clowns in a Honda shot at us. Not to mention some or all of them cracked you over the head and broke your memory banks, which is why my parents sent you off with me in the first place. The least you can do is listen when I give you instructions that are for your own good."

There was a beat of silence.

"I'm finished," she said.

"Do you feel better?"

"Yes."

"I apologize." He moved around behind her and began to knead her shoulders, then her neck and spine.

In the time it took to draw her next breath she went from burning mad to just burning.

"I did not mean to make light of my situation, or to give the impression that your life is so inconsequential that my presence is not an imposition."

She moved away before she lost more than her anger, like some of her clothes. "I'm hungry, how about you?"

Conn didn't say anything, but the air between them seemed to crackle.

It would be so easy to cross that supercharged foot of distance and throw herself into the inferno. And it would be the most difficult thing she would ever do. She wasn't an impulsive person. Or an open one. That wasn't to say she shut people out by choice. Rather, it wasn't in her nature to let people in easily.

Besides, the man didn't even know himself, so how could she know anything about him? Except that there were people who wanted to harm him, if not kill him, and while he might be a floater as an amnesiac, there was a core of steel in him, an ability to go from harmless to threatening in the space of a heartbeat that didn't come from being an engineer or a mechanic. Whatever his occupation was when he was in touch with reality, it was something people like her didn't want to know about.

WHEN RAE TOLD HIM THEY WERE GOING TO THE Somerset Collection, Conn thought it was something people purchased for no discernible purpose, like the little pewter figurines of knights and conjurers that were sold at the faire. Turned out it was a pair of large buildings on either side of a wide thoroughfare called Big Beaver, the two connected with a walkway made of glass that stretched above the road.

Rae guided the Hummer beneath the walkway, then turned a huge half-circle to end up behind one of the buildings. They went beneath a concrete roof covering a large parking lot, and Rae drove up and down the aisles until she found a space she could maneuver the huge vehicle into.

"Okay, now we just have to pray nobody parks too close," she said, opening her door and stepping out just as they heard the screech of rubber on pavement.

Conn twisted around in his seat, making the shift from

calm to alert even before he saw the Honda slide to a stop, blocking them in. All the windows were shiny new glass, but the car wasn't blue anymore, at least not all of it. It was a rainbow palette of replaced body parts, green quarter panels, red hood, the remaining blue parts dented and crumpled.

Conn looked to Rae—their eyes met as they came to an instantaneous and simultaneous conclusion. And since Rae was already vulnerable, he shot out of the Hummer, rounding the front of it. He wrapped his hand around hers and took off running, between cars, working their way to the building, keeping himself between her and the Honda racing after them.

He kept them out of the wide driving lanes, not easy with the huge columns holding up the roof and drivers who parked too close to their neighbors, but the only way to neutralize the car was to get inside. That meant crossing the main drive between the cars and the mall entrance. He pulled Rae out into the yellow-lined crosswalk without hesitation, the Honda racing toward them. Conn poured on the speed, slinging an arm around Rae's waist and boosting her up. His feet hit the curb just as the Honda blasted by behind them, tires galumphing on the curb as the driver jerked to a stop across the narrow lane that led to the delivery door for the pizza restaurant just inside the mall.

Conn let go of Rae long enough to muscle the big door open. She scooted in under his arm as two guys piled out of the Honda, then stopped to look back at the third, heaving his bulk out of the driver's seat. He hitched his pants up under his impressive belly and took a position by the rear bumper. Waiting for them to come out.

Rae caught Conn by the wrist and tried to drag him into the mall. He pulled her into the restaurant instead, some sort of fusion pizza place. He could circle through there, he decided, come out the delivery door and surprise the third guy. The third guy wasn't going to chase them on foot, and if Conn could get his hands on a knife, he wouldn't be driving, either, not with a couple of slashed tires.

The other two guys followed, all four of them winding
their way through the tables and booths at a fast walk. The
hostess trailed along behind with menus, customers, and
waitstaff staring as they went by. Conn burst through the
swinging doors that led to the kitchen, and it smelled good
in there. Really good. There were bound to be knives, too,
but his stomach was growling—and two bad guys were
right behind them.

The kitchen staff was yelling, pots and pans clanged to
the floor, and things were frying and steaming and apparently not in the right way, considering how the cooks
were racing around looking frantic and blocking off their
pursuers in the process.

Conn spied what he wanted, towing Rae between a
stainless steel table and a vat of hot oil along one wall. He
snatched up a carving knife with his right hand, dipping
his left into a wire basket suspended over the vat. He
swiped his arm along the counter in the process, knocking
things over as he went, but he'd seen the same kind of oil
vat at the faire, and he had a decent idea what to expect
from the basket.

"Ouch," he said, juggling the crispy brown chunk he'd
snagged until it cooled enough for him to take a bite.
"Scottish chicken."

"Forget about your stomach," Rae said, apparently
reading his mind yet again since she was pulling him toward the door at the back of the kitchen. "I'm more interested in the knife. For the tires, right?"

"Yep."

But one of the bad guys made it to the delivery door
before them, yelling, "Cut them off, Harry," the other guy
already moving away to do just that.

Conn backtracked, shoving the cooks aside and sweeping racks out of his way and into the other guy's path.
Restaurant workers shouted, dishes and flatware crashed
to the floor, and a little curl of smoke emanated from the
general direction of the deep fryer. The fire alarm began
to wail and cell phones came out just as Conn pulled Rae
through the door and back into the dining area.

They slalomed around tables and booths, back through the restaurant and out into the mall, Conn feeling like he was in one of his nightly memory flashes, still not remembering everything, but also not stopping to think. He stepped onto the moving stairway, taking the steps two at a time and boosting Rae up in front of him, scanning their surroundings.

The Somerset Collection offered everything the high-end shopper could want: valet parking, three levels of stores that sold everything from caramel apples to shirts with strange and disturbing messages blazoned across them. Options for people being chased by potential murderers were few and far between.

"Any ideas?" he said to Rae as they hit the top of the stairway and started off at a fast walk.

"Moe and Larry don't seem to care if they catch us in here," she said, sounding worried.

"Moe and Larry?"

"Stooges," she said with a slight smile, "for lack of better names to call them."

"Moe and Harry," Conn said as if he understood a tenth of what she'd said. "One of them is named Harry."

"They're keeping up but not closing in."

"Yeah," Conn said, sounding grim, even to his own ears. If he'd been alone, he would have confronted the threat and eliminated it. If he'd been sure he was the only target. He couldn't take the chance they'd kidnap Rae to get to him, and he didn't ask himself how he knew that. It was what men had done to women since the world began. "We need to lose them, find a place to hide until they get tired of looking. Is there a way out up here?"

"I'm not that familiar with the mall."

"We can't go out the door we came in, not with the third Stooge waiting for us."

"Exactly what I was thinking," Rae said. "But maybe we should concentrate on the two guys coming up the escalator behind us."

They took off again, up the next escalator, which seemed to lead onto a floor of small food purveyors, kind of like the stalls at the faire, but a definite step up in variety and quality. There weren't any turkey legs in sight, for one thing, which meant no smoke, so he could smell everything else. His mouth began to water.

But Moe and Harry were right behind them, coming up the stairway.

Conn forgot about food completely, picking a direction at random and heading that way, staying behind Rae as much as possible without letting her know he was doing it. She might be a stranger to this kind of danger, but she was too quick-witted to miss the implications of his behavior, and too independent-minded to allow it. But he'd be damned if she got hurt on his account.

At least their pursuers seemed disinclined to pull weapons, which meant all he had to do was get away from them long enough to get back to the car. Easier said than done. They were in a well-lighted place, too sparsely occupied to provide them cover, so no ducking into one of the shiny, glass-fronted stores and hiding until the bad guys passed them by. And then it got worse.

A skinny man, a kid really, in a dark blue outfit fell in behind their pursuers, lifting a small device to his mouth and talking into it.

"Mall cop," Rae said.

Conn heard the word *cop*, remembered her using it as a substitute for *sheriff* and poured on the speed, dragging her along behind him, heading toward a big store that seemed to take up one whole end of the mall. There had to be a way to get lost in there.

"Wait," Rae shouted, tugging on his arm with both hands, "this way."

Conn didn't question her decision. She had to know more about the place than he did, so he followed her down the moving stairway again, pursued by two men who were probably responsible for his memory loss, a low budget sheriff, and a couple of kids with saggy black pants, silver rings through various facial features, and a boatload of curiosity. All they needed was a queen and a couple of courtiers and they'd have a decent parade.

He was still looking over his shoulder when Rae changed direction again. He turned back around just in time to nearly run face-first into the corner of a wall, ducking his head just in time to take the glancing blow on his temple. His ears rang and his vision blurred, but he shook it off, especially since the wall turned out to be the side of the glass walkway he'd seen from the road below.

"It's really too bad a good conk on the head doesn't solve your problem," Rae said.

Conn just aimed her forward and gave her a light shove. The walkway was a wide, brightly lit, sparsely traveled thoroughfare with moving sidewalks on either side. They ran down the center, nowhere to hide and no way out except the twin building at the opposite end. Conn blocked Rae as much as he could, and not just from attack. He didn't want the guys chasing them to see her face and connect her with Annie and Nelson. She thought she couldn't be found, but he wasn't willing to risk it.

"There has to be an exit here somewhere," she said when they came out the other end of the walkway into the south section of the mall. "All we have to do is find it."

Conn shook his head. "There doesn't seem to be much chance we'll lose these guys."

"If we can get back to the Hummer, they're toast."

"Toast?" Conn repeated, momentarily sidetracked by his grumbling belly.

"Run now, eat later," Rae yelled at him, glancing behind her. "Run now or you may not get to eat later."

"Thanks, I needed that motivation," Conn said. "I wasn't really taking these guys seriously."

"They don't have swords or guns, or a car, for that matter," Rae said, "but they're persistent. And they could sic the mall cop on us as a last resort."

"What can the mall cop do?"

"He can call the real cops."

Now *that*, Conn thought, was a motivator. He still didn't understand why the Blisses were so adamant about not wanting the police involved, but he agreed with them on a level that went beyond the memory problem. Sort of like the way he knew the sun was shining, even though there were clouds in the sky.

"He was talking into something," Conn said, remembering that first glimpse, right before he'd run into the wall. Which still hurt.

"Who?" Rae asked him, sounding breathless now that he'd picked up the pace. "Talking into what?"

"The kid in blue, and I don't know."

She looked over her shoulder. Conn moved to block her again.

"You keep doing that. Why?"

"Chivalry," he said, which was nothing but the truth, and whether she chose to believe it or not, Rae opted not to quibble.

"There's a parking structure on this side, too," she said, pausing at a lighted monolith that said INFORMATION at the top of it. She consulted it for a moment, but what really caught her attention was the fact that Harry and Moe had stopped a short distance away. "They're playing cat and mouse. They don't want an altercation in here with witnesses."

"They'd prefer to get us outside."

"Well, we can't stay in here," Rae said. "That thing the mall cop was talking into was a radio. If the real police aren't already here they're coming."

"Where's the exit?" Conn said, taking her by the hand with a renewed sense of urgency.

Rae pulled him off in a new direction. "They're just going to follow us."

Conn didn't figure he needed to comment on that.

"Okay," she said, "but I don't get it. Once we're outside, they're not going to play nice anymore."

"How fast can you run?"

Rae looked down at her shoes, which were some sort of shiny brown leather, but at least they were flat. "As fast as I have to," she said, meeting his eyes with determination.

"Good, then run," he said, taking her by the hand and pulling her through the exit door, which led onto the roof of a parking structure, a concrete monstrosity like the one where she worked. This one was packed with rows of vehicles along the same line as the Hummer, but a bit smaller. Great cover, unlike the ramp curving down to the next level.

As soon as they cleared the door, Conn headed straight for the ramp, making it to the bend just as Harry and Moe slammed out of the mall. "Stop," one of them yelled, squeezing off a shot that whizzed by just as they rounded the corner. The bullet thunked into the concrete wall.

"They shot at us," Rae said, breathless and wide-eyed.

Conn didn't waste his energy on talk, pulling her between two parked cars and slipping through the iron railings in front of them. They ended up on another sloped ramp, Harry and Moe's pounding footsteps echoing off the concrete close behind them.

The Stooges didn't seem to be in very good physical condition, but Rae wasn't exactly making the pursuit a challenge. Not her fault, Conn reminded himself as they worked their way down to the ground floor of the structure, unable to put any real distance between themselves and death. She couldn't possibly be prepared for this kind of footrace, not to mention she seemed to be having trouble with her footwear.

She slipped again; Conn dragged her upright. She hesitated for a second, then kicked her shoes off, hopping on one foot then the other until she was down to blue socks with little clocks on them.

"Those were Rockports," she said forlornly.

"Those were useless," Conn said, "at least for running."

"They were slip-ons," she protested breathlessly. "Brand-new, stiff ones. It wasn't their fault."

"They're just shoes."

She sent him a look meant to promise retribution. It only made him smile. "I'll buy you another pair."

"With what?"

That question stopped him, at least mentally. His feet kept moving, but it took a second for his brain to catch up. "I'll make you another pair."

"How about we get across the road in one piece first," she said, and when she would have stopped at the edge of the six-lane divided highway that separated the two sides of the mall, Conn took one assessing look at traffic and dragged her straight out into it. Cars swerved around them or jerked to a stop with a shriek of brakes and rubber, then they were across the east-bound lanes and on the grass-covered median.

Rae was tearing at the hand he had locked around her wrist, but she couldn't pry him loose. He dragged her into the west-bound lanes, but there didn't seem to be any traffic, the cars all pulling over before they got close. Conn heard a wailing noise, growing steadily louder.

"Siren," Rae gasped out, one hand on her side, stopping to bend at the waist as they made it to the other side of the road, right about where she'd driven the Hummer into the mall when they'd first arrived. "Fire truck." She pointed down the road and there was a huge red vehicle turning at the cross street that ran beside the mall. "Bad guys."

Conn looked over his shoulder. Harry and Moe were finally making it across the east-bound side of Big Beaver, having stopped at the curb and waited for traffic to clear.

"We're almost there," he said, breathing hard himself but nowhere near played out. He let go of Rae's wrist and wrapped his arm around her waist instead, running flat out even though he had to practically carry her at that speed.

Instead of following the road around the mall as they had in the Hummer, Rae pointed to the main entrance. Conn took her that way, slamming through the heavy door without slowing, running around a fountain that consisted of a huge ball slowly rotating on a thin layer of water. Any other time Conn would have stopped to examine the fountain, but he could only marvel at it as they raced by, dodging women with strollers, slow-moving shoppers on cell phones, and groups of youngsters wandering around with no discernible destination. In less than a minute they ran by the pizza restaurant, patrons and employees streaming through the entrance and into the mall to mill around in little knots, staring at the smoke pouring out at ceiling level.

Conn pushed through the heavy exit doors and saw the fire truck pull up, the shrieking of the siren nearly deafening under the concrete parking deck before it cut off. A cloud of greasy black smoke rolled along the cement ceiling, but it wasn't curiosity that brought Conn to a halt. Rae elbowed him in the side. It surprised him, and he was just out of breath enough to stop and let her go.

"The pizza restaurant is on fire," she said. "It's our fault."

She drew close to his side, an instinctive gesture that made Conn want to put his arm around her again. He didn't. Maybe if they hadn't been in jeopardy he would have allowed himself to comfort her. In his current frame of mind, protecting her physically was his responsibility. Letting her depend on him emotionally seemed as dangerous to his welfare as the men chasing them—men who came out of the mall just then.

"It's their fault," Conn said, just as Harry and Moe spied them on the other side of the drive. They started across, but the sound of shattering glass brought them up short.

Conn searched for the origin of the sound, but all he saw was a crowd of men in bulky yellow and black jackets milling around. Them and the front of a light blue car. "Is that what I think it is?" he asked Rae.

"It is if you think the firemen are jamming their hose through the Honda's front seat windows because it's blocking the door to the restaurant."

Sure enough a hose with a big metal end appeared out of the driver's-side window, two firemen pulling it into the restaurant while the big guy who'd been driving the Honda stood to one side, rocking nervously from foot to foot. He saw his cohorts and raced over.

Harry looked over at them, meeting Conn's eyes for a long minute—there was a promise in his gaze. "Stay with them, Joe," he said to his partner, then he turned back to the Honda. A police officer stopped him before he could get in the way of the firemen.

"This your car?" Conn heard the officer say.

"Shouldn'ta parked it here," one of the hose jockeys yelled.

The officer pulled out his ticket pad. "What's your name?"

"Harry Mosconi" was all Conn caught, because he saw the second pursuer heading in their direction, the driver lumbering along behind him.

Conn put Rae behind him again, waiting for them to cross the street.

"You couldn't best me with swords," Conn said when they were close enough so he didn't have to speak loud enough for the nearby gawkers to overhear. "Do you think to fare better with bare fists?"

Joe stopped a couple yards away, inching to one side in an attempt to get a look at Rae.

Conn locked her behind him with one arm, despite her protests and struggles. "If I let her go, it will be to deal with you."

Joe thought about that for all of a second before he backed off, snagging his friend by the collar and pulling him toward the Honda.

Rae shoved at Conn, and when he let her go and turned around, she was glaring daggers at him.

"What was that all about?"

Conn herded her toward the Hummer. "I thought it best they not see your face," he said.

"Why not?"

Because no one seeing her could mistake her relationship to Annie Bliss, and if they determined that much they might be able to find her. He should have known she'd already reasoned it out. Thankfully she failed to make the connection to her parents, likely because she'd done such a good job distancing herself from them.

"It's not like they can identify me just by seeing my face," she said. "I'm not famous—or infamous. I don't have a mug shot or anything."

"Mug shot?"

"Mug shot," she repeated. "*Mug* is slang for face, I have no idea why, and cameras shoot pictures, so *mug shot* is what they call the pictures they take of criminals when they're arrested. So they have a picture to identify them with. Hey, maybe you have a mug shot somewhere."

"You think I'm a criminal?"

"Since you don't know who you are, you have to admit it's a possibility. Although it doesn't help. Even if you have a mug shot there's no telling where it is. And if it's federal we can't get to it at all."

"Don't sound so disheartened," Conn said.

"Disheartened? I'm hoping you'll turn out to be Public Enemy Number One, so the FBI will ride in on their white horses and take you off my hands."

She climbed into the driver's seat of the Hummer, looking like she couldn't wait to be rid of him, while Conn . . . had no idea who he was or what kind of man he might be. Unless his dreams *were* memory flashes, and then he was pretty sure she wouldn't like the man he was.

Neither would he.

chapter
10

"HOW DID THEY FIND US?" RAE ASKED CONN when they were out of the parking lot and on their way back to safe territory. At least she hoped it was safe territory. "They don't know who I am. If they did they'd have come after us at my house. And if they don't know who I am or where I live, they can't possibly know where I work, which means they couldn't have been lying in wait for me to show up there."

Conn stared out the window. Not exactly the help she was hoping for.

"Feel free to chime in anytime," she prompted.

Still nothing. Back to floater mentality.

"Come on, I need some help here. Tap into that guy you are when we're in danger. You know—driven, decisive, suspicious. That guy doesn't just know how to deal with trouble, he anticipates it."

"You seem to have considered all the possibilities."

"No, I don't think I have. That's what I need you for."

"If I thought they knew who you were I would not have gone to such lengths to keep your face hidden," he explained with the patience of a kindergarten teacher. "And I agree with the rest of your reasoning, except—"

Rae's cell phone chimed. "Hold that thought," she said to Conn, digging her phone out and looking at the display. She considered letting it go to voice mail, but her mother would only keep calling until she got an answer. And Rae didn't appreciate being patronized by a delusional gypsy.

"Hi, Mom," she said into the phone.

"Hello, Sunny. How's it going?"

"I've been better," she said, trying to decide how much to tell her mother. Heck, she didn't even know what to tell her mother. Annie and Nelson already knew someone was after Conn. Getting chased again really wasn't anything new. Then again, she doubted her parents had shared everything with her.

"You sound out of breath," Annie said.

"We're in the car, on our way to the grocery store. Look, Mom—"

"Grocery store," Annie repeated on a disappointed breath of air. "Well, that is the way to a man's heart."

"You have *got* to be kidding."

"You know," Annie said, "there's a lot of other interesting real estate there besides Conn's stomach. I say go for a nice leisurely tour."

Rae let her shoulders slump a little, distracted from the get-information-from-Mom program by the same old contention. "Is that why you didn't send Conn any clothes?"

There was a beat of silence, acknowledgment of a direct hit. "Just trying to encourage you to try something new," Annie said tightly.

"Don't you mean someone?" Rae cut her gaze toward the passenger seat.

"Conn's a nice boy. You should loosen up and enjoy yourself a little."

"'Loose' being the operative word? I've only known him twenty-four hours." Not to mention there were guys trying to kill him—or seriously maim him at the very least—and she was in the damage path. Which reminded her, "Listen, Mom, those guys who attacked Conn—"

"I should let you go," Annie said, "it's dangerous to drive and talk on a cell phone," and she disconnected.

Rae snapped the phone closed and dropped it in her purse, slowing to take the ramp onto I-75. "Except?" she said to Conn, picking up the conversation her mother had interrupted.

"What?"

"Right before I answered the phone, I was trying to figure out how Harry and Joe found us. You agreed with what I said about them not knowing who I was. Except . . ."

"Except what?" Conn said, still looking confused.

"That's what I want to know."

"Then just finish the sentence."

"It was your sentence," she reminded him.

"It was?"

"Who's on first?" Rae said, frustrated not only with his inability to understand but his complete lack of concern about it.

"First what?"

"It's a classic Laurel and Hardy routine."

He spread his hands.

"Never mind."

"You say that a lot. You roll your eyes and sigh and look at me like . . . that."

Rae snorted, which was not on his list. Neither was swearing, and once she realized that several choice words came to mind, not to mention phrases. "Give me another twenty-four hours, I'll be cussing a blue streak."

Conn frowned. "How do you speak in color?"

"Keep asking me questions like that, and you're bound to find out."

THEY MADE IT BACK TO GROSSE POINTE IN UNDER twenty minutes, exchanging even fewer words. None of them were blue.

Rae pulled into a parking lot at the corner of Kercheval and Notre Dame, in the heart of the downtown shopping area called the Village. She turned the Hummer off and just sat there a moment, savoring the silence, which had a lot to do with the complete lack of new circumstances for Conn to make into a comedy routine.

"Is it a good idea to leave the vehicle here?" he finally asked.

"Hummers aren't unusual for this area, so it really doesn't stand out," Rae said. And anyway, the Honda wasn't coming after them anytime soon. "First thing tomorrow morning I'm getting rid of this thing, though."

"So where's the food?" Conn wanted to know, his stomach being the only thing he felt any urgency about unless they were being chased.

"You need some clothes."

"After the food, right?"

Rae set off, in the direction opposite the market. It took a few seconds, but Conn caught up with her, looking resigned.

Kercheval was the main thoroughfare through Grosse Pointe, lined with the businesses and restaurants that comprised the three blocks of the downtown area. There were only two stores within walking distance that sold men's clothing. One of those handled businesswear: tweed, silk, serge, no denim. The other specialized in outdoor gear, specifically mountaineering.

"I don't know," Conn said when they walked through the door and he was confronted by displays of camping and climbing equipment, and, with winter coming on, skis and snowboards.

"Let's see," Rae said, "there's no denim—or leather, for that matter—but waterproof, windproof, and thermal seems to be right up your alley. And don't ask me what I mean by that, or tell me you don't have an alley, it's just a figure of speech."

A young woman with a name badge that said KIKI stepped out from behind a rack of thermal underwear, took one look at Conn, and rushed over to him. "Hel-lo, lover," she said, bunching up the pair of long johns in her hands as she sized him up.

"What ho," Conn said, not exactly immune to her charms, which were all too obvious.

Not that Rae blamed him. She even found herself fascinated by the girl's ability to get outdoor clothing that tight and low cut.

"Did he just call you a ho?" the sales attendant behind the register asked.

"He can call me anything he wants," Kiki said.

"I apologize if I gave offense with my turn of phrase."

"Mmmm, muscles and manners," Kiki purred, circling around him, which brought her face-to-face with Rae. "Oh," she said like she had a mouthful of climbing chalk.

"Yep, I'm with him." Rae slipped a finger into the side belt loop of his jeans and towed him toward the fitting room.

"I'll be happy to help you," the girl said, following them. "With anything."

"Nope." Rae surveyed her other options, which consisted of a kid who was probably still in high school and a woman with the body of a gymnast and the face of a forty-year-old. Rae pegged her for early thirties. Wind and sun were hell on the skin. The kid would have been Rae's first choice, but he was clearly intimidated, so Rae went with the woman, Betsy, according to her name tag.

Conn's physique wasn't lost on Betsy, either, but at least she wasn't drooling.

"Cargo pants," she said to Betsy. "What do you think? Thirty in the waist, thirty-eight length?"

"Waist sounds right," Betsy said, "forty length, which is the top end of what we carry." She retrieved a pair of pants and handed them to Rae. "Black, unlined, and the cloth is a nice, breathable, everyday blend, sturdy and soundless when he moves."

Rae looked at her, one eyebrow raised.

"Men don't usually like it when their pants rub together and make noise."

"O-kay," she said, handing the pants to Conn and sending him into the little dressing room.

She stood there with Betsy, listening to the rustle of cloth and trying not to imagine what was going on—or coming off—behind the door.

Betsy looked over at her, cheeks pink, clearly on the same wavelength. "I think I'll get some shirts," she said, and fled to the other side of the store.

"They fit," Conn called out.

"Come out and let me see," Rae said, which had more to do with the fact that she'd sneaked a look at the price tag, and she wasn't paying that much for a pair of pants until she knew they were right. And boy, were they right, snug around the hips and butt, making the most of Conn's long legs despite the pockets at his thighs and calves.

Something made noise next to her, and Rae tore her eyes off his backside long enough to note that Betsy and her coworker were back, the latter letting her breath leak out on a raspy sigh. Even the high school kid had edged over to check out the fit of Conn's pants, which was probably a shame since he already seemed to have self-esteem issues.

"How many do you want?" Betsy asked Rae, never taking her eyes off Conn.

"Four. All black." It seemed the only appropriate color somehow.

"Good call." Betsy handed her a couple of shirts, one long-sleeved, one short, both extra large and made of some knit material that must have incorporated gold, considering the price.

"Better than cotton," Betsy said. "More expensive, sure, but this fabric has the breathability and warmth of wool, while still being washable."

"Right, give me six, all short-sleeved."

"You got it," Betsy said, her eyes on Conn's biceps.

Rae pointed to the dressing room, and Conn went back in. There were more rustling noises, but Betsy seemed to find it a lot easier to concentrate. So did Rae. She'd already seen him without a shirt.

"He'll need a jacket," she said.

Betsy scurried off, and Rae picked up socks and boxers, piling them on the counter and calculating the hit to
her credit card. It was necessary, but she still winced
when Betsy returned with a jacket costing more than
Rae's one and only pair of Manolos. Which reminded her.
"Shoes," she said when Conn came out of the dressing
room and handed her the cargo pants, which she dumped
on the counter immediately because they were still warm
from his body, and the urge was to rub them against her
cheek instead.

Conn sat where Betsy indicated, trying on a couple different styles of hiking boots. "Stiff," he observed, oblivi-
ous to sending Kiki and Betsy into slack-jawed hormonal
overload.

Rae had to admit, if she hadn't been somewhat immune to him, she'd have been incapacitated by that mental picture, too.

"Time to check out," she said, deliberately walking between the lust-stricken and the object of their dementia,
which broke the spell. For the most part.

Betsy rang her up, so at least they could escape the
store, which couldn't happen too soon for Rae—even if
she had a feeling the grocery store would be Scene Two
of Connor Larkin Does Grosse Pointe.

The Hummer was on the way, so they dropped the
bags and hit the Kroger. Conn walked in, and his eyes lit
up like a five-year-old's in a toy store.

The Village Kroger wasn't the newest incarnation of a
grocery store, the kind that included a Starbucks and offered hand-rolled sushi. It was small and cramped, but it'd
taken over an additional storefront not long before, and the
wall between had been knocked down. The space had been
given over completely to wine and liquor. Rae steered clear
of that area; she had enough trouble without adding alcohol
to the mix.

The aisles ran diagonally in the main part of the store,
to make the most of the small space and still leave areas
for produce, meat, and deli. The place was crowded on a

Sunday afternoon, everyone from maids in uniform to women dressed in couture. Rae barely noticed the other patrons. The other patrons noticed them.

They got to the checkout, their cart loaded with more food than Rae bought in six months. She could almost feel the blessed peace and quiet of her house—

"Is she a barbarian?" Conn asked her.

Rae followed the direction of his gaze to a woman dressed in a full-length fur coat. She'd borrowed the rest of her fashion sense from Olivia Newton-John, right down to the headband and blue eye shadow.

Her attitude could best be described as prickly. Until she got a good look at Conn. "Barbarian, huh?" she said. "There's nothing wrong with a little role playing."

"Could you make an effort not to be so damned memorable?" Rae said, then rolled her eyes. He couldn't do anything about his height, or his muscles, or those laser-sharp blue eyes and ruggedly handsome face. "At least stop talking like a living anachronism."

"Anak—what?"

"Try to speak like everyone else."

"Why does the opinion of this strange woman concern you?"

"It shouldn't— It doesn't," she said, feeling as wrung out as she sounded. She'd always hated being different, but what did it really matter? She didn't know that woman in the fur coat. Sure, she might run into her in the market one day in the future, but the woman undoubtedly wouldn't remember her, and not just because their social and economic spheres were miles apart. She hadn't taken her eyes off Conn.

"Talk however you want," she said with a shrug she actually meant rather than one intended to hide how much the situation bothered her. That felt good, too. "I have a feeling I'd be back on the circuit with my parents in no time if I spent too long with you."

"Would that be so bad?"

"Yes," she said, not having to think about that one at all. It felt good to let some things go, just not the career and stability she'd worked so hard to achieve. "I like my life. And it won't always be lonely," she added hastily because she knew what he was about to say. "There'll be a man someday, maybe a couple of kids."

Conn started to pile their purchases on the conveyor, including several packages of frozen chicken nuggets. He even used the plastic divider like he'd seen the woman before him do. "I'm surprised you haven't found that man yet," he said. "You must notice the attention you draw."

"They look, but they rarely approach, and the ones who do always turn out to be . . . wrong for me."

"You're closed off."

"Yes," she said, "I am." Her experiences with men had taught her to be cynical about their motives. But then, her childhood had lacked the kind of socialization an eighteen-year-old would have gotten from a public school education. She'd been naïve, and a hell of a target, at eighteen.

"If it was me," the cashier said, "I'd open whatever he wanted me to."

Rae ran her credit card through the reader, pushed the appropriate buttons, and signed on the little electronic line.

"I'm just saying," the cashier persisted, her eyes on Conn.

"Is the advice extra?" Rae asked her.

"Honey, if you need that kind of advice, there's no hope for you."

Rae snatched the receipt and shooed Conn out of the way, pushing the cart out of the store.

"Did I hear that woman say we could open something?" he asked her.

Rae grabbed the first item that came to hand, a package of Oreos, ripped it open, and handed it to him. Good thing he was clueless most of the time, she thought, as she beeped the Hummer open and started loading groceries in the back. If he had any idea of the effect he had on women, her included, he wouldn't be munching obliviously on cookies. He'd be nibbling on her instead. And she'd be letting him.

chapter
11

CONN WAS WEARING THE BLACK PANTS RAE HAD
bought for him earlier, the ones with all the pockets. The
rest of his clothing was black, too, and he was wet from
head to toe. Dripping. But the real problem was his hands.
One of them held a long, wicked-looking knife with a
blade two inches wide, one side of it serrated. The other
hand held a gun.

He was hunkered down at the very edge of a village
surrounded by jungle, one shoulder pressed to the trunk of
a huge tree. He eased around, lifted a device to his eyes
and saw men dressed as he was, faces smeared with
stripes of black paint, working their way silently between
the crudely built huts, signaling to one another to coordi-
nate their movements.

And then the night exploded, rocket blasts punctuated
by staccato bursts of gunfire, desperate shouts, and the
screams of the hurt and dying. Those who'd chosen to be a
part of the conflict, and those who hadn't.

Conn waited for a streak of light, chose a target not
dressed in black, and in the space between heartbeats he
squeezed the trigger. The gun jammed. He threw it aside,

flipping the knife to his right hand, even though he knew
it was no use against large artillery and automatic weaponry. And even though the men being slaughtered weren't
his mission, he left cover, put himself in the chaos of gunfire and death, moving in close to his victims, slashing a
throat or jamming the knife between ribs, hearing the
grunts of his victims, their eyes going flat and dead even
as he moved on, searching for the next target. He caught
movement out of the corner of his eye, flipping the knife
and catching it by the tip as he turned and let it fly, just as
a rocket blast illuminated the face of a child—

He jerked awake, already off the couch before his surroundings registered, and then he stayed on his feet, went
through the kitchen and out the back door, scrubbing his
hands back through his hair. The feelings lingered, de-
spair and self-loathing, but the scene was fading from his
waking mind, lost to an illness he didn't understand. And
didn't want to, just as he didn't want to know what had
happened to that child.

But he knew what had happened to that child. And
who was responsible. There was only one way that situation could have played out.

His breath steamed on the air. He wore only cotton
boxers, but the cold outside couldn't compete with the
one within. He stood there in the dark and quiet, letting
the peace of the place wash over him, through him. But
the dream lingered. The affliction that seemed such an
irritant for Rae Blissfield became his last line of defense
as he slipped the ugliness behind it and stepped back on
the other side.

"Is everything all right?"

He didn't turn, didn't have to when Rae stepped up beside him, wearing her fuzzy white robe. She settled into a
metal chair, pulling her knees up and tucking the robe
around her bare feet.

"I heard the door open," she said, resting her chin on
her knees. "Trouble sleeping?"

"Dreams."

"Memories?"

"God, I hope not." But he knew they were, and it was becoming harder to pull himself back from the ugliness each time.

"Bad, huh?"

"You have no idea."

"Maybe that's why you're not remembering," Rae said. "Maybe it's not just that there was something terrible in your life, maybe you were . . ."

"Terrible?" He didn't disagree, but he couldn't shrug her off, either.

"You have to admit it's a real possibility that you're not a nice guy, right? You react to trouble like you're no stranger to it. And those guys chasing you, they could have shot us today, but they didn't. Maybe . . . maybe they're not the bad guys." Maybe that was why her parents had made her promise to keep the police out of this, Rae thought. Not that Annie and Nelson would protect a criminal, but they had . . . unusual ideas about what constituted right and wrong.

Conn bent, picked up a handful of dead leaves, and crumbled them in his fist. "I see no merit in speculation."

Considering the path of her thoughts, Rae wholeheartedly agreed. If Conn was a criminal, she didn't want to know why her parents were protecting him. "How about breakfast? You always feel better when your stomach is full."

Conn took in her soft smile, a smile that accepted without judgment, without pity. She was willing to give him the benefit of the doubt, that smile said, but when she held out a hand he didn't take it.

She kept saving him, and he didn't want to get used to being saved. Not by her. He had no doubt he could protect her from the men chasing him, but when it came to returning the favor in ways that really counted, he had a feeling he wouldn't be so successful.

THE DEALERSHIP WHERE RAE HAD BOUGHT HER CAR, and where it was currently being serviced, was located in

Troy, on a side street that curved around from West Ma-
ple Road to North Crooks.

Thanks to Conn's early morning upheaval, they arrived
long before the office was open. The service department
was in full swing, though, so Rae pulled into the lot and
parked by the service entrance. She didn't get out of the
vehicle.

"Worried about the Stooges?" Conn asked her.

"The mall is less than a mile from here," she said. "They
found us once, by accident from all appearances."

"Then it's unlikely they will be so lucky twice in two
days."

"True, and the real problem is them." She pointed at a
pair of black Lincoln squad cars, white stripes along their
sides bearing the seal of the city and the words "Troy Police Department," parked at the curb in front of the main
office.

Cole sat up straight in his seat. "Do you think they're
here for us?"

"Why don't you sit tight and I'll go find out." She
opened the driver's-side door and hopped out, literally,
then looked back in at Conn. "Aren't you going to ask me
how one sits tight?"

"I think I can figure it out this time."

Rae grinned at him, then took herself off in the direction of the police cruisers, going right to the source. She
didn't even have to ask any questions. It was pretty clear
what had happened, and when she joined the circle of
gawkers, it turned out that most of them worked there.
Just listening to them talk filled in the rest of the blanks.

"They were broken into last night," she told Conn when
she got back to the Hummer.

"Broken?" he said, craning his neck see the front of the
office.

"Someone went into the dealership illegally after
hours. To steal things. From where I was standing I could
see one of the computers on the floor by the door, but they
didn't get away with it, and from what I heard nothing

was actually stolen. The police responded to the silent alarm too fast."

Conn didn't have anything to say about that, but he must have been scenting trouble, because his expression had gone flat, the blue of his eyes going impossibly sharper as he scanned the dealership.

"You think this has something to do with us," she said.

"Don't you?"

Rae clambered into the Hummer, but she left the door open, folding one foot under her so she could sit facing Conn. "If we stick with the assumption that they don't know who I am, the only way they could trace us would be the dealer plates . . . Shit."

Conn twisted around. "Where?"

Rae pointed to the multi-colored Honda, parked just inside the driveway, the driver's and front passenger's side windows covered with plastic and duct tape.

"It doesn't look like anyone is in there," Conn said.

"Hard to see, considering the makeshift windows, but I'm willing to bet they're there. They probably got stuck when the police showed up. And we stumbled right into their laps. I guess they don't want to start anything with the Boys in Blue right there."

"Boys in—"

"The police. Blue uniforms."

"Right. We can't sit here forever."

"Neither will the police. As soon as they leave Harry and Joe are coming for us."

"Then we leave now. We already know this vehicle is proof against their worst."

Rae sighed. "I'm getting really tired of this."

"Then change the rules," Conn said, as if it were the obvious course.

"Change the rules?"

"Like this." Conn got out of the van, sauntered into the service bay and up to the little counter where the orders were written up.

Rae froze, all her breath leaking out at the idea of

Conn working without a net. She fired up the Hummer,
jammed it into gear, and wheeled it into a tight turn, floor-
ing it into a parking space she'd never have been able to
navigate without desperation on her side.

She got inside just as the counter guy, whose name, according to the embroidered patch on his pocket, was Jim,
said to Conn, "Can I help you with something, Mac?"

"Who's Mac?" Conn asked him.

"He's with me," Rae said. "I'm here to see if my Jaguar is ready."

"Name?" Jim said, standing a little straighter, which
made sense when the other customer said, "What about
my van?" and Jim pointed behind him to a sign that said,
DEALERSHIP CUSTOMERS HAVE PREFERENCE.

"I'm a customer, too," the other guy protested.

"You're here for an oil change. Not the same thing."

"If I don't get the oil changed in this thing every
three thousand miles like clockwork it breaks down.
This is the only place open this early, and time is money
when you're self-employed. I ain't losing half a workday waiting."

"That's all right," Conn said. "We're in no hurry."

"Fine with me, Mac." Jim turned back to ask the other
customer for his mileage, then rolled his eyes when he
didn't get the answer he wanted. "What, you've never
gotten your oil changed before, genius?" he said, heading
out to the parking lot, the less-than-apologetic customer
trailing along behind him.

"We're not in a hurry?" Rae said to Conn.

He shrugged, but this time she could tell he was up to
something. His shoulders were loose, but his eyes were
focused, watching Jim and his customer stop at a white
delivery van parked a couple spots down from the Hummer with a HOW'S MY DRIVING? sign on the back.

Jim opened the door and bent into the van, getting the
mileage, Rae presumed. She turned back to Conn, just in
time to see him reach over the edge of the desk and pick
up the keys lying on the partially filled out work order.

"No," Rae said, keeping her voice down, staring at the mechanics in the other service bays.

By the time she'd assured herself Conn's larceny had gone unnoticed, he was headed out to the parking lot. She caught up with him at the door and dragged him to a stop. It wasn't easy. "We are not stealing that van."

"Do you have a better idea?"

He was already shaking his head before she said, "The police—"

"We only go far enough to lose the Stooges, then we leave the van and double back here. No one will be harmed."

She blew out a breath. "That's it. I give up. I'm going to jail, but at least it will be peaceful."

"At last, you learn to find the silver lining," Conn said, grinning. "Can I drive?"

"Let me put it this way, I want to be alive to go to jail." She took the keys, but Conn was running the rest of the show. Except he didn't seem to realize that. "We should probably go before Jim comes back and notices the keys missing."

He bowed slightly, gesturing her to go ahead.

"This is your operation. You go first."

The word *operation* seemed to do the trick. Conn stopped smiling and started moving. He led her across the parking lot as if they were headed for the Hummer, passing Jim and his customer, still bickering, on the way back. As soon as they were out of sight of the guys in the Honda, Conn caught her by the wrist, towing her around to the passenger side of the white HOW'S MY DRIVING? van. As soon as Jim and the driver had finished with the odometer reading and closed the driver's-side door, Conn stuffed Rae in, and climbed in behind her. Rae moved over into the driver's seat.

So far so good, she thought, firing up the van before she could have second thoughts. She eased it out of the space, driving down to the end of the parking aisle, away from the open service bay. They would have gotten away with it, if they hadn't needed to go right by the Honda to get out. And if the Honda hadn't been full of guys who wanted to stop them—even with the police sitting mere yards away.

They were almost on top of the Honda, still moving at a speed designed to evade notice, when the Honda's driver popped up behind the wheel. His gaze locked with Rae's.

She didn't hesitate, putting the gas pedal to the floor. The van sputtered and coughed, barely picking up speed, which meant its front bumper and the Honda's got to the same place at the same time. The van shuddered to the sound of metal shrieking, and for a second they were hung up on the other car's bumper before they tore free and shot toward the driveway.

The Honda, minus its front bumper, the hood partially buckled, makeshift plastic windows flapping, swung out behind them. A few seconds later she heard sirens.

"The Honda is chasing us," she said to Conn, needlessly since he was watching it in the side mirror. "So are the police."

"Lose them."

Rae had a feeling that order was more about the cops than the Honda. She made a left on North Crooks Road, headed for Big Beaver and the entrance ramp to I-75. It would have been the quickest way to get rid of the Honda, if not for the van, which was old and clearly not well-maintained, still sputtering and coughing its way up to speed. The police were another story. The police weren't known for giving up.

It was a concern for Rae, even before they got on the highway, which was bumper-to-bumper, stop-and-go rush-hour traffic, the kind of traffic that freaked her out even when she wasn't being chased by the police.

She swerved around cars, cutting the wheel right and left, shifting the van into spaces that didn't look big enough for a moped. The Honda, being smaller and more maneuverable, forged its own path, trying to come up beside them. The two squad cars were bringing up the rear, one parked on the Honda's back bumper, the other sticking with the van. Even though they were running full lights and sirens the other vehicles couldn't get out of anyone's way.

And then the radio bolted to the dash started to squawk, a man's voice yelling about phone calls and lawsuits and unemployment.

Conn reached for the handset.

"People must be calling the toll-free number." Rae flipped the radio off. "Best we stay out of it. They'll figure it out later." She saw brake lights up ahead, three lanes of them, and shook her head. "We're not going to outrun the police," she said to Conn.

"Not in this," he said, sounding disgusted. "If we still had the Hummer—"

"It has nothing to do with what we're driving. It's rush hour, and trust me, that isn't what it sounds like. There are so many cars on the road we won't get anywhere fast, and I won't put other lives in danger by trying to. Besides, these things never end well for the people who aren't in uniform. The police can call out as many squad cars as they want. Sooner or later we'll be caught, and it won't be pretty."

If Conn had been driving, they'd have kept running, that much was clear. But Rae was at the wheel, so she bullied her way over to the right lane and shot off at the next exit, blasting through a yellow light that was just turning red, trapping the squad car at the intersection. She took the turnaround and got back on the highway, going southbound now, staying in the right lane until she saw the sign for Big Beaver. She got off there and took a left, pulling into the Troy Police Station not far beyond. The Honda kept going, one of the squad cars from the dealership hot on its back bumper. The other car screeched into the lot behind the van.

Rae was already parking at the curb by the entrance, and she wasn't waiting for the chase officers. They'd pull weapons and get out handcuffs, and she wasn't about to be cuffed and arrested in public, not to mention

the part where she'd probably have to lay facedown on
the ground.

"Trust me, this is our only option," she said to Conn.
She jumped out of the van, Conn right behind her. They
went inside, and when the officer at the counter stepped
up and asked what he could do for them, Rae said, "I just
stole a van. But I have a really good reason."

chapter 12

THE POLICE WERE HAVING A HARD TIME WITH
the whole stealing-a-van-to-get-away-from-the-guys-in-
the-Honda justification. Especially since they'd lost the
Honda. They *really* had a hard time with Conn's memory loss.

They'd taken his fingerprints and run them against
every known database with no luck. Rae had to give it to
the Troy Police: They were thorough. And stubborn. She
was getting a kick out of the show, though.

They were sitting in a small office, she and Conn on
one side of the desk, a Detective Hershowitz on the other.
He was rapidly losing patience.

"Where are you from?" he asked Conn for the third
time. When he didn't get an answer, he said, "Clamming
up isn't going to do you any good."

"Clamming up?"

"He means you're not answering his questions."

"Why doesn't he say that then?" Conn said, arms
crossed, face set into a frown, not bothering to hide his
irritation. Since they'd stepped foot in the place, he'd
acted . . . not superior, exactly, but definitely dismissive.

If he kept it up they were the ones who'd get dismissed. Right into a cell.

"He has a hard time with sayings," she told the detective.

"He has a hard time with his hearing, if you ask me."

"I meant slang and colloquialisms. Like 'a bird in the hand is worth two in the bush.'"

"Especially if you're hungry," Conn added.

"Not helping," Rae said under her voice.

Detective Hershowitz sat silently through the Laurel and Hardy routine. He wasn't amused. "You should be grateful you're not handcuffed or in a holding cell."

"We are," Rae said. "*Very* grateful. Especially about the handcuffs."

"Don't like handcuffs, huh?" Detective Hershowitz asked, leaning in her direction and shifting from stern to . . . not so stern. With an overtone of *Ick*. "Bad associations?" he asked her. "I mean, you don't have any record or anything, so . . ." His eyes shifted in Conn's direction, went hard again. "King Kong like to get rough?"

"Hey, personal! And he is not my boyfriend."

"Boy?"

Rae whipped around. "Now is not the time to worry about how manly we think you are."

"So what's the deal with you two? Him not being your boyfriend, why are you together? He doesn't need an accountant, he needs a psychiatrist."

"Uhhhh . . . I should get that," Rae said, when her phone, sitting on the desk with all their other possessions, rang.

Hershowitz slapped a hand on hers, then picked up the phone himself. She was praying the call wasn't from her parents.

It wasn't. The way Hershowitz sat up straight in his chair was her first clue. Her second came when he handed the phone to Conn.

Rae intercepted it. "Who is this?"

"Put Larkin on."

"Not until you tell me who you are and where you're from."

"I'm the guy who can have you thrown into a cell and charged with any number of crimes, regardless of what you actually did and what the local yokels decide to do about it."

"It's for you," she said, handing the phone to Conn. "If this guy is an example of your friends, I can see why you wouldn't want your memory back."

But she moved in close so she could hear both sides of the conversation. Conn didn't discourage her.

"You missed your last check-in," the grump on the other end of the call said. "I was about to send someone after you—until your prints turned up in the system, then I was pretty sure you were dead."

"Who is this?" Conn asked him.

"You're joking, right? It's Mike."

"No, Mike, he's not joking," Rae said. "He got hit over the head a week ago, and lost his memory."

"Jesus, Conn, you're letting a ci— You're letting her listen in? You really have lost your memory. What if she's one of them?"

Rae snatched the phone out of Conn's hand, saying, "Let me handle this," when he wanted to move in close. "One of whom?" she said into the phone.

"A criminal," Mike said.

"That's interesting, because I was wondering the same thing, Mike. How do we know you're not the criminal?"

"Because I'm not," he said with the kind of authority and a lack of patience that told her he was an important guy. It didn't tell her he was on the up and up, so either he worked for some law enforcement agency, probably federal, or he was with the mafia.

Either way it wasn't good for her.

"Put Larkin back on," he said in a voice that sounded like he was chewing rock.

Rae looked at Hershowitz, then at Conn, not sure what to do. Conn didn't have a clue what was what. He needed her. On the other hand, she had a pretty good idea she didn't want any part of whatever Conn was mixed up in.

And then she remembered her parents. "Look," she said into the phone.

"Handcuffs, jail cell, serious criminal charges," Mike said. "Any of that meaningful to you?"

Rae huffed out a breath, handing the phone to Conn again, and this time she didn't bother to listen in. She just didn't have the heart to find out any sooner than necessary what new detour her life was going to take.

Conn did a lot of listening, said a couple of "uh-huhs," and handed the phone to Detective Hershowitz. "Mike says to keep my head down and work on getting my memory back until he can send someone."

"Did he tell you what's going on?"

Conn shook his head. "He said he isn't telling me anything, not even who he is, until I remember how to keep my mouth shut."

Rae bit back her frustration. She wanted *answers*, dammit, but every time she thought she might get some fate conspired to leave her clueless and stranded with a man who was nothing but trouble. On every imaginable level.

"You can go," Hershowitz said. "Just don't steal any more cars."

"Any chance you'll tell me what that Mike guy said to you?"

"He said I could arrest you if you made a nuisance of yourself."

Rae didn't need to be told twice. She gathered her things together, retrieved her phone from the detective, and herded Conn out of the detective's office.

"Well," she said when they were in the lobby, "you must be a good guy."

"You doubted me? I'm wounded."

"Right, you're destroyed. Sorry. So what does 'good guy' mean? You were with my parents' group doing undercover work? Which means there's some sort of criminal activity going on there?"

"I don't remember."

"Let's go ask my mom and dad."

Conn caught her by the upper arm. "Harry and his friends will be watching the faire."

"But my parents—"

"Are fine. If they were a target they would have had trouble already. If we go back there, we will only bring it to them."

Rae dug deep and managed to calm herself, mostly because what Conn said made sense. They'd sent Conn away for his safety, but she knew that if they were in danger, they'd have pulled up stakes and taken off, too. Still . . . "Maybe we should send the police."

"And tell them what? There are outlaws at the Renaissance faire?"

Rae huffed out a breath, crossing her arms. "They'll think we're pulling a prank."

"If you mean jesting, aye, you're right."

"And what about Harry and Joe? They broke into the dealership to get my name and address, but they botched it. Otherwise they'd have been on their way to my house. All they have to do is pose as reporters, or bribe someone at the dealership. Jim looked bribable. Heck, Jim will probably give them my address for free after the trouble we caused."

"Then we leave."

"What will that solve?"

"We'll be safe—"

"That's just geography. You have to get your memory back. That's the only solution."

"How do you suggest I do that?" Conn said, every bit as angry and frustrated as she was, for all he kept his voice completely flat.

"Stop fighting it. Stop being all Zen and go-with-the-flow and laid-back. Pretend you're in danger—which you are, by the way—and get a clue." She was yelling at him by the time she finished that sentence, and all the police were staring at her. So she used it to her advantage. "Can someone call us a cab?"

* * *

CONN WAS STILL ANGRY, STEWING THE ENTIRE CAB
ride back to her house. "We're just going to pack some
things and then we'll go away for a few days," she said
once she'd paid the cab and it was gone.

He didn't answer, or look at her. And he didn't shrug.
She missed the shrug.

"I'm sorry I went to the police."

"You broke a promise," he said.

"They were going to catch us anyway. I just made it so
we could talk to them on our terms."

Conn rolled his shoulders. "Do you think it wise for us
to be here?"

Progress, she thought, even if he still wasn't looking
at her. "Even if the Stooges know the police let us go,
which they can't possibly, and even if they know where
I live, they're probably lying low until the heat dies
down . . . they're staying home until they think the authorities have stopped looking for them."

She moved into her bedroom while she talked to throw
some clothes in an overnight bag, then to the bathroom,
and then to Conn's room. She didn't figure he was worried about clothes since she could hear him banging
around in the kitchen, probably trying to bring every
crumb of food in the place.

"There's just one problem," she called out, dropping
the bags in the living room on the way to the kitchen.
"We don't have a car—oh."

Harry stood by the kitchen door, flanked by Joe and
the chubby, balding man who seemed to be their desig-
nated driver. Harry had a gun pointed at Conn.

"Good plan," Conn said to her.

"I'm an accountant," she snapped. "You're the . . . whatever you are."

"Exactly. I don't know what I am. Why else would I
let a woman tell me what to do?"

"A woman! Who do you think gave birth to you, genius? No, don't answer that. I'm sure she was a paragon,
despite the way you turned out."

Conn opened his mouth, but nothing came out. His eyes said it all.

Rae almost backed off. She would have backed off, but he said, "It wouldn't have hurt you to turn out a bit more like your mother wanted: relaxed, accepting, accommodating—"

"Accommodating! Who's been taking care of you the last couple of days? And I don't recall you saying *thank you*, either. Accommodating, hah," and she started to storm off.

"Hey!"

Rae rounded on Harry, and got a face full of gun.

"Yeah, that's right, I'm in charge."

"I bet *your* mother would be proud," Rae said.

Harry's gun faltered, just for a second. Out of the corner of her eye Rae saw Conn's muscles bunch, and she realized he hadn't taken his eyes off Harry, not even when they were arguing—well, not entirely. And then Harry got over the crack about his mother, the gun stopped shaking, and Conn went back to waiting for an opening because, Rae finally understood, that's what he was doing.

And she was going to help him.

"I apologize for bringing your mother into this," she said to Harry, "but it was a long weekend. Really long. And I only spent half of it with him."

"We've been dealing with him for a lot longer. And thanks to you we had to chase him all over the metro area, so if anyone has the right to be mad, it's us."

"Yeah," the third man chimed in. "We had to spend hours on the floor of that stupid Honda this morning."

Rae snorted out a laugh. "Don't blame that on me. It's your own fault for being such incompetent criminals."

"Our fault," Harry sputtered.

It probably wasn't the best strategy to tick off the guy holding the gun, but she got the distinct impression she was supposed to be distracting the bad guys. It had something to do with the way Conn was easing to one side, putting himself in position to take Harry out. Or maybe he was just getting out of the line of fire.

"You botched the robbery at the dealership and got stuck there," she said, deciding to trust Conn. He might be laid-back, but he wasn't a coward. "You guys are like the Three Stooges: Harry, Joe and . . ." She looked at the heavy guy.

"Kemp," he supplied, a goofy grin curving his mouth. "Hey, she's right, we do sound like the Three Stooges. Harry, Joe, and Kemp."

"I thought the third Stooge was Curly."

"Shemp was a late replacement for Curly," Kemp said. "Larry, Moe, and Shemp."

"Shut up," Harry said. "We have a job to do, let's get on with it."

"Do you really think you can do this without messing it up?"

"You're the reason everything is screwed up."

"It's not my fault you parked outside the mall and got stuck by the fire truck."

"We found you, didn't we?"

"Yeah, how did you find us?" Rae asked, and not just for distraction value. She was seriously interested.

"It was just dumb luck," Kemp said. "We had to pick up some money to get the glass fixed—" Harry gave him a shot to the arm. "Ouch! Hey!"

Rae couldn't help laughing. "If that wasn't a Three Stooges move, I don't know what is. Maybe botching the robbery at the dealership and getting stuck there, but hey, at least you got my address—"

Harry's gaze flicked away from hers, just a split second but enough to tell her she was on to something.

"You didn't get my address, did you?"

"Nah," Kemp said, rubbing his arm and shooting Harry a mutinous look. "We went back and bribed the service manager."

"Shut up!"

"Why, Harry? They ain't gonna be talking to anyone."

Rae's blood ran cold, the more so because Kemp wasn't saying that as a scare tactic, he was just a goofball who knew the score and couldn't help blurting it out. She resisted the urge to look in Conn's direction, though, moving to the stool at her kitchen island, which just happened to be in the opposite direction from him.

"Jim figured out who you was because you left the Hummer there," Kemp was saying.

"Yeah," Harry put in, "he didn't take much convincing, either. He was pretty pissed that you stole the van right out from under his nose."

"Now who's a Stooge?"

"I don't know," Rae said. "I wasn't stupid enough to drive a Honda onto UAW property."

That was the last straw for Harry. His eyes went crazy and stayed that way. He lifted the gun, just as Conn struck, chopping down on his wrist. Conn caught the gun as Harry dropped it, flipping it to Rae and facing off against Harry, Joe, and Kemp, hand-to-hand.

It wasn't a very long fight. Rae didn't even have to wrestle with the possibility of using the gun because it was over in seconds. Conn punched Harry in the face, backhanding Joe at the same time. Both men went down as Kemp waded in and punched Conn on the side of the head. Conn staggered a little, looking woozy like he had during the sword fight. Then he shook his head and turned to Kemp. Rae had to give Kemp credit, he lifted his fists and stepped in. He might even have been threatening, if he hadn't been wincing already.

Conn slapped a hand on Kemp's chest and shoved him onto his ass. "Get out," he said, "and take your friends with you."

Kemp nodded, never taking his eyes off Conn, as he scooped a hand into Joe's armpit.

Harry stumbled to his feet, working his jaw side to side. He sent Conn a look he knew he couldn't back up without the gun. "This isn't over," he said. Hooking Joe's other arm, he and Kemp assisted their semi-conscious partner toward the kitchen door.

"Took you long enough," Rae said to Conn once they were gone.

"I wanted to see how long you could talk before Harry shot you just to shut you up."

"I wouldn't be so cocky. He'll probably shoot you on sight the next time."

"Then I will just have to make certain there isn't a next time."

"How are you going to do that?"

Conn grinned. "*How* is your part of the operation."

"You're putting your fate into the hands of a woman?"

"No, I'm putting my fate into the hands of my partner."

"Partner?"

"As in team. We make a pretty good one. I mean, you knew exactly what I was thinking. Before. Why I was insulting you."

"Partner," Rae said, sinking down on one of the stools at her kitchen island. "I'm speechless."

Conn grinned. "Now I can die a happy man."

"Not if I have anything to say about it." Rae stood, gathering up the overnight bag with their things when a thought occurred to her. "Now, all we need is some wheels."

chapter
13

"I NEED TO BORROW A CAR, MR. PENNWORTHY.
It's a matter of life and death."

"After the way he talked to me?" Mr. Pennworthy hooked a thumb in Conn's direction.

Conn could have cared less. He was busy taking in his surroundings. Not that Rae could blame him. Her house was a step up from a typical subdivision home. Mr. Pennworthy lived in the closest thing to a castle America could boast. It sat behind her house and four of her neighbors—three stories of Tudor-style construction dating back to a time when men like Ford and Dodge were tapping into the American Dream to build fortunes.

Conn hadn't spoken since Mr. Pennworthy had opened the door and invited them in, but his face said it all. The foyer was pretty impressive, Rae had to admit, from the marble beneath their feet to the ornate, coffered ceiling two floors above their heads, a Waterford chandelier suspended within the sweep of the double staircase.

"Where do you keep the Armory?" Conn finally said, turning to Rae. "We should borrow some weapons, as well."

"Armory? Weapons?" Mr. Pennworthy goggled at Conn. "I don't have any weapons here."

"Is that not a suit of armor?" Conn brushed past him, headed for a room that had probably been a ballroom ninety years before. Now it was a formal dining room, and Conn was right, there was a suit of armor at the far side, just visible from the foyer.

"This is very poorly made," Conn said, stopping in front of the arm and bending to study the right gauntlet. "Not authentic. See here?" He straightened, pointing to the large chest plate.

"I don't see anything," Rae said.

"Me either," Mr. Pennworthy chimed in, more interested in the appraisal than the intrusion.

"You see nothing because there is nothing to see. It simply does not match. Nor does this gorget—that's the neck guard. It is not in the same style as the breastplate and the greaves." He pointed at the lower leg pieces.

"Then it's a reproduction. A fake. Not an actual suit of armor."

Mr. Pennworthy looked like he was going to pop a vein, probably the one throbbing on his forehead. "I have papers authenticating this armor," he said.

"He has papers," Rae repeated. She sidled up close to Conn. "And we need a car."

"I don't know about papers," Conn said.

Rae lifted her eyes heavenward. God ignored her, too.

"Anyone can write anything," Conn continued. "That doesn't make it the truth. But it's not entirely a loss. See here?" He pulled Mr. Pennworthy forward and made sure he was following. "This breastplate has been repaired."

"I knew about that," Mr. Pennworthy said.

"It's a real repair, made by a real armorer, probably the same one who made the breastplate."

"But . . . I thought you said . . ."

"I said it isn't a complete fraud. The breastplate, helm, greaves, all the large pieces are authentic. The gauntlets are not. The smaller, more intricate pieces are more easily lost and degraded by time and weather if not properly cared for. The gorget is from another suit entirely."

"So the suit was cobbled together."

"Aye."

"I'd sue," Mr. Pennworthy grumbled, "if I knew where to find the criminal who sold it to me."

"So you didn't get it from a reputable dealer."

Mr. Pennworthy didn't dignify Rae's observation with a comment.

"This is good armor," Conn said. "The flaws only make it more interesting."

Mr. Pennworthy took another look at the armor, seeing it through Conn's eyes. "You're right," he finally said.

"This has all been really fascinating," Rae said, "but we still need a car. Please, Mr. Pennworthy, it's really important."

He smiled, an impossibly sweet smile from such an old grouch. "I know that," he said, patting her cheek. "You wouldn't have asked otherwise. And I wouldn't say yes if you weren't the least objectionable neighbor I've ever had, and since I've lived here forty years, that's saying something."

"Thank you," Rae said, completely floored.

Mr. Pennworthy led them through the house, plucking a key ring from one of at least a dozen hooks by a doorway in the kitchen. He opened the door, which led onto a garage bigger than her house, filled with everything from sports cars to trucks.

He dropped the key ring, with no keys on it, into Rae's hand and said, "Take the Cadillac. I don't know what's going on, but there's no reason you can't be comfortable while you're at it. And if you need anything, just push the little red button."

THE CADILLAC TURNED OUT TO BE A BRAND-NEW STS-V, which Rae decided had something to do with the engine being a V-8. There was throaty roar and a slight vibration when she stepped on the gas pedal, both muted by the leather and wood interior.

She navigated them onto I-75, heading north, the Caddy eating up the miles. The sky was blue and cloudless, the sunroof was open, and surround sound filled the interior with the soft strains of classical music.

"Enjoying the ride?" she said to Conn, then regretted it since he'd been half asleep. "I'm sorry. You should rest while you have the chance. I know you didn't get much sleep last night."

"Neither did you."

"I only had an early wake-up call. I got the impression it was a long night for you."

He shrugged that off.

Rae went with it. "So how do you know so much about armor?"

"I'm an armorer."

"We both know that's not really the case."

"Do we?" Conn said, sounding bleak.

Rae exhaled heavily, tired more in spirit than mind. "I know you don't want to talk about it, but we can't keep running away."

Conn crossed his arms, settling back into his seat.

"Those guys are going to catch up to us again."

"And I will best them again."

"Not if they shoot you first, which they're likely to do, now that you've humiliated them twice." She took his smile as an acknowledgment, and his silence as an invitation. "You must work for some sort of law enforcement agency," she said, "likely federal since you crossed numerous state lines with my parents' traveling group. FBI, DEA, NSA, or some other acronym I've never heard of." All of which were laughable, knowing the kind of people her parents were, and the kind of people they surrounded themselves with. But whoever Conn was, he also knew a hell of a lot about medieval armor. More than background information for an undercover operative.

"Speculation again? 'Tis a bad habit with you."

"As ignoring reality is with you. You can't sit back

forever and expect everything to work out the way you want it to."

"I see no purpose in rushing."

Rae hunched her shoulders, then made the effort to relax them again. They had a long trip ahead, even if it was all highway driving. "I don't get that. There's too much to do to just float through life."

"Why?"

"I have goals, things I want to accomplish."

"Will those things make you happy? Because you're not happy now."

"Well." Rae searched, but there didn't seem to be a response to that, at least not one she could put into words. There were a lot of feelings, all muddled up inside her, a confusing whirl of fear and discomfort and indignation. But mostly there was disappointment, because he was right.

Whatever else Connor Larkin might be, he had this way of cutting right to the heart of any matter. He'd certainly pegged her, and not who she told herself she was, or the woman she let other people see. Somehow, in less than three days, he'd come to know *her*, the little girl who'd grown up as Sunny and felt out of place, and the adult who'd renamed herself Rae and still hadn't quite found her true place in life. But she'd gotten closer, she reminded herself. She was on the way to finding herself, and standing still wasn't going to get her there.

She chose not to say as much to Conn. He'd only make her doubt herself again, probably in less than ten words.

They drove awhile in silence. Rae was just beginning to relax when her cell went off: "Money, money, money, money, MONEY," the ring tone she used for P.I.G.

"Hello?" she said into the phone, tentative until she heard Morris Greenblatt's voice on the other end. And then she didn't relax completely because he wouldn't be calling her if there wasn't a problem.

"Mr. Ratcliffe called this morning," he said, confirming her worst suspicions since Ratcliffe was one of her biggest and most demanding clients, not to mention he'd been with the firm since its founding so he knew Putnam and Ibold personally. "He's waiting for his third-quarter financial statements and tax estimate."

"It's a bit soon for those to be ready. I still have some work to do on them."

"I told him as much," Greenblatt said, "but he wants them by Friday."

"I can do that," Rae said, hoping she was right and knowing she wasn't since she'd brought clothes and food but no work files. And the chances of getting her life back were nonexistent as long as she was saddled with Sir Blanksalot.

"Three more of your clients left messages as well, but I won't bother you with them right now. Just make sure Mr. Ratcliffe gets what he wants."

Or else, Mr. Greenblatt's tone implied. Or else she wouldn't have to worry about making partner again this year. Or having a job, for that matter.

"I will, Mr. Greenblatt. Thank you."

"Ms. Blissfield? Rae."

"Yes?"

"Is . . . is everything all right? It sounds like you're in a car."

"Everything is fine," she said, ignoring the part about the car. "The statements will be ready." She winced a bit, told herself she'd find a way to make that the truth.

"Bad news?" Conn asked as she disconnected and slipped her phone back into her purse.

"Just my job," she said, "one of those accomplishments that are making me so unhappy."

"Then quit."

"I was being facetious. No, never mind. I know what you think of my job." And she didn't want to hear it again. She was tired of feeling wrong for wanting a house and security, and okay, so she wasn't happy, she was lonely, but Connor Larkin wasn't the cure for that. And she'd be fine. Just as soon as she made partner she could relax a little, and when she wasn't working eighty hours a week anymore she'd have time for a life. And then she'd be happy.

She glanced over at Conn. He looked like he heard everything she'd just thought. And he wasn't buying it. "What do you know, anyway?" she demanded. "You think I'm deluding myself that a partnership is what I want? What about you? You won't get your memory back. Not can't. *Won't*. What does it say about a man when he doesn't want to know who he is?"

Conn didn't respond, but he didn't shrug her off, either. For the first time since she'd met him he looked troubled. She regretted destroying his tranquility, even though she knew his peace of mind was costing them. Costing her.

"I'm sorry, Conn, but we aren't going to be safe again until you start facing . . . everything. Yourself."

"That was your place of work. On the phone just now."

"Yes, but it's not about that— Okay, it's partly about that." She was pushing him to be honest with himself. He deserved the same from her. "I want my life back, but it's not just that. I'm not . . . this." She gestured around her, but the plush interior of the Cadillac didn't quite send the message she intended. "I don't like having people chase me, or come into my house and threaten me with guns. I don't like being worried and confused and *afraid* all the time.

"I know you think I'm unhappy, but I like stability. I like having a job, I like giving my clients what they want, and you're right, it's boring sometimes—a lot of the time, actually. And sure, the partners at my firm are way too anal, and maybe, just once, I'd like to take all my clients' money and plunk it down at the casino because, hell, playing the stock market is just as much of a gamble, and the casino would be a lot more fun."

"So why don't you?"

"Because I'm an adult, and adults have responsibilities. That's why it's called work. It's not supposed to be fun all the time. There are people counting on me, and right now I'm letting them down. So are you."

"Do you think so?"

"You're not here by accident, Conn. That guy on the phone. Mike. He told you to get your memory back, right?"

"Right. Except I don't know how."

"Just relax." Rae shook her head. "I can't believe I just said that to you. You could teach the Dalai Lama how to be at peace. You don't sweat anything, let alone the small stuff."

"Sweat?" Conn sniffed at his armpits.

She rolled her eyes. "The only thing you're fighting is yourself. You keep having these dreams but you fight your way out of them. Heck, you've barely slept the last two nights."

"Your point?" Conn asked, the tone of his voice a warning she ignored.

"I'm willing to bet they're not just dreams. They're memories, and you need to stop running away from them."

Conn mulled that for a minute, then nodded. His expression was calm, but a muscle in his jaw clenched and released, clenched and released.

Rae didn't know what he saw in those dreams, but she was glad she wasn't the one who had to face them.

EVEN WITH A STOP FOR A QUICK LUNCH, MACKINAW City was less than four hours out of Detroit. The city huddled in the shadow of the Mackinac Bridge, which stretched over the Straits of Mackinac, connecting Michigan's Lower and Upper Peninsulas. Fort Michilimackinac, an authentic colonial-era fort, sat on the Lake Michigan side at the southern foot of the bridge, the Lower Peninsula side. But what seemed to interest Rae the most, Conn noticed, was a series of docks with large boats coming and going at regular intervals from the commercial part of the city. She'd parked the car there by the docks and gone into a little office, coming back out a few minutes later with papers appearing similar to the ones handed out upon entrance to the Renaissance faire in Holly Grove.

"I kept an eye on the highway behind us," she said, consulting the folded paper in her hands, "and I never saw the Honda. I don't think we can relax completely, but there's no reason we can't have a little fun while we're here."

"What did you have in mind?"

"Ever been to Mackinac Island? What am I saying, even if you had you wouldn't remember it."

"What is so fun about Mackinac Island?"

"No cars allowed. Everyone gets around on foot or horseback, or by carriage or bicycle."

Conn didn't see where that was such a treat, but he followed her to a window where she bought tickets, then went to stand in a queue that consisted of them and a handful of people who did not appear to be tourists.

"They're probably locals," she said.

Conn decided the look on his face must still be skeptical because she said, "Really, it's a popular vacation spot in Michigan, although people usually come earlier in the season." She stared into the gunmetal sky, wrapping her arms around herself.

"It turned cold," he said.

"Can't be more than sixty degrees, and there's a cold front moving in from the north. At least that was the forecast on the radio."

She wore only a thin coat that seemed poor proof against the cold and even less against the wind gusting in off the water. He suffered from little of either, thanks to the jacket she'd purchased for him. His cold came from inside.

Rae was right; he had to face the dreams that weren't dreams. Problem was, he didn't know how to bring it about. He was asleep when the dreams came. By the time he realized he was fighting his way out, the opportunity to face the truth had been lost.

Conn moved in behind her, sheltering her from the

wind, but wanting to take comfort as much as give it. He rested his hands on her shoulders, just rested them there. She smiled up at him, which was all the warmth he could have asked for. And more than he deserved.

The man at the gangplank waved them forward, saying listlessly, "Last ferry of the day," and taking the tickets Rae handed him. Conn wanted to sit inside, with the few other passengers, where it was warm. Rae wasn't having any part of that.

"If this thing capsizes," she said as she climbed the stairs just inside the entrance, "I'd rather risk hypothermia and have a fighting chance than drown trapped inside a glass coffin."

"The water is much warmer than the air," Conn said as they came out into the open, and the wind, even stiffer on the completely exposed upper deck, hit him full in the face. "You're more likely to freeze to death up here."

But when the boat started up, he was glad they were out there. The view was amazing, even when the boat began to move and the wind all but knocked him off his feet. He braced himself behind the railing at the very front of the boat and took it all in, the clean scent of the water, the gulls wheeling and shrieking overhead, looking for a handout. The bridge was dark against the cloudy sky, the city they'd just left receding as the boat eased out of the harbor.

"I changed my mind," Rae yelled. "Just shout *I'm king of the world* and let's go inside."

"What?"

"I'm going to stand in the stairwell, out of the wind."

Conn stayed there another minute, but he knew even if Rae was out of the wind she was still freezing. He turned to go sit with her, and found Harry and Joe standing behind him.

"Rae," Conn said, but his eyes were on Harry's gun—a different gun since the first one was in Rae's trash can.

"She's kind of busy," Harry said, hooking a thumb over his shoulder.

Rae was by the railing about halfway down the upper

deck, squaring off against Kemp. She looked up and caught Conn's eyes. She was furious. It took real work to keep the smile off his face.

"You do exactly what I tell you," Harry said, "or she's toast."

Even if he hadn't heard that saying before, there was no mistaking the way Harry brandished his gun. "She gets anywhere near a toaster and you're dead," Conn told him.

"You just come with us and nobody will get hurt."

Conn pointed at Kemp. "He leaves first, or I'm not going anywhere."

Harry exhaled heavily. "Why can't this ever be easy?"

Joe shook his head. Everyone ignored him.

"Look," Harry said, "we just want to know who you are and where you're from."

"Didn't you get the bulletin?" Rae yelled at him. "He doesn't know any of that stuff. He lost his memory when you conked him over the head."

"Hit him again," Kemp suggested. "See if that gets his brains unscrambled."

"That only works in the movies," Rae and Conn said at the same time and with the same exasperation.

"Whatever," Harry said. "We'll just keep you company until your memory comes back. And just in case you need some incentive, I think Red should hang around, too."

"Hey," she shouted at Harry, "I have a job, you know."

"So do I," Harry shouted back. "And a gun."

"I am really tired of this," Rae said.

"Yeah, well, what are you gonna do about it?"

"This." And she kicked Kemp in the balls.

He went down hard. Harry and Joe both sucked in their breath, hunching automatically. Conn did the same.

"Well?" Rae shrieked at him. "What are you waiting for? Go medieval on their asses."

Conn lunged at Harry. Harry shot once, the bullet going wide, then there was a click and nothing.

Ray spread her hands. "Only one bullet?"

Conn shook his head and grabbed Harry. Joe grabbed

him, which barely slowed him down as he quickstepped
Harry to the railing at the back of the ferry and tossed him
over. Joe took one look at Conn, who was turning to deal
with him, and jumped in after his friend.

"Huh," Rae said, joining him at the railing to watch
Harry and Joe bob off into the distance. "I wonder if they
can swim."

"Bloodthirsty," Conn said.

"Drowning doesn't actually involve blood."

"It appears they can at least float, so drowning is
probably too much to hope for. Although no one on this
ferry seems to have noticed that two men have gone overboard."

"We're not more than a half a mile from shore, three-
quarters tops, and you said the water is warmer than the air,
so they'll survive. And I think they could use some company." She looked back at Kemp, still on the deck and turning blue. Probably not from the air temperature.

"I'm not sure he's breathing yet," Conn said. He might
have known she'd perk up at that.

"What?" she said, just his expression enough to make
her defensive. "I told you I was tired of being chased."

"They're not the real problem," Conn pointed out.
"They're working for someone, and if we get rid of them
permanently, someone else will come."

Rae sighed. "Someone who's not a Stooge. Maybe we
should ask Kemp what's going on."

"I don't know," Kemp groaned out. "Harry is the only
one who talks to the boss."

Conn mulled that for a moment. "Do you think he's
telling the truth?"

"I think Harry is the brains of the outfit," Rae said. She
ambled over to Kemp, prodding him with her foot on his
thigh, dangerously close to familiar territory. "How did
you find us?"

"OnStar," Kemp said, his voice almost back down to a
normal octave. "We saw you take off in the old guy's
Caddy. Harry has some contacts and he managed to keep

tabs on you. We stayed far enough back so you wouldn't spot the Honda, and here we are."

"That's probably all we're going to get out of him," Rae said to Conn.

Conn pointed to the back of the boat. "Go sit back there," he instructed Kemp, "and if you know what's good for you, you'll take the return trip."

"Sure," Kemp said, "but it won't do you any good. Harry isn't going to give up until he does what he has to do." He looked at Rae. His expression could best be described as avid. "And I'm going to enjoy helping him."

chapter
14

CONN AND RAE MADE THE REST OF THE FERRY
ride on the top deck, snuggled together to conserve body
heat. Kemp was huddled alone in the front of the boat, sitting on the deck with his back against the railing. Where he
could keep an eye on Rae's feet.

When they docked at Mackinac Island, Rae and Conn
disembarked. Kemp was still on board when it left for the
mainland again, and since there wouldn't be another ferry
that night, Rae relaxed for the first time in three days. It
didn't last long.

As they walked away from the dock, Conn slung an
arm around her shoulders and pulled her close to his side.

"For warmth," he said.

"Uh-huh," Rae said back, but she didn't shove him off.
Because she *was* cold.

And Conn was just trying to help. That's why he was
holding her so closely. If his attitude had changed, if he
was . . . a little overly protective since he'd seen Kemp
threatening her, it was just her imagination. He'd always
been solicitous, after all.

Not that she was complaining—well, her conscience

was kicking up a bit of a fuss, and that annoying little voice of caution was yammering at her. But she'd decided to ignore both, and just bask. It had been a long time since she'd been in a relationship, let alone one that grew close enough for this kind of intimacy, and she didn't mean sex. It was amazing to spend time with someone and not feel a need to talk, to just . . . be. And sure it had only been three days, but she was never again going to scoff at one of those movie heroines for getting involved with a man too fast. There was something about danger that made you stop worrying and overthinking, that allowed you to just be in the moment. And in this moment, she was enjoying herself and damn the consequences.

Conn wasn't as sanguine about the future, at least the immediate future, which was as far ahead as he thought. "They'll be waiting for us when we get back," he said. "They know we'll be prepared for them today. Tomorrow is another story."

"Tomorrow we can take the ferry to St. Ignace. It's over there." Rae pointed northwest, in the general direction of the other city that serviced the island. "The Upper Peninsula."

Conn shrugged off the matter of geography, but it was a tight, edgy imitation of his usual brush-off. "They can split their forces."

"I'm not sure Harry will let the other two out of his sight for that long. Although Kemp does follow instructions pretty well."

That earned her a slight smile, a little squeeze going along with it. "He's no match for you."

Rae smiled back, but she wasn't all that confident. "Next time he won't get that close." Heck, next time he'd probably bring a weapon. But she'd worry about that next time.

"Necessities," she said when they came out onto the main street. She looked left and right, found what she wanted, and set off in that direction, Conn following along. "It's an ATM, Automated Teller."

"We had those at the faire," he said, standing aside

while she fed her card in and punched buttons. "Why do you need so much money?"

"Tipping, ferry tickets, in case you get hungry." She took out the maximum, and retrieved the receipt and her card.

She'd be broke in no time if this kept up. Especially if she lost her job. And she wasn't thinking about that either, Rae decided. There was nothing she could do about it, so driving herself crazy was foolish.

Philosophy by Larkin. She slid a glance at Conn, but the grim amusement she felt was for herself. Her mother had been trying Rae's entire life to get her to adopt a more relaxed outlook. Conn had accomplished it in three days. Rae would have gotten a good laugh about it if she didn't know it was exactly what her mother had been hoping when she'd saddled her with him.

In any other small town she'd have visited the Chamber of Commerce next, but since the day she'd settled in Michigan, she'd heard about the Grand Hotel. She'd always wanted to stay there, and it offered the added bonus of limiting access to those with reservations. Not that she thought private grounds and a dress code would keep Harry and company out if they really wanted to get in; the place probably wasn't run like Fort Knox. But it would be more difficult, at least.

She made a phone call and secured a reservation at the Grand, not difficult considering the thinness of the tourist crowds and the rates, which ranged in price from a couple hundred dollars per person per night for an interior room with no windows, to a four-bedroom cottage that started at fifty-eight thousand dollars a month. But at least there were perks.

"Good news," for Conn anyway, "the reservation includes dinner and breakfast."

His stomach growled right on cue. "What are we waiting for?"

"The proper wardrobe, and the only place to get it without knowing the town is up there." She pointed to the hotel.

The Grand Hotel occupied a high bluff overlooking the Straits of Mackinac, with the commercial section of town stretched out down the hill to the east, and the hotel's nine-hole golf course filling the vee between the two.

The hotel had hosted five U.S. Presidents, two movie crews, and countless celebrities and other persons of note in its three hundred eighty-five rooms, no two of which were decorated alike.

They walked up the hill to the point where the road was blocked off, and waited until their reservation was verified and they were politely reminded of the evening dress code in force for all areas of the hotel. Rae followed Conn up the steps to the front porch, stretching six hundred and sixty feet along the front of the hotel behind columns that soared three stories to the overhanging top floor. Planters ran the entire length of the porch, filled with geraniums fading with the season.

They didn't take the time to enjoy the flowers or the porch, or the view out over the Straits of Mackinac. Clothes were the first order of business, and only because they needed the clothes to get warm and fed, and, at least on Rae's part, to find an escape from the mental exhaustion. She was tired of being chased by bad guys, and she hated what it was doing to her. Even if Kemp had deserved what he'd gotten.

They hit the gift shop, or maybe it would be more accurate to say the gift shop hit her, right in the credit card. She had to take several deep breaths when she sneaked a peek at the price tags, but seeing Conn in dress slacks and shirt, a jacket and tie, was worth it, especially when they arrived at the doorway of the dining room. All eyes in the room, men and women, were glued to him. He had a presence that was undeniable. Too bad he was a loon, and she wasn't just talking about the amnesia. She was pretty sure he wouldn't turn out to be a gypsy like her parents, but spies were another kind of gypsy entirely, and not the harmless kind, so she had even less chance of a future with him..

And she was getting so far ahead of herself Einstein would want to study her.

"Why are you smiling?" he asked her.

"I may be paying this off for the next year, but it's almost worth it."

Conn leaned down to whisper in her ear. "I can take the almost out of that statement."

"That's some ego you've got there, Robin Hood."

"I've never had any complaints."

"That's either a sign of your memory coming back, or just the typical male delusion that you're all gods between the sheets."

He frowned. "It's not my memory."

"Then you might have had complaints," she teased.

"Perhaps, but that was the past. What counts is now."

Great, he was probably a womanizer, too—a world-traveling spy with a God complex where women were concerned and a need to prove it continually. That might be ungracious, but he'd kissed her when she'd been a complete stranger. And he hadn't touched her since, at least not with that kind of intent. "I think I'm safe," she said.

"Do you?"

She met his eyes again and felt like she'd caught on fire. She was on the verge of asking him how hungry he was when the hostess showed up and planted herself in front of Conn.

"The dining room is crowded tonight," she said to him.

Rae tipped her head to look around the doorway. Maybe five tables were occupied in a room that held at least thirty.

"Maybe you'd prefer room service," the hostess said, dropping her voice, and her eyes. The only thing that could've made it more suggestive would be if she'd handed him a room key and offered to bring the food herself.

And then she took a step back and started to babble, her eyes going wide. Rae took one look at Conn's face and nearly took a step back herself.

"If you are offering an apology," he said to the hostess, "it should not be to me."

She turned to Rae, her mouth dropping open. "Oh, my gosh, I didn't even see you there. I'm so sorry."

"Never mind," Rae said, "it's understandable."

"Thank you," the hostess said, careful to keep her eyes off Conn as she led them to a table. "I really am sorry," she added before she left them. "I'd tell you it's because I've been stuck on this island all summer with the same handful of eligible bachelors, but honey, you don't have to be stuck on an island to appreciate him."

No, but being stuck with him made the island seem a whole lot smaller.

It was a good thing the meal plan was included because Conn ate everything in sight, including most of Rae's meal when she pushed it aside, too tied up in knots to do more than pick at it.

"Something ails you?" he asked her.

"Just nerves, I guess."

"Harry?"

Conn, she thought, even as she nodded because his assumption was easier than the truth, and then she blurted out, "I only got one room," before she could stop herself, hoist on her own petard because of that damned honesty her parents had drummed into her.

Conn smiled, slow and easy. And suggestively. "Don't get the wrong idea," she said. "I don't have . . . designs on you."

Although if it felt this warm in the dining room when he was only smiling at her, she could imagine what it would be like in a room with a bed—and not because of his mouth, or his hands, or his body. Well, not only because of those things. It was Conn, who he was inside, calm and centered. Even when they were in danger there was a quietness about him, a confidence that made her feel secure, while she second-guessed everything, every decision . . .

"I can get another room—"

"No. It would be a mistake for us to separate."

"That's what I expected you to say, but I think—"

"You think too much," he said, so completely in synch with her thought process it scared the hell out of her.

How did you fight someone who seemed to be inside your own mind? "What I'm thinking about right now is taking a walk on the beach," she said, because what she needed most at the moment was distance, and if she couldn't get that, she'd settle for a distraction.

"It's cold out there," Conn reminded her.

"Exactly."

Even if Conn would have let her walk on a wide-open, unprotected beach, the closest thing the island boasted was a rocky shoreline, and that was quite a hike from the hotel. He was okay with a visit to the wide front porch. It didn't help. Neither did watching television, or reading, or taking a shower. And Conn wouldn't let her get another room. Harry was getting desperate, he said, and even though there was almost no chance Harry swam to shore or managed to find an alternate way to get to the island after dark, Conn wasn't letting her out of his sight. Considering the fact that neither of them had gotten a wink of sleep so far, let alone closed their eyes, he was as good as his word.

Rae stood at the window, gazing out over the water. No big-city light pollution stained the night sky, and since the clouds had blown out when the cold front came in, it seemed like the entire Milky Way was visible.

Conn came to stand at the other side of the window, and she blinked because for a moment he was washed in that silver light. The whole knight-in-shining-armor thing flashed across her mind and she didn't roll her eyes. She didn't feel like an idiot for not rolling her eyes, either. Considering the upheaval inside her there wasn't a whole lot of room left over for feeling like an idiot. But she was pretty sure that wouldn't last long.

Conn hadn't said a word, he hadn't even looked at her. But she wanted him to. She wanted him to do more than look. She wanted him to touch her, and to know what it did to her when he put his hands on her. She wanted to touch him back, with more than just her hands, to feel him against her, bare skin to bare skin, to lose her breath and let her mind blur and her bones melt. She wanted his arms around her and his mouth on hers, she wanted him inside her, to be as close to him as she could get, for as long as she could have him.

It wasn't the cautious choice, or the wise one. It wasn't even a choice, she realized. It was a chance. The only one she was going to get. They didn't have a future. All they had was now, and now was only going to last until he got his memory back.

And yet that space between them, a mere eighteen inches of cool air, could have been the Grand Canyon. Conn wasn't making that distance any easier to cross. He turned from the view out the window, leaned one shoulder on the wall, and watched her.

He'd invited her in every way he could. Now he was forcing her to make the next move. There'd be no out later on, no saying her thoughts had been muddled, or that he'd worn down her defenses. He was daring her. She'd never been a sucker for a dare, but she stepped forward, just one step before he met her halfway, folding her into his arms and bringing her against him.

She rested her cheek against his bare chest, the scent of him, soap and man, drifting to her with each breath she took. His skin was warm against hers, his heart a comforting drumbeat. They stood that way for a while in the silver light before Conn stepped back, his hands loose at her waist where her camisole met the waistband of the boxers she routinely slept in.

There was a question in his eyes.

Rae answered it by lifting her camisole up and over her head. She should have been self-conscious, but his hands were there, skimming over her ribs, her breasts, lifting to frame her face. He bent to kiss her, just his hands and mouth touching her, but when she tried to deepen the kiss, to answer the need raging inside her, he stepped back again, dropped to his knees, and gathered her close.

He rested his cheek on her bare stomach, making her tremble so much she could barely stand. Conn steadied her, held her up effortlessly, his mouth cruising along her stomach just above her waistband, nibbling little kisses,

each one a spear of pleasure, a promise of more, a tease
that drove her crazy.

She fisted both hands in his hair and pulled his head
back until he looked at her, his eyes dark and so wild it
was another assault on her senses, a mental assault that
had her imagining what he wanted to do to her and antici-
pating what she'd do to him. And as she held his gaze,
she could see he knew what she was thinking. A rumble
of sound came from him, strained laughter turning feral as
he took one nipple into his mouth. She bowed back, her
hands going to his shoulders to brace herself as he moved
to her other breast, and she was devastated again, every
nerve on fire, blind and deaf to everything but the need as
she reached higher and higher . . . And then he was gone.

Her breath sobbed out, the need still buzzing inside her
like a living thing. Then Conn was there again, sweeping
her up into his arms and carrying her to the bed. She
didn't want to let go, but her muscles were still quivering
and he was undeniable as he slipped her arms from
around his neck. She felt her boxers and panties slip off,
felt the bed dip and then he was warm against her, his
mouth on her belly as he worked his way down and sent
her flying again. She fisted her hands in the bedclothes,
reality narrowing down to the rasp of his stubbled cheeks
against her thighs, the hot slide of his tongue, the skilled
invasion of his fingers as the world exploded, the air sear-
ing into her lungs as pleasure raced through her, inde-
scribably intense and nearly unbearable. And though she
begged him to stop he showed her no mercy, scooping his
hands under her bottom and driving her higher still, until
she shattered into a million bits of heat and light that
ebbed and flowed, wave into wave, until she was utterly
spent.

And yet she wanted to do for him what he'd done for
her, so she made the mighty effort to drag herself up, one
touch enough to energize her again. She used her hands
and mouth as he had, teasing kisses and inciting touches,
pushing his hands away when he tried to take control
again. Each groan was music to her, the rasp of his breath

and the pounding of his heart a thrill because she knew it was for her. She kissed his mouth but wouldn't let him take the kiss deep. She explored his chest, the ridges of muscle on his belly, laughing softly as they quivered under her touch.

But as she slipped lower he pulled her back up, whispering against her mouth, "I cannot bear it."

"You're the strongest man I've ever known," she said.

"Not where you're concerned," he said, urging her gently but inexorably down onto the bed. "Not after wanting you from the first moment I saw you." He swept a hand from her hip down to her knee, lifting it and opening her to him. "One taste and I knew my life would be . . . less, until I could taste you again, until I could join with you and make you mine." And he rose above her, filled her even as his mouth took hers and his body began to move.

A part of her wanted to object to the ring of possession in his voice, the way his arms tightened, the antiquated notion of a man owning a woman. Even if her mind hadn't gone fuzzy, even if she could have spoken, she wouldn't have because there was also a part of her that was thrilled at being *his*. Some might see it as a weakness to surrender, but one of the most amazing strengths a woman had was the ability to make a man tremble for her, to feel his strength and know he was holding it back for her sake.

Conn could have taken his own pleasure; he'd already seen to hers. But he made love like he did everything else, slowly, thoroughly, taking his time to learn and savor, and giving her no choice but to do the same.

His eyes stayed on hers, their fingers intertwined as he moved. She matched the slow, excruciating rhythm, feeling the frantic beating of his heart, the exquisite friction of his body moving on hers, in hers, driving the pleasure up and drawing it out until she was on the edge but not going over because when she did she wanted him to be with her. And then she saw his eyes go blank and she let herself fall, gave up her last shred of control as he slipped deep inside her one last time and locked himself there, his body shuddering as hers convulsed around him.

   She held him close, not letting him go even after the fireworks faded and she came back to herself, because it wasn't just sex. Her breathing had already slowed, and her pulse would get back to normal, but her heart would never be the same.

chapter
15

CONN JERKED AWAKE AS HE ALWAYS DID, HIS ears ringing with imaginary gunfire, the screams of the wounded and dying, his hand fisted as around a knife handle. The face of a child, eyes wide and terrified.

He struggled with the remains of the nightmare, but he wasn't holding it at bay, not completely. If he hadn't been so exhausted, so wrapped up in the woman in his arms, he wouldn't have been able to hold it at bay at all.

But Rae was there with him. He dropped a kiss on her shoulder, lightly, and she shifted onto her back, welcomed him, so open and free and loving that he couldn't stay in the dark place.

"Another dream?" she asked him, her voice soft in the darkness.

He gathered her close, resting his chin on top of her head. She didn't push. They both knew the stakes involved in getting his memory back, and that he should have been making the effort. But she didn't push, so he didn't push.

She offered, and he accepted, helping her as she slipped on top of him. He put his hands on her hips, slid

them up to her breasts as she began to move. Then he
lifted at the waist so he could wind his hands in her hair,
so he could take her mouth and nuzzle her neck, so he
could hear the way her breath broke when he drew a nipple into his mouth.

They came to peak together, in such perfect accord
already it should have given him pause. He refused to
dwell on it, though. When Rae eased down beside him
he gathered her against him, her back to his front, and
buried his nose in her hair to drink in her scent and
memorize the way she fit into his arms. The future
would surely take them in separate directions, but now,
tonight, she was his. They belonged to each other, and
the world was right.

CONN'S SHOWER THE NEXT MORNING CONSISTING,
as it did, of hot water, slippery soap, and a lot of naked
redhead, was going down as one of the truly amazing
memories of his life, old or new. It appeared it would be
the last of its kind, at least with Rae Blissfield.

She hadn't looked at him once since they'd left the
bath, dressing in silence and adding their new things to
the small bag she'd brought from her home. He knew she
was wrung out, tired from the lack of sleep and wincing
every now and then from overused muscles. He felt the
same, but he couldn't regret the night they'd shared. And
he'd be damned if he let her.

He crossed the room and lifted her chin until their eyes
met. "You are not this woman. Embarrassed—" He touched
her hair, back up in an ugly bun. "—closed off."

"I'm not embarrassed." But she brushed his hand
away, her cheeks heating as she turned back to her packing. "Not exactly. It's just . . . Last night . . . I've never
been with anyone like that, or been like that with anyone,
before."

Conn wrapped her in his arms, laughing a little, but
wanting her again, impossibly. "I've never, either."

Rae pulled back enough to look up at him, half hopeful.

"I don't need my memory back to know it."

She smiled, brighter than the sun and incredibly sweet. "I wish we could stay here awhile longer."

Conn looked around the room. "This is only a place. This," he rested his hand over her heart, "is where you live."

She went quiet, wistful, and when she lifted her face to his again, he could tell she was troubled.

"What is it?"

"Last night . . . You have some scars. Quite a few, actually, little round ones." Her hand slipped over his T-shirt, pausing when she said, "Here and here. Does it have anything to do with the dreams? No, don't shrug this off, Conn."

He wanted to do just that, but even if he could have refused her, the time had come to face the unpleasant. "In the dreams, it's night, but there is a lot of flashing light and noise—"

"Gunfire?"

"It's constant, a thunder that never stops. And there are men dressed in trousers and shirts, all black, and they wear heavy boots, or sometimes they wear clothing in shades of tan and brown, like sand—"

"Uniforms," Rae said. "They are soldiers. It's a war you're seeing, although there's no way to know which one. It sounds like more than one, all jumbled up in your memory."

Conn sank into a chair because he needed to sit for a moment, and because he didn't want her to see it, he bent to put on his shoes. He should have known the pretense was futile.

"Are you dizzy?"

He shook his head, the muddled feeling going away because denying its existence to Rae was enough to chase it off. Still, the reassuring smile he attempted fell short. "If I was dizzy, it would be from lack of food after so much . . . exertion."

"Conn—"

He stood. "It cannot be forced."

She took the hand he held out; he collected the bag from the bed.

"Let's go break our fast," he said, his stomach growling.

"Maybe we should call ahead," she teased, "and make sure there's enough food for the rest of the island."

"IT'S WARMER TODAY," CONN SAID WHEN THEY stepped out onto the wide drive behind the hotel.

The sun shone, bright in the sky and almost blinding off the water. There wasn't a cloud overhead, just the one they'd be walking into. "They'll be waiting for us when we get off the ferry," Rae said.

"They will."

A carriage pulled up to take them to the docks, compliments of the Grand Hotel. The driver climbed down from the front seat and collected their bag from Conn. "I'm Eddie," he said, taking it behind the carriage. He'd just finished securing it when they heard a commotion coming from the stable not far away.

Eddie stared in that direction, then took off running. Rae looked at Conn, and they came to the same conclusion. Conn handed her into the front seat of the carriage, then raced around to jump into the other side, taking up the reins as three or four horses came out of the stable and bolted in different directions. The stable hands came out behind them . . . Okay, not all of them worked for the hotel.

"Harry, Joe, and Kemp," Rae said, watching them struggle with a horse apiece. Harry and Joe managed to get on board. Kemp's horse was too much for him. It took off, dragging Kemp a dozen yards before he let go of the reins and windmilled to a stop in a graceless heap.

"Even the Three Stooges could do better than that," Rae said, snorting out a laugh when Joe listed to the side and sort of flopped out of the saddle.

Harry wasn't having as much trouble. Harry was actually catching up with them. Joe was climbing back on his horse, too.

"Go," Rae said to Conn, keeping her eyes on the bad guys, especially Kemp, who climbed to his feet, took one look at Harry and Joe still arguing with their mounts, and headed for a bicycle rack outside the hotel's rear entrance.

"I should know how to do this," Conn said.

That got her attention. She turned forward, took one look at Conn, staring at the leather straps in his hands and looking clueless, and rolled her eyes. "Hand them over," she said, "and push that forward." She pointed at the brake lever on Conn's left. Once he'd disengaged the brake she snapped the reins to slap the horses on the butts and get them into motion.

"How?" Conn asked as the carriage jerked forward, then settled into a smooth roll.

"With my childhood?" Rae glanced over at him, smiling slightly. "I can also dance the Scottish Sword Dance, read palms, and juggle."

"Can you make this thing go faster? And why are we going downhill?"

"The horses are used to walking," Rae said, snapping the reins again to no avail. Except one of the horses turned its head and gave her a dirty look. "And we're going downhill because just about everything is downhill from the Grand Hotel, including our only way off the island. Plus I thought it would be easier for the horses."

"They have horses, too," Conn pointed out, "and theirs aren't pulling all this weight."

"You'd better be talking about the carriage."

Conn gave her a look, not seeing the humor in the situation. Especially when Kemp and his bicycle passed them.

"He's heading to the docks to cut us off," Rae said. "Any ideas?"

"They won't try anything as long as we're in town, surrounded by witnesses."

"And after that?"

"There were maps in the lobby," Conn said. "I looked at them."

"Those were historical, not current. And you didn't study them."

He shrugged. "Didn't need to."

"Great, you can't remember anything about yourself, but I'm supposed to believe you took one glance at a map of Mackinac Island and memorized the layout. A historical map, no less. It was probably a century old."

"Not much has changed here in a hundred years' time."

"The forgetful leading the ignorant." She blew out a breath. "Lead on, Bourne."

Conn didn't roll his eyes, but she could tell he wanted to. "Continue through town," he said.

"Maybe we should rethink the route through town. All those innocent bystanders."

"Do you have a better idea?"

The coach lurched and a voice said, "I do. Pull over and get out."

Rae glanced over her shoulder and saw Eddie, who was just a kid really, probably not more than eighteen years old, in the backseat. "Where did you come from?"

He snorted. "An old lady with a walker could catch this thing. You're going like, two miles an hour, so I jumped in."

"Then you won't have any trouble jumping back out," Conn said.

"No way. These guys are my responsibility."

The horses seemed to perk up at the sound of his voice. Their pace definitely picked up. Slightly.

"We promise not to hurt the horses," Conn said. "Get out."

Rae had to give the kid credit. He went dead white the second Conn looked at him, but he reached over the backseat, grabbed something Rae couldn't see, and tried to hit Conn over the head with it.

Conn blocked the blow and tried to shove him out of the carriage.

"Wait! He can help us."

Conn had Eddie by the front of his shirt, ready to toss

him overboard. He held on for another half minute, then said, "Sit down and behave," letting go with enough of a shove to have the kid hitting the back of the seat with a little *oomph*. "The next person who hits me over the head is going to die," he said to Rae when he settled back into his seat.

"Okay, but he can tell us where we can lose Harry and Joe."

"Yeah," Eddie said, sounding sullen, "I can tell you how to lose those other guys. But why would I want to?"

"Because those guys want to kill us, and they're not cops."

"How do I know that? They're not even trying to catch up. Hell, I'm not even sure they're following us."

He had a point since Harry and Joe were keeping their horses to a sedate walk. They even managed to look innocent—well, Harry managed it. Joe looked a little panicked.

"Everyone heads into town," the kid was saying, "and the Hulk up there in the front seat doesn't strike me as a good guy. I mean, he did steal my coach."

"Cops introduce themselves with badges," Rae said. "Cops would knock on the door of our room, or wait for us at the ferry and arrest us. They wouldn't steal horses and engage in hot pursuit."

"Hot pursuit? This is more like directional coincidence." There was a moment of silence, all of them conceding Eddie's point. Then he said, "Do you guys have badges?"

"No," Rae began.

Conn took over. "You don't have much choice but to trust us, kid. We haven't tried to hurt you—"

"Except the part where you wanted to toss me from a moving vehicle."

"You tried to hit me over the head," Conn said through clenched teeth.

"Look, Eddie, I know they don't seem dangerous," Rae said, sending Conn a warning look. "They won't try anything as long as we're in town."

"No witnesses."

"Exactly, but the minute we stop we're in trouble. And since you're with us, and they won't know what we said to you, you're not safe, either."

"I'm just an innocent bystander."

"I believe you, but what do you think your chances of convincing them are?"

Eddie looked over his shoulder.

"You're a witness now, and you know what happens to witnesses in the movies."

"Not really."

"Trust me, you don't want to find out firsthand. Help us get away, they'll follow us, and you'll be safe."

"There's no way we're going to lose them in this," Eddie said. "And we're running out of town. That cross street up ahead is it."

Rae peered ahead and saw the street he was talking about, nothing but woods on the other side.

"Where does that road going off at a right angle lead?" Conn asked.

"Fort Mackinac, then around the hotel golf course and into the state park. There's another golf course there, and the airport."

"Airport?"

"Yeah, the island has a small airport, but it's all uphill from here. Hey, I have an idea." Eddie pulled out a cell phone and started texting, talking at the same time, which was pretty good since multi-tasking was a skill Rae would have sworn he didn't possess. Then again, he'd exceeded all her expectations in their short acquaintance. "Take a left when you get to the dead end," he said.

"Are you sure?"

"Absolutely. My friends can ride circles around these guys."

"I don't think it's a good idea to bring more . . . Okay," she said when a couple horses appeared out of nowhere.

"They were riding in the park," Eddie explained. He half stood, gesticulating wildly at the horses behind the carriage.

The horses moved in between them and their pursuers.

Harry took out a gun and pointed it at them.

Eddie's friends bolted, not that anyone could blame them, and Eddie slid down in the seat so nothing was visible but the tips of his gelled hair. "That would have worked without the gun."

"That's it," Conn said, climbing into the backseat. "Keep your head down," he said to Rae, "and you get on the floor."

Eddie didn't have to be told twice. Rae was having a little trouble with his instructions since it was hard to guide the horses without being able to see where they were going.

Harry and Joe were getting impatient, too, now that they'd left the potential for harming innocent tourists behind them. And it wasn't just Harry. Joe was armed this time, too, but it was Harry who fired and missed as Conn climbed onto the back of the carriage. Conn chose his moment and jumped, swiping Joe completely off his horse but only hitting Harry hard enough to knock him sideways. His gun went off again, but Harry was already listing badly to his right. He made it another fifty yards or so before gravity won.

Harry flopped onto the grass at the side of the road, but he didn't stay down, springing to his feet and squeezing off another shot. He scared his horse and Joe's away but the shot missed Conn and everyone in the carriage because Conn ran off at an angle, zigzagging to confound Harry's aim, circling back around to the road when he was sure he was out of gunshot range.

Rae had stopped the carriage not far in front of him, and when he got in she pointed to a bullet hole in the side of it, not six inches from her head.

Conn went cold, but he hid it. "If it's any consolation," he said, "they grazed me."

"What!"

He stuck his finger through a hole in the leg of his pants, about mid-thigh. "Just caught me enough to leave a welt."

"Well," Rae said, "at least they didn't hit you in the head."

Conn looked over his shoulder and saw Harry coming. Somehow he'd caught one of the horses. "Don't worry," he said, exhaling heavily, "there's still time."

chapter
16

"TWO DOWN, ONE TO GO," RAE SAID, SETTING THE carriage in motion.

"But he's the one with the gun," Eddie observed.

Conn didn't say anything. He was busy thinking of a way out of this mess, and coming to only one conclusion.

"Airport," he finally said. "Get there fast."

"Tell it to the horses," Rae said.

"You just have to know what you're doing." Eddie stood up, and when they didn't get the hint, he said, "Let me drive."

Since Eddie was in her way, Rae slid over into Conn's lap. As much as Conn enjoyed that, he couldn't afford the distraction. He eased out from underneath her and plopped her into the front seat he'd vacated, climbing into the back so he could stay between her and Harry in case Harry decided to take potshots at them again.

Eddie coaxed his equine friends into a gentle gallop. Harry, listing from side to side on his reluctant mount, fell behind. By the time he caught up they were at the airport, and Conn was already boosting Rae into a small plane sitting on the tarmac. She wasn't going willingly.

"Can you fly this thing?" she wanted to know, bracing her hands on the edge of the doorway.

"Yes." He peeled her hand off the door and stuffed her inside, tossed her bag in after her, then followed her through the door.

"That's what you thought about the carriage. Then you handed me the reins."

He buckled himself into the pilot's seat. "Your point?"

"Flying a plane wasn't something I learned on the Renaissance circuit."

"I know how to fly," he said, flipping switches and starting up the plane.

"Your memory is back?"

Yes, he thought, but he said, "No." Snap decision, but his gut told him it was the right one, and he usually went with his gut.

If he told Rae he was Conn the FBI agent, not Conn the Armorer, she'd start asking questions, and when he refused to answer those questions she'd get pissed and try to ditch him. He couldn't protect her if she ditched him.

That meant he was going to have to pretend he was just a floater with no memory of who he really was. He tried to convince himself it was just another undercover op. He'd passed himself off as someone else dozens of times and gotten away with it. This was no different.

He looked over at Rae and stopped lying to himself. This one *was* different, if for no other reason than his ultimate goal on every previous mission had been to keep himself alive. True, on every previous mission the other people involved had been criminals, but he'd have sacrificed the mission to save his own butt.

For the first time, he knew there was one life more important than his own. He wasn't sure how he felt about that, but it sure as hell didn't instill him with confidence. And if he didn't believe he was going to get through this, he probably wouldn't. And neither would she.

"Hello," Rae shouted at him, "are you paying attention?"

Conn took a deep breath and tried to channel his inner

Renaissance man. He was only partially successful. He nailed the tone if not the style of speech. "It's not like we're going to run into anything up here."

"It's not up here I'm worried about, it's down there."

No shit, Conn thought, but his alter ego wouldn't have said that. His alter ego would have shrugged it off, so that was what he did. It wasn't easy to put sarcasm into a shrug, but he gave it a shot, and he must have managed it because when he glanced over she was studying him. So he smiled at her and popped up an eyebrow, and she blushed. It was a shameless exploitation of their night together, but you used what you had. And if you felt crappy about it, you just ate that.

Then again, she didn't let it go, so how crappy could he feel?

"Really," she said, peering down at the Mackinac Bridge and the deceptively pretty straits below, "you can land this thing, right?"

Conn held up a hand and let the plane bobble a little.

Rae locked her hands around the yoke in front of her and sent him a look. But she also shut up.

Quiet was good because Conn needed to think. Not about flying the plane, he knew how to fly the plane. He even knew how to land it. *How* he knew was the issue.

There'd been no pain, no warning signs, no *aha* moment. He'd gotten into the carriage, picked up the reins, and drawn a blank. Blank was nothing new, except for the last handful of days blank had referred to the twenty-first century. Suddenly, just when he'd needed to tap in to that medieval store of knowledge, it was gone. But he'd taken one look at the plane and known he could fly it. Handy, since it was the only way they were going to shake Harry loose.

Problem was, how did he explain it? He'd gotten them out of immediate trouble, and that was going to fly—no pun intended—for a little while, but Rae wasn't stupid; as soon as the emergency was over she'd want to know how he'd pulled it off.

"So what's going on with you?"

Or maybe she wouldn't wait that long. So, moment of truth. He could stick with the first lie, which would save him from having to tell her any more lies. Or he could tell her the truth—which would be so much worse.

"I, uh . . ."

"Damn it, Conn," she said, "you can't land the plane, can you? You did that 'danger mode' thing where you think you know everything, you shoved me into this plane, and now we're going to die."

She looked around, then got out of her seat and started digging through shelves and storage lockers.

"What are you doing?"

"I'm looking for the driver's manual."

"Driver's manual?"

"There have to be instructions some—yes!" She plopped back into the copilot's seat and started flipping through a bound book. "Okay, first we radio in a mayday."

"I don't think it's a good idea to tell the police where we're landing."

"True, but on the other hand they'll call in emergency vehicles, and that sounds like the right way to go."

Conn reached over and ripped the radio's handset out of the control panel.

"That's a no, then," Rae said, giving Conn a moment of guilt when he realized how hard she was working to keep from panicking.

"Just tell me what to do."

"We need to find a place to land." She peered out the window, not looking very hopeful.

They'd passed over the straits; Mackinaw City was spread out below them for a moment before the small cluster of buildings gave way to trees. Nothing but trees, leaves past the brightest colors of fall but still thick enough that nothing was visible on the ground unless they were right over it. But Conn knew the highway was down there somewhere.

"I-75," Rae said, just as he banked the plane to the right—wobbling it again to remind her he didn't know what he was doing.

He had to give her credit, her hand closed around his arm and went white knuckled, but only for a second before she got hold of herself. "Thank God it's a weekday and traffic is light. Look for a straight stretch—"

The engine began to sputter.

Her eyes cut to his. "Don't tell me, we're out of gas."

Conn looked at the gauge and came to the same conclusion. The plane had probably been on the runway because it had just arrived and was waiting to be refueled.

She looked at the manual again. "U-u-u-mmm," she said, her voice shaking as much as her hands.

Conn reached over and rubbed the back of her neck. "We can do this."

She took a deep breath and let it out. "People are always landing planes on highways, right?"

"If you say so."

"You're the one who got us into this situation. Time to put your money where your mouth is. That means prove what you said about being able to land this thing."

"I know—" Conn stopped himself before he gave away the farm. "What's next?"

"The throttle controls altitude," Rae said, too intent on the instructions to notice his verbal slip. "That's the throttle." She started to point to a bright blue lever, then got sidetracked. "Landing gear. When—" She started paging through the manual.

Conn didn't figure they had any time to waste. "It's labeled," he said.

"But I don't know if we should turn it on yet."

"Only one way to find out." He put the gear down, feeling the plane shudder a little, but more interested in the road rushing up at them, the two lanes looking impossibly narrow as the engine gave a last cough and went silent. "Keep reading."

There wasn't a lot of traffic on a weekday morning, but Conn had chosen the southbound lanes so whatever cars came along would be heading the same direction and hopefully see them in plenty of time to get out of their way. He wrestled with the wheel, just the sound of the air rushing by them as he fought to make a glider out of a plane that was never meant to be one.

Rae started to talk about balancing the throttle with the control stick, decreasing their altitude, and applying flaps. Conn made sure he didn't anticipate her directions too much, pulling the yoke toward him to slow the plane down to around seventy knots, keeping the nose up as they dropped under twenty-five feet. No need to kill the throttle since the engines had already stopped. He let the back wheels drop to the roadway, deliberately hard.

Rae gave a little cry and grabbed his arm.

He shook her off. "Gotta land the plane," he growled, the plane dropping to the pavement again, softer this time. He pushed up slightly on the wheel to bring the nose down. The front wheel touched down, rubber squealing as he applied the brake.

When the plane finally came to a stop, he looked over at Rae, white as a sheet. He clapped her on the back and she wheezed in a breath, some of her color returning. It took another minute, and a lot more deep breathing—on both their parts—before she said, "What now?"

Conn answered her question by taking her hand and pulling her out of the plane. If she was okay enough to talk, she was okay enough to walk. There were a couple of cars behind the plane, but they were too far back to see much, not even if they were male or female since part of Rae's return to reality had been putting her hair up in that ugly bun again.

He retrieved their things and towed her through the ditch, boosted her over the ancient farm fence on the other side, and followed her into the forest.

"Mackinaw City will be this way," she said, heading north. "Do you think those guys are watching the car?"

"I'm more concerned about the dogs," Conn said.

She stopped and looked back at him.

He shrugged. "In my day they would have brought out the hounds to track outlaws."

Rae didn't have a comeback for that, at least not a verbal one. Her pace picked up, though, so Conn got the distinct impression she didn't want to risk coming face-to-face— or face-to-muzzle—with any potential pursuers.

Conn was just glad she didn't ask any questions. He needed to think, to put everything that had happened in the last few days together with what he'd discovered before he'd lost his memory and see how the new picture shaped up. He wasn't going to be able to do that until he factored Rae into the equation.

Considering the situation, he was lucky to be free and alive. He had Rae to thank for that—and what he'd done was the furthest thing from thanking her. Getting involved with her had been a mistake, one he'd never have made if he'd been himself. Not that he had any regrets.

Every moment with her had been incredible, but what she'd given him was more than sex. She'd given him back himself. Before Rae, every time he'd come close to a breakthrough he'd smothered the restlessness, the flashbacks of death and war—almost post-traumatic stress because he'd been doing this since he was a kid: marines, Special Forces, then FBI. He'd made a deliberate decision to be a guy without that kind of past, hell, to be a guy with no past because that was better than the one he lived with.

There'd been no need for that last night because Rae had been there. He'd lost himself in her. Even when morning came he'd made her his world, and it had become such a habit not to try to remember he hadn't realized he was back, that he was Connor Larkin, FBI agent, until Harry, Joe, and Kemp showed up, and a label popped into his head.

Counterfeiters.

And Annie and Nelson Bliss were in it, right up to their tie-dyed headbands.

It was Conn's job to shut down the operation, and it should have been a piece of cake, which was why Mike Kovaleski, his handler, had put him on it. Conn had been tired of the ugliness of his past, soul-deep tired. A bunch of latter-day hippies living on the fringe of society, who didn't want to file tax returns, let alone obey laws, shouldn't have posed a problem for him. They probably figured no one would care if they made a little cash. Literally.

Turned out it was a whole lot more complicated. Somebody-was-playing-puppet-master complicated. No way had Rae's parents hired Harry, for one thing. No way had they hit him over the head, then rescued him from the mud and nursed him and his broken brain. And no way would they hire a trio of bumbling enforcers to hide their crime, let alone sic them on their own daughter.

And now the bumbling enforcers were taking potshots at them, which told Conn two things: The mastermind was getting panicky, opting to take him out without discovering who he was and what he knew. And the mastermind was in Detroit. Otherwise the situation would have escalated earlier.

It was time to stop pussyfooting around and close this case. It might be a simplistic view of things, but it was more than he'd known yesterday, and progress was progress. He had to find out who was running the show before Rae discovered what was going on. He'd still have to arrest her parents, there was no getting around that. But she'd be safe. That was the mission: Get the bad guys and keep the civilians from getting hurt.

Their feelings didn't count.

Unfortunately, he had to pretend to still be into Rae without actually doing anything about it. Keep his distance without appearing to keep his distance. So she didn't get suspicious.

He'd probably need Merlin to pull it off. Too bad he didn't believe in magic anymore.

RAE FOLLOWED CONN THROUGH THE WOODS, GRATEful, at least, that she was dressed for it. He set a brutal pace, stopping every now and again to let her catch up. She might have been angry, she might have complained. She might have found a handy place to sit until she was rested and the hell with everything else. The thought of dogs kept her going. Not that she didn't like dogs, she just assumed the ones that would be sent after them would be more reminiscent of Cujo than Lassie.

Although, it would be a good distraction from Conn, since the only thing that seemed to keep her from wanting to jump him was danger. Take now, for instance, watching him stride through the woods, arms swinging and butt flexing. It was ... invigorating. A little line of sweat darkened the back of his T-shirt even though the temperature hadn't broken the sixty-degree mark. It made her want to strip off the shirt, and the pants, and—

"I didn't realize we were so far out of the city," she said in a desperate effort to stop thinking about sex in the woods.

Conn didn't say anything. Conn was saving his breath for walking. She made a conscious effort to do the same—and to keep her eyes off him. She had a lot to think about anyway. Harry and his cronies, sure, but first and foremost, everything had changed. Oh, not Conn, he was just in danger mode. And not her, not really. What had changed was *them*.

Rae allowed herself a smile only because she knew he couldn't see it, couldn't see the wistfulness, the secret joy, the voluptuousness she'd never felt before.

The temptation was to hold on to all of that, even if holding on meant not trying to quantify or qualify their relationship. Not trying to look ahead. But that wasn't her nature. She'd never taken the term "bean counter" as an insult. It was what she did and who she was. She embraced that, but for once in her life she was content to live in the moment, not weighing risk and return, not holding back until she was absolutely certain she'd get back what she'd put in.

Conn's memory would return soon enough, and she would have to watch him walk away. She couldn't even dread it because it meant he could deal with the people who were after him. But it was going to hurt like hell.

"We're back," Conn said over his shoulder, and she put all the anxiety over the future away.

One thing at a time, she told herself, the first being getting to Mr. Pennworthy's car without cops or dogs finding them.

Conn had stopped behind some pines that turned out to form a sort of boundary at the back of a little house.

Rae peered through the aromatic boughs and didn't see anyone. She kept her voice down anyway. "The car is on the other side of the city, and I-75 is still between here and there. We should keep moving until we find an underpass—a road that goes beneath the highway," she added automatically, having gotten used to explaining those kinds of terms to Conn. "Without being seen, if possible. Maybe you should slouch or something."

Conn met her eyes for the first time since they'd left the plane, and he was smiling. "Maybe you should cover up that hair."

"You didn't feel that way last night," she said, regretting the words as soon as they were out because his eyes darkened, grew intense, and she forgot where they were and what they were doing.

Conn wasn't helping. "We could wait until full dark," he said. He didn't leave much mystery about how he expected to fill the hours between then and now.

Tempting, but her desire was tempered by the possibility of discovery, especially this close to civilization. And she didn't mean the sex police. The regular police were more of a concern, or maybe the FAA would get involved, since they'd stolen the plane. And then there were Harry, Joe, and Kemp. Among others. "Remember the dogs?"

"If there were going to be hounds, they'd be a problem by now."

"It's dinnertime," Rae countered, "and it's not barbecue weather, so most people should be indoors."

His eyes lit up, and his stomach growled. So much for her irresistibility.

"Don't even think about it," she said. "We'll stop to eat after we put a few miles between us and incarceration. I'll even go for Scottish chicken. As long as we don't get caught. If we do we'll be eating jail food."

"Have a little faith," Conn said, and he set off, moving in the general direction of the highway, following the line of trees.

Rae followed him through the woods edging the city. He didn't really give her a choice, but she was getting tired of the macho attitude. She trotted a little, went past him, and took the lead.

"If there are bullets, that's where they're coming from," Conn said.

"I'm tired of being Guinevere."

"That would make me King Arthur."

"He came to a bad end."

"He was borne off by beautiful woman to an island to live for eternity."

"But he was stabbed with a sword first. I'm not sure being borne off to an island by beautiful women is worth being skewered."

"I don't know about the skewering, but having one woman give me a hard time is bad enough. Three? For eternity? Not worth immortality."

"I've been giving you a hard time? Since I met you I've been chased, shot at, arrested, and nearly killed in a plane crash."

Conn looked like he wanted to argue, especially about the plane, and she had to admit he had bragging rights after that landing. But they came to a narrow, rutted dirt lane that ran parallel to the highway, with a strip of weeds growing in the center, knee-high, and he turned to study the area, his eyes going laser sharp.

"Not exactly a high traffic area," Rae observed.

"True, but it will appear less suspicious if we pretend to be a couple out for an evening stroll," he said.

"With our luggage?"

Conn slung the strap of her bag over his shoulder, adjusting it so the bag hung behind him. Then he took her hand, twining his fingers with hers.

Rae had never been one for fairy tales, having grown up in a life that capitalized on them, not to mention the part where she knew what life was like behind Mother

Goose's whitewash job, people not bathing for months, covered in lice and fleas, living in squalor.

Being hand in hand with Conn was her idea of a fantasy, and if she didn't pull her hand from his it didn't mean she was getting sucked into the illusion. He was right about the pretense. People would look at them and see exactly what Conn wanted them to see. Unless those people were Harry, Joe, and Kemp.

chapter
17

MACKINAW CITY WASN'T THAT LARGE, AND I-75
soared through the middle of it, ramping up to the bridge
approach, so it was hard to miss. Good thing, since skin-
to-skin contact with Rae was wreaking havoc on Conn's
ability to run the op. He was grateful his pattern of speech
had been getting gradually less stilted over the last couple
of days as he'd come closer to retrieving his memory,
because he'd slipped more than once.

Rae hadn't noticed. He chose not to read anything into
that.

That first dirt lane brought them to a paved road that led
beneath I-75. Direction wasn't a mystery with the bridge
looming overhead, and before they knew it they were out
of the bridge's shadow and walking along the divided lane
leading into the touristcentric area of the city: a maze of
shops, restaurants, and entertainment that led, ultimately, to
the docks along the shoreline.

"Do you think the car is being watched?" Rae asked.

Under normal circumstances Conn would have said,
Yes, and let it go at that. His alter ego was regrettably
wordy. Even more regrettably, he had to keep up the pre-

tense. "I think we should attempt to discover what happened after we left the island. Harry and his friends may not be at liberty to attempt an ambush at the car."

"You think the police arrested them?"

"Unless they grew wings." Conn headed for the nearest shop.

Rae pulled him back. "You're too memorable," and before he could argue, she put up her hood and went inside.

Conn let her go, but he put a foot on the door to hold it slightly open so he could hear the conversation without being seen.

Rae wandered around, aimlessly browsing for a couple minutes before she approached the checkout counter, plucking a pair of earrings from a rack and holding them up to her ears. "I hear there was some commotion on the island today," she said to the bored girl picking at her nail polish behind the cash register.

"Yeah," the girl said, "some guys stole horses from the Grand Hotel and, like, chased this carriage all over the island. With guns."

"Was anyone hurt?"

"Nah. The driver took them on single-handedly, like John Wayne or something. The people in the carriage, like, totally stole a plane and flew it off the island. They landed it about ten miles away from here, like, right in the middle of I-75."

"Really," Rae said.

"Yeah, I heard it was some guy built like the Hulk and a lady with red hair . . ."

"Shit," Conn said under his breath as Rae shot out of the store and took off at a fast walk.

"You heard all that, right?"

"Aye," Conn said, letting her lead the way into the maze of boutiques and restaurants. As soon as they were out of sight of that first shop, Conn slowed to a more leisurely pace so they didn't draw more attention. "So much for you being the unremarkable one."

"You wouldn't have gotten that much out of her. She'd have taken one look at you and—"

Conn popped up an eyebrow.

"Okay, you could have found out whatever you wanted to know, but not by asking questions."

"There are many ways to get information, but I would not want to cross that particular line."

Rae didn't say anything, but Conn thought he caught the beginning of a smile before she looked away. It gave him a little ego boost, knowing she was jealous, but then there was the downside. Her feelings. But it was too late to do anything about it, except try not to encourage her.

They'd been working their way toward the docks, and the parking lot where they'd left Mr. Pennworthy's car. When they found themselves at the last line of buildings, ready to step out into the open, Conn caught Rae's arm.

She didn't argue with him. She looked like she understood his hesitation, if not the exact reason for it. "I don't see anyone around the car."

"That's what troubles me," he said.

The car was parked in a wide-open lot, no other vehicles around it, owing to the lateness of the day, and the season, and the scarcity of tourists. He didn't see anyone lurking nearby, and the closest building was too far off to be used as cover. The sun was low in the western sky. Not much natural light made it past the buildings. All they had to do was cross the parking lot, get in the car, and drive away. Nothing to it. That was exactly what bothered Conn.

There'd been a pretty big ruckus on Mackinac Island earlier, complete with a horse chase and gunfire, not to mention a stolen airplane that was currently blocking the southbound lanes of a major interstate highway. Only half the combatants were in police custody, and it made sense that the authorities would be watching the ferry yards at Mackinaw City and St. Ignace in the hope they could collar the hijackers. Just because he didn't see them didn't mean they weren't there.

Their options were limited. If there'd been a bus station in Mackinaw City, and if it weren't being watched, the ticket agent would have instructions to be on the lookout

for them. And he and Rae were anything but mistakable.
They could steal a car, but he preferred to take their
chances with the Cadillac. It was a prime example of Detroit technology, perfectly maintained, with an engine
more powerful than anything he was likely to stumble
across in a small town where most of the residents
worked the tourist industry for slightly over minimum
wage. Especially since the tourists, who might have pro-
vided something worthwhile to steal, were all snug at
home, getting ready for winter.

Now, if he could only figure out a way to get behind
the wheel . . . Not a good idea to push that agenda, he
decided, not after the plane. No way could he sneak that
kind of skill by Rae twice. He'd barely made it the first
time. And Rae wasn't such a bad driver, judging by their
two previous auto-related altercations. Not that he could
warn her of the possibilities since Conn the Armorer
couldn't possibly anticipate the actions of twenty-first-
century law enforcement.

He took Rae by the hand and stepped out into the open,
crossing the parking lot. They were at the car, and she
was coding them in, when the lights came on. The lights
came from two cars.

"Shit," he said, losing precious seconds while he wrestled with the urge to race around the car and get behind
the wheel himself. He finally yanked open the passenger
door, yelling, "Let's go."

She opened the driver's-side door and looked in at
him. "Can't your friend get us out of this?"

Conn grabbed her arm and pulled her into the car. "I
don't know how to get in touch with him," he lied.

Rae just sat there, staring at the police cruisers bearing
down on them.

"Either you drive or I will."

She pushed the keyless ignition, and shot it into DRIVE
as soon as the engine roared to life, giving the car enough
gas to make the tires spin out on the gravel as she
wheeled it toward the road.

The two cruisers swung out behind them, sirens screaming as they sped back through the area Conn and Rae had just covered on foot.

"I-75?" Conn asked her.

"That's our best bet, don't you think?"

"Not southbound."

She looked over at him, jerking the steering wheel to the right just as one of the cruisers pulled up next to him. The deputy driving it took evasive action and ran into a light pole.

"One down, one to go," Conn said, grinning.

"I was just trying to change lanes," Rae said, looking panicky. "Do you think he's hurt? He's hurt. Oh my God, I killed a police officer."

"Air bag went off," Conn said, then closed his eyes and called himself every kind of idiot there was for mentioning something no medieval armorer would know about. If she hadn't been busy worrying about killing a cop he'd've been toast. "He's fine," Conn said. "The car won't be moving anytime soon, though." He looked over his shoulder. "The other guy seems to be okay with staying behind us."

"That's because we have nowhere to go," Rae said, taking the northbound ramp onto I-75. "Except the bridge."

Conn reached over and set his left hand on top of her right hand, leaving it there until she stopped shaking.

"You okay?"

She nodded, giving him a slight smile. It came out more like a grimace, but at least she'd tried. It said something about her state of mind.

"He's not following us onto the bridge," Rae said.

Sure enough, the cruiser had stopped at the Lower Peninsula entrance to the northbound side, pulling across the two lanes of traffic to stop any other vehicles from crossing the bridge.

"What are they up to?"

"My guess," Conn said, "is that they have the other side of the bridge blocked."

Rae blew out a breath, but she stayed calm. "They're

trying to keep innocent bystanders from getting hurt. And it's not like we can go anywhere but forward."

She had a point there. They couldn't cut over to the southbound lanes, and it had to be at least a couple hundred feet to the water. Even if they could get the Caddy over the side, they'd never survive the fall.

They passed the southern tower, moving onto the center span. Even when they'd crested the hill there was nothing to see, no taillights in front of them, and since the sun had completely set, and they were still a couple of miles from the far end, not even the hint of the vehicle blocking their way was visible. Conn still knew it was going to be there.

So did Rae, but instead of slowing down when the vehicle came into sight, she sped up. Even worse, it was a pickup truck, the seal on its side illegible at that distance but a clear indication that it represented a sheriff's department—not to mention the equivalent of a brick wall at the speed they were going.

"Rae," he said, keeping his voice calm so he didn't upset her. "Maybe we should stop."

"If I hit the back end of the pickup really hard, I can punch it out of the way and keep going."

"Maybe, but—"

"It always works in the movies."

"I don't doubt the mechanics of your plan. But even if the police car that hit the pole a few minutes ago had been driveable, the officer was unable—"

"Because of the air bag." Rae smacked herself in the head with the heel of her hand. "Stupid. So we stop, and then what? He'll have a gun."

"So did Harry," Conn reminded her.

"Right." Rae did another one of her deep-breathing exercises, slowing the car as they passed the second tower and started the final descent.

She was about a quarter mile from the truck, going less than twenty miles an hour, when Conn opened the passenger door and rolled out, letting momentum take him to his feet again. He stayed low, keeping the bulk of the car between himself and the police officer getting out of the pickup.

The Caddy rolled to a stop, Conn catching up to it just as the officer approached the driver's side and ordered Rae out of the car. By the time he caught sight of Conn in his peripheral vision it was over, Conn clouting him on the jaw hard enough to put him out.

He didn't waste any time, dragging the officer up into a fireman's carry and dumping him in the bed of his pickup, then jumping in the cab and pulling it up far enough so the Cadillac could get by. The radio was already squawking for a response.

"What the hell was that?"

Conn turned around in time for Rae to punch him on the arm. "Ouch," he said, just registering the aches and bruises from the stunt he'd pulled.

"Don't ever do that again."

He rubbed his arm. "I won't if you won't."

"You scared me half to death."

"Yell and walk," Conn said, nudging her back to the Caddy. "We don't have much time before the deputy on the other side decides to come over here and find out why he's not getting an answer."

"I think it's too late already."

"Fuck."

That got a reaction from Rae, although it was nonverbal.

"It seemed to be appropriate to the circumstances."

"I'll say."

Conn climbed into the passenger seat of the Cadillac, Rae barely waiting until he was completely in before she took off. "Now what do we do?"

"Drive. And lose him," he said, shooting a glance at the cop car bearing down on them, and wishing he was behind the wheel. Then again, Rae hadn't done too badly.

She took off, but she couldn't seem to lose the squad car on the curving back roads. He couldn't catch up to them, either, but it was just a matter of time before he called in reinforcements.

"We can't do this forever," Conn said.

Rae kept her focus on the road, but she must have agreed, because she poured on the speed, taking the next curve practically on two wheels.

Conn braced himself, marveling at the cornering ability of the Cadillac but keeping an eye out the back window. The cruiser was falling behind, coming into the curve just as Rae steered out of it. By the time she made it around the next bend, the cop was still out of sight. She went another couple of miles, keeping to an insane speed, then taking a left at a narrow dirt lane leading into the forest. She went a couple hundred yards and turned off the lights and engine.

They both turned around in time to see the squad car cruise to a stop at the entrance to the lane. He sat there a minute, long enough for Conn to start thinking about what he'd do if it came to a confrontation. Then he zoomed off, his tires squealing a little on the blacktop road.

Conn had just begun to relax when Rae clutched at him. "Watch the nails," he said, peeling her claws out of his arm. He looked over to find her pointing out the window with her other hand.

They were surrounded by men in camouflage, almost all of them with a bow slung over their shoulders.

"That explains why the sheriff took off."

"Great," Rae said. "There's never a cop around when you need one."

chapter 18

CONN REACHED FOR THE DOOR HANDLE.

Rae squeezed his arm. "Do you think that's a good idea? If we stay in the car, and there's any trouble, I can run them down."

"I think they'd get back up."

Rae smiled slightly. "I'm pretty sure they're human, despite appearances."

"I suppose if I told you to stay here, you wouldn't listen, either."

Rae turned the headlights back on and opened her door. "You keep mistaking me for one of those mousy, oppressed sixteenth-century women who were afraid of big, strong men."

"Well, beating a woman was legal, and if that didn't work, you could always be burned as a witch."

"Renaissance, huh." Rae got out of the car.

Conn got out as well. They both stayed behind the doors.

"What do you trolls want?" one of the men called out.

"Trolls?" Conn asked.

"We're not trolls," Rae said.

They all looked at the car. "Definitely trolls," the same

man said. "That's what we call anybody living in the Lower Peninsula—below the bridge."

"Clever," Rae said. "If we're trolls, what are you?"

"Yoopers."

She frowned.

"Yoopers," a kid about eighteen repeated, "as in *U.P.* Upper Peninsula. Jeez, trolls are stupid."

"And Yoopers don't have any manners."

"Why are you antagonizing them?" Conn said under his breath.

"Why are you so calm?" Rae shot back. "These guys aren't here for a square dance, they're armed and dangerous."

"I think she just insulted us with that square dance comment, Billy," the guy who'd spoken before—the guy who seemed to be the head Yooper—said conversationally to the man standing next to him.

"I think you're right, Jonas," Billy said back. "That definitely felt insulting. I think she owes us an apology."

"Oh, for Pete's sake, I didn't mean anything by it," Rae said. "And you called me a troll, so I think we're even."

"Does that sound like an apology, Billy?"

"No, it most certainly does not, Jonas." And Billy stepped forward.

Conn was around the door and grabbing him by the neck before anyone else could move. He took Billy's bow and quiver and shoved him into the dirt, nocking an arrow and shooting it into the ground between Jonas's feet, then shooting twice more, his aim perfect. Rae's heart was pounding a mile a minute, and she doubted the whole episode had taken three beats.

Jonas held up his hands to show he didn't mean any harm, then stepped forward and helped Billy to his feet. Jonas seemed pretty calm, but Rae took a quick survey of the other faces and figured she and Conn were about to star in a remake of *Deliverance*, minus the canoe and the catchy soundtrack.

"He's lost his memory," Rae said, hoping an explanation would help. "He thinks he's a sixteenth-century armorer."

"We can fix that," one of the supporting characters yelled out. "Let's hit him over the head."

The others laughed, but there was a sinister undertone that told her it probably wouldn't stop with Conn's head, and he wouldn't be able to take enough Yoopers out before they were on him. And okay, now she was thinking like she was from the sixteenth century.

"Look, we didn't mean to trespass," she said, trying to sound as sincere and nonthreatening as possible. "Just let us go and we'll never come back."

Jonas rubbed his jaw. "First, tell us why the cops were after you."

Rae looked at Conn.

He bumped up a shoulder, which she took for agreement. "Like I said, Conn lost his memory."

"Conn?" the eighteen-year-old said. "Cool name."

"It's short for Connor—and why am I explaining that to you? My parents travel around the country working Renaissance faires."

"They have one of those over to Ironwood," the kid chimed in, adding for the benefit of the trolls, "that's all the way to the other side of the U.P. Hey, do you dress up in one of them wench outfits?"

The peanut gallery seemed to get a kick out of that idea, laughing and leering, which struck a nerve.

"Do you want an explanation or a fashion show, cupcake?"

"There she goes, getting all insulting again," Billy said.

"She is kind of touchy," Jonas agreed.

Conn crossed his arms. "You have no idea."

"Explaining, here," Rae said tightly.

The morons all quieted down, and she gave Conn a look that said she was including him in that group. "A week or so ago, a couple of guys conked Conn over the head and he lost his memory," she continued. "They've been trying to catch him ever since and finish the job."

"Why do they want you dead?" Jonas asked Conn.

"Don't know," Conn said, "but they caught up to us on Mackinac Island this morning."

"Hey, wait a minute." Billy sidled up to Jonas. "I bet they're the ones who stole that plane we heard about. Landed it right in the middle of I-75."

"Cool," the kid said, still mired in the seventies, slang-wise.

The rest of the troop chimed in, equally impressed with their larcenous activities.

"I take it you don't like the people on Mackinac Island," Rae observed.

"It ain't the residents," Billy said, "it's them rich trolls, buying up all the waterfront real estate and lording it over ever'body else. They do the same up here, buying hunting lodges and traipsing around in their sissy orange clothes, shooting up the countryside with no concern for whose backyard they're in."

"So . . . You'll let us go, right?"

"We'll do better than that."

THE YOOPERS LIVED IN A TINY COLLECTION OF BUILD-ings Conn hesitated to call a town. A dozen or so houses huddled around a gas station/market/pizzeria, all in one small structure, with a potholed dirt road running in front of it. Jonas's wife was at her sister's in Munising for the week, he'd said, helping with a new baby. So Jonas bunked at Billy's for the night, graciously surrendering his home to Conn and Rae.

Conn didn't like it. There was no way in hell these guys didn't know the local heat. Hell, they were probably cousins or something. That didn't mean they liked each other, but they'd close ranks against outsiders, and he and Rae were definitely outsiders. Rich trolls. Just look at the car they were driving, and the clothes they were wearing probably cost more than the Yoopers made in a month. His certainly did; he'd seen the price tags, and while that might not have made an impression on the floater he'd been, he got it now, and it wouldn't be lost on people who spent a lot of time in outdoor gear.

Put it all together and it spelled one thing: Reward. It might look like Jonas had made a neighborly gesture, but Conn would bet his left nut they were being watched, and once enough time had passed, Jonas was going to contact his cousin the county sheriff and play *Let's Make a Deal*.

He went to the tiny square window in the front door and peered out. There wasn't a lot of light in the small settlement, but he caught the slight silver shimmer of someone's breath steaming on the cold night air. There was a man hunkered in the shadows against the house across from Jonas's, and when he shifted to find a more comfortable position, Conn saw the unmistakable silhouette of a long gun barrel, probably a hunting rifle, lying across the crook of his elbow. Conn wasn't sure they'd actually shoot, but then he wasn't willing to stake his life on it.

"What are you doing?"

"Nothing," Conn said to Rae. There was no point in alarming her until it was necessary. She did fine once they were in danger, but she didn't have the nerves for waiting out a threat.

"I'm tired," she said around a yawn. "Let's go to bed."

And right there was the other problem with having Jonas's house to themselves. That whole balancing act, where he needed to establish some distance from Rae while seeming to do just the opposite, was kind of difficult when they were alone together.

"I'll join you in a few minutes," he said, but when Rae disappeared into the bedroom, he went into the kitchen instead, searching through the cupboards and drawers and having no luck.

He was forced to admit to himself that what he wanted would most likely be in the bedroom. He didn't mean Rae, although she was the first thing he saw, lying back against the pillows, still fully clothed, thankfully. She smiled when he came in, and it wasn't easy, but he went to the dresser and started to rummage through the drawers.

"What are you looking for?"

Conn all but jumped out of his shoes, the sound of Rae's voice and the light touch of her hand on his back a complete shock since he'd been trying so hard to ignore her.

"If you tell me, maybe I can help."

"I'd tell you if I knew," he said tightly.

"Oh. Sure."

He heard the hurt in her voice, but he didn't look at her. If he saw the hurt on her face he was a goner. He moved on to the closet, finally coming across something useful, a hunting knife—a well-balanced hunting knife, he thought, hefting it.

"Okay," Rae said, "what's going on?"

Conn had intended to wait, but on further consideration he decided it would be best to move now, and not just to defuse the bedroom situation. He had no idea what the Yoopers were planning, or how often they intended to change the watch. Waiting meant risks he couldn't begin to guess, but he knew one thing: He'd need all the facts before they could make a clean getaway.

"Conn!" Rae snapped. "Talk to me."

"Something feels . . . wrong," he said.

"Oh, thank God. I mean, I felt that way, too." She looked up, her eyes narrowing in on his slight smirk. The color came up in her face again, and suddenly all the danger didn't seem to be outside.

He pulled her into the front room, easing the curtain aside on the window. "There, at the corner of the house directly across from this one."

"I don't see anything."

"Look again. His breath is steaming." He didn't point out the gun barrel.

"Got him," she said, glancing over her shoulder. "What are they up to?"

Her face was close to his, too close, and it took a second or two for Conn to remember what was at stake and resist the temptation.

"They're watching this house, right?"

And here was the tricky part, Conn thought, focusing back in on what was really important. He had to get Rae to figure it all out for herself without letting on that he was nudging her in the right direction.

"That would be my guess."

"Do you think they told the sheriff we're here?"

"If they had, we'd be in jail by now."

"So, they haven't told the sheriff, but they're keeping us here. Why?"

"In my time, there would be a demand for ransom," he said carefully.

"Even if they knew who to ransom us to . . . Damn." She slipped away from him, pacing across the small room as she worked it out. "They're trying to get a reward. Which means they told the sheriff they know where we are. And since I doubt the sheriff is a fool, that means he'll be around before too long to check it out."

Shit, even he hadn't considered that. "Then we'd better be on our way."

"How?"

"This I know how to accomplish," he said. "Get our things together, stay here, and wait for my signal."

"You're not going to . . ." She pointed at the knife in his hand. "You know."

"I won't kill him, but he's not going to cause us a problem anytime soon."

For once she followed instructions, taking off to get their bag. Conn headed straight for the kitchen. The house had two doors, both the front and a side door visible from the watcher's vantage point. There was a window over the kitchen sink that looked out the back of the house, the panes sliding right to left. Conn boosted himself onto the edge of the counter, lifted out both panes, and set them inside, then forced the storm window out of the frame.

He climbed through and circled around, coming up behind the Yooper on guard and cracking him at the base of the skull with the handle of Jonas's knife. The guy slumped against the side of the building, out for the count. Billy.

That meant Jonas was alone in Billy's house, probably

negotiating their worth. Trouble was, Conn didn't know which building that was. So he slipped from house to house, keeping to the shadows and peeking in windows. The third house was a tiny, honest-to-God log cabin that turned out to be one room for everything: bedroom, kitchen—even the bathtub was out in the open, just a curtain that probably hid a toilet in the corner. And Jonas was there.

Conn backed up two steps and kicked in the front door. Jonas spun around, saw him, and lunged to the right. Conn flipped the knife, caught it by the tip and let it fly, pinning Jonas's sleeve to the wall, his fingers inches from the rifle propped in the corner of the cabin, not far from where he'd been sitting.

Conn snatched the gun before Jonas could snag it with the other hand. He tossed it on the bed across the room. By the time he turned back Jonas was trying to lever the knife out of the wall with his left hand. He wasn't having much luck.

Conn returned to Jonas and pulled the knife out of the wall. "Looks like I got more than sleeve," he said, wiping the knife on Jonas's pants.

Jonas rolled his sleeve back and examined the slight gash in the meaty part of his forearm, halfway between his wrist and his elbow. "Just caught the edge of my arm. I'll live."

Conn grunted a commentary, one that didn't include any level of apology. "So what are we worth?"

Jonas smirked a little. "That ain't been decided yet."

"Because the sheriff is on his way here to take us off your hands," Conn informed him. "What, not smiling any-more? Did you really think we were going to be held up by you?"

Jonas took that for a rhetorical question.

Conn tied Jonas to the chair, using electrical cords ripped from every appliance in the place.

"You can't leave me here."

"You won't be alone for long," Conn said. "But the sheriff is going to be pissed when he gets here and finds out we're gone because you got greedy."

"Maybe you should worry about yourself," Jonas said.

"A backwater sheriff is no trouble."

Jonas laughed. "I meant you lying about your memory problem. Your lady friend isn't going to be happy when she finds out. And women are way scarier than the law any day."

chapter
19

RAE HAD BEEN HALFWAY THROUGH THE KITCHEN window when Conn came in the front door, Billy slung over his shoulder like the week's dry cleaning. He slammed Billy into a chair, hard enough to knock him out, if he hadn't already been unconscious, then collected Rae off the windowsill.

"Predictable," he said, setting her feet on the floor and stepping away, all in one quick move that reminded Rae of the way he'd avoided her in the bedroom moments before.

Well, if he wanted a fight, she'd give him one. "What do you think ordering me around is, if not predictable?"

"What exactly were you planning to do?"

"I don't know, stop Jonas from shooting you?"

"He wants to ransom us, not shoot us."

"Then I probably would have been successful."

Conn shook his head, taking the bag from her, going back through the house, and opening the front door.

"What's wro—"

He put a hand over her mouth, pulling away almost immediately. "Yell at me later. I'm going to push the car far enough so it doesn't alert attention when it starts. You're going to steer it."

"So much for not ordering me around," Rae said, but she kept her voice down, as he had.

As soon as they stepped outside, Conn all but disappeared into the night, moving so silently in his dark clothes she wouldn't have had a clue where to go if not for the occasional light and the fact that she remembered where they'd left the car.

When they arrived and she'd coded it open, he tossed the bag in and went to the back of the car. Rae slid into the front seat and put the car in gear. It began to move almost immediately. They'd gone more than a mile, and Rae was about to risk Conn's anger again when he jumped in the front seat.

He wasn't even breathing hard. "You can start the car now."

She did, resisting the urge to floor it and get the hell out of there. Instead she brought up the GPS. "What about the bridge? Do you think the sheriff will still be waiting there?"

"I doubt it. They think Jonas has us stashed somewhere, so why would they lose sleep waiting for us to cross the bridge?"

He had a point, even if he did get it across in that superior man-is-the-master-race tone of voice that always ticked her off, not to mention making her want to argue with him just because he was being an ass. Which always ended up biting her in hers, because he was almost always proved to be right.

And of course he was. They crossed the bridge with no problem, but Rae left I-75 as soon as the GPS gave them an alternate route that didn't mean wandering around the Upper Michigan backwoods any longer than necessary.

"Best not to push our luck," she said to Conn. "The sheriff may know we're gone by now. If they put out an alert every state cop between here and the Ohio border will be on the lookout for us."

"I'm not arguing," Conn said, settling back into his seat and closing his eyes.

"Not unless you count the passive-aggressive kind of argument."

She glanced over at him then back at the road, doing a double-take and finding his face as calm as ever. She told herself it was just the faint wash of dashboard light that had canted his expression toward pissed off for a second, since he couldn't possibly understand a term like passive-aggressive.

"Is everything all right?"

"I don't know."

He exhaled heavily. "It's been a long day."

It had been a long three days. As apologies went it wasn't the most eloquent, but she got his point. They were both tired and touchy.

"We can't go back to your house," Conn said, "and we can't keep running."

"And that leaves what? The Renaissance festival?"

"Do we have any other choice?"

"But that's where all this started . . . Oh. My parents."

"They may know something that will help me," Conn said, not sounding all that happy about the prospect.

Rae could identify. Facing her mother after . . . everything . . . wasn't on the top of her list of fun activities.

"It'll be after midnight by the time we get there."

Conn's gut was telling him to get on with the mission. But his gut wasn't talking loud enough. "If we arrive after your parents retire, we'll have to sleep in the car."

"Not very comfortable."

"No, and I do prefer to be comfortable."

"I think I can find you a bed," Rae said.

"If you can find me a bed, I'll do the rest."

She looked over at him, smiled. "Not if I have anything to say about it."

He tried, really tried, to get that picture out of his head, but even if he could've managed it and fought off the craving that came along with it, he just didn't see how he could avoid spending the night in her arms without telling her the truth. But then, he'd always known he had the kind of job that required sacrifice. Sometimes you had to take one for the team.

RAE KEPT TO THE BACK ROADS, WORKING HER WAY steadily south. They passed dozens of motels, but she thought they'd be too memorable in a small town where everyone knew everyone else on sight. So she kept driving until she got to Frankenmuth, where there were several large hotels and, due to the huge outlet mall close by, even in the fall there were decent-sized crowds.

Founded in the mid-1800s by a Bavarian missionary and his congregation, Frankenmuth had become a tourist mecca, famous for tulips, Christmas ornaments, and home-style chicken dinners. Tulips were out of season, they by-passed Bronner's, the world's largest Christmas store, and Conn had worked his way through a mountain of fried chicken, buttered noodles, mashed potatoes and gravy, stuffing, and the vegetable of the day.

Rae had made a fairly good rendering of Snoopy in mashed potatoes, with a gravy Woodstock. The rest of her dinner migrated from one side of the plate to the other. Not much of it made the trip to her stomach, but not because of nerves. Because of anticipation.

For once in her life she was living in the moment, accepting Conn for who he was. Just for tonight, she hoped his memory never came back. She had plans for him tonight, plans that had begun with her sliding her hands under his shirt, smoothing her palms over his back as he struggled to unlock their hotel room door with suddenly clumsy hands.

Now she slipped her arms around him, took the key card, and swiped it. Conn hit the door handle, pulled her into the room behind him, and had her up against the door before it closed all the way. He took her mouth, his hands on her everywhere, his body hard and hot against hers.

She went under between one heartbeat and the next, aroused on so many levels there was no choice but to taste and smell and *feel*.

And then he was gone, the absence so shocking it took her a second to realize he was pulling her clothes off, and then she returned the favor, hands fumbling, pulse racing, tripping over her own feet because his mouth was back on hers, feasting as he backed her across the room. They fell on the bed, rolling together, legs tangling, and then Conn was driving her to peak, knowing how and where to touch her so it felt incredibly good, unbelievably perfect, until she came apart, helpless under his hands and his mouth.

Then he was inside her, before she could begin to recover, pushing her again, impossibly higher but drawing it out, too, making every stroke an event, his mouth on hers, at her breasts, both hands under her bottom, scooping her up so she had to take him deeper, so deep she would have screamed at the sheer bliss if she'd had any breath. And then the orgasm rolled over her, rocketed through her, and she did cry out because it was too much, a million bits of heat and light and waves of pleasure before she collapsed, spent, breath and heart racing, skin slick and tingling from head to toe.

Conn sank down beside her. The air was cold on her bare skin, but she laughed because her bra was still hooked and peeled down inside out, the straps pinning her arms to her sides. Conn was only half out of his jeans and boxers, one shoe and sock still on because he'd only taken the time to peel one leg out.

Rae sat up and took off her bra, running a hand over his clothed thigh. "I'm flattered," she said.

Conn laughed, too, getting rid of the rest of his clothes, then gathering her close. "I like hearing you laugh," he said, sounding bemused, probably, Rae thought, because she wasn't a laugher.

It sobered her a little, realizing how much she'd changed in the few short days since Conn had invaded her life. And she wasn't the only one. "I guess we're both a little bit different."

"Are we?"

She shrugged, tucking her head under his chin. It had been different this time, making love with Conn. He'd been intense, driving her to peak, not giving her a moment to catch her breath before he took her again. Not that she objected to being taken. What women didn't want to be overpowered once in a while by a man who knew how to temper his strength?

There'd been a focus this time, though, the feeling he'd been striving for the destination rather than savoring the journey. As if he was still in danger mode. She liked danger mode, but she liked it when he was laid-back, too. She couldn't say that to him, though.

He tipped her chin up, and even in the meager light from the window she could tell he knew what was on her mind. It was a little scary, but also liberating, knowing he understood her so completely that she didn't have to explain herself.

And then he kissed her, gently, thoroughly. It was incredible and familiar, and while she was a woman who appreciated the tried and true, just now she was into variety. She wanted him every way she could have him. She didn't know how long Conn would be in her life, and she refused to waste a moment.

She smiled against his mouth, shifting until she was straddling him. Conn wasn't going to be taken, though. He came up to his knees, his hands around her waist as he moved behind her, pulling her back so she was sitting on his thighs. His hands were on her breasts, his mouth hot at the nape of her neck. She slipped her hand down, curling her fingers around him, hard and thick between her legs, and he groaned. She felt his hands tremble, the muscles of his thighs quivering just at her touch, making her feel strong and humble at the same time. And then he slipped inside her and began to move, surging into her, his hands sure at her waist as she eased forward to brace herself, to take him deeper, until he touched something that made her go blind and deaf, that stole her breath and sent her soaring.

She cried out as he came into her over and over, harder and faster with each thrust. He curled over her and around her, as his hand slipped down between her legs and stroked over the center of her. He drove himself deep one last time, his groan a rumble of joy and triumph as he went over, and her body tightened around him as she flew high, floating back down to find herself curled in his arms, her back to his front. Her head was pillowed on his shoulder, one of his arms wrapped around her waist, the fingertips of his other hand making lazy circles on her belly.

He sighed, his breath warm at her temple, his arms tightening as if to pull her closer, and when he couldn't, he slipped one leg over hers instead and made a sound of contentment deep in his throat, an "mmmmmm," that told her he was feeling everything she was, and it shattered the walls around her heart.

chapter 20

AFGHANISTAN, FIRST WAVE BEFORE THE TALIBAN had been chased into the mountains, when the fighting had been town by town, and sometimes street by street. Conn was there again, in that village with the crumbling huts and the artillery and machine-gun fire, and the kid with the wide, terrified eyes. Running out of a shack filled with explosives. He hadn't known that at first. He still didn't know if the kid had been a suicide bomber or an innocent dupe, but Conn was right back there, breaking the first rule of any mission, reacting without thinking. He'd dropped the knife he'd been about to throw, shouted at his nearest team member and dove for the kid. He didn't get there in time.

He woke up, not with a jerk like he had before, and definitely not hard enough to wake Rae, who was still wrapped in his arms. Or maybe she was exhausted, but even remembering why wasn't enough to block out the rest of the flashback. His warning had saved his unit, given them time to take cover. He'd been the only one wounded. The scars along his side and back that Rae had noticed were from shrapnel, not bullets. The real damage had yet to heal.

He nuzzled his face into Rae's neck, and she sighed softly, settling herself more firmly against him. And the memories faded.

What would it be like, he wondered, to get in the car tomorrow and keep driving south, past Holly Grove, across the Michigan border, just the two of them, until they landed on some beach with blue water stretching to the horizon. What would it be like to throw Rae's cell phone out the car window, forget Mike Kovaleski, the FBI, and his obligation to arrest her parents for violating federal law? To forget that when he did Rae would hate him.

It was a nice fantasy, but he dealt in reality. If he took off the Bureau would just send another agent, and the Blisses would be arrested anyway. And Rae wasn't a runner. Even if he could convince her to go with him, she'd ask . . . no, she'd *demand* an explanation, and telling her the truth wasn't good for her life expectancy. As justifications went, it was a hell of a good one, being that it was true.

He eased his arm from beneath Rae's head and slipped out of bed, not looking back once he'd assured himself she was fast asleep. Her purse was on the nightstand. He fished her phone out, cat-footed it into the bathroom, and dialed his handler. It was barely seven A.M., but Mike would pick up. Mike always picked up.

"This better be good," he said, sounding like his normal, gruff self.

"Don't you ever sleep?" Conn asked, keeping his voice low.

"Not when the safety of the free world is in my hands."

"If that's true we're all doomed."

"Only when my agents get their brains scrambled—which I assume is no longer the case."

"Sunnyside up again," Conn said tersely.

"The op?"

"I'm on my way back to the faire. We were on Mackinac Island, a couple hundred miles away, when my memory came back. That was yesterday. This is the first chance

I've had to check in." And he was justifying it because he felt like shit for going behind Rae's back, even knowing he did it for her sake.

"Mackinac Island," Mike said. "Great Lakes, big hotel, no cars."

"That's the place."

"Who's we? Still with the Blissfield woman?"

"Yeah."

"Spill it."

"She's the daughter of Annie and Nelson Bliss. They pawned me off on her for my own safety."

"And now she's in trouble."

"Now she's my responsibility. But I don't think the bad guys know she's related to the Blisses. She was born on the road, and when she went to college she applied for a birth certificate using the different last name."

"I checked her out," Mike said. "There's no connection between her and the parents, but I bet the mastermind of the counterfeiting ring could find her if he asked the right questions."

"The Blisses and their friends are damned secretive," Conn said, "suspicious of everyone and very protective of one another. They have no respect for authority, and that includes federal, state, and local. Hell, that includes dog catchers and librarians."

"People like that give me the runs," Mike said. "What else?"

"The bad guys showed up while we were on the island, in a carriage, headed to the ferry docks. They stole a couple of horses and came after us."

Mike grunted out his opinion of that. "Sounds like a real Wild West fiasco."

"Yeah, all they were missing were the black hats. It was touch and go for a couple of minutes."

"And yet here you are talking to me."

"There's a small airport on the island. I, uh, commandeered a plane."

"And I'm all that stands between you and a jail cell."

"Rae, too," Conn said. "Her prints are in the system in Troy, remember? The last thing I need is for local boys in blue to get in the middle of this. Or the state cops."

"I'll clean it up," Mike said. "What else?"

"Run the name Harry Mosconi."

Conn heard buttons clicking then Mike said, "First dive, not much. Regular guy, wife and two kids, one in college, one in high school. Worked at an auto plant until sixteen months ago when he got laid off after eighteen years. Had a DUI eight months ago."

"No connections to organized crime?"

"There're Mosconis peppered throughout known mob lists, but no Harry in Detroit. No direct connection 'tween him and any of the others. But I'll keep looking. And, Larkin?"

"Yeah."

"Welcome back, man."

"Yeah," Conn said again, because it was the easy comeback. "Can you—"

"Conn?" Rae called. "Who are you talking to?"

"Shit. I'll reach out when I can," he said to Mike, then he disconnected and deleted all record of the call from the cell phone.

"Everything all right?" Rae asked him when he came out of the bathroom. "I thought I heard you talking in there."

"Everything is fine." Except her phone was still in his hand instead of her purse. And then it went off, singing about money. He held it up, thinking fast. "This thing was making noise. I tried to answer it without waking you."

She jumped out of bed and snatched it out of his hand, fumbling it in her haste. The ring tone told her it was work, the readout gave her the rest of the bad news. "Mr. Putnam, one of my bosses." But she didn't answer it, pacing, the phone clutched in her fist, until it went silent. She waited a couple minutes before she opened it and began pushing buttons—accessing her messages—not happy ones, Conn figured when she got that pinched look around her mouth and eyes.

She closed the phone carefully, and cleared her throat. "There's no record of the call you took."

Conn came and looked over her shoulder. "I pushed that button," he said, "and that one."

"You must have deleted it by accident. Do you remember who it was from?"

"No."

She did her deep breathing routine. "It had to be Putnam. A couple of my clients are anxious to get their quarterly statements."

Conn felt a moment of guilt, both for lying to her and for causing her trouble at work. "I thought they agreed you could work at home for the week."

"They did, but this isn't exactly home, and the only numbers I've looked at have been on credit card receipts. Which I won't be able to pay if I lose my job."

"What can I do?"

"That's a pretty good start," Rae said, relaxing back against him, at which point Conn noticed he'd begun to rub her shoulders without even realizing he was doing it.

She looked up at him. "It's still early. Let's go back to bed."

Conn closed his eyes and dug deep. He should at least start to establish some distance, get his head back in the mission and leave his body out of this, unless it was to put that body between hers and danger.

But he leaned over to kiss her, putting the mission away one last time, and losing himself in her.

THEY LEFT FRANKENMUTH AFTER BREAKFAST AND went straight to Grosse Pointe to pick up her files. She hadn't argued with Conn when he pointed out that her house wasn't safe if Harry and company got out of jail. He'd conceded that she wouldn't be content to stay in hiding if it meant putting her job in further jeopardy. He even helped her pack up her work papers, although she had to take over after he fumbled a stack of files. She shooed him away, gathering everything off the floor and sorting it into the jacket again, then packed some clean clothing for herself, since Conn was already carrying around just about everything he owned.

By the time she got outside he was checking over her Jaguar, which the dealership had dropped off in her driveway. Every door was open, so was the trunk, and Conn was on his knees on the driver's side, the upper half of his body inside the car. He'd piled an assortment of items on the driveway next to the vehicle, things they'd left in the Hummer, Rae noticed on closer inspection.

"What are you doing?"

Conn pulled his head out, stared up at her for a second, then shrugged. "I've never seen one of these before."

"And the seats are fascinating?"

"Everything is fascinating."

Rae shook her head and dumped the box of files and her overnight bag into the trunk. By the time she climbed into the driver's seat and adjusted it to her liking, Conn had put all the stuff from the driveway into the trunk and hopped into the passenger seat.

They left the Cadillac at her house, so Harry and his friends wouldn't bother Mr. Pennworthy. Rae steered the Jaguar into Holly Grove a little before noon, driving up the long, rutted dirt road until they came to a barrier made of wooden sawhorses and a lackadaisical teenager wearing a Robin Hood hat with a red feather, a Dracula cape, and a bored expression. He perked up slightly when he spotted Conn.

"Cool wheels, dude," he said when he'd ambled around to Conn's window. "Where you been—oh. Dude, trading up," he finished with a wide smile as his eyes landed on Rae. "Nice."

Conn grinned over at her. "Not all the time."

"Trading up?" Rae said.

"It's a long story."

"There was a blonde a few weeks back," the kid said. "Had a laugh like a hyena, but she was almost as pretty as you."

Conn gave Rae a once-over, a teasing glint in his eyes. "It's a toss-up. I like the red hair better."

Rae rolled her eyes, but she was trying not to smile. "If you two are done objectifying me . . ." She let the car inch forward.

"I'm going, I'm going . . ." the teenager said, but he stuck around long enough to say to Conn, "Man, she's impatient."

"This kid could give a snail lessons," she said, watching him wander back to the sawhorses.

He picked up the end of one where the two met in the center of the road and swung it out of the way before he shuffled back to the other and did the same. Then he waved them through with a bow and a flourish. Rae didn't miss the sarcasm, but she had other things on her mind.

"Nervous?" Conn asked her.

She realized she had a death grip on the steering wheel and forced her fingers to unlock.

"Harry won't expect us to come back here," Conn said, "if he's even out of jail."

Rae blew out a breath. "I'm sure you're right." But she didn't feel any better, because Harry wasn't the only menace she was facing. Annie Bliss could take on Harry and win every time, no gun necessary.

They pulled up in front of the Airstream, and a beat later the door crashed open, hard enough to bang against the trailer. Her parents came out, her dad pulling open Rae's door almost before she had time to shut off the engine, both of them hugging her at the same time.

"What's all this?" Rae said. "I mean, I missed you guys, too, but it's only been a few days."

"You didn't call." Annie shot Conn a look that promised something dire, then hugged Rae again.

"Why didn't you call me?"

"Your mother wanted to," Nelson said, putting his arm around his wife's shoulders and patting her, "but we didn't because we knew you were fine."

Annie didn't look like she knew it, but she smiled

anyway. "We were just wondering how it was going, not that we thought you wouldn't look out for Conn."

"It wasn't all me." She glanced over at Conn.

"We make a pretty good team," he said.

Annie smiled brightly. Rae wasn't buying it. She knew that smile: It was her mother's *something's not right but putting a brave face on it* smile. She also knew there was no point calling Annie on it.

"Have you eaten?"

"In Frankenmuth," Rae said, "this morning."

"Frankenmuth? The Christmas town?"

"It's been an interesting few days."

"We can't wait to hear about it," Annie said.

And she wouldn't leave them alone until she did, Rae knew.

They all trooped into the Airstream. Rae took a deep breath, prepared to give them the high points, but Conn butted in, telling them a carefully edited version of the story. He left out the sex, which Rae had intended to do as well. But he left out the guns, too.

"I'm just glad you're back," Annie said when he'd finished.

Conn nodded, straightening away from the door where he'd been leaning and putting his hand on the knob instead. "I'll leave you to your family time."

Rae followed him out the door. "That was quite the sanitized version of events."

"There was no need to alarm your parents. They would only feel guilty for putting you in that position."

She nodded. "So . . . where are you going?"

"My tent. You should stay here tonight."

"Why—"

"It's best," Conn said. "Respectful."

"And old fashioned— What am I saying? You think you're from the sixteenth century. But it didn't bother you last night."

"I should not have taken advantage."

"You weren't the only one taking advantage," Rae reminded him.

She'd been teasing, trying to put them back on easy footing. But he wasn't looking at her. There was a distance in his manner that stung, but she had her pride. If he didn't want her around, she'd oblige him. "I'll get out of your hair, then."

"Rae."

She stopped, but she didn't turn back.

"Saturday. You should stay with me in the booth."

That got her attention. "Are you serious? Harry and his friends will show up sooner or later."

He shrugged. "I need to work—"

"So do I. There are two more messages on my phone from Mr. Putnam. A couple of my clients are raising hell, and he can't do anything because I have their files. If I don't have something to show them soon, I'll be out of a job."

"If Harry and his friends get their hands on you, letting your clients down will be the least of your worries," Conn said. "You need to stay with me until we know where they are and what they plan to do next."

But they wouldn't be sleeping together, that much was clear from the chill in his voice. Not that she was surprised. They'd enjoyed each other for a time, but now that time had come to an end. It wasn't as if she hadn't been expecting it, and she shouldn't be taking it personally. But she was. It hurt like hell.

And she wasn't about to let him know that.

"Fine," she said, because he made sense, at least about Harry and Joe and Kemp. And because she'd make her own decisions.

"You'll stay close?"

She pointed to the picnic table in front of her parents' trailer. "I'll be right there, working, for the rest of the day. I can e-mail the completed statements to my assistant and she can get them to the clients."

"Then we have an agreement."

She nodded and turned toward the Jaguar to collect her files and laptop.

"Rae . . ."

"What?"

"I'm not sure how to word this."

She looked over her shoulder at him. "Give it a stab."

"We're back in familiar surroundings, with people we both know."

Rae relaxed a little. His memory problem had become so commonplace to her that she kept forgetting about it, not to mention the antiquated beliefs that came along with it. "You don't want to offend anyone, or give them the wrong impression. About us."

He nodded, looking relieved.

"You're a nice man, Connor Larkin."

His gaze shifted to hers. He seemed to want to say something, and he did. She just expected it to be something more meaningful than, "I'll see you later."

But she wasn't feeling rejected anymore, so she'd take what she could get.

BRIGHT AND EARLY SATURDAY MORNING RAE FOUND herself wearing her mother's idea of appropriate attire, which consisted of a Kelly green dress with a leather corset over it and a light peach tunic beneath. Her hair was down and she wore a circlet of flowers, the ribbons blowing in a breeze that was on the uncomfortable side of cool. Not a good thing considering her braless state. Then again, she was still wearing underwear, so she decided to be grateful. Thinking positive, that was the key.

The sun was shining in a sky dotted with puffy white clouds, fake knights were getting ready to joust a few hundred yards away to the shouts of "huzzah" from the crowd, and she'd actually managed to put in a decent day's work yesterday, hard as it had been to focus on numbers when being an accountant felt so completely useless.

Now she stood in Conn's booth—the part without the forge—playing sales wench, which was pretty much her worst nightmare. For a man who claimed he needed to work, Conn had done precious little of it, taking off after each scheduled demonstration and returning just before the next one. He brought back a snack or something to drink each time, but Rae was chafing at being left there, supposedly for her own safety, while the man who claimed to be concerned about her was nowhere in the vicinity. Not that her irritation ever lasted long.

Currently he was making . . . she could care less. Neither could the crowd of women gathered around watching him. Not that she blamed them. She remembered what it was like to see him for the first time in leather pants and not much else, bare muscles sweaty and rippling. Familiarity hadn't blunted his impact on her.

"Can I see that dagger?"

She turned back to the man pretending to shop for one of Conn's weapons. He wasn't actually pointing at anything since his eyes weren't on the display—at least not the goods in the case in front of her.

"Do you mean this one?" she asked sweetly, pulling a lethally sharp dagger out of its leather sheath and holding it in his line of sight, right about breast level.

"That's one of my favorites," Conn said, coming up beside her. "It's good for, say, putting out eyes."

The man's gaze traveled up, locking on Conn's face. "It's, uh . . . really nice."

"You must be talking about the knife," Conn said, because the man's eyes had fixed on Rae's cleavage again.

"Cash or credit?" Rae asked him.

"Oh, John, you're not buying that," a pleasant, PTA-type woman said from a couple feet down the counter, which was as close as she could get to her husband in the crush of sighing women.

Conn turned his smile on her. "It's a beautifully crafted weapon, madam. A chatelaine would have worn this kind of knife in a sheath hung at her waist, or," his voice deepened, "in the case of the Celtic warrior woman, strapped at her thigh."

She blushed, but she didn't say another word as her husband got out his wallet and plunked down a Visa card.

"That was a peacekeeping sale if I ever saw one," Conn said after they were gone.

Rae laughed. "You're shameless."

His eyes dropped to her breasts. "My tactics were no different than yours."

"I wasn't using any tactics. It's this dress." She tugged on the gathered neckline of the peach undertunic, then gave up with a little shrug. "It definitely makes the most of what I've got."

Conn looked around at the male portion of their fan club. "If it made any more I'd have to fight some of these guys off."

"Maybe I should strap one of those knives to my thigh and fight my own battles."

He popped up a brow. "You don't think one of those knives would stop me."

"Probably not, but it might be fun trying."

His eyes darkened, and he moved closer. Rae held her ground, ignoring the crowd of onlookers cluing in to the sexual tension behind the counter. She was lost to everything but Conn and the way she needed him—

A throat was cleared, loudly, not that it took much volume, what with the crowd gone completely silent.

They jerked apart. Rae took in their audience and felt her face heat. But since the entertainment was over, and the joust was beginning, most of the onlookers dispersed, until the only ones left were a pretty blond woman who looked like she belonged on reality TV, and a man who was as tall as Conn, and almost as muscular. And Annie Bliss, the three of them standing on the other side of the dirt path in front of Conn's forge.

Annie came over and crooked a finger at Conn. He joined her down the counter a little way, his head coming up when Annie gestured to the couple and said something Rae couldn't hear. Conn looked startled for a second, then his expression went blank.

Rae gave up on pretending to respect his privacy. "Do you know them?" she asked, joining him.

"I don't think so."

"They seem to know you. Her especially."

Conn glanced over at the blonde.

"She does look worried about you," Annie said. "It might be a good idea for you to talk to her. Maybe she can jog something loose. In your head."

Conn stared at Annie a second, then walked over to the blonde and her companion.

"Subtle, Mom."

"This is family entertainment," her mother shot back. "Despite the dress," she added when Rae glanced down at her overflowing décolletage. "You guys were one heaving breath away from X-rated."

"You've been shoving me at him since day one. Why the sudden change of heart?"

Annie sniffed. "We'll talk about it later."

"Yes, we will." But what concerned her now was the conversation happening under the trees on the other side of the path.

"Every man has a past," Annie said quietly. "Sometimes it makes the future impossible. Certain futures, anyway."

"I'm not holding out hope for a future with Connor Larkin," Rae said.

"You're all about the future, Sunny," Annie said sadly.

"Sometimes people change."

"Not that much."

chapter
21

"WHATEVER YOU DO, DON'T HUG ME," CONN SAID when he was close enough to Harmony Swift to get his point across.

"I'm supposed to be a tourist," she said.

"I'm supposed to have amnesia."

Harmony's smile had faltered; that news brought it back full force, and that was saying something. A man passing by walked into a tree, which was probably nothing compared to what his wife was going to do to him when she got him alone.

"Amnesia, huh? Don't know who you are?"

"Worse than that. I think I really am a sixteenth-century armorer."

Harmony started laughing, so she turned her face into Cole's shoulder. He put his arm around her, patting her on the back as if comforting her. "It's not like we were going to blow your cover," Cole said. "I'm a civilian, but I know what covert means."

"Yeah, I remember."

Harmony Swift was a former FBI agent. She'd broken Cole out of jail to help her rescue another agent who'd been kidnapped and held for ransom. Along the way, Harmony had come out on the bad end of a run-in with a Russian *Mafiya* operative named Irina, and Mike Kovaleski had sent her to Conn while she recuperated enough to finish the op. Conn had known her longer than that, though. She was like the little sister he'd never had.

"Mike should've called you off," he said. "I talked to him this morning, told him my memory was back."

"He did call us off," Cole said, "but we were already in town, and Harmony insisted on hunting you down. The last time she went after one of her FBI friends she dragged me from Pennsylvania to L.A."

"It wouldn't have been such an ordeal if you'd've come along peaceably," Harmony said.

"Which is why I decided not to fight the inevitable this time."

"If you two are done reminiscing, you can take off. It was nice seeing you, but I have a lot going on right now."

"Aw, and we were having so much fun." Harmony brandished the shopping bag in her hand. "I even bought this plastic faux-granite gargoyle's head. So I'd look like a tourist."

"The fanny pack accomplished that," Conn said.

"It's designer."

"I'm not surprised." Under normal circumstances she wouldn't be caught dead with a fanny pack. It was a safe bet that the lacy tank and khaki short pants she was wearing were at least three figures. Apiece. Her underwear probably cost more than that, and the shoes would make a dent in the national debt. That was what came of growing up in close proximity to Rodeo Drive, not to mention having the wherewithal to shop there.

"It's still a fanny pack," he said.

She looked at it and wrinkled her nose. "I know. The things I do for friendship. But seriously, is everything all right?" she asked, her eyes lifting, but not to his, focusing instead over his shoulder.

Conn didn't need to turn around to know Rae was watching them. Watching and wondering. "It's under control."

"Doesn't look under control," Cole said. He wasn't a wordy guy, preferring to cut right to the point.

Conn glanced over his shoulder and saw Rae waiting for the crowded path to clear so she could join them.

"Civilians," Harmony scoffed, "they never follow instructions." And she stepped forward, whacking Conn over the head with the bag in her hand.

"Ouch," he said.

"That only works in the movies," Rae said. She held out a hand. "Rae Blissfield."

"Harmony Swift and Cole Hackett," Harmony said, shifting aside so Cole could shake Rae's hand as well. "We're friends of Conn's, but he doesn't seem to remember us."

"How did you know he was here?"

"We traveled with the group for a little while," Harmony said without hesitation. "Spent some time in winter camp in Colorado Springs."

"Then you know my parents," Rae said. "Annie and Nelson Bliss."

"They're your parents?" Harmony stepped forward and gave Rae a hug. "Annie helped me out, big-time, not too long ago. They're the best."

"I remember when you wore that getup," Cole said to Harmony.

If he and Rae had been looking at each other like that, Conn thought, watching Cole and Harmony have visual sex, it was a good thing Annie had broken them up before the booth burst into flames.

"We should be going," Cole said, but Harmony broke their connection first.

"You have a customer," she said to Rae, ignoring her own faint embarrassment for the bigger picture. Ever the consummate agent.

Rae looked over her shoulder then back, clearly reluctant to leave.

"Kids," Cole added, "playing with the knives."

That did it. She whipped around in a swirl of Kelly green and shot across the path.

"That was mean," Harmony said to Cole. "I'm proud of you."

Cole bumped up a shoulder. "Your lie was good, mine was better."

"But I'm the one who has to deal with the fallout."

"Gravy," Cole said.

Harmony rolled her eyes. "Be careful, Conn, and I'm not talking about the bad guys."

Conn glanced over his shoulder. "She's very intuitive."

"Only about you, I'll bet."

"Go away," Conn said to Harmony, only half-teasing. "Call Mike and let him know I'm good." At least as far as the mission was concerned. Seeing Harmony and Cole again, knowing how close they'd come to death, just being together on the same mission . . .

Turning Rae loose wasn't an option; it would only make her the easier target. He had to finish this op, ferret out the head of the counterfeiting ring, and cut it off before Rae got hurt. And he didn't mean the kind of hurt that would come from watching her parents go to jail. He couldn't spare her that. He could make sure she was around to do everything in her power to help them.

He'd spent the entire previous day trying to pick up from where he'd left off before he lost his memory, without much luck. He needed the map Rae had found in his tent a week ago, the one where some of the booths were circled. That map represented months' worth of legwork, ruling out merchants until he'd pared the possibilities down to the point where, even without turning one of the ring members, he was only days away from closing the case.

Problem was, he didn't know what Rae had done with the map. He was pretty sure it wasn't in her files, he was positive it wasn't in her car, but he couldn't ask her about it. If he asked her about it, she'd want to know why it mattered. He couldn't tell her why it mattered because then she'd know his memory was back. He didn't bother to remind himself why he couldn't tell her his memory was back. Her safety depended on it, and her safety was always uppermost in his mind.

While she'd been up to her hairline in other peoples'
finances yesterday, Conn had gotten himself a fresh map
and made an effort to reproduce the one he'd lost, with
partial success. There were dozens of booths, and he
couldn't remember exactly which ones had still been suspect. Chances were good that he never would, and while
it frustrated him to think he might have lost some of his
short-term memory permanently, he counted himself for-
tunate he'd been able to retrieve as much as he had. And
even if he'd had the map he'd marked up, wandering
around while the place was deserted would have made
him too conspicuous. The guilty parties would be nervous; he needed the crowds of tourists as cover, so he'd
made an effort that morning, between armor-making
demonstrations, to check out the likely culprits. He hadn't
accomplished much. Except to piss off Rae.

"Conn?"

He blinked, making the shift from Rae to the op just that
fast. "The exit is that way," he said to Harmony, pointing in
the general flow of foot traffic.

She held his eyes for a long moment, but all she said
was, "Consider yourself hugged."

"You've got our number," Cole added.

Conn waved them off.

"Fine, be all macho and solitary," Harmony said. "But
don't get yourself killed. This is one story, classified or
not, that I'm looking forward to hearing."

RAE STAYED BEHIND THE COUNTER IN CONN'S
booth, knowing that was where he wanted her and wondering why. She kept one eye on the never-ending stream
of weapons aficionados, mostly teenage boys addicted to
Japanese anime. Intense interest in weapons, no money to
buy them, which made it easy to keep the rest of her focus
on Conn's interaction with Harmony Swift and Cole
Hackett. And the fact that something about it was off.

Sure, there'd been an instant rush of jealousy. Harmony Swift was beautiful, and she obviously loved Conn.

But not in the way Rae . . . not in the way she loved him, Rae admitted to herself. She blew out a breath, slumping against the wall behind her as the truth sank in. Not that it was much of a surprise. She'd been lonely, and Conn had been a revelation. Everything that was missing from her life. But Conn wasn't real. Even he knew that.

So she pushed the emotions away—the love, and the pain. She was going to get hurt. She could sit around waiting for it, or she could stop thinking with her emotions, stop seeing what she wanted to see. And when she took off the heart-shaped glasses and looked back over the last few days, a picture formed, all the little things coming together. Conn's speech was more clipped, less filled with historical clichés. His manner was more consistently intense as well, not just when they were in danger, but the sex . . . It was different, too, still amazing—no doubt it would be the best of her life—but different from that first time.

And then there was the look in his eyes when he'd seen Harmony Swift. Because he'd recognized her. And then he'd lied about it.

So why didn't she feel anything? She'd gone completely numb, no tears, no sense of betrayal, no homicidal urges. Good thing, since she was confronting Conn over a long counter filled with really sharp weapons.

"They seemed to be nice people," Rae said.

Conn shrugged.

"So when did your memory come back?"

"What?" Conn asked as if she'd wanted to know the temperature.

It might have worked if she hadn't been looking him straight in the eye. And he knew it.

He scrubbed a hand over his face, his eyes lifting to stare off, over her head.

"When?"

His gaze shifted back to hers. "Mackinac Island. Before the plane."

Okay, now she was feeling something—pissed off. She walked out of the booth, heading for the faire workers' entrance at the back of the grounds, less than a hundred yards away.

Conn caught her just as she was going through the gate. "I'm telling the truth, Rae."

"Better late than never? Is that supposed to make me feel better?"

"I woke up and it was just there."

"And so was I."

Conn had the grace to look sheepish. He did not look apologetic.

"Let go of my arm."

For a second she thought he'd refuse. Then he let her go. It hurt, desperately. She couldn't bear to stand there and listen to him justify using sex to keep her in the dark, but she wanted him to fight for the opportunity. And he let her just walk away.

She found herself at her parents' trailer without knowing how she got there. She didn't take the time to change, just snagged her purse off the table and turned to go back out. Conn stood in the doorway, filling it completely.

"Get out of my way."

"No," he said, calm, implacable, almost back to Conn the Floater.

But she knew the difference now. "I'm leaving."

He snatched her purse and took out the Jaguar's keys. "Not without these."

Her vision went red around the edges, fury being a much safer emotion to deal with than the deep, dark well of pain just beneath.

"I'm on a case." The appeal for understanding in his voice only infuriated her more.

"And I'm just a tool, I get it."

"You're not a tool. I got you into this, and it's my job to keep you safe."

"So I'm a responsibility," she said bitterly. "That makes it so much better."

"I didn't mean it that way."

She shoved him out of the way and left the trailer, but he caught her wrist, his touch like a knife to her heart because, foolishly, she wanted him to take her in his arms and make it all go away. After everything, she still wanted him.

"Don't you want an explanation?"

More than she wanted her next breath, and to her own shame, she'd probably believe him. She looked at his hand, locked around her wrist, stared at it until he let her go. It was the hardest thing she'd ever done, but she lifted her eyes to his. She'd be damned if she hid.

"I'm sure whatever you're doing is classified."

"It is."

"Then your explanation would only be more lies." And this time, when she walked away, he let her go.

CONN WAS IN THE FORGE, BANGING ON A PIECE OF steel that had long gone cold. He didn't care. The perpetual crowd of women were gathered around, oohing and aahing. He *really* didn't care about them.

When Annie Bliss showed up, he knew he was in for it. He didn't give a damn about her, either.

"Where's Rae?" she said.

He ignored her.

She stomped to the front of the enclosure and folded out the wooden shutters with the closed sign on them. Conn picked up the mangled steel with his tongs, ignoring the chorus of angry female voices on the other side.

Annie put herself between him and the fire, jamming her hands on her hips. "Where's my daughter?"

"I don't know."

All the blood drained out of Annie's face. Conn might have felt bad, if there'd been any room around the anger.

"You promised to keep an eye on her."

"I got a little sidetracked when you sent Harmony and Cole over here."

"I thought they would help you with your memory . . . wait," she clutched at his arm. "It's back, isn't it?"

"Yeah," he snapped out, pissed at himself more than her because he hadn't been able to hide the truth from Rae. It didn't matter that she'd been able to practically

read his mind since day one. It didn't matter that with his
memory gone he hadn't known the importance of keeping
his distance from her, let alone carrying on with his mission. His memory was back, had been back long enough
for him to get his footing and make the right choices for
everyone involved. Instead, he'd made mistakes, selfish
ones, right down the line.

"Does Rae know?" Annie asked him.

"Rae knows."

"She didn't take it well."

"I had to confiscate her car keys."

Annie sank back against the edge of the firebox. Conn
took her by the upper arms and moved her to his work-
bench. Letting her catch on fire would not make Rae
happy. Then again—

"How much does she know?"

It might not be long before Rae wished her parents into
the same hell she'd probably doomed him to. "She wasn't
interested in explanations," Conn said.

Annie pulled her phone out of a hidden pocket in her
skirt and called Nelson. At least that's what Conn assumed, since she sent the party on the other end of the
phone to their trailer to see if Rae was there. And after
she'd disconnected, Annie got to her feet, and Conn knew
he was in for it again.

But he'd be damned if he stood there and took it. "She'll
be safe."

"It's a little late for that," Annie said. "We trusted you—"

"I need to know what's going on with the counterfeiting operation."

"I need to talk about Rae. What happened between the
two of you?"

"None of your business," Conn said.

"She's my daughter."

"And if you weren't printing money in the back room,
she wouldn't be in this mess."

That did it. Annie snapped her mouth shut, looking
like she wanted to hurt him. But her eyes teared up.

Conn stepped forward, hesitating when he realized what he was about to do.

Annie took the decision out of his hands by throwing her arms around him.

So much for establishing distance, Conn thought, patting her back awkwardly.

"I'm sorry," she said, stepping back. "You're right. We got ourselves into this mess, and dragged you and Rae in with us."

"I got myself in," Conn reminded her. "And I'm going to get myself and Rae out."

Annie sat again. "But not Nelson and me."

What could he say? Much as he wanted to reassure her, he wouldn't lie. The Blisses were going to get arrested, maybe do some jail time. The U.S. government had an unforgiving nature when it came to counterfeiters. No matter the circumstances, it was a crime they usually insisted on punishing with something more than probation.

Nelson raced through the open back of the booth, out of breath, clutching at his side. "Sun," he gasped, "Sunny . . . gone. Took . . ."

Annie flew off the bench and grabbed him by the shirtfront, shaking him. "Someone took Sunny?"

He shook his head. "Airstream . . . she took it."

"*Christ.*" Conn slammed his fist into the shutters, startling a shriek out of an elderly woman who was walking by.

Nelson cracked the shutter open and said, "Sorry," then tried to calm his wife, who was having a panic attack.

Conn was busy trying not to lose his head. It took all of his training, and a reminder that if Harry had Rae he wouldn't harm her. She would be leverage to Harry. Kemp was another story. Kemp would want payback.

"Shut up," he said to the Blisses, pulling out his cell phone, retrieved from his tent last night. Rae didn't answer. Not meaningful, considering she wanted him dead.

"Maybe she'll pick up for you," he said to Annie. "Call her."

"That's not exactly medieval," a voice said from the other side of the shutters. "Maybe you should try carrier pigeon."

Conn closed his eyes. He didn't have to see the face to know who the voice belonged to. "What are you, the cavalry?"

The left shutter popped open, and a man vaulted over the low rail. Tall, dark hair, shit-eating grin. "You're the one who looks like he belongs on a horse," he said to Conn, but his eyes were on Nelson and Annie.

"They're all right," Conn said.

"Do they have names?"

"Where are my manners?"

"You never had any, but you have a way with sarcasm." He stepped forward and held his hand out.

Nelson took it, then Annie, both of them looking a little shell-shocked.

"James Aloysius Smith the Third," he said. "My friends call me Trip."

"You don't have any friends," Conn said.

"Casualty of my lifestyle. Yours, too." He gave Conn a once-over, taking in the no shirt/leather pants ensemble. "Once upon a time."

Conn rolled his shoulders. "This is turning into a cluster . . ." He looked at Annie and Nelson, watching them with great interest. He would have pulled Trip aside and finished their conversation in private, but what was the point? "Why did Mike send you?"

"He's FBI, too," Annie said, breathing a sigh of relief.

Trip held Conn's eyes, one eyebrow lifting.

"They're acting as CIs," Conn said. "Answer my question."

Trip bumped up a shoulder. "Mike probably figured it wouldn't hurt for me to scope out the sitch, as the kids say."

Conn's first instinct was to send him packing, but he didn't have the luxury of pride. "Since you're here, you can hang out for a while, keep an eye on the *sitch*. Fill him in," he said to the Blisses.

Nelson caught his arm. "You're going after her? That's not a good idea."

"I'm the only one who can," Conn said.

"I can't wait to hear this fairy tale," he heard Trip say as he walked away.

At least Annie and Nelson didn't know all the details. It wasn't much, as silver linings went, but he'd take anything he could get.

chapter
22

IT FELT GOOD TO BE HOME, TO BE DRESSED IN HER own clothes and sitting at her desk in her home office. It was way after lunchtime. Her stomach was growling but she couldn't imagine putting anything in it. She was angry and exhausted, but she felt like she was getting her feet under her again. Now if she could only get her mind on work—

Her cell phone chimed. Her mother, she saw on the display. She shut it off. The house phone rang almost immediately.

Rae put her head down on her desk. She really didn't want to talk to anyone. She didn't even want to think anymore, let alone feel. And if she didn't answer the phone she wasn't going to get any peace because her mother would keep calling.

She picked up the cordless handset and pushed the TALK button. "I'm not coming back."

"That's too bad," Annie said, "because your father and I have nowhere to sleep tonight."

"Get my keys from Conn and come get the Airstream."

"Really, Sunny, you took it, you should bring it back."

"Nope, but thanks for calling."

"Wait," her mother said, sounding unusually hesitant. "I hope you know how much we love you."

That took Rae off guard. Not that her parents loved her. She knew that. So why did her mother feel a need to be so dramatic about it? "Of course I know you love me," she said. "And I love you guys, too. So why am I going to be mad at you?"

Annie laughed softly, but it was strained and unnatural. "Just don't forget that we've only ever wanted you to be happy."

Rae didn't know how to answer that. Her definition of happiness and her mother's were so far apart. "I know you mean well," she said at last. Then she looked up and saw Conn standing in the doorway to her home office. "I have to go, Mom."

"Rae? Conn is on his way to your house," Annie said on a rush.

"He's already here." And Rae disconnected.

"I know you're pissed off," Conn said, "but I didn't think you'd be this stupid. I checked on Harry and Joe. They're out of jail, and if this isn't the first stop on their hit parade, it's the second. And you've got that damned trailer sitting in front of your house like a neon NO VACANCY sign."

"I hope Harry and his friends show up."

"But not me."

There didn't seem to be a need to agree with that, but it wasn't for the reason Conn thought. She was afraid she couldn't resist him.

She pointed to the door. "You can take the Airstream if it makes you feel better."

"I came here to explain, and that's what I intend to do."

"Suit yourself." She got up and came around the desk. At least she tried to.

He blocked her in, and before she could backpedal his hands were on her, framing her face.

"That won't work anymore," she said, even though she wanted him to kiss her more than she wanted her next breath.

He didn't, just rested his forehead against hers. "I came here to explain. It's the least I can do."

She pulled free, slipped around him and out of the room, amazed that she managed it with every muscle in her body trembling. "You don't owe me anything."

"I owe you my protection."

"I don't need it."

"You don't have a choice," he said, following her into the kitchen.

Rae didn't miss the part where he stationed himself between her and the back door. Like she was idiotic enough to run from a man twice her size and strength.

"It's me or protective custody, and before you commit yourself you might want to consider your parents."

She went to the refrigerator and took out a bottle of water. She didn't offer Conn any.

"Did you use them, too?" She'd wanted to hurt him, which was foolish since you couldn't hurt someone who had no feelings. But that wasn't why he was avoiding her eyes. "Who are you, and what do my parents have to do with any of this?"

Rae had expected him to prevaricate. He looked her square in the eyes and said, "I'm FBI. Your parents are counterfeiters, along with several of their friends."

She went deaf for a second, blind and breathless, too, as though all the air had been sucked out of the room. "You're lying," she finally managed to strangle out, the words thin and weak, even to her own ears.

"Think about it," Conn said. "A bunch of people on the fringe who don't want to file tax returns, let alone obey laws. They thought they could get away with making a bit of cash. Literally."

Rae didn't want to believe it. Unfortunately it was just the kind of thing her parents would do for just the reason he'd given. And then there was the cloth she'd seen on her father's loom, God, not even a week ago. She didn't even try to absorb how much her life had changed in six short days, beginning with Conn in her bed and ending with her parents being . . . She couldn't bring herself to call them felons yet. But the cloth on her father's loom had been stiff, almost paper consistency, the ink swirled on it copper or green depending on how the light hit it. Just like the new bills the government was printing. There was the iPhone, too, and her mother's hesitation and uncertainty on the phone just moments before.

Rae leaned back against the kitchen island, all the breath leaking out of her. But she couldn't stand still. She opened the water bottle and didn't drink. Her mind was moving a million miles a second. She couldn't hold on to a single thought.

Until she noticed the pity on Conn's face. It wasn't a thought she settled on, though. It was a feeling, and the feeling was fury. She refused to give him the satisfaction. "You dropped the bomb," she said when she could keep her voice steady, "now clean up the mess."

Conn shook his head. "You constantly amaze me."

"You constantly lie to me. Try not to."

"The sarcasm I was expecting. I just figured there'd be tears and shouting and, you know, violence first."

"Yeah, I'm a constant surprise," Rae said, still pacing because she was pretty sure she hadn't heard the worst. "Move on."

"This is all classified, Rae. I'm telling you because—"

"Don't."

Conn scrubbed a hand back through his hair.

Rae looked away. She didn't want to see the sympathy on his face, just like she didn't want to hear any justifications. She had to do what he was doing. She had to keep emotion out of this, or she wouldn't get through it. "Start talking," she said, "and don't leave anything out."

"I was born on a rainy morning in July."

"Even the heavens wept."

He grinned. "You said don't leave anything out."

"Your birth is over-sharing."

"What's your view on Special Forces?"

"Sounds pertinent."

"That's what brought me here," Conn said, turning serious. "Marines, then Special Forces until I opted out. The only thing I was fit for in the private sector was cop or bodyguard or security of some kind. I didn't want that."

"So you joined the FBI?"

He shrugged, a gesture that almost made her miss Conn the Armorer before she remembered he didn't really exist.

"No confusion, no fuckups," he said. *No kids with bombs strapped to them, no civilians who turned out to be enemy combatants, no split-second decisions where he had to make a judgment call and kill based on it.* "I wanted to know who the bad guys are and go after them,"

"And my parents are the bad guys?"

"They broke the law."

"There have to be mitigating circumstances."

"It won't matter. Printing money is the exclusive province of the Unites States government, and they have no tolerance, no sense of humor, and no mercy when it comes to dealing with counterfeiters."

"You picked some really terrifying bad guys."

"I don't pick the missions, they pick me. The U.S. Secret Service has exclusive jurisdiction in counterfeiting cases, but they needed someone with special talents, so Mike Kovaleski, my handler, agreed to loan me to them. I have a degree in history, with a minor in major global conflict."

"There's a shocker."

"Before I came I did a lot of research on medieval history, thinking it would be necessary."

"And once you got here you realized these things bear no resemblance whatsoever to what the Renaissance was really like."

"True, but when I got cracked over the head all that medieval stuff was right there, waiting to fill in the gaps in my memory."

"My parents didn't hit you over the head."

"If you're asking me if Annie and Nelson are on my suspect list, the answer is yes."

"Why would they hit you then take care of you?"

"I don't believe they're responsible for organizing the crime."

"They wouldn't hire Harry and Joe and Kemp, either."

"Again, I agree with you, but they're counterfeiting, Rae. They might not be the ringleaders, but they're participating. It makes them suspects."

"But you agree there's someone else involved."

"Yes."

"Who?"

"Can't say. Yet."

Rae studied his face, and she didn't like what she saw. "You're not telling me the truth."

"I don't know what the truth is," Conn said. "Not all of it anyway."

"Then I suggest we find out."

"We?"

She huffed out a breath. "You don't think I'm going to sit back while my parents are up to their necks in trouble."

"Whatever is going on, it's getting serious. I can't keep an eye on you and wrap this mess up at the same time."

Rae pushed to her feet. "Let me make it easy for you. I'm not your problem."

"I got you into this."

"My parents got me into this."

"The op is heating up," Conn said, slowly and clearly.

"If you think being deliberately patronizing is going to put me off, guess again."

"You're being bullheaded. Harry and his friends have gone from fists to guns in the space of a week."

"I know. I was there. They may come off as Stooges, but if they were trying to kill us, we'd be dead. Look, there's no point in arguing," she said when Conn tried to do just that. "I'll take the Airstream back, you follow me in the car."

"Then what?"

"Then we find my parents and get some answers."

"Don't you think I tried that already?"

She met his eyes. "I didn't."

* * *

RAE BACKED THE AIRSTREAM INTO THE SAME SPOT
it had occupied before she'd borrowed it, and okay, it took
her three tries, but she had to give her parents credit. They
were right there, waiting for her, along with a really attractive, dangerous-looking man. A man who was dressed as a
tourist, but had FBI written all over him. Thanks to Conn,
she recognized it now.

Her mother climbed into the old rattletrap of a pickup
they used to haul the trailer from place to place. Her father
came around to the driver's window, already open thanks
to the lack of air-conditioning. Conn and the stranger
stayed where they were.

"I don't want to talk about it," Rae said.

"Give us a chance to explain, Sunny—"

"Stop." Rae shoved both hands through her hair, scooping it up and jamming in a clip she dug from her purse. "I
only want to know one thing. If you knew Conn was an
FBI agent on a *mission*, a man who is completely wrong
for me, why did you keep shoving me at him?"

"I thought it was the best way to make you run in the
other direction. But we didn't know he was FBI."

Rae gave her mother a look.

"We knew he was hiding something," Nelson put in,
"but who here isn't? We knew he wouldn't hurt you, but
your mother was only trying to protect you."

"When will you stop treating me like a child?"

"You'll always be my child."

"I'm your daughter," Rae said. "Your *grown* daughter.
There's a difference."

She reached for the door handle, but for once her father wasn't standing aside.

"Sunny," he said quietly, putting his hand on her shoulder. "You're not the kind of woman who runs away when
things get tough."

Rae laughed, but it was harsh and humorless. "I'm exactly that kind of woman. I ran away when I was eighteen."

"You stepped out on your own."

"Did I? I wonder how much of that was bravery and how much was manipulation."

Nelson shook his head. "I've never been disappointed in you before now," he said. And he walked away.

Later, Rae knew, that would devastate her, but at the moment she was too angry to be moved by it.

Then again, her face wasn't wet because of Conn.

chapter
23

CONN LEFT RAE AND HER PARENTS TO THEIR FAM-
ily moment. He decided it was a good sign that he didn't
hear any yelling. But then, they hadn't gotten to him yet.

Trip wandered over and stood at his right side. Conn
took a step to the left.

Trip snorted out a laugh. "You're probably going to
need a friend."

"In this line of work?"

"This is just a job," Trip said.

"It's not just a job, it's a lifestyle."

"Only for as long as you want it to be."

"Maybe you should get some ugly glasses and a couch,
and hang out a shingle."

"I could definitely come up with some new approaches
to anger management. Probably not court sanctioned,
though."

Nelson walked away from the pickup, looking like death
warmed over. A minute later Annie jumped out of the front
seat, digging her phone out of her skirt pocket. Rae exited
the driver's door and came around the front of the pickup,
heading straight for Conn.

"Hold that thought," he said to Trip. Anger management was definitely going to be an issue.

"I know that look," he said to Rae when she planted herself in front of him. "Your mind is made up."

"Yep."

"I could take her off your hands," Trip offered Conn.

"It'll take more than a couch and a line of bullshit to survive her," Conn said.

"Don't spare my feelings just because I'm standing right here," Rae said, and when Trip turned to her, she popped up an eyebrow, daring him to comment.

"On second thought," he said, "you're on your own, Larkin. Besides, Mike reached out. Puff MacArthur is getting out of jail tomorrow. Since you have this under control, I have an urge to make his acquaintance."

"Lucius 'Puff of Smoke' MacArthur? He must be in his sixties by now."

"And he's sitting on the location of a cache of stolen loot."

"He spent the last twenty-five years incarcerated with the worst criminals in the country, and none of them could convince him to give it up. Not to mention every local, state, and federal law enforcement officer will want to close this case."

Trip grinned, and it was diabolical. "None of them are me." And he took off.

"No ego there," Rae said, watching Trip walk off toward the parking lot. "Maybe you should go with him, teach him how to pretend to be something he's not."

"He already knows."

She snorted softly. "It's probably required training for you people."

"It's more of a prerequisite for employment."

"They're making a lot of movies in Michigan now. Tax breaks. You should stick around, see where your talents take you. Better pay and less gunfire—okay, you'd be a puffed up, muscle-bound action hero, but at least the bad guys would be shooting blanks, and you'd always get to win."

"Are you done?"

"Not even close."

"We have other things to talk about," Conn said. "All of us, and unless I miss my guess, your mom is calling your dad."

Rae let her chin drop to her chest, just for a second or two, so mentally exhausted and emotionally wrung out all she could think about was walking away. She wanted to lose herself in crowds of people who had nothing more earth-shattering on their minds than enjoying an Indian summer.

But she wasn't going to put this behind her by running away from it. Her father was right about that much.

Nelson must not have gone far because he walked back into the clearing next to the Airstream, Annie holding his hand.

Rae teared up immediately. "Dad I—"

Nelson folded her into a hug. "I should be the one apologizing to you," he said. "I had no right to say you were a disappointment, considering what we've gotten you into."

"Let's just figure out what to do next. Okay?"

Annie wiped away her tears, laughing as Nelson hugged her hard, rocking her a little and saying, "It'll be all right."

Conn reached out and drew Rae back against him, rubbing her shoulders.

She pulled away. "Somebody fill me in," she said, an invitation that clearly wasn't meant for him since she established a safe distance from him, both physically and visually, keeping her eyes on her parents.

"I had just figured out your parents were involved when I was hit over the head," Conn said.

"Don't look at us," Annie said.

"It had to be Harry," Rae said.

Annie looked confused. "Harry? We don't know any Harry."

Rae stepped in front of her father. "Dad? Care to tell me the truth?"

Conn knew exactly why she was challenging her father, but he stood back and let her handle it because Nelson was no match for his daughter. Hell, Conn admitted, neither was he.

"All right," Nelson said, taking exactly two seconds to cave in. "We'll never get out of this if we don't tell you what's going on. Although I'm not sure I understand how we got involved in the first place."

"We were coerced," Annie snapped.

"Start at the beginning," Conn said, "the first time you were contacted."

"It was about a year and a half ago, after the faire in North Carolina. You remember it, Sunny."

"Raleigh," she said. "What happened?"

"We do know Harry. He approached us . . . He asked—"

"He beat around the bush," Annie put in, "and when we figured out what he was suggesting and turned him down, he started making threats against our friends."

"Annie wanted to call a meeting and tell everyone what was going on, let them decide for themselves. Harry said if we spilled the beans, they'd pick a target at random, and we'd never see it coming. And if we still didn't cooperate—" Nelson folded his wife's hand into his. "—Annie would be next. We held him off while we tried to figure a way out, but then Dill Pickle Sally's brakes went out on the road between St. Louis and Minneapolis, and she'd just had them fixed. Thank heaven it was a nice, straight stretch of road or who knows what might have happened. Harry called us right after . . ." Nelson shook himself a little as he put aside the frightening memory. And got defensive. "It's just making a little money. The U.S. government prints up a new batch whenever it suits them. Hell, it's not even backed by any real assets anymore, so why should they be in charge?"

Rae flicked a glance at Conn. He could see she wanted to answer that question, but she kept her head in the game.

"They never threatened Rae, right?"

"They don't know about Sunny," Annie said. "That's why we sent you off with her, remember? So you'd be safe until you got your memory back."

Conn knew that, but at the time it hadn't made an impression. He hadn't known about the operation, let alone who he was. Now it bothered him. "A daughter is a pretty big detail to miss. The kind of people who are usually behind this sort of crime don't make mistakes like that."

"The kind of people?" Rae asked. "Are you talking about the mafia?"

Annie went white. "There's mafia in Detroit?"

"There's mafia in every big city," Conn said. "Harry's last name is Mosconi. No criminal record but my bet would be that Harry isn't made yet, so he probably hasn't hit the grid before now. If this is his big play, he won't let anything or anyone stand in his way."

The Blisses were quiet, absorbing that awful thought.

"He's definitely up to something," Nelson finally said. "They used to ask for a new batch of ink every couple of months. Two weeks ago they told us to prepare twice the usual amount. They want it before we leave Holly Grove."

Conn didn't even have to think about what that meant. He'd made a mess of things, but there was hope because, like all crooks, greed got 'em every time. "They're going to shut down the operation, after one last big push."

"What's the chance they'll leave witnesses behind?" Nelson asked.

"None."

Nelson sank down to the ground, waving his wife and daughter off when they tried to help him.

"You okay?" Conn asked.

"Yeah." He held his hand out and let Conn pull him to his feet. "I feel like an idiot."

"Don't. They would have made any threat or promise it took to get you on board. You were doomed the moment they decided you'd be useful."

"That's the part that doesn't make any sense. How would they even know about us?"

Conn shrugged. "Can't say. But it's ingenious. Find a group of nonconformists who are a community, but also tend to be wary of each other and untrusting of authority. This group also happens to have the set of skills necessary to make the ink, to engrave the plates, and to print the money. Thousands of people go through these Renaissance festivals so the money gets spread out quickly, and in a different city every few days or weeks, which means the authorities waste time looking for the source after it's already moved on."

"What about the paper?" Rae asked him. "You didn't mention the paper."

"They probably have a line on the paper. I doubt there's anyone here who could make it—"

"Nelson could."

"I'm sure you're good," Conn said to him, "but there's a watermark and a security thread running through the paper. Get either one of those wrong and the whole thing is a bust."

"And you think it's the mafia?"

"Who else could pull it off? The key for them is keeping all the pieces of the operation ignorant of one another. They threaten you each individually with whatever is most precious to you, and you're alone. You can't get together, get that safety-in-numbers bravado thing going, and mess up their operation. Like I said, pretty damn tight, and the mafia has the expertise and experience to know just how to handle this kind of operation."

"Great," Rae said, "if you're done admiring the mastermind, can we focus on how to catch him?"

"Or her," Annie said. "Women are just as capable as men . . ."

"Not really the time for a feminist speech, Mom." Not to mention the mafia wasn't really an equal opportunity employer.

Annie smiled crookedly. "Gotta get it in while I can."

"Where's your optimism?" Rae asked her.

"I don't know how we're going to get through this one."

Rae looked to Conn for some reassurance. He couldn't give her any. "Let's stop the counterfeiters and worry about the rest later."

If everyone was alive. Conn had a pretty good idea he

wasn't the only one thinking that. The minute they started
rocking the boat, this thing was going to heat up, big-
time.

"The first thing we have to do . . ." Nelson said to Conn.

"Don't even think about it," Rae said. "They may not
have known about me when this started, but they do
now."

"They don't know you're our daughter," Annie said.

"Are you sure?"

"Even if they don't know she's your daughter," Conn
said, "they know she's involved."

"Because of us." This time it was Annie who sat, although she chose the picnic table bench. "Oh, Sunny, I'm
so sorry."

"Don't be." She looked at Conn, and whatever else
was going on in her head, at least he could see she had no
regrets.

Considering what they faced, it was small consolation.
Her parents he needed; they were cogs in the counterfeiting wheel, and if they disappeared all hell would break
loose, not to mention he couldn't discover the other participants without them. Rae was superfluous. He should
put her in protective custody. She talked big, but he knew
Trip could handle her.

The sorry truth was he didn't feel comfortable letting
Rae out of his sight. It was a mistake. A big one. He
couldn't afford the distraction. And then there was the
problem she had with following instructions. But there was
no way he'd shake her loose—and before that warm, fuzzy
feeling blooming around his breastbone got too big for its
britches, he reminded himself that her motivations didn't
include him. She wanted to be there for her parents.

Conn could respect that. But it was damned inconve-
nient, and it would be hell keeping her safe and watching
his own back at the same time. And Rae wasn't the only
one who needed his protection. He'd gone into this op
thinking the Renaissance nuts were the bad guys—and
they weren't all that bad, even if they were breaking the
law. But there was a real bad guy out there, and he—or

she—had them by the short hairs. If Conn didn't do his job right somebody was going to get hurt, maybe killed.

And it would be on him.

"The paper isn't in play," he said, shaking off the fear. *If you can't control it, don't let it control you.* "We know where the ink is coming from, that just leaves the plates and the printing press. Of the two, the plates are the important piece. The operation can be shut down any second, but if we get our hands on the plates, someone will talk to save themselves. Even then it's just the word of a bunch of—"

"The word you're looking for is *kooks*," Annie said.

"—*people* who don't conform and probably have police records anyway."

"Except you're not a kook," Nelson pointed out. "You're FBI."

"Which is why they'll have to kill me to pull it off."

Rae's expression went even grimmer. "We have to get our hands on the plates, before Harry and Joe figure out what we're up to and beat us to them. If they haven't already."

chapter
24

"SO, WHERE'S THE MAP?"

"Map?" Rae traded a look with her parents, but since Conn had directed the question to her, she wound up going back to him for the explanation. And then it hit her. "The map!" She thunked herself on the forehead and ran into the trailer.

She came back, brandishing the map they'd found in Conn's tent. "Is this what you were looking for in my car?"

"And your house, and your files. And then I tried to re-create it, but some of it's gone—" He rapped his knuckles on the side of his head. "—for good, I think."

"It was in the pocket of the jeans I borrowed from my mom," Rae said, "but you couldn't just ask for it, right? I mean, that would have meant telling me the truth about your memory coming back, and why you're here."

"After which you would have taken off, making it impossible for me to protect you."

Rae buried both hands in her hair, a wordless sound of frustration bursting out of her. "Why do men think it's all right to lie to a woman for her own good?" she said, drilling a finger into his chest. "Did it ever occur to you that telling me the truth, treating me like an adult, *trusting* me to understand the situation and just deal with it would be the right course of action? And sure, I took off, but maybe that was because you, all of you," she corrected, including her parents, "were deciding what I should do and how I should do it. Time," she said as she poked him again, "for a new program. You worry about your mission and let me worry about me."

"We can't stop worrying just because you want us to," Annie pointed out, but quietly.

"Fine," Rae shot back, "worry all you want. Just keep it to yourself." She spun away from Conn, unfolded the map, and slapped it on the picnic table.

"I checked out a few places already," she said as he and her parents came over, each of them pinning down a corner against the brisk wind. "And before you give me hell, Mom and Dad, Conn and I came back that first day because I thought we might be able to figure out who was giving him trouble and resolve the problem. Clearly that was naïve on my part, but I had no idea you were involved in a federal crime."

"But some of these people will recognize you," Annie said.

"That was more than ten years ago, and anyway I made sure to steer clear of the ones I know."

"Good thinking," Conn said with just a hint of sarcasm, his voice carefully modulated otherwise. "Who have you already talked to?"

Rae met his eyes and saw the anger seething just under the surface. He didn't appreciate being put in his place, well, too damn bad. She'd been manipulated by all three of them; she had a right to make her position clear, and if it offended him, so what? He didn't plan to stick around, so it wasn't like his resentment would be a problem for long.

"I went to this place first," she said, pointing to Earth Enchanted, "Onyx Chalcedony. Paranoid but harmless. I'd be surprised if she's involved."

"That would be our take as well," Nelson said. "Onyx

is afraid of her own shadow. Too twitchy to bring into an operation like this."

Since everyone seemed to be in agreement, Rae moved on. "Next place was Paper Moon."

"Hans Lockner. Nasty little stinker of a man who frequently drinks himself into a stupor, picks fights with other men, and makes lewd suggestions to women."

"Thanks for the character assessment, Mom," Rae said, "but I'm pretty sure he isn't involved since he offered to, uh, show me the back room."

Conn's hand fisted on his corner of the map.

Rae chose not to read into his reaction, for her own peace of mind. She'd already let him go; no point in getting her hopes up now. "If he was printing money back there he wouldn't be so quick to extend invitations. And I doubt he can get his mind out of his codpiece long enough to do anything as tricky as printing money right under everyone's noses. Besides, there's no way he could keep a secret like this, especially when it's something he could use to score with women. Counterfeiting is pretty sexy." She held up a hand when her parents exchanged a look and the temperature seemed to go up a couple of degrees. "Pretend I didn't say that.

"In any event, the last place I checked out was called Mettle Works. Cornelia Ferdic. Not exactly corporate America, but she was probably the most normal of the three."

"She does some pretty amazing work in metal," Nelson said.

"I could see her as the engraver," Conn said, "which is why her booth isn't already crossed off. I ruled out all the proprietors who had established home bases and didn't travel with the group, and then I went booth by booth, ruling out the ones with the wrong skills until I was left with a half-dozen possibilities. Jewelers who make their own designs, and anyone else who works with metals and might have the skill to engrave the plates. Under other circumstances I would have included the armorer.

"Then there's the printer," he continued. "Most counterfeit money nowadays is made using sophisticated computer equipment and color copiers, but the best bills are still printed the old-fashioned way, on a printing press. I'm no expert, but the Secret Service said the bills appearing on the Renaissance circuit are press bills."

"There are quite a few booths that sell paper goods," Nelson put in, "horoscopes, posters of castles and dragons, Celtic symbols, and the meaning of names."

"Only a few of them actually print their own wares, and since the bills are being distributed on site, it makes sense that the printer will also be doing the aging, so we look for someone with the capability of washing the bills."

"We?"

"You want to help, Rae, the first step is to search the rest of the circled booths and the campsites of whoever runs them, identify the conspirators, and get our hands on the plates. I need a face-to-face with one of the Stooges. Harry or Joe would be my first choices, since my money is on Kemp not knowing anything. We get the plates, they'll have to come after us."

"Us?" Nelson repeated.

"We're all in play."

"We can't all be together all the time," Rae pointed out. "It will be faster if we split up."

"No."

"But—"

"You said we could trust you to handle the truth. The truth is you're a liability, Rae. Your parents should be safe until the operation is completely shut down. Harry and his friends can use you to hold the rest of us hostage. That means you stick with me or I call Trip and put you in protective custody."

Rae didn't have a choice, and she knew it, so she had to settle for silent and cranky. If her glare had any effect on Conn he didn't show it.

"You take the engravers," he said to Nelson and Annie. "Don't get confrontational. Keep the conversation light and see if you can get a feel for whether or not they're involved, without letting them know what you're doing."

"Rae would probably tell you I'm a master at manipulation," Annie said.

She might have yesterday; today she just wanted them to be safe.

It must have showed on her face, because Annie said, "We know these people pretty well. Nelson and I will get to the bottom of this."

"Nope. No getting to the bottom of anything," Conn said. "If you think you know who made the plates call me before you take it any further."

"But—"

"No buts, Mom. Conn is the expert. You need to listen to him."

"We *all* need to listen to him," Nelson said. But he wasn't looking at his wife.

Rae got the message, loud and clear. "I'm going with him, aren't I?"

Nobody had a response to that.

"It's just past lunchtime," Conn said. "Everyone should be at their booths."

He took off. Rae felt no need to keep up. She hugged her parents, then headed in the direction Conn had gone. He was waiting for her a little way up the path. She passed him and kept walking.

"How long are you going to stay mad at me?" he asked, falling into step with her.

"I'm not mad at you."

"You're mad at somebody."

He had that right. "Let's leave the postmortem on our . . . relationship for another time," *like never*, "and concentrate on finding the plates."

"So you can be rid of me?"

Rae rounded on him, stopping dead in the middle of the path. "Are we going to pretend that's not part of your agenda?"

She had him there, she could see it on his face, but she couldn't say there was any satisfaction in it. He'd used her, he'd used her parents, and when it was all over he'd walk away with a clean conscience because he was going to make sure they were still alive, even if it meant jail time for a few harmless people who'd been dragged into breaking the law against their will.

It pissed her off. All of it, including the part where Conn didn't give a damn about mitigating circumstances. Especially that part. But when he skirted her and the gawkers, and set off down the path again, she swallowed her resentment and went with him. So what if it hurt like hell to be anywhere near him? So what if she felt like a fool for trusting him, and for falling in love with him? Her parents needed her to help close down the counterfeiting ring, and she'd be damned if she let them down.

THIS OP HAD GONE FROM BAD TO WORSE, CONN thought, working his way around a mountain of frustration only to come up against a wall of failure. At least it felt like failure. He and Rae had spent the rest of the day going from booth to booth with nothing to show for it. No more booths—at least no more questionable ones since they'd eliminated all the circled ones on his map, one way or another, and come up empty-handed. No plates. Annie and Nelson had laid the groundwork with the potential engravers, they said, but they couldn't say for sure who it was yet.

That left the campsites, but by the time they were done with the booths it had been too late for that. The reenactors had been closing up shop and wandering back to their campsites, and since it was Saturday night, with another long workday on tap for Sunday, they were in for the night. Quiet evening meal, no celebrating, turning in early.

Conn might have given that a try—turning in early—except there was no one else to keep an eye on Rae and her parents. And he never slept much anyway.

He was heading back from another circuit of the camp when a shadow slipped out of the Bliss's Airstream. He reacted without thinking, two steps bringing him up behind the shadow, one arm went around the shoulders and over the mouth, the other secured the target's right arm. He realized almost immediately it was Rae. He didn't let her go. "What are you doing out here?"

She lashed out with her left fist, connected with his thigh, and said a sulky, "Ouch," rubbing at her right arm when Conn released her.

Conn, on the other hand, fisted his hand around the heat where her lips had touched his skin. But that was an impulse, a reaction, and a foolish indulgence when there were possibly armed assailants in the vicinity. "You were supposed to stay with your parents. I don't think Harry and his henchmen will bother them." Which was the only reason he'd felt secure enough to leave for even the brief time it took to check the campsite.

"My dad is a buzz saw when he sleeps. I don't know how my mom stands it."

Love, Conn thought, then took a big mental step back from that precipice. His life was about violence, about bad people doing bad things, and the sometimes bad things he had to do to stop them. If there was an emotional angle, it would be greed, or fanaticism or just plain selfishness on the part of his adversary. For his side of it, there was righting a wrong, the satisfaction of putting one more criminal in a place where they couldn't hurt anyone, except other criminals.

Now here he was thinking about love—hell, not just love, the kind of love that lasted a lifetime and made allowances for annoying habits. He could have faced the reason for his sudden shift in outlook, especially since it was standing not three feet away. Admitting Rae had gotten to him wouldn't be doing either of them any favors. If he admitted that, he'd start thinking about possibilities and what-ifs. He'd start thinking about tomorrow and the rest of his life, and making changes. Problem was, you couldn't change your past.

He wouldn't even be considering it if not for this idiotic operation. A few months with the Renaissance fanatics, not to mention a good blow to the head, and he was going soft. Next thing he knew he'd be wearing tie-dye and flashing everyone the peace sign and—

"Did you hear that?" Rae asked him, her voice low.

—completely losing his edge. Conn walked a few steps off so she wasn't jamming his senses, but he didn't hear anything . . . at least anything unusual. There was a radio playing somewhere, muffled, a slight wind rattled tree branches and swirled the dead leaves on the ground, the faint whoosh of traffic drifted to him from Dixie Highway.

"What?"

"I thought I heard someone call out, but it was faint."

"Direction?"

"Your guess is as good as mine."

Conn argued with himself for a few seconds, then decided it would be stupid to go racing off into the darkness with no idea where to look or what he was looking for, and a better than even chance it might be someone trying to distract him long enough to get to Rae.

"It was probably nothing," she said.

"Maybe. I can't go campsite to campsite asking questions."

"No, you'd only alarm everyone. Besides, these people don't exactly keep regular hours. It was probably just one of the night owls." But she rubbed her arms and looked over her shoulder, clearly uneasy.

"You should get some rest," Conn said. "I think this thing is going to come to a head soon, tomorrow, the next day, definitely not long now."

"What about you? You can't stay up all night. I know it's your job, but you won't be any good to anyone if you're exhausted."

"My job." He blew out a breath. Maybe it was the darkness that made it easier to speak, maybe the exhaustion. He was definitely tired of keeping it bottled up inside him, and he needed Rae to know the truth. Maybe if he told her the truth she'd establish the distance he was having so much trouble keeping. "Let me tell you about my job.

"My unit's last long-term assignment was in the early days of Afghanistan, before the country was secured. After that we went wherever they sent us, always short missions, always a different place, always ugly."

"The nightmares."

He flashed her a look and said, "Yeah," on an outrush of breath. "It was . . ."

Classified, Rae thought, but she couldn't bring herself to be sarcastic, not when he looked so torn up. His face was all hard planes and angles, and there was a bitterness in his voice, a bleakness in his eyes that the darkness couldn't hide.

"It doesn't matter where it happened. In my nightmares it was all jumbled up, different ops, different places. Maybe if I'd seen it the same way, time after time, I would have gotten the real memory back sooner. But it always played out the same way."

She kept her eyes off his face, trying to filter what he said without getting dragged into the emotion in his voice. He might just be playing a part, she reminded herself. It could be merely another layer of lies to support his undercover activities, the same as his role at the Renaissance faire. But if he was acting, he was doing a damn good job. Those nightmares hadn't been scripted. How could they be? Nobody was good enough to fake that kind of torment while in a deep sleep.

"We infiltrated this village," he was saying, "middle of nowhere, dead of night, supposed to be a terrorist haven. We figured it would be mostly men, maybe a few women living and working like poor farmers as a front for one of the guerrilla cells. But there was this kid, maybe ten years old. He came out of a shack, waving his arms and shouting.

"The fight was full-on already, guns, grenades, one of the enemy combatants had a rocket launcher. I couldn't hear what the kid was shouting, but I've never seen anyone so terrified. All I can figure is there must have been chemicals or gas stored in that shack." His jaw clenched, just once, before he continued. "There was no way I was going to be heard over the radio, so I broke cover and went for the nearest guy in my unit, just as the shack exploded."

Conn passed a hand over his side. He must not have realized he was doing it because when she said, "Those aren't bullet wounds," he dropped his hand, his face going set and hard.

"Shrapnel. Barely missed my heart, they told me. We didn't lose one single man that night. The kid wasn't so lucky." He didn't say anything for a minute, then, "I passed five yards in front of him."

"You made a choice."

"Yeah."

And a child had died. How did she not feel sorry for him now? And how would feeling sorry for him change anything about her situation, or her parents? Or his, for that matter?

"I'm sorry, Conn. I wish there was something else I could say."

"There isn't anything else to say. It happened, I've moved on."

"No, you haven't," she said, stung at the dismissal in his voice. He dropped a bomb like that and expected her to . . . what? Take it in stride? Act like it was no big deal that she knew he walked around with that kind of weight on his conscience? Not hardly. "Maybe you're getting from day to day, but you haven't put it behind you."

"It can't be changed."

"No, but it can't be ignored, either. You've been doing that and look where it's gotten you."

"So what do you suggest?"

"Take it out, look at it, feel it, Conn, until you can believe that you did what you had to do and forgive yourself. Yes, the actions of your unit had an unbelievably terrible outcome, but how many lives did you save that day. How many have you saved since? You've taken criminals off the streets, drug dealers who might still be walking around free to hurt other kids if not for you."

He looked at her finally, and it was devastating. The

emptiness in his eyes made hers fill with tears. Of sympathy, yes, but there was frustration and anger, too.

"His death is on the hands of the people who put him in that village. People who knew he'd be in danger and didn't care. You can feel guilty about it the rest of your life, Conn, but that just makes it about you, not him. Just like this conversation is about you."

"If you can't handle this—"

"You don't want me to handle it. You want me to walk away? Fine, I'll walk away, but I don't know why it matters when you're already gone."

chapter
25

"WE'RE NOT ACTUALLY GONNA TORTURE THIS guy, are we?"

"Until he cries like a baby," Harry said, pulling Joe aside. "We went to a lot of trouble to get our hands on this guy." Hell, they'd almost been caught. Twice. Larkin had been wandering the camp, and they'd nearly run right into him when they were wrestling Hans Lockner out to the car. And if the Blissfield woman hadn't shown up to distract him, Larkin would probably have stumbled across them while they were tossing Hans's place. Joe understood stealth, his problem was attention span. He'd made a lot of noise in between reminders. "We let him stew down here all night, and he's still not talking. It's time to get serious."

"It's the crack of dawn. I got, like, four hours of sleep. I'm tired."

"Then keep your yap shut and let me handle this," Harry whispered. "I'm trying to scare the crap out of him here, and it won't work so good if you make me admit I don't want to hit him."

"Well, I ain't hitting him. Blood makes me barf."

"You hit Larkin."

"That was mostly an accident. I tripped him so you and Kemp could get him on the ground and tie him up, remember? He hit his head when he fell. There was a lot of blood."

"Oh. Right. There doesn't have to be any blood. You could kick him."

"Sure, just let me change into my steel-toed boots."

"Really?"

"No. I'm not kicking him, either."

"Maybe you ought to pull some Three Stooges stunts," Hans Lockner said. "Try to poke my eyes out, hit me in the stomach, then conk me on the head when I double over."

"I'm getting tired of the Stooges crap," Joe said. "Maybe I will hit him."

"Oh, puh-leeze. I heard you talking over there. You don't like blood, and I'm a bleeder."

Hans owned and ran a shop called Paper Moon, which specialized in prints of damsels in distress. He made the prints right there in the back of the small wooden building where he sold them, and when he wasn't printing copies of dragons assailing Druid priestesses in the forest, he was making money. Except when he was tied to a chair in the basement of Joe's house in Redford.

Despite their close call, kidnapping Hans had been a raging success, especially as compared to their last attempt. As things stood, however, they were on track to get just as much information from him as they'd gotten from Connor Larkin.

Harry might have worried that he was barking up the wrong tree, but Hans was the guy who printed the money, which meant Hans had been in possession of the plates last.

"It's your ass or mine," Harry said, the memory of past failure as much an incentive as the consequences of missing the boat again. "Cough up the plates, and don't tell us they're in your trailer. We already looked there. We want the truth, or the next thing coming out of your mouth will be your teeth."

"Go ahead, hit me."

Harry looked at Joe. Joe looked back. Neither of them moved.

"I didn't sign up for this," Joe said.

"Yes you did, and we got no choice if you want to eat tomorrow. You got laid off, same as me." It hadn't seemed so bleak at first. With unemployment and subpay they'd pulled down ninety percent of their pay sitting on their butts. But the layoff had become permanent when the union bartered their jobs away during the subsequent contract talks, and then the economy went to shit. There were no other jobs, unless you went into another profession. Hell, Harry thought, he hadn't wanted to go to college when he was eighteen. No way was he going back at fifty-three.

When the simple delivery job had turned into something more . . . troubling, he'd said to himself, *How hard could it be to threaten some ding-dongs who liked to play dress-up?* Even when Larkin had come on the scene, he'd only been one guy—built like a bulldozer, sure, but there were three of them and only one of him.

The whole thing had turned to crap, though, and the Mackinac Island jail was just a taste of the humiliation they were in for, the difference between Marshmallow Fluff and a crust of maggot-ridden bread. First they found out Larkin was some kind of secret agent, and they'd blown their one chance to find out how deep the shit really was. Then the big boss refused to shut down the operation. No, he wanted to make one last big score. With Larkin's posse ready to ride in like John Wayne and the cavalry trouncing the fucking Indians. And to top it all off, they were expected to kill the participants *and* the witnesses. Actually put people in their graves. And they couldn't even smack around one obnoxious jackass to save their own necks.

Then again, there was more than one way to defrock a re-enactor.

"You got any liquor in the house?" he said to Joe.

"Got some Jack left over from last New Year's."

"Well?"

Joe shoved his hands into his pockets and ambled up the stairs.

"Liquor ain't gonna help," Hans said.

"Shut the fuck up."

"Okay, but I thought the point here was to get me to talk."

"Everybody's a comedian."

"Not everybody. Some of us are Stooges. And that's not Jack Daniel's," he added when Joe returned with a dusty bottle that held a few inches of murky brown liquid. "You don't expect me to drink that."

"Nope." But it gave Harry great pleasure to plug Hans's nose and pour the contents of the bottle down his throat.

Harry had a feeling Hans's blood was already about twenty proof since it didn't take him all that long to get good and sloshed. Unfortunately he also got belligerent. Turned out Hans was a mean drunk.

"Go fruk y'sel," he slurred when Harry asked him where the plates were.

"We know you had them last."

"So wha'? Been print'n money onna side, too. Din't even notice."

"Jesus," Joe said, "why didn't we think of that?"

"Shtup'd pricksh."

"I wanna hit him now."

"He wouldn't feel it, Joe."

"I would."

"Focus," Harry said. "We need to get the plates or we're toast."

Joe gave Hans an open-handed shot to the chest. No blood drawn, but Hans's chair went flying over backward.

"Fruck," he shouted, sounding like the booze was wearing off. Or maybe the pain was cutting through. He rolled around without managing to improve his situation at all. "Feels like you broke my wrists. Fucking asshole."

Joe leaned over, got right in Hans's face. "*I want. The fucking. Plates. Now.*"

Hans tried to spit at him. It splatted back on his own face.

"Not a good idea when you're on your back and there's, you know, *gravity*," Joe said, booting Hans in the side, but without much intent since Hans barely grunted.

"You done?" Harry asked him.

Joe fisted his hands and glared at Hans. "Not until we get the plates."

"Cut it out, you're scaring me," Harry deadpanned. "Any ideas? Other than beating the crap out of him, which ain't gonna do any good now that he's feeling no pain."

"The booze was your idea."

"You think you can do better, go right ahead."

Joe mulled it over for a minute, eyes rolling back in his head like he was trying to read the thoughts as they scrolled across his brain. It must have worked because his eyes rotated forward again, and he looked like there ought to be a lightbulb popping on over his head. "Be right back," he said, taking the basement stairs two at a time and disappearing before Harry could ask him what the bright idea was.

When he came back, a couple of little white pills stamped with cloverleaf lay in the palm of his hand.

"It looks like aspirin. What good's that gonna do?"

"It's not aspirin, it's E, you know, Ecstasy. Kid next door is into all this garbage, says it will make anybody do anything you want."

"Isn't that the sex drug?"

"I think it works for that, too. Mostly, he said it's a mood elevator."

"That couldn't hurt. Give him some."

Joe didn't follow instructions. He just looked at the pills in his hand.

"What's wrong?"

"I'm not sure how much to give him."

Harry just shook his head and pinched one of the pills off Joe's palm. Hans clenched his teeth shut. Hans definitely did not want his mood elevated.

"Hold his nose shut," Joe suggested.

"You do it, and when he opens his mouth to breathe I'll toss the pill down his throat."

They grabbed Hans by the arms and hoisted him and his chair back to an upright position. Joe got behind him and clamped his thumb and forefinger around Hans's nose. Hans opened his lips and sucked in a breath, letting it whistle back out again through teeth he'd clamped shut. "Dumb asses," he said. He was grinning from ear to ear.

Harry lost it. He gave Joe a shot to the shoulder that broke his hold on Hans's nose, knocked Hans and his chair over again, and kneeled on his neck until he gasped for air. In went the pill, and Hans swallowed it before he knew what was happening. The fact that he almost choked on it was just gravy.

"How long do you think it will take?" Joe asked a couple hours later.

"Seems like there should've been some change by now." Harry walked over to Hans. "How you doing?"

"I'm lying on a cold cement floor with my hands and feet tied to a chair. How about we switch places and you can see firsthand how I'm doing, you *fucking moron*."

"I think he needs more time," Joe said.

"I think he needs more E." And since Harry was in charge, they repeated the process, minus the part where he had to kneel on Hans's neck. Hans might be fully sauced and partially cooked, but he wasn't forgetful or stupid.

Joe consulted his watch. It was after nine A.M., with no end in sight. "Let's go have breakfast," he said. "I got some nice, fresh sausage. He should be ready to talk by the time we're done."

"I want some sausage," Hans said as they started up the stairs.

"We want the plates," Harry said.

"Shove the fucking plates up your fucking ass," Hans shouted.

Harry chose not to respond.

"Give me some fucking sausage. I'm starving here."

"Yeah, you look it," Joe yelled down to Hans before he shut the basement door and left Hans alone, still cursing and screaming.

They'd barely worked their way through scrambled

eggs, sausage, and toast before the silence from the basement became deafening.

"You think the second pill was overkill?" Joe asked.

"I hope it wasn't any kind of kill." Harry made a beeline for the door to the basement, taking the stairs two at a time and breathing a sigh of relief when Hans turned his head and smiled at him.

Smiled at him. That was a good sign. He thought.

"Hey, how you doin'?" Hans said in a nighttime deejay kind of voice.

Harry stopped so fast Joe ran into him.

"What's wrong?"

"I don't think his mood's the only thing that's been elevated," Harry said.

"I'll tell you where the plates are if you get me a broad."

"A broad?" Joe repeated. Joe was a little slow on the uptake.

Hans thrust his hips a couple of times. "A broad, dumbass."

Joe stared at Hans's bulging crotch. "Jeez, he's all sexed up."

"That's right, baby face. Put on a dress or untie my hands—at least one of them."

Joe made a sound in the back of his throat that pretty much summed up their mutual disgust, but didn't begin to address Harry's frustration.

"Christ," he said, "all I want is the freaking plates."

"Tree," Hans shouted like he had Tourette's. "They're in the tree." Then he passed out.

Harry and Joe traded a look, then Joe walked over and nudged Hans with the toe of his beat-up Nike. Hans snorted out a breath and settled into a nice steady snoring pattern.

"Should we pick him up?" Joe said.

Harry shrugged. "He seems to be pretty comfortable."

"What tree do you think he was talking about?"

"Has to be at the nutfest," Harry said. He pulled out his cell phone and called Kemp to come and watch Hans. "Soon as he gets here," Harry said to Joe, "we head back to the festival. Should get there just before lunch-time."

Joe, master of the obvious, said, "There's a lotta trees there," and when Harry scowled at him, he added hastily, "but I bet we can figure out where Hans stashed the plates in no time. We just have to think like him."

"Great," Harry said, "all I have to do is stick my finger in a light socket and kill off a bunch of brain cells, and I'll be all set."

chapter 26

SUNDAY MORNING ARRIVED ON A STIFF NORTH-
easterly wind, bringing a sharp drop in temperature,
clouds that seemed to be all talk and no action, and a
mean case of second-guessing on Conn's part.

"We already checked out all the booths on the map,"
Rae reminded him.

"Except these two."

"I was in Paper Moon, and I thought you ruled out Madame Zaretsky based on my parents' opinion that it wasn't
her."

"I have a gut feeling."

Rae rolled her eyes, since one of those booths was
Hans Lockner's, and the other was probably just a smoke
screen. Conn seemed hell-bent on making Hans's acquaintance, so there was no point in arguing about it.

Madame Zaretsky read palms and tarot out of a tent
pitched not far from the tilting grounds where the "jousts"
were held, but away from the permanent booths ringing
the Grove. She looked like the typical palm reader: gypsy
dress, scarf wrapped around her graying hair, gold coin
earrings brushing her shoulders. In real life she was a

grandmother of twelve, named Edith Whipple, from New Jersey. With really bad eyesight, and an equally bad accent. Her predictions, however, tended to be spot-on. She'd been traveling with the group on and off for as long as Rae could remember. The tourists didn't really buy her shtick. The circuit gypsies claimed she had a cosmic gift. But then, they tended to be a superstitious lot.

A girl in her early teens sat on the threadbare velvet ottoman across the table from Madame, a fog-filled crystal ball between them. The girl got up and joined a group of friends standing nearby, all of them blushing and giggling as they wandered off. Judging by the sidelong glances going Conn's way, Rae figured it wasn't all about the reading.

Conn nudged Rae toward the ottoman. Rae had no intention of putting her butt on that stool. She already knew how her future was going to play out—at least in the short term, short being however long it took her to get over Connor Larkin.

"Sit, sit," Madame Zaretsky said, peering up in the general direction of Conn's face.

Conn crossed his arms and glared at Rae.

"He's shy," Rae said to Madame.

"He ees afrrrraid?"

Conn blew out a breath, folded his long body onto the stool, and laid his hand, palm up, on the table. But he was looking at Rae.

She popped up an eyebrow and stared back until he turned his attention to the task at hand—which was keeping Madame Zaretsky busy while Rae searched the premises for a printing press. Not that Madame was much of a challenge since she had to practically put her face in Conn's hand just to see it.

"Verrrry interrrrresting," Madame said, tracing the lines on Conn's palm with her finger. "The road you walk is not easy, or straight."

Or truthful, Rae thought as she slipped behind Madame and pretended to browse the stacks of tarot cards and aromatherapy candles, the bins of stones possessing various useful properties, and the racks of preprinted zodiacs and personality charts. Madame Zaretsky also printed horoscopes to order, one hour or less.

Rae took a quick glance around, and when it was clear she slipped into the tent. There was no printing press, just a computer with a screen saver running. When Rae put her hand on the mouse, a menu popped up for state-of-the-art publishing software, and there was a printer that looked pretty sophisticated and expensive to her untrained eye. But when she brought up the list of files there were only three, and none of them contained artwork for counterfeit money.

Besides the computer, there wasn't much else inside the tent except a bigger table where Madame worked up the special-order horoscopes and apparently ate her lunch, since the remains of something unidentifiable but definitely food-based was spread out on one end.

She eased out of the tent, just in time to hear the end of Conn's palm reading.

"You arrre not long for this life," Madame was saying. She traced the lifeline on Conn's palm, which curled from his wrist, around the pad of his thumb to the index finger side of his hand. "See here where the line breaks? You are in a time of great upheaval. You will not overcome."

Rae's heart skipped. She drew in her breath and held it against the sudden pain. Even if Madame Zaretsky's accuracy hadn't been well proven, Rae had never considered Conn's danger, not really anyway. He seemed so . . . impervious, so rock solid. She'd seen him fight off men with swords, for Pete's sake. But he was as mortal as the next man. He could be hurt. He could be killed.

The thought of it devastated her. She knew he would leave; she'd come to terms with it. But in her mind's eye she'd always seen him going on with his life. She'd resented him for it, but maybe it was for the best after all. She wasn't the kind of woman who could live day-to-day, never knowing if the man she loved would come home to her at the end of his next assignment. This way she could always think of him as he was now—alive, vital. And more than a little snarky.

"I'm not going to kick it today, am I?"

"You mock me now," Madame said in her faux-Russian accent. "But you will remember Madame Zarrretsky long after you leave."

"If I believe you, *long* isn't a concept that applies to me." Conn tucked a five-dollar bill into Madame's hand as he got to his feet. "Next time," he said when he joined Rae, "it's your turn to be the distraction."

"But you do it so well," Rae said, not entirely sarcastic since he'd done a pretty damn good job of distracting her. "It's not Madame Zaretsky. She has a pretty sophisticated computer set up in the tent, and the latest in print shop software, but I don't think she has the knowledge to use it for forgeries. She didn't even password protect the system, and I couldn't find anything suspicious."

"She was a long shot anyway. An elderly woman with bad eyes? Not a good bet for this kind of enterprise."

"She says artificial lenses interfere with the 'sight,'" Rae told him. "But she wears glasses the rest of the time."

"Still crossing her off the list."

"She has a pretty good track record, you know."

"Are you saying you believe her?"

"My mother calls her the Jeane Dixon of the Renaissance circuit."

"Who's Jeane Dixon?"

"She predicted the assassination of John Kennedy."

"Anything more recent?"

Rae frowned, coming up empty.

"I'll be careful," Conn said, deadpan voice, bland expression, not taking Rae or Madame Zaretsky seriously.

Fine, Rae thought, she'd tried. If he wanted to play fast and loose with his life, well, it was his life to play fast and loose with.

"Answer your phone," Madame Zaretsky called after them.

Conn took out his cell phone, just in time for it to ring.

He frowned over his shoulder at Madame, who was smiling, probably because she'd expected that reaction even if she couldn't see it.

"Yeah," he said into the phone. He listened for a few seconds, then said, "Go to your booth and act normal . . . I'm sure . . . Rae's fine. We're both fine, and we can finish our part of this faster if we know you're safe." And he snapped the phone closed.

"My mother?" Rae said.

He chose not to state the obvious. "They identified the engraver. Cornelia Ferdic."

"No. Really? She didn't strike me as the type."

"How about your parents? Ever think they'd be involved in something like this?"

She got his point, even if she chose not to say as much. "So I take it she doesn't have the plates."

"No." Conn reached out and tapped the pendant Rae had bought from Cornelia less than a week before. "Judging by her merchandise, she's good enough to make them."

He hadn't actually touched her, but her heart was pounding so hard, just at the close call, that Rae had to struggle to focus on what he was saying. Concentrating on the life-and-death stuff put it all back into perspective. Keeping her eyes off him helped.

"Your parents have done their part so I sent them back to work. Best to keep everything as normal as possible, while we close the rest of the circle." Conn pulled out his cell phone and speed dialed, not bothering with a greeting. "Cornelia Ferdic," he said into the phone. "She's been with the group . . ."

"Not more than ten years," Rae supplied. "She joined up after I went off to college."

Conn relayed that information into the phone, then said, "Yeah, I know the Secret Service checked the group out before I was sent, and they came up empty. There were a lot of people to check out, especially when you factor how they come and go. Do me a favor and put one of our guys on it. Have him peel back another layer or

two on this woman. Those plates are just too damn good
for her to be a beginner." And he disconnected.

"That was your FBI handler?"

"Yeah. He's going to check Ferdic out and get back to
me."

Rae frowned. "You really think she's some sort of pro-
fessional counterfeiter?"

"There's no way those plates are novice work, especially if they were made in the time frame your parents
gave me. The Secret Service ran background checks on
everyone affiliated with the group, and they came up with
nothing. Now that we have a name, it's worth taking a
deeper look. If we don't find anything, it's just a little
time lost."

"And if you do find something?"

"It could give us a direction on the guys who are running the show. Get this over with faster."

"By all means," Rae said dryly. "We wouldn't want to
trespass on your time any longer than necessary."

Conn ignored the sarcasm. "If we cut off the head of
the snake, the rest of it will die with no collateral damage.
The other players won't get off scot-free, but at least
they'll be alive."

If there was a way to keep her parents safe, Rae was all
for that. She headed for the next booth on their list, but
Conn took off on a tangent that ultimately led directly to
Hans Lockner's booth, Paper Moon.

Rae pulled Conn to a stop a hundred yards away. "Is
this really necessary?"

"Because he's a pervert, and I want to smash his face
in?"

"Because being a pervert doesn't make him a criminal." She grinned. "But it does mean he has good taste."

"He strikes me as the kind of guy who goes for quan-
tity, not quality."

Rae could have taken that as an insult, but she was too
busy cluing in to the physical subtext beneath Conn's
words, the muscle working in his jaw, the way he stared,
blue eyes laser sharp, at Hans's booth, the general aura of

leashed control. If she hadn't known better, she'd have said Conn had something against Hans Lockner, and it wasn't about the case. The case was his job; this was personal.

He flashed her a look that had her jumping to conclusions she had no business landing on under the current circumstances. And then he made a beeline for the booth, his strides too long for her to keep up.

A teenager with black eyeliner and multiple piercings stood at the counter. When Rae walked in he was huffing out breath. "Don't bother, man," he said to Conn. "I been waiting here for, like, ever." He tossed down a print of a dragon hovering over a frail-looking woman, her skirts blowing in an artistic wind and leaving nothing to the viewer's imagination. "Dude who runs this place oughta be glad I'm not of a larcenous inclination," and he stomped out.

Conn leaned over the counter, then walked behind it. "Kid's right," he said. "There's nobody here, but this guy isn't even trying to hide what he's doing."

Rae joined him in the back room, in time to watch him pull back a huge gray tarp and reveal what she figured must be a printing press. "Everyone minds their own business around here," she said, deciding not to think about Hans's estimation of her intelligence if he thought she'd ignore a hulking piece of machinery just because it was under a tarp. Then again, Hans probably thought he could dazzle her with his attributes. Yuck.

Conn started at one end of the contraption and worked his way methodically to the other end, flipping a switch that made the machine whir to life, spitting out a sheet of paper without a single mark on it.

"Fuck," he said, scrubbing a hand back through his hair.

"No plates, I take it."

"No plates." He turned the machine off and replaced the tarp.

When he started to search the small back room, Rae went to work helping him, the two of them circling the place methodically. They came up empty-handed.

"It's almost dinnertime," Rae said. "If we're going to search his campsite we'll have to hurry. A lot of the regulars will be heading back there soon."

Hans owned a pop-up camper that he dragged around behind a rusted-out Chevy pickup. When Rae and Conn got there they found the place trashed, even beyond the best efforts of a complete slob. Furniture was overturned; food boxes were sliced open and emptied on the table, counter, and floor; and every storage compartment in the place was open and vomiting its contents.

"Do you think they found the plates?" Rae asked Conn.

"No. They would have stopped searching."

"Unless the plates were the last place they looked."

"It's always the last place you look," Conn said, "but the odds are against them having to tear everything apart, so we go on the premise the plates weren't found."

Rae followed him outside and watched him kneel to peer under the pop-up, then the Chevy. He climbed up to look on top of both, then jumped to the ground.

"They'd be close," he said, turning in a slow circle and surveying their surroundings.

Rae made a beeline for the nearest tree, an old beech with gray bark and a hollow base. She didn't look there, though, instead climbing the stubs of long-shed branches until she was high enough to reach into the canopy of yellow leaves starting to fall. "I learned this from an old guy who traveled with us when I was a kid," she said. "He was a hobo for part of his life, and he used to hide everything he owned in a tree at night."

She felt around in the crotch of the first row of branches, then the next highest level. Nothing. She climbed down and moved on to another beech, not far from the first, Conn boosting her up this time. His hands lingered on her waist, slipping down to her thighs to steady her once she found her footing on a low branch.

Rae scrambled up out of reach, before she forgot that Conn's objective was solving the case so he could put her into his past, before she let herself slide down, into his arms, before she begged him to love her back, just for a moment, even if it was a lie.

"Are the plates up there?"

She smiled a little, darkly amused by her own stupidity, mooning over a man who saw her, at best, as an unwelcome burden. For as short a time as possible, which brought her full circle and gave her a swift kick in the pride. Conn didn't want her around, the hell with him.

She searched the branches above her head, grinning when she felt plastic-covered cloth wrapped around something hard and rectangular.

She almost bobbled it when Conn wrapped his hands around her hips to help her down, and since her focus shifted from finding the plates to getting his hands off her she tossed him the bundle. "Good news. You're one step closer to getting rid of me."

Conn took out a pocket knife and slit the wrappings along one side, peeling them back far enough to reveal a pair of metal plates taped together. "You'd make a pretty good detective," he said.

"I'm just an accountant with an interesting background. And I've had enough of the FBI."

"And I could do without the hostility."

"Then you're in the wrong line of work."

chapter 27

"LARKIN IS FBI."

"You sure?"

"We overheard him talking to the woman he's with."

There was silence from the other end of the phone, as Harry's boss digested that news, then said, "What else?"

Harry did a preemptive grimace and said, "He has the plates," rushing to add, "the printer spilled, but by the time we got back to the nutfest, Larkin was already there."

"Get the plates, then deal with the witnesses."

"Deal?"

"Who's going to take care of your family if you go to jail?"

Harry didn't voice an answer, but he was shrieking, "No," into the silence in his own head. *He just wanted a job, for Christ's sake, a normal job with a normal pay-check and a list of functions that did not include car chases, torture, or breaking federal laws. Not to mention murder. Jesus, how would he look his wife and kids in the eyes after that?*

"If you're done whining—"

"Watch it, or I might decide to leave everyone else alone and *deal* with you."

"Don't be an idiot. If anything happens to me, I've made sure your name will come up in the murder investigation."

"I never agreed to kill anyone."

"But you will."

Yeah, he would, Harry decided. His heart was heavy, so was his conscience, but jail wasn't an option Going to the feds and turning informant crossed his mind, but that would probably certainly end in jail time, and worse, his family would find out he was a criminal. He just couldn't face that. "I want a larger share, or you do your own dirty work."

"It always comes down to money," Morris Greenblatt said with a papery accountant's chuckle.

"Keep laughing," Harry shot back, "but don't forget you're no better than me."

"I'm the one who put this whole operation together. Without me you'd be panhandling on a street corner."

That didn't sound as bad to Harry as it had a few months ago. Too bad he'd opted to put his nuts in a wringer. "Okay, Einstein, explain to me how we're going to get those plates?"

"Use your imagination."

"In my imagination this guy is still built like a truck, and now that he has his memory back, he'll be ready for us."

"Don't sweat it," Greenblatt said, "I have a secret weapon."

CONN TOOK ANNIE'S CELL AND COPIED A NUMBER into his. "I'll call Harry in the morning, let him know we have the plates, and set up a meet. The three of you are going to—"

"Have your back," Rae said.

Conn cut his eyes skyward, but God wasn't in a facilitating mood. Conn knew that, because it was the fourth time he'd tried to convince the Blisses—father, mother, and daughter—to stay somewhere safe while his negotiations with Harry and the Stooges played out. And it was the fourth time they'd refused to listen to reason. As if he hadn't done this sort of thing dozens of times before.

"I've done this sort of thing dozens of times before," he said—out loud this time. It had more effect that way, or it would have if he'd been dealing with reasonable people. "I'm still here."

"There are three of them and one of you," Annie said. "Remind you of anything? Now that you've got your memory back, I mean."

"There's no call for sarcasm."

"How about food?" Nelson set a tray of hamburgers and hot dogs on the table, alongside Annie's potato salad and the corn he'd taken off the grill a few minutes before.

"Will you be more agreeable once you've had dinner?"

"No." Rae took a hamburger, dumped some ketchup on it, and then ignored it altogether, along with the rest of the food she put on her plate.

"There's nothing you can do to help," Conn said, sliding her plate over in front of him.

"Hey!"

"You're not going to eat it anyway."

She pulled her plate away from him and took a bite of the burger, just to spite him. She raised her eyes to his as she finished chewing and swallowed, the corners of her mouth lifting in reluctant amusement.

Conn felt something shift inside him, like a puzzle piece settling softly into place and completing a picture that was a complete revelation, but at the same time somehow familiar. He wanted to stay in that moment, even as he told himself no good could come of it.

So what if they connected on levels he didn't want to explore? So what if he saw something in Rae's eyes in unguarded moments? She didn't trust him, and she was right not to. He wasn't suited for anything but what he was doing, and even if she would've been willing to go with him, he'd never ask her to walk away from the home and life she'd worked so hard to create just so he had a warm place to land between missions.

"We were talking about this death wish you have," Rae said, not about to be sidetracked.

"I don't take unnecessary risks, but I can't watch your back and mine at the same time. With you hanging around my chances of coming through this in one piece drop drastically."

Rae pushed her plate away again. "Don't spare my feelings."

"I'm the expert, remember?"

"You said it yourself, sweetheart."

"Thanks, Mom," Rae said, still holding Conn's eyes. "I guess that means you and Dad are going to make yourselves scarce, too."

"Oh, well . . ."

Rae's phone went off. Even if Conn hadn't recognized the money song she used for her bosses, the look on her face would have given it away. She flipped the phone open and put it to her ear, her expression changing to one of cautious relief. "Mr. Greenblatt?"

Her gaze shifted to Conn's, she sank her teeth into her bottom lip, and he almost forgot what he was trying to do. Almost. Possible death was pretty hard to lose sight of.

"Can you hold on a minute?" she said into the phone, then put her finger over the mouthpiece. "There's a new client coming in for a meeting tomorrow. The governor is giving big tax breaks to film companies that open studios in Michigan."

"Tell him you'll be there."

"But—"

"You still want to make partner, right? He's giving you a sign of confidence."

She started to shake her head.

Damn her and her stubbornness. "The debate is over. I don't work with a partner, and I sure as hell don't work with a team."

Rae lifted her chin, putting the phone up to her ear. "I'll see you in the morning, Mr. Greenblatt," she said, getting to her feet and keeping her eyes on Conn's until she turned and walked away.

"Well, son," Nelson said, "you got what you wanted."

Yeah, Conn thought, he'd gotten what he wanted. Rae wouldn't be around to split his attention tomorrow. Now all he had to do was figure out how to stop thinking about how pissed off she was.

JUST AFTER DARK A HUGE BONFIRE WAS LIT IN THE center of camp. Lawn chairs, camp stools, and hollow logs ringed the fire, occupied by the members of the Bliss's traveling group, most of them still in costume. If not for the various motor vehicles and somewhat modern campers parked in the gloom beyond the firelight, it might have been the sixteenth century. Conn's attitude certainly fit the picture.

"Still mad at me?" he said, parking himself on the ground beside her low beach chair.

"You're a jerk."

"Is that the best you can do?"

"You don't deserve my best."

"C'mon, take a couple of cheap shots. It'll make you feel better."

It would make her feel better. The question was, what was Conn getting out of it? "I thought you wanted to be alone."

"I want to work alone," he said.

"The two sort of go together."

"That would have a lot more oomph if you tacked *jerk* on the end."

She gave him a dirty look. "We done here?"

"Not until you get your head out of your ass. This is getting serious, Rae. Harry and his friends may come off as Stooges, but they'll kill for those plates."

"And I don't have the necessary training. I got that earlier. When you told me you didn't want a partner anymore. And yet here you are."

He blew out a breath, staring into the fire for a minute.

"What do you want?"

"It would be easier for me to concentrate on what I have to do if you weren't mad at me."

"Fine. Or as you so charmingly put it, my head is out of my ass. Harry and his friends are all yours. Hell, take on the whole mafia for all I care." Rae kept her voice down; she even managed to sound like she'd come to terms with his high-handed, obnoxious, insulting ultimatum. Then she tried to cap it off with a dramatic exit, but the low beach chair tripped her up and she fell back into it, crossing her arms and not caring if Conn knew she was actually fuming.

"Need some help?" he said, not making much of an effort to hide his amusement.

"I'd say yes, but I know you have a problem with teamwork."

She boosted herself out of the chair, temper taking her to her feet in one jack-in-the-box move. Temper took her out of the circle of firelight and into the blessed darkness beyond. Stubbornness kept her from doing anything rash. She stayed in the shadows at the edge of the fire, watching the re-enactors quietly celebrate another successful weekend, and refusing to give Connor Larkin the satisfaction of knowing he'd sent her running again—and really, he hadn't. She was hurt and angry, but taking it out on Conn wasn't going to change that any more than distance from him would.

Besides, it wasn't any more his fault that it was hers. Sure, he was an undercover agent, but he hadn't known that a week ago. And sure, he'd gotten his memory back and kept it from her, and yeah, it ticked her off, but she wouldn't appreciate him interfering in her work if she was in the midst of an accounting emergency . . . Okay, accounting wasn't exactly a life-or-death career path, but it was the principle of the thing. Her job was to sit at a desk and protect people from the IRS, his was to carry a gun and protect democracy, or at least capitalism. Both their lives were on the line, and in both cases failure meant unemployment, but she would only lose her job, and maybe her house. Conn might be moving to a much smaller piece of real estate. Six feet under.

The Renaissance folk were as exhausted as any so-called normal person after a long couple of days of work. Considering the week Rae had just been through, she could identify. Her problem, however, was with tomorrow.

Her parents had already gone off to bed, others trailing out of the firelight in ones and twos, including Conn. He'd pitched his tent outside the entrance to the Airstream. Rae hesitated between the two, torn. She wanted to clear the air with Conn, just in case, but she was pretty sure that wasn't her only motivation

Conn took the decision out of her hands. "I'm not asleep," he said, flipping open the front flap.

The moon was nearly full, enough light leaking through the trees to see his expression, including the surprise when she said, "I owe you an apology."

"For?"

"You're doing what you think is right."

"But you still don't agree with it."

"I still think you're being an idiot. But it's your life to gamble with."

"Then the apology is really about your conscience. That and you have no confidence in my job skills."

"Well, you're being a *jerk*, and I think that's about you pushing me away in case something goes wrong tomorrow."

"Why would I do that?"

She crawled into the tent, shoved him onto his back, and laid her body on his. "This is why," she said, taking his mouth but not letting him deepen the kiss. "You can pretend—" No, she wouldn't be that woman who asked for reassurances, even obliquely. Her feelings were her feelings; they didn't give her the right to push him into an emotional corner. She could show him how she felt, though. She couldn't help it, really, pouring herself into another kiss, offering him more than her body. Offering him everything she was.

And Conn accepted, without hesitation and without words. It stung, made the joy a little bittersweet until she gave herself to sensation, to the slide of his hands over her skin as they slipped clothing off, the feel of him against her, strong and sure, the pull of his mouth at her breast as his fingers slipped between her legs and entered her, and the building of pleasure, layer on layer, drawing her into a knot of coiled need, winding tighter and tighter until his mouth replaced his fingers and she unraveled, Conn drawing the orgasm out to an impossible length that left her spent, but wanting to curl into herself so she could hold on to that magic just a little longer.

Conn was there, though, gathering her close, holding her almost too tightly. If she could have, she would have brought him closer still. She would have crawled inside his skin so he could never leave her behind. She had to settle for nuzzling her face into the crook of his neck, absorbing his heat, breathing his scent, listening to his heartbeat under her ear.

They stayed that way for a little while, Rae not letting herself read anything into the embrace. Conn couldn't be worried about the next day; he was never uncertain. And she already knew he cared for her, the friends-with-benefits-but-no-future kind of caring. Not enough to call it love, but enough to be gentle, and gentle he was. He made love to her slowly, as he'd done that first time, with the intensity that stole her breath, and a tenderness that made her heart ache.

His hands and mouth were everywhere at once—her neck, her breasts, her center. He joined his body to hers, a long, slow slide that made her toes curl and her back arch and every cell she had come alive. He pulled her knee up and went deeper, keeping to that same agonizingly slow pace until she shoved at his shoulders and he rolled to his back, taking her with him.

Rae rose over him, filled with an urgency she'd never felt before, not just a physical drive, but an emotional one. And the emotion was anger. She slammed her body against his, balancing on the razor's edge between a nearly unbearable level of pleasure and complete sensory overload, rocking her body into his, harder and faster,

more desperate with each stroke until he grabbed her hips
and said gently, "Let go," and she did, felt him go over as
her climax blasted through her, a collision of sensation
and emotion too intense to bear, let alone hide.

She eased down beside Conn, but any hope he wouldn't
notice her upset flew out the window when he wiped a tear
from her cheek.

"What's this?" he said softly.

"It's been a hell of a day," she said, swallowing hard
and willing the tears back.

"I'm sorry for the way I handled things today, but you
have to trust that I'm right."

"I do. You're the one with the trust issues."

"I know," he said on a heavy exhale. "I guess I'll have
to work on that."

If he was still around after tomorrow.

Neither of them said it, but it hung between them all
the same.

"Tomorrow morning I'll take you home to get your
files, then I'll take you to work," he said.

"See? You don't trust me."

"It's not mistrust, it's just . . . I don't need any distractions tomorrow. It'll help me to know you're safe while
the meet goes down."

Rae digested that for a few seconds, then said, "Okay,"
without actually coming to terms with what it might
mean. In the matter of hopeless causes, ignorance was
definitely bliss.

She sat up, but Conn pulled her back down next to
him.

"Worried about my safety again?" she teased.

"Yeah, it's your safety I'm thinking about."

"Okay," she said, settling down beside him, "because
being an accountant is dangerous, so I need all the protection I can get."

chapter
28

CONN WOKE ALONE EARLY MONDAY MORNING.
Despite his solitude he stayed where he was, replaying the
night before and smiling. Rae had slipped out of the tent
in the early morning hours. He'd known she was leaving
and chose not to stop her. She needed the distance and so
did he. Much as he would have enjoyed starting the day
the way he'd ended the last one, it wasn't exactly condu-
cive to keeping his head in the game. Just remembering
Rae, naked and warm, that amazing red hair tousled, her
eyes sleepy and inviting . . . And what the hell was he
supposed to be thinking about?

She came out of the Airstream, bright smile, bright
eyes, no sign of sadness or resentment, and he gave up on
reloading his former train of thought.

"What's your problem?" she asked him when he
crawled out of his tent.

He wiped the frown off his face, although he couldn't
quite make it to her level of chipper. "I expected less
Sunny and more Rae."

"Ouch."

"You know what I mean."

She bumped up a shoulder. "What would be the point? You have a life, I have a life."

"Yeah, we both have lives," Conn said, irritated.

"There's no *we*. You said it more than once."

"Not like that."

"Maybe not, but you got your message across anyway, and I understand that's the way it has to be."

She didn't have to sound so damn happy about it. He sure as hell wasn't happy about it. He wasn't exactly sure what he felt, but happy wasn't anywhere on the list.

"Get your purse," he said, "I'll take you back to your life."

"Okay," she said, with what he swore was a slight smirk.

He ignored the smirk. "Where are your parents? They're coming with us."

"Let's go find them."

She nipped into the trailer and retrieved her purse, and they headed straight for her parents' booth. Sure enough they were there, packing up.

"The festival has a couple more weeks to run," Rae said.

Annie reached for the packing tape. "We thought it would be best to call it a day here."

Conn looked around the crude wooden building. Most of the textiles and clothing they hawked were still on display. The back room was empty, so was Nelson's loom. They'd gotten rid of the evidence against them. He looked at Rae and knew she'd come to the same conclusion.

"It won't matter," he said.

And there was the sadness he'd expected to see earlier. But it was her disappointment that made him look away.

They followed Annie and Nelson out of the booth and through the eerily deserted Grove. Pennants waved, booths were filled with merchandise, and the stages beckoned. The place was like a hooker in suburbia at noon, he decided—all tarted up and no john in sight.

There was, however, activity at the staff entrance, which was also the service entrance. A UPS truck was parked to one side, and people, some of them in Renaissance garb for a reason Conn couldn't begin to fathom when there were no tourists around, were queued up to ship merchandise or sort through the stack the driver had already off-loaded.

A couple other trucks were parked there as well, a small U-Haul and a similarly-sized white truck with TWO MEN AND A HAND TRUCK printed on it in Home Depot press-on black lettering. Some sort of small-time home-based business, Conn guessed.

He tuned in to the activity in the small Grove, keeping one eye and one ear on the Blisses, not that they were doing any talking.

"Loosen up," he said under his voice. "You look like there's a firing squad in your future."

"There's probably a jail cell," Rae snapped, although she kept her voice down, too. "You're clearly not going to do anything about it."

"That's for the lawyers."

"Cop-out."

"Let's just worry about today, shall we?" Nelson said, always the voice of reason.

Rae went silent and sulky.

From the corner of his eye, Conn caught movement from the U-haul, shifting his eyes in that direction and turning his head only enough to get a better look—at Kemp exiting the driver's door.

Conn put Rae and her disappointment out of his mind. Words would only be an empty reassurance anyway. The best he could do for her was finish this thing and stand for her parents when the time came.

Kemp was wearing a brown cape and a bald cap, trying to be Friar Tuck. Rae and her parents didn't notice him, which was only more justification for wanting them far away from the op today—no sense of danger, although Rae looked over at him, her "Conn" radar apparently humming. He lifted a brow in question, radiating *Nothing wrong here* for all he was worth.

Nelson put an arm around her shoulders and said

something, and she turned away. Conn was thinking fast and moving slow, dragging his feet while he took stock and made a game plan.

Being short and camouflaged, Kemp blended in with the small crowd. He kept his head down, trying to look innocent, and completely missing Rae and her parents. Conn kept track of the shiny pink plastic scalp with the fringe of faux hair. Not a problem from his height.

The U-Haul was for moving Lockner's printing press, but Kemp was going to have a problem—besides figuring out a way to move the thing by himself. Kemp was about to have a close encounter with a cattle prod . . . Okay, Conn wasn't going to actually torture him, unless scare tactics counted.

He caught up with Rae and her parents, handing Nelson the keys to the Jaguar. "Take Rae to work, then find yourself a crowded place to spend the day," he said. "There's a mall not far from her office building. That'll work."

"You said you were going to take me." Rae stepped close and lowered her voice. "You said you needed to know I was safe."

She had him there, and for a moment it worried him that Harry and Joe were wandering around somewhere, concocting who knew what harebrained schemes. What worried him more was that Rae wouldn't cooperate.

"Fine," he said. "Go to the Airstream. I'll be there in ten minutes."

"What are you going to do?"

"Just go. I'll be right behind you. Trust me."

Those last two words did it. She snapped her mouth shut, regarded him out of narrowed eyes for another few seconds, then turned at her father's urging and walked off with them.

Conn did an about-face, located the fake scalp, and weaved his way around everyone else so he could come up behind Kemp, saying, "Hey, man, it's been a long time," pretending to hug him but locking his hand around the back of Kemp's neck. He felt Kemp's muscles bunch and said, "Don't even think of it," letting his light jacket gape open.

Kemp took a look at the gun holster beneath Conn's left arm and aborted whatever misguided hopes he had for escape. Conn quick-stepped him to the Airstream, but five adults, one of them with Kemp's girth, exceeded the available space, so Conn cut right to the chase.

"This is why I need you to go with your parents," he said to Rae. "Kemp is going to tell me everything he knows."

"I don't know anything," Kemp said.

"Shut up or I'll sic her on you."

Rae played along, glaring at Kemp. When her eyes dropped to his crotch, he hunched, knees clenched together, shuffling backward as far as he could, which was all of two inches before he came up against the galley cabinets.

Then Rae turned her glare on him, and Conn resisted the urge to do a duck-and-cover routine of his own, except the body part he would have covered was a lot higher than his crotch. That body part was also covered by heavy muscle, but that didn't seem to be much protection against Rae.

"Are you going to torture him?" she asked.

"Only if he makes it necessary."

"I hope you're feeling uncooperative," she said to Kemp, looking avid. "Conn has a really excellent collection of knives."

Kemp looked a little green, but Conn had to hand it to him. "I'm not telling him anything," he said to Rae.

"Is there any way you can take pictures? Maybe video?"

Okay, now she was scaring him. "Maybe I should let you question him."

"Don't you mean interrogate?"

"It's a good thing she has to go to work," Conn said to Kemp, not to mention reminding Rae.

"Yeah, you have to go to work," Kemp said, visibly relieved, almost cheerful at the idea of Rae taking herself elsewhere.

"We only work on the weekends," Annie said, and not

because she was trying to cut in on Rae's fun. She looked like she wouldn't mind getting a piece of Kemp.

Kemp was wise enough to keep his mouth shut.

Conn thought that was a good idea, catching Nelson's eye and trying to let him know without words—and the messy female emotions they would spark—that the safety of his woman was in his hands.

"Let's go," Nelson said with steel in his voice.

It caught all of them off guard, but not for long.

"You promised to take me," Rae said to Conn.

"You can't break a promise," Kemp said. "And you should walk her right to the door, make sure she gets there okay."

"Then again, I hate to interfere with your work," she said, more for Kemp's sake than anything else. Her eyes, when they met Conn's, were troubled.

He took the gun out of his holster, flipped off the safety, and handed it to Nelson, checking to make sure there was a bullet in the chamber. "If he moves, shoot him."

"I'll assume you don't mean I should hit him anywhere . . . final."

"Man," Kemp said, "your whole family is crazy."

Rae looked like she was about to prove him right. "Save something for me," Conn said, pulling her down the hallway and into the bedroom.

"You're not actually going to torture him," she said when they were out of sight. "He doesn't know anything."

"He knows where Harry and Joe are. Since Harry isn't answering his phone, it's a start."

"Oh. Then you are going to take on all three of them."

"Not at the same time."

"Okay," she said, but that look was in her eyes again, and it wasn't the worry that bothered him, it was what the worry might push her into doing—namely, getting herself in trouble in a misguided attempt to help him.

"I'm giving you my cell phone number," he said, knowing it would give her peace of mind, even if she was too proud to use it. "I promise to call you later."

"You promised to take me to work, too."

"Kemp won't keep, and your boss is expecting you."

"The hell with my boss."

"Nope."

"Nope?"

"Nope, I'm not having this argument again."

She crossed her arms and huffed out a breath, but Conn knew she was replaying the discussion they'd had last night. She could go to work, or she could be stubborn, and if anything went wrong, she'd have to wonder if sticking around had been the right decision.

"Fine," she said, "but I'm expecting a progress report before lunch. And if you don't call me, I'm coming back here to find out why."

"I thought you trusted me."

"I do. It's the bad guys I don't trust."

CONN TOOK KEMP INTO THE WOODS, FEELING LIKE a fool when he tied him to a tree.

"What are we doing out here?" Kemp asked him, clearly grasping at straws since he knew exactly what they were doing out there.

"Just making sure we're far enough from the activity in the Grove so we won't attract attention when the yelling starts."

"Yelling?"

"You said you weren't going to tell me anything. That means I'll have to persuade you, and I'm not talking about dinner and drinks."

"W-what are you going to do?"

Conn bent to his left ankle and removed a knife from the sheath there. It wasn't a big knife, but then nothing in life was about size, it was about what you did with what you had. He had no intention of actually torturing Kemp. The trick was to look like you were capable of torturing someone. A little crazy didn't hurt, either.

Testing the edge of the knife on his biceps got both points across. Kemp started to babble, talking about how he'd worked at an auto plant for twenty years before he lost his job, staring, white-faced, at the thin line of blood trickling down Conn's arm.

"I don't have any other skills," Kemp said, stopping to swallow convulsively.

"So you became mob muscle."

"Mob?"

"Mafia."

Kemp's mouth dropped open, and if his eyes widened any farther he'd be able to see behind him without turning his head.

"I take it that's a surprise to you."

"Harry never said . . . He kept the identity of the boss a secret."

"Doesn't mean you're completely ignorant."

"But if I tell you—" His voice dropped to a whisper, his eyes darting around the woods. "—won't they kill me and cut out my tongue?"

"Maybe you should worry about what I'm going to do to you."

Kemp's eyes shifted to Conn's bloody biceps, but he clammed up anyway.

Conn leaned into his line of vision. "Let me put it this way: I'm going to find out who's behind this one way or another. You make it harder on me, and when I do find them I'll make sure they think you fingered them."

"But I don't—I only drove the car."

Not much to work with, but it was all he had. "Tell me where you went."

"Here mostly."

Conn cast his eyes to the heavens. "Where else?"

"We followed you. That chick's house, the one you were with. Mackinac Island."

Conn paced away, then back, something nagging at the edge of his mind. And then it hit him. "You just said you followed us, but that day at the mall—"

"Oh, that . . . We ran into you coming out of that parking structure."

"Why were you in the parking structure to begin with?"

"Harry had to pick up a check to pay for the glass in his car. The glass your girlfriend got broken by luring us to that union hall."

"Did you see what business Harry went into?"

Kemp shook his head. "He had me take him to the top floor and told me to let the car idle by the elevator since it wasn't running so hot."

The top floor. Kemp kept bitching, but Conn had checked out of the conversation, his brain working a mile a minute, culling bits and pieces out of his memory from the past week. Rae wondering how Harry had followed them from the parking structure attached to her firm's building to the mall. After she'd taken the elevator to the top floor. Her boss asking her where she was, what she was doing, and who she was doing it with, when all he should have been interested in was whether or not her work was getting done. And Harry and company in that same parking structure, Kemp letting the car idle on the top floor? That took it beyond coincidence. Especially when he recalled Annie wondering how the mastermind had found out about their group.

"Shut up," he snapped at Kemp, pissed at himself because if he'd been in his right mind he'd have made the connection that day. And sure, it might be far-fetched that a CPA was behind the counterfeiting, and he didn't have anything but coincidence and supposition to go on, but it made too much sense to ignore. He considered calling Mike to run it by him, but he knew Mike would tell him not to break an ankle jumping to conclusions. And he couldn't take the time because Rae was probably sitting at her desk, in the office of the head counterfeiter.

Hell, finding her sitting at her desk would be a relief. All he had to do was get there.

chapter
29

ANNIE AND NELSON HAD DRIVEN RAE TO HER
house to get her files and change into something work-
appropriate. It felt good to be in a skirt and suit jacket
again, to be sitting behind her desk. Being able to concentrate would have been a nice bonus, but she was
fighting her way through the brain bounce without
dwelling on her relationship with Conn. It helped to focus on the bright side, which, surprisingly, wasn't all
that difficult to find.

The past week had been a revelation—not that she
wanted to be chased around by homicidal goofballs—but,
in a weird way, she'd kind of enjoyed it. Sure, there'd
been fear, but there'd been excitement, too, and she could
stand a little of that in her life. Rae had no clear idea what
that meant, but she could say with certainty that a partnership with P.I.G. wasn't it. In the meanwhile, though, she
had a job to do. Conn might not need her, but her clients
did.

She finished putting her files away and got down to
work. Having a goal always settled her. Step one was
getting her clients' quarterly taxes done, and then she'd

move on to step two. Step two was TBD. To Be Determined. And figuring that out, she decided was going to be half the fun.

Still, when her cell rang, she pounced on it. Flying without a net was still a new, and not entirely comfortable, concept. "Conn?" she said, plugging her other ear because she was having a hard time hearing him.

His voice was muffled, but she thought she heard him yell, "Shut the fuck up," followed by a few seconds of silence before he came back on the line, loud and clear. "I want you out of there," he said.

"I can't. My parents went to the mall to 'wallow in American consumerism,' as my dad put it. Mom planned to drag him around all morning, and I promised I'd get one of the assistants to drop me there so I could meet them at the food court for lunch, which isn't for another hour. Why do you want me to leave now?"

And then she made the leap. "You think one of the partners here is a counterfeiter? Or all of them? Not possible, especially Ibold, since he's about eighty years old." But she listened to him repeat what he'd gotten from Kemp, and she felt a chill snake down her spine. It could be Putnam or Greenblatt.

"Did you tell them about your parents?" Conn asked her.

"Not right away, but I wear things made from my father's cloth . . . blouses, scarves. I couldn't tell you the specific date, or even what piece of clothing it was, but I remember an assistant asked me once where I shopped, and I told her my father made textiles, using organic dyes. And what the assistants know, the partners know."

"Right. You have to leave."

"Because they know about my blouses? That's not proof."

"We can worry about proof later. I'm calling your parents—"

"No. It'll only raise questions if they show up here again. I'll leave."

"Promise me," Conn said.

"I promise I'll leave," Rae replied without hesitation. She just didn't say when.

IF ONE OF HER BOSSES WAS BEHIND THE COUNTER-feiting, Rae needed to know, and while she was at it, she could collect the evidence Conn would need to prove it. Of course, it also meant she'd gotten her parents into this mess, not the other way around. But she'd deal with that when she had to.

Ibold never came into the office anymore. Putnam had gone to a meeting downtown, and Greenblatt had taken the morning off to handle some personal business. The assistants had scattered as soon as the bosses left the building. She didn't blame them. They were kept on a pretty tight leash, especially this time of the year; the only break they got besides a half-hour lunch was when the partners were away.

Rae picked up a couple of files, just in case, and went to Putnam's office, slipping inside without being seen. She locked the door behind her and dropped the files. None of his desk drawers were locked, neither was his file cabinet. She rifled through them, careful not to leave any sign of a disturbance. She found nothing indicating he was involved in a criminal enterprise. The top of his desk was immaculate, but she checked behind his computer screen, on the sides of the hard drive, under his blotter, lifting his keyboard in the process. *Bingo*.

All the computers in the firm were hooked into a cen-tral hard drive system, the V drive, the virtual vault where every client's financial records were kept. Some of those files, the ones for their biggest clients, were password protected. A small square of paper was taped to the un-derside of Putnam's keyboard. On it were all his pass-words.

Rae jotted them down on one of the file folders she'd brought with her and hurried back to her desk, worried more about speed than anyone seeing her come out of Putnam's office. She signed out of her user ID and signed in under his, opening the protected files and searching through them as thoroughly as she could with one eye on the clock. She found nothing unusual, no files for clients she didn't recognize—nothing in those files raised a red flag.

Even Putnam's personal accounts were clean, as far as she could tell. The balances were impressive, but she could tie his income to the firm's income with no trouble. She ran through the firm's books again, and stuck with her first assessment. Profits were down year after year, the firm investment fund had really taken a beating on the stock market, and considering that she knew most of P.I.G.'s business, it was clear that Putnam wasn't laundering counterfeit money through his legitimate operations. Which made no sense.

She could understand why he didn't wash all the money through P.I.G.'s accounts. There had to be thousands, and in the current economy—and especially in Michigan, one of the hardest hit states—it would raise IRS eyebrows if their business wasn't suffering. But some of that counterfeit money should have been funneled through the firm; it was just too damn convenient not to do it.

She sneaked into Morris Greenblatt's office, but he was more careful with his passwords, so she was stymied there. All the clients' files were in the vault . . . in the vault. She got to her feet and ran into Mr. Putnam's office again, retrieved a key from his top desk drawer, and took it to a room next door, also called the vault. Depending on who you talked to, the physical vault was either a small storage room or a big closet. Since all the current work was done on computer, it wasn't used much anymore except as an archive for the pre-electronic and current printed records they had to keep on hand in case of audit.

Several aisles of storage shelves filled the room, four high, packed with twenty-five years' worth of boxes. Time was short, but she fought the urge to tear into the first row, asking herself instead where she would've put something she wanted to keep hidden but lay her hands on quickly. Not the bottom or top shelves, not the aisle with the most recent records. She eased down the narrow passage along the wall, going all the way to the back and working her way forward.

She didn't do a box-by-box search, just looked for the unusual. She found it in the third aisle from the back, a box that, unlike all the others, wasn't dust-covered. She opened it and on top lay an old-fashioned ledger, bound in heavy brown cardboard and filled with green ledger pages. The entries were from 1977, but when she lifted it to put it aside, a little rectangular USB flash drive fell out of the spine. And her heart began to pound.

She ran back to her office and shut the door, dropping the ledger she hadn't realized she'd brought along on the floor next to her chair, and tossing the drive on her desk like a hot potato. She stared at it for a full minute, and when she could breathe again, when her stomach dropped out of her throat, she plugged the drive into her computer, put her hand on the wireless mouse on its under-the-desktop shelf, and accessed the drive. Up popped a password prompt.

If she'd had to guess between the two active partners, she'd have pegged Putnam for the guilty party over Greenblatt any day, if only because Morris Greenblatt had always been nice to her, and Putnam didn't have a friendly bone in his body. What surprised her was that none of Putnam's passwords worked. So she tried them again. And struck out again. She blew out a breath, glancing at the cell phone sitting on her desk—the cell phone with Conn's number in it. She didn't figure he was any more of a computer expert than she was, but he had a lot more experience at this espionage stuff. And he'd tell her to get her backside out of there.

Conn was right, but she couldn't walk away, even with that USB drive in her hand. The authorities would certainly be able to get around the password lock, but as soon as the drive was found missing all other evidence would be destroyed. Rae wanted to make damn sure the guilty party went down, and since her career of choice involved balancing accounts to the penny, and she'd spent many a night doing just that, she put her faith in her own expertise, making absolutely sure she had proof of who was behind the counterfeiting before she walked out the door and lost her last opportunity.

Putnam's usual passwords weren't working, and she didn't have Greenblatt's. And maybe she didn't need them. She tried the obvious tie-ins: *counterfeit, Renaissance, mastermind*, nothing worked. She sat back again, thought of Conn, then put him and everything else out of her mind, her eyes landing on the ledger sitting next to her chair. She stared at it absently, not really seeing it until she ran out of other possibilities. And then it struck her that something didn't fit.

She picked up the ledger and set it on her desk, flipping through the pages and frowning, not really sure she was seeing what she was seeing. She took a deep breath, typed in a password, and the file opened up.

Rae started working her way through the files, following the trail, like Hansel and Gretel's breadcrumbs. "Dammit," she said as the picture started to form, "dammit, dammit, *dammit*."

"Something wrong?"

Rae looked up and practically fell out of her chair. "No, Mr. Greenblatt," she said, her hand creeping to the mouse. "Everything is fine." She shut the files down and kept clicking, watching the screen in her peripheral vision so she could keep her focus on Morris Greenblatt.

His eyes dropped to the ledger sitting open on her desk, and she knew that he knew she'd found the flash drive.

"You're really too smart for your own good," Greenblatt said cheerfully.

"You're not going to try to convince me I'm wrong?"

"What would be the point? You've already seen the files. And you were never leaving here anyway."

"What's that supposed to mean?" she asked, hoping to buy herself a few seconds more. Her phone was on the left side of her desk, away from the door and behind her computer monitor where Greenblatt couldn't see it. She inched her hand over it and hit the callback, the phone dialing Conn since his was the last number.

She heard Conn's voice, but Greenblatt heard it, too, and for a small, round man with really short legs he could move pretty damn fast. She lifted the phone to her ear, trying to get out from behind her desk and talk at the same time, not doing either well because Greenblatt got to her first, snatching the phone and shoving her back into her chair. And she didn't remember what she'd said. Or if Conn had even heard her.

RAE HAD PROMISED TO LEAVE THE OFFICE. CONN knew her track record with following instructions, which was why he'd climbed behind the wheel of Kemp's U-Haul and headed straight to Troy. The engine ran rough and loud, but every now and then he heard a thump from the back of the truck when he rounded a corner or stopped short. That would be Kemp. Conn probably should have felt bad about it, but then he could have left the guy tied to a tree.

He tried to call Rae; she didn't pick up, so he gave it five minutes and tried again. Nothing. He kept calling every few minutes, getting more desperate, almost desperate enough to blow through the next red light. He didn't, the overused truck shuddering to a stop on bald tires. Kemp started yelling, just as Conn's phone rang.

He slammed his fist into the back of the cab and shouted, "Shut the fuck up," as he answered his phone with the other hand.

"Conn," Rae said, "I'm still at the office. It's—"

"What?" Conn said, struggling to hear over the engine. "Rae? *Shit*." The call disconnected, and he panicked. It was a new feeling for him.

He sat at the light, even after it turned green, ignoring the honking horns of the motorists behind him, trying to call Rae back with no luck and then fighting to think. He had to get control, had to put himself back in a cold, emotionally dead place. Otherwise they wouldn't get through this.

But emotional death was beyond him. He hit the gas, shooting through the light just as it turned red, wringing every bit of horsepower from the moving van, in complete disregard for the speed limit until he got to the highway interchange, then taking the ramp for I-75 practically on two wheels.

Conn forced himself to run the facts like it was any other case. *I'm still at the office.* That's what Rae had said. She'd been about to tell him the identity of the mastermind when the call cut off, which meant she'd probably been incapacitated in some way. *Dammit*, she should have listened to him—

He cut that thought off, took the anger, and the fear, and forced them under a layer of calm so he could think. If she'd been taken, her captor would have her cell. And Conn's number was the last one dialed.

He stopped trying to call Rae. It was the hardest thing he'd ever done, but he put the phone on the seat beside him and waited. It rang, just as the exit sign for Big Beaver Road came into sight.

He flipped the phone open, and a muffled voice said, "I want the plates or the girl dies."

"Very dramatic," Conn said, swinging the van off the highway, heading for Rae's office building because he didn't know where else to go. "One problem. I hand over the plates and she's dead anyway. Me, too."

"Oh, well, uh . . ."

Okay, definitely a man, but not Harry or Joe or Kemp. He had to be talking to the mastermind, Conn thought, working hard again not to lose it at the idea of Rae being held against her will, maybe hurt— "Let me talk to Rae."

"No."

"I hear her voice in the next ten seconds," Conn said, "or I call my handler and turn over the plates, and the printing press. And Kemp. How long do you think it will be before he talks?"

"He doesn't know anything."

"He knew enough for me to narrow my search down to your firm."

"What firm?"

"Putnam, Ibold, and Greenblatt. I know Harry Mosconi went there for a check to fix the glass in his Honda, and since Rae said Ibold has one foot in the grave it must be Putnam or Greenblatt."

The call disconnected.

"Shit." Conn redialed.

No answer.

He wheeled the U-Haul into the parking structure drive, realized at the last minute that it wouldn't fit inside, and slid it to a stop across the two lanes comprising the entrance and exit, barely missing a Buick that slipped out in front of the U-Haul at the last second. A Lexus pulled up at the exit, the driver giving the horn a brief little hey-you're-blocking-the-exit toot. When Conn jumped out of the van, the Lexus's window whirred down and a sour-looking woman peered out.

"I'm going to call the police," she said.

Conn kept walking, throwing, "You do that," over his shoulder as he passed her car by.

He hit the elevator, hands on the door so when they parted at Rae's floor he was through before they'd opened all the way. He shoved through the glass doors etched with P.I.G., skirted the receptionist's desk and worked his way through the suite. Until he came to Rae's office. He stopped there, caught by the light, fresh scent of her perfume on the air, seeing her in the little touches. Rae considered herself a number cruncher, cool, all business. But she was also a woman who hung brightly colored suncatchers full of dried flowers in her window, and draped a swatch of what he assumed was one of her father's woven textiles over the file cabinet in her office. She was a woman who'd taken in a complete stranger who needed help, and wanted her parents to see her as the person she'd become, not the child they'd raised. And she was a woman who'd been let down by all three of them.

Conn couldn't speak for Annie and Nelson, but he sure

as hell wasn't letting her down again. He put his feet in motion, finding four women of various ages gathered in the front of the suite. They drew back a little when he came toward them.

"Any of you know where Rae Blissfield is?" he asked them. "Is there anyone around besides secretaries?"

One of the women drew herself up, clearly insulted. "We're not secretaries," she said.

"We're administrative assistants," another chimed in helpfully.

"You can call yourself Topsy and spin in circles for all I care, I just want to know where Rae Blissfield went."

"Oh," the helpful administrative assistant said. "She left with Mr. Greenblatt about ten minutes ago. He said they had a meeting."

Conn didn't bother to ask where. He slammed through the doors, took the elevator back down, and found a Troy police officer talking to the Lexus driver.

"There he is," she crowed.

The cop straightened away from the car window, putting himself in Conn's path.

Conn flipped his badge out of his pocket and flashed it at the cop. "FBI," he said, giving the cranky old bat in the Lexus a dismissive glance.

The officer hooked a thumb in the general direction of the U-Haul. "Is there somebody in the back of that thing?"

"Yeah." Conn took the keys out of his pocket, stripped one off the ring, and flipped it to the cop. "Hang onto him for me, would you?"

He didn't wait for an answer, going around the truck and getting into the police cruiser. The officer followed him, his hand hovering over his sidearm.

"You gonna shoot me?" Conn asked him.

The cop blew out a breath. "No, but I'll need an explanation for my squad commander."

Conn gunned the engine. "My mission is classified. But I'll try not to hurt your car." And he took off, tires squealing, half his focus on the road, the other half on the computer, looking up Morris Greenblatt's address.

It wasn't far, and he didn't expect to find Rae there. But he had to look, just like he had to check out Harry Mosconi's place—no Rae, but it wasn't empty, either. A woman answered the door, late thirties, pretty, a couple of kids in the ten-to-fifteen age bracket behind her, all three of them staring at the police cruiser but keeping their curiosity to themselves.

As soon as he saw her he knew Rae wasn't there. Mosconi's wife screamed PTA, home-baked cookies, and bedtime stories. The kids were well-behaved, the house was neat as a pin, hell, even the dog sniffed him politely then sat and wagged its tail.

Nice family, Conn thought as he headed back to the car. It was a shame Harry was going to jail for the rest of his life.

Harry's wife supplied Joe's last name, along with Kemp's, since they were cousins. The police computer gave him the locations. Conn was on his way when his cell rang. He picked it up, fumbling it a little, before he managed to answer.

"Conn? It's Annie."

Even if he'd checked the readout he still would have taken their call. He had no clue what to tell Rae's parents, but he couldn't leave them hanging.

"I can't get Rae," Annie was saying, a little breathless and nerved up. "She's not answering her cell or her office phone, and she didn't meet us—"

"Let me talk to Nelson," Conn said, her worry too much to handle on top of his own. "There's a police station not far from the mall," he said when Nelson came on the line. "Go there and wait for me."

"But—"

"Don't go inside. Don't even get out of the car. I'll be there in about an hour." Unless he found Rae. He'd have some major ass-kicking to do then. It would probably delay him a few minutes.

He grinned. Having a target for all the emotional crap jumping around inside him was a nice little fantasy that put him almost back to normal again. Normal being really pissed off, especially when he got to Joe's house, a little bungalow it took five minutes to search and find deserted.

The same went for Kemp's hole-in-the-wall apartment, although it proved harder to rule out. The place was a garbage scow, one room of trash and smell, except for the bathroom, and if it was as ill-kept as the rest of the place, and Rae was in there, she'd be screaming bloody murder unless . . .

Conn found himself at the bathroom door with no consideration for whether or not he was up to date on his tetanus booster. The bathroom was empty. Unless he counted bacterial life.

He stood there a moment, struggling with the urge to trash the place, not that anyone would notice. He forced himself to think instead, but there was no reason he couldn't move, too. He went out to the cruiser and headed back toward Troy, which let him feel like he was doing something even if he wasn't. That was pretty much where the forward progress ended. Until he made it back to the Troy police station and had a brilliant idea.

He pointed the cruiser toward Rae's Jaguar, parked in the corner of the lot farthest from the door. Annie and Nelson were out of the Jag before he made it into the next parking space. Conn got out and held up a hand. They stopped in their tracks. He kept walking, across the parking lot, through the front door, only stopping for the cop on desk duty, one Sergeant Melnick, because it wouldn't help him to piss off the locals.

He held up his badge and said, "I'm here to collect the prisoner you're holding for me. Kemper Salerno."

"The guy from the U-Haul?"

"Yeah."

"The U-Haul my officer had to drive in here because you commandeered his squad car?"

"It was an emergency," Conn said.

"And here I thought it was just another fed clusterfuck."

Conn took a deep breath. Even if he could have gotten the words out, an apology would have thrown off the en-

tire federal/local dynamic it had taken decades to establish. "You've got no reason to hold him," he said.

"Guantanamo Bay mean anything to you?"

"Okay, so we have a track record. You gonna hand
him over or what?"

Melnick gave it some thought, then gestured Conn to
follow him. "Like you said, we got no reason to hold him."

They went into the bowels of the station, arriving at
the holding cells. Melnick instructed the guard on duty to
retrieve Kemp. He came back empty-handed.

"Prisoner refuses to come out of the cell," he said.
"Guy says he'll confess to anything we want as long as
we don't make him go with the fed."

Conn exchanged a look with Melnick, who said, "You
want him, go get him." The other cop was helpful enough
to hold out the key to Kemp's cell.

Conn took it, consigning Kemp to the lowest level of
hell for making him into a laughingstock.

Kemp was huddled on the cot in his cell, completely
covered by a gray, industrial-grade blanket that couldn't
begin to camouflage his doughy form.

"Get your ass out of there," Conn said, unlocking the
door.

"No."

Conn went into the cell, hauled Kemp off the cot, and
shoved him toward the door. Kemp fisted his hands around
the bars at either side of the door, so Conn pinched the
nerves in his shoulders until his hands spasmed and let go,
flopping uselessly at the ends of his arms.

Kemp braced his feet in the opening and dropped onto
his ass. And he began to shout. "Help!" he yelled. "He
tied me to a tree. He's going to torture me."

Conn hauled Kemp upright by the collar of his shirt,
planted his foot on Kemp's ass, and shoved with every
ounce of muscle he possessed. Kemp shot out of the cell
like a champagne cork, bounced off the opposite wall, and
fell on his face.

"Looks like torture to me," Melnick said, having come
into the holding cell area to watch the show.

The guard nodded solemnly.

Kemp got on all fours and tried to dive between Conn's legs, back into the cell. Conn scissored his legs together, trapping Kemp at the neck. He gurgled a little, so Conn caught him by the waistband of his jeans and hauled him back out into the narrow hallway.

"Jesus," he said, "I just want you to make a phone call."

Kemp rolled on to his back and peered up. "Promise you won't hurt me?"

"Yeah." But he didn't tell Kemp who was waiting for him in the parking lot. He did handcuff him.

They got to the car, Annie stepped out, and Kemp tried to run. Conn took him by the collar and cuffs and stuffed him into the backseat of the Jaguar, following him in.

"Where to?" Nelson asked.

"Holly Grove. There's a tree there with Kemp's name on it. Unless he makes this phone call."

Annie turned around and looked at Kemp; that was all it took. Conn had been in some nasty situations in his life, but confronted with that face, he had to admit he'd do whatever was asked of him.

He handed Kemp his own cell, retrieved along with the rest of his personal effects. Kemp dialed and handed the phone to Conn.

"You didn't have to use Kemp's phone for the caller ID," Harry said once Conn had identified himself. "I would have picked up for you."

"Just covering all my bases," Conn said. He'd needed to retrieve Kemp anyway, and frankly he was tired of coming up empty-handed. Harry knew Kemp was in custody, and Kemp would rat him out without a second thought.

"My wife says you were at the house."

"You have a nice family," Conn said.

"You're not married to her. I'm already in hot water, and she doesn't even know what I did yet."

"What if I offered you a way to cool that water off?"

"You want me to find out where your girlfriend is."

"Yeah," Conn said, not even wincing at the label. He

had bigger problems than how the bad guys characterized his relationship with Rae.

"I'll try," Harry was saying, "but Greenblatt has gone berserk. He wants the plates and he's not exactly trusting us to get them for him."

"So is that a yes?"

"Can you keep me out of jail?"

"I can't promise that."

Harry was silent.

"You could disappear," Conn said.

"Either way I'm gone from my family, but at least I'd be free."

"But you'd still have to live with your conscience."

chapter
30

IT WAS DARK, ALMOST PITCH-BLACK, AND QUIET except for the rattle of the chain around her ankle when Rae shifted position. She was hunched on a lumpy mattress covered with a dirty blanket that had stopped making her skin crawl days ago. At least she thought it was days. It could have been hours or weeks, hard to measure time in the complete absence of light and sound.

One thing she knew, she was never going to hear the words *solitary confinement* again and envy the recipient a chance to get away from it all. Sensory deprivation was bad enough; being alone with her own thoughts for hours on end was torture. If she'd been a wolf, she'd have chewed off her foot by now. Not that she minded being in her own head, but she was a make-lemonade-out-of-lemons kind of person, a woman who needed to act in the face of adversity. It was damned hard to find anything positive about her predicament, and impossible to take action shackled to a bed.

Her parents must be frantic, and Conn . . . Best not to think about him. If anything would push her over the edge, it was the stew of emotions that made up her rela-

tionship with Connor Larkin, and her inability to sort
them out, let alone articulate them—and not because she
had a problem speaking her mind. Because she had a
problem speaking her heart.

Not something she would need to worry about unless
she got free, which wasn't likely to happen anytime soon.
Short of chewing off her foot.

She was imprisoned in Hans Lockner's small trailer, one
room, except for the bathroom. All the windows were covered, and her chain wasn't long enough to reach any of
them. The tiny bathroom had no windows at all, and she
only got in there when Morris Greenblatt let her. Not that
she had to use it much. He'd drugged her the first time she
ate, so she hadn't been eating, only drinking water when
she could get into the bathroom and get it straight from the
tap. And yelling hadn't gotten her anything but a sore
throat, and eventually another look at Greenblatt's gun.

It galled her. All of it. From the moment Morris had
come into her office and held her at gunpoint, she'd felt
like a failure. The man was six inches shorter than her,
sixty pounds overweight, and he'd probably burst a blood
vessel if he had to run more than ten feet. But Smith &
Wesson were the great equalizers, and she'd found herself
out of the office and in the backseat of his car, hands and
feet secured, gagged, and shoved over sideways.

She'd struggled upright just as Morris drove them out
of the parking structure, barely missing getting creamed
by a U-Haul pulling in. Shame, she thought now, as she
had then. If the U-Haul had hit them she'd probably be in
the hospital, but at least she wouldn't be a hostage on the
verge of death. And as if that wasn't enough, she was
spending her last hours in the place she detested the most:
the Renaissance festival. Close enough to feel Conn's
presence, but no way to get to him.

Frustration was the least of what she was feeling; there
was a cold, murderous rage building inside her, and it
wasn't all aimed at her captor.

Greenblatt had left his car in the overflow lot, a mile
away through thick woods, and walked her into the night,

keeping a death grip on her arm and the gun shoved into her ribs. She might have fought back under other circumstances, but in the pitch dark, on uneven ground, there'd been a pretty good chance he'd shoot her accidentally one of the times he stumbled. And he'd stumbled a lot. She had the bruises to prove it. Considering his frame of mind, she was lucky she wasn't dead. He'd been on the edge when he kidnapped her, as the days passed and he didn't get what he wanted; she could all but smell the desperation. She'd never understood that phrase before, but now she knew it was a combination of sweat, stale cologne, and clothing that hadn't been changed in a long, long time.

A light flipped on, Greenblatt's distinct shape just a silhouette against it. "Take these."

Rae blinked and held up a hand, but he didn't wait for her eyes to adjust before he tossed a bundle of clothing into her lap.

She unwound the bundle and held it up, rolling her eyes. "No. Way," she said, her voice rusty. It wasn't enough to be held prisoner for a week in a ratty trailer where the only alone time she got was in a windowless bathroom. It wasn't enough to be chained to a filthy bed in a pitch-black room while he sat there in the dark . . . breathing and creeping her out almost the entire time. It wasn't enough that she, a person who counted things for a living, didn't even know what day it was, that she was practically dying of thirst and starvation, all the while she was mere feet from Conn and her parents, with no hope of rescue. Now she had to dress like a wench?

Morris cocked his gun.

"Go ahead," she said, "you're going to kill me anyway." She could see the struggle on his face. He didn't plan on letting her out of this alive, but he needed her cooperation. And her only hope was to get out of the trailer.

"If you promise to behave," Morris said, "you can take a shower."

She cut her eyes toward the bacteria breeding ground that was the trailer's bathroom. "In there?"

"That or nothing."

Rae heaved a breath. "Unlock me."

"Uh-uh." He tossed her the key.

She unlocked the cuff around her ankle and looked up at him.

He met her stare, moved his gun hand an inch to the right, and squeezed off a shot.

Rae eyed the tiny spot of anemic daylight coming through the new hole in the wall and decided she wasn't okay with dying. At least not unless she could take Morris Greenblatt with her.

She showered in the stingy trickle of water, careful not to touch the sides, then let herself air dry, and although she nearly froze to death, she used the time to wrack her brain again. Her brain let her down, not that she blamed it; she just didn't have the frame of reference it took to deal with an armed and desperate counterfeiter. She did, Rae thought, have the ability to adapt to circumstance and take advantage of opportunity. And she had a little desperation of her own to draw on.

She slipped into the wench dress; she despised it, but at least it was clean. Morris, when she joined him, looked ridiculous in tunic and tights. Except for the gun he held under cover of his cape. The gun looked pretty damn serious, especially as the smell of cordite still hung on the fetid air.

He held out a plastic tie. Rae bit down on her frustration and took it, putting it around her wrists and letting Morris tighten it.When he came at her with a gag, though, she balked.

"I'll behave, I promise."

"I can't risk it," Morris said.

"Why don't you call this off? I won't say anything. Neither will my parents or anyone else. They'll go to jail if they talk."

It sounded reasonable to Rae, even if it was her idea. Morris seemed to consider it, too, but just when she began to have hope, he shook his head.

"Too late for that. It was too late when your boyfriend got involved."

"He's not my boyfriend."

"You better hope he has feelings for you, because I'm trading you for the plates."

"He won't give them up."

"Then I'm sorry for you."

"Not sorry enough to overcome your greed and selfishness."

"I can't go to jail."

"Let me loose and you won't have to."

Morris studied her face for a minute, smirking at what he saw there. "You think you can kill me with your bare hands?" he asked her. "It's not as easy as you think, killing."

"No," Rae said, "it just takes a certain kind of person."

He rubbed his forehead, ashamed, and Rae attacked, leading with all her fury and fear and hopelessness. It wasn't much of a struggle, not with her hands tied, but she got in a couple good hits. She was also gagged before it was all over, but Morris was limping. And she hadn't gotten shot, which she took as a minor miracle since he'd never let go of the gun.

He shoved her out the door, into a sunrise that had barely limped over the horizon only to disappear beneath an unrelieved layer of heavy, gray clouds. It was chilly and drizzling, and not much light made it through the canopy of dead leaves still on the trees.

Morris walked her around the outside of the faire grounds. Rae kept her eyes on where she was placing her feet, until he stopped, and then she looked up—way up—and said, "You have got to be kidding."

CORNELIA FERDIC WAS A MAN. BETTER YET, SHE WAS a man with a past, and that past was counterfeiting. Frederick Cornelius, aka Cornelia Ferdic, had spent eighteen and a half years of a twenty-five-year sentence in federal prison for a bogus set of twenty-dollar-bill plates so good they were on display at the Bureau of Engraving and Printing in Washington, D.C. He'd only gotten better in the last quarter century. He'd come out of the closet, too, but going around in drag didn't hamper his skill with metal, and it had turned out to be a pretty good red herring.

Mike's call about Cornelia wound up being the high point of a week Conn spent moving a hundred miles an hour and getting nowhere fast. Greenblatt had completely dropped out of his own life, and Harry had proven to be no help whatsoever. Hans Lockner had fallen off the radar, only to reappear in a hospital psych ward. He'd been dumped at the emergency room entrance by some well-meaning friend who hadn't stuck around long enough to offer an explanation as to how Hans had gotten comatose on a combination of alcohol and Ecstasy, leaving the doctors to suspect suicide. Conn had a feeling Greenblatt's Stooges might have been involved.

None of it brought him any closer to finding Rae.

Annie and Nelson weren't giving him hell, but he felt it every time he saw the hope and anguish in their eyes. They blamed themselves. Conn knew he was really at fault. He'd screwed up this operation from start to finish. Getting Rae hurt, a woman he . . . Getting a civilian hurt would only be the capper.

A sleepless Friday night rolled into an overcast Saturday morning. The temperature had dropped into the forties, and all the leaves seemed to have fallen from the trees overnight. When Conn's phone rang he was prowling the faire grounds not long after the place opened for the day at ten A.M. His gut was already talking, big-time, so he didn't bother to check the phone's display.

It was no surprise to hear Morris Greenblatt's voice. What surprised Conn was the wave of fury, so violent it hazed his vision with red and had his hands fisting. The crack of the phone he was on the verge of crushing brought him back, far enough to keep him from destroying his one connection to Rae.

"Did you hear me?" Morris asked, sounding impatient.

"You're bringing Rae to the faire grounds around noon," Conn repeated. "Where should I meet you?"

"You'll know. Bring the plates." And Morris disconnected.

Conn made a phone call, said, "Holly Grove, now," and hung up without waiting for a response. He was halfway back to the Airstream when he ran into Nelson Bliss.

Nelson took one look at his face and said, "Now?"

"Greenblatt said noon. I don't know about you, but I don't trust him."

"He has to get in," Nelson pointed out needlessly.

"There are too many ways into the place," Conn said. "We can't cover them all."

"The hell we can't." Nelson took off at a slow run, already on his phone and barking orders.

He made one call after another, not stopping to let Conn in on the game plan as he went from booth to booth handing out instructions.

"What can I do?" Conn finally asked, dragging him to a stop.

"You can sit back and let me handle this."

"I can't—"

Nelson grasped him by the upper arms, giving him a little shake. "We got our daughter into this," he said, on the ragged edge of control himself but doing a hell of a lot better job at handling the craziness than Conn was doing. "You've done everything you can. This is our place, these are our people. Let us do this, Conn."

By the time they got back to the Airstream an hour later, there was a crowd of re-enactors surrounding the picnic table. Annie came into the clearing, lugging a box that turned out to hold a stack of flyers depicting Rae as a damsel in distress being held by the "vyle crymynal" Morris Greenblatt. A reward was offered, a list of booths given, and Nelson handed Conn a stack of flyers.

"Now you can help," he said. "We passed these out to the parking attendants."

"He wouldn't tell me to meet him here if he didn't

have a way in that allowed him to avoid the cops and parking attendants and the people at the entrance. Hell, maybe they're already here." The thought of it, the notion that Rae was already there, right under his nose, had him fighting off a desperate stew of emotion, the urge to put his fist through something.

"That's why we're offering a reward for the tourists. These flyers are already being handed out with the maps and pamphlets distributed at the entrance, and they're being hung at every booth. He's not getting by us."

Conn scrubbed his hands through his hair, swallowing back the rage, not fighting it off but shoving it down deep, to a place that was cold because rage, ice-cold fury, was a hell of a weapon and he wanted to be able to pull it out when he needed it most.

Annie and Nelson went out into the festival: Nelson to loiter at the public entrance, Annie to stake out the participant's gate. The crowds were thin, owing to the weather, but not as thin as they would have been if it hadn't been the last weekend of the festival.

Conn the Armorer walked the faire, systematically, covering every inch of ground, even looking into the back rooms of the booths, as he worked his way from the front grounds to the back. He wore his buff-colored leather pants, the boots—with knives in either one, and a brown leather vest, and a sword—a real one, and to hell with the rules that stated no one could carry a real weapon. Morris Greenblatt would sure as hell be armed. Not that it was going to matter.

He carried the plates in a leather bag slung crosswise over his shoulder, hiding the gun stuffed into his waistband. He drew a lot of looks from the paying guests, most of them female. Everything seemed normal, including his rising frustration level, and then he noticed a steady stream of foot traffic heading toward the back of the place. Not that unusual, since that was where the joust took place, and the joust was a big draw for the crowds. Except the joust wasn't for another two hours.

"What's going on?" Conn asked one of the tourists passing by.

"There's a medieval weapons demonstration at noon."

"Right." He was supposed to be demonstrating the longsword. His heart began to race, his gut telling him he was in the right place at the right time.

He kept to a walk, a fast one, his long legs taking him in the direction of the crowd. Behind the last line of food booths at the far end of the jousting grounds a gate led to an open area surrounded by sparse woods.

Conn rounded the corner and stopped dead. Racks set up along the back of the row of booths held swords and crossbows, maces, war hammers, battle axes, and the first primitive bombs that were hand-worked metal shells filled with dynamite that had to be placed by hand at the base of a castle wall in order to be effective.

What caught Conn, what everyone stared at, was a catapult, a siege engine used to throw really big rocks at castle walls. In more recent years they'd been used by performance artists to toss everything from washing machines to cows. He had the feeling, though, that the living thing struggling in the catapult's basket wasn't bovine. His blood ran cold when he spotted Morris Greenblatt by the trigger. Harry Mosconi stood behind Morris.

Conn made eye contact with Harry. Harry looked away. No help there.

Rae popped up in the basket, gagged, hands secured behind her.

"Hand over the plates, and I'll let her go," Morris said.

Conn dragged his gaze off Rae, met Greenblatt's eyes. "We both know that's a lie."

Greenblatt took a step back, but he didn't get far enough from the catapult for Conn to feel like he could get there first.

"Hey," someone in the crowd shouted, "that the guy from the wanted poster?" The rest of the onlookers started to mutter about the reward.

Greenblatt edged closer to the trigger, looking like he

thought a distraction might be in order before the crowd got any more unruly. "I want the plates."

"No."

"Just give me the plates," Morris said, almost blubbering in desperation. "I'll disappear, everyone will be safe, I promise."

Conn looked up at Rae. She shook her head. They'd always been in accord, but he didn't know if she was telling him not to give up the plates, or if she was saying she knew he couldn't give them up, and she wanted him to think again. Bottom line, it was his decision, and the choice was between her and the job, which meant there was no winning this one. If he chose the operation, he'd lose Rae, and if he chose her, he lost Greenblatt and the plates.

"Don't make me do this," Morris said, dragging Conn back to the only choice that really mattered. Keeping Rae alive and unhurt.

"Nobody's making you do this but you," he said.

"I can't go to jail."

"Whatever happens here today, Morris, you're going to jail. If I don't put you there, someone else will, and they won't need the plates to do it. We have all the players rounded up, and they're all going to testify against you."

"Do it," someone in the crowd yelled, sounding a little worse for a visit to the beer tent, which didn't stop the rest of the tourists from picking up the chant.

It was all Morris Greenblatt needed to hear.

chapter
31

MORRIS'S EYES WERE WHEELING, FROM CONN TO the crowd, dozens of voices shouting some variation of "Let 'er rip." His hand edged toward the trigger, just as Conn raced for the catapult and leaped. The first jump took him onto the six-foot-tall wheel, the second put him on the long arm. From there he scrambled into the basket, scooping Rae into his arms and tearing off her gag.

She worked her jaw, but what came out of her mouth shocked the hell out of him, because what came out of her mouth was "I love you," not "What took you so long," or "I don't need to be rescued," but "I love you." And then she added, "I just wanted you to know. In case we die," so when Morris hit the trigger, and they flew into the air, momentum pushing them back for a split second until the arc was completed and the arm slammed against the crossbar, vaulting them over the heads of the crowd in a roar of sound and swirl of color, Conn should have been estimating their trajectory, judging their landing site, and working out a way to live through it. Instead he was thinking about her, loving him, so that when they skimmed over a row of trees and the ground started rush-

ing up at them he had no more than a split second to twist
around so he hit first, to provide whatever cushion he
could. And to thank God when he saw the pretty little
pond beneath them.

He let Rae go at the last minute, splashing down a
couple feet away, into brackish, weed-choked, frigid water. Conn fought his way toward the light above his head,
broke the surface, and sucked in air as he spun in a circle.
Rae didn't come back up.

He floundered over to the spot he'd seen her go under,
a swirl of mud on the surface telling him he had the right
place as he dove down, reaching around blind in the murk
until his fingers encountered something soft. Lungs
screaming, he dove deeper, buried his hand in that soft-
ness and pulled, kicking for the surface and the air that
was cold enough to cut his lungs like a knife but was still
far better than drowning. Rae broke the surface a second
later, clutching at him and coughing up half the pond.

Conn wrapped his arm around her and struck out for
the shore. It wasn't the best way to conduct a rescue, but
he couldn't bring himself to let her go. He dragged her up
the muddy bank, but she was far from rescued, shivering,
bone white, probably close to hypothermia. He took a
knife out of his boot and cut the bonds on her wrists,
chafing them between his hands to get the blood flowing.

She looked up at him, smiling through tears. "You
chose me over the operation."

"I talked to Harry when you went missing. He's a decent guy, despite everything. I'm pretty sure he dealt with
Morris. It's his only chance to help himself out. He'll still
get arrested, but I promised I'd go to bat for him."

He held out a hand. She ignored it, trying to struggle to
her feet without his help. She made it as far as her knees
before she gave up, and still she didn't turn to him for
assistance.

Conn began to get an inkling he'd done something
wrong.

"Why are you just standing there?" she said. "Go get
Morris. I'm sure Harry has him all tied up for you."

And there it was, Conn thought. She wanted him to put her before the operation and he had . . . Okay, so he'd hedged his bets. "I saved your life," he reminded her, "at risk to my own."

"The water did that."

"Without my extra weight in that basket you'd have overshot the water. Not to mention the part where you were sinking instead of swimming."

"This dress weighs twenty pounds when it's dry. I was tied up in that damn basket for half the day in a soaking drizzle, bound and gagged. And then there's the part where I went into the pond."

"You're welcome," Conn said.

Rae fought the rest of the way upright, bunching up her sodden skirts.

"Your feet are bare."

"Greenblatt took my shoes."

"If you ask nice, I could carry you back to the faire."

"That'll be the day." She set off, picking her way carefully, sucking in a breath every other step because it was impossible not to land on a tree branch or rock hidden by the dead undergrowth.

"Offer still stands," he called after her. "You don't even have to say *pretty please*."

She looked back at him, eyes narrowed.

Conn crossed his arms, but he didn't grin until she turned forward again, laughing outright when he heard her mutter, "Jackass."

In three strides he swept her off her feet, slung her belly down over his shoulder, and carried her back to the open ground around the catapult. The crowd cheered, women sighed, and best of all, Morris was being held by Harry Mosconi and several men, an unexpected side benefit of their wanted poster. Conn hadn't expected the tourists to actually apprehend Greenblatt, just report the sighting. But he'd take it.

He set Rae on her feet, stepping back so the swing she took at him whiffed by and threw her off balance. The onlookers laughed, thinking it was part of the show.

One look at Rae's face would have told them differently, but she directed all her fury at Conn. He understood why she might be irritated, but the murderous depth of her rage baffled him.

"Why are you so mad?" he asked her.

She whipped around, picking her way across the muddy ground to retrieve her shoes from where Greenblatt had stashed them behind the catapult.

Conn caught up to her, took her by the arm. "You're alive, Morris isn't going anywhere, neither is Harry. Kemp is already in custody, and it won't be a problem to pick up Joe."

"Well," she snapped, tugging her arm free. "Everything worked out fine for you. All you have to do is arrest my parents and the others who were coerced into committing the actual crime, and you're all set." And off she went, muddy feet jammed into the Italian leather pumps she must have been wearing a week ago at work, making a sucking sound with every step she took.

She should have looked comical, hell, she should have been steaming, she was so hot. Conn couldn't find it in himself to so much as crack a smile—at the mental picture or the actual one.

"Rae," he called after her with no idea what he could possibly say.

She stopped, looked over her shoulder. "You can't help who you are, Conn, I always knew that." She searched his face, and he knew she was waiting for him to say something.

He closed the distance between them, held her gaze even when he wanted to look away from the pain he saw there. "A lot happened in a short period of time," he began, still searching for the right words. "We were under a lot of pressure, in danger, those things can color your feelings."

"Color your feelings? What feelings are you talking about, exactly?"

"That's what we both need to find out."

"I'm not having any problem identifying my feelings."

"Yeah, neither am I."

A tide of red rushed up her neck and into her face, except for the skin beneath her eyes, which was still bruised-looking. For the first time, he thought about something besides his own fear and frustration, the sense of impotence that had gripped him for the last five days. She must have felt all of that and more, must have wondered when he was going to come for her, and even when he hadn't until it was almost too late, there'd been no recriminations. She'd told him she loved him. And she trusted him. She hadn't put that into words, but her actions said it all.

And what did he do? He laughed at her, ignored her feelings, and then trivialized them. He wanted to fix it, to make her understand that it wasn't as simple as saying the words. He just didn't know how.

"I'm only saying we should both take some time, make sure it wasn't just the danger before we make any big decisions."

She huffed out a soft laugh, but there was no humor in the slight smile on her face. What he saw was pity, and not for her own sake. "If you don't know what you're feeling for me, the answer is nothing."

"That's not true."

"Nothing strong enough to build a relationship on."

"Is that what you want?" he demanded, angry at the way she was looking at him, the sorrow and finality in her voice. "Are you moving to D.C. so you can wait for me between missions?"

"If that was an invitation, you need to work on the delivery."

Conn pressed his lips together, damned if he spoke and damned if he didn't.

"And just for the record, I'm not angling for an invitation. I'm not that pathetic."

Annie stepped between them. "This is silly," she said to Rae. "I know you hate it when I interfere. Conn doesn't like it either, but you need to know how he spent the last week."

"It doesn't matter."

"You're being an ass, too," Annie told him. "You worked around the clock, barely slept, ate nothing, all you thought about was finding Rae."

"It's my job to make sure nobody gets hurt."

"And I'm just another civilian."

He met her eyes. There was a long moment where she thought he would speak, where she *knew* he'd tell her she was wrong. She could see it in his eyes, she told herself, all but read it on his thoughts.

He only nodded.

So much for being in tune with Connor Larkin, she thought as the pain crashed over her in a wave so intense she nearly doubled over and retched.

"He put his life at risk for you, Sunny."

"Mom, *please*."

Annie stepped back.

Rae pushed down the irritation, took a breath that was like swallowing razor blades. The pain steadied her enough to lift her gaze to Conn's. "Thank you for rescuing me. I'm glad you're all right, and I hope—" She swallowed before her voice broke and humiliated her. "—I hope everything works out for you."

"That sounds final."

"Final is what you want."

"I want some time—"

"To convince yourself there's nothing between us. Let me spare you the agonizing. Good-bye."

She stepped back, Annie and Nelson moving to flank her. She could see it pissed Conn off, but she needed the support so she didn't throw herself into his arms and beg him not to leave. In a day filled with humiliations that would be the biggest one of all.

chapter
32

INSTEAD OF GOING TO COLORADO SPRINGS, THEIR usual winter camp, Rae's parents had been living with her while the rest of the case played out—compliments of the federal court system that prohibited them from leaving the state. It wasn't as horrible as she thought it would be. It was horrible in a whole different way. They were finally giving her some space, but there was an unfortunate trade-off.

The federal court was in Flint, once a General Motors boomtown, now fallen on hard times. It wasn't bad enough that they were on their way to her parents' sentencing hearing . . . the shuttered plants and air of quiet dejection never failed to affect them when they drove through the city. Rae, for her part, always thought about what she'd survived and counted her blessings. Her parents took a trip down memory lane, too. Invariably they arrived at a different mental destination.

"I'm sorry, Rae," Annie said. Nelson didn't weigh in verbally, but Rae could feel him radiating guilt.

After six months of mea culpas and silent regret, she'd had enough. "I wish you'd stop apologizing, Mom. And Dad . . . It's not like you did any of this on purpose."

"But we asked you to take Conn in, and then we—I—pushed you at him."

"And I don't have a mind of my own, right? I can't be trusted to make decisions, but if I do make a decision and it turns out to be wrong, I need you to take the blame."

"Rae—"

"No, Dad, just listen. I know you feel responsible for what happened—"

"We are responsible."

"And I had nothing to do with it? Greenblatt hatched this plan after he found out about you and the rest of your group. Because of me, because I took a job with his firm."

That had come out within hours of Morris Greenblatt's arrest, how he'd worked for Putnam and Ibold all those years, not really getting anywhere, even after he'd made partner. How he'd grown more and more disgusted, and more hopeless because, at his age, he was stuck at P.I.G. Morris had already known a guy at the Bureau of Engraving and Printing, a guy with a line on the paper and a fondness for playing the ponies, if not the skill or luck to come out ahead. And then Morris had found out about Rae's parents.

He'd only been spitballing, Morris had said, tossing around what-ifs with his friend. The paper was the hardest part of any counterfeit operation because of the security strip. Get that wrong and the whole thing fell apart, but once that hurdle was crossed it had all fallen into place. Such a pretty picture he hadn't seen how it could go wrong.

"Greenblatt already had that friend at the Treasury—" Nelson began.

"And no way to come up with a set of plates, or get his hands on the dye, until he hired me. And you only agreed to participate after you were threatened."

"Getting you tangled up with Conn—"

"Sure, you're responsible for asking me to take Conn in. But you didn't have all the facts. You were only trying to do what was right. And I could have said no." She caught her mother's eye in the rearview and nearly smiled over her expression. "I could have said no," she repeated. "I didn't, and every time you take responsibility for my decision," *her weakness*, "to get involved with Conn, you put me on the level of a child. It's time for that to stop. I love you, and you'll always be my parents, but I'm nearly thirty years old. I've been on my own for almost half my life and if you can't treat me as a rational, self-sufficient adult—"

"We can," Nelson said, shooting his wife a look over his shoulder. "We will."

"You can't ask us not to worry," Annie said.

Rae did smile then, over the sullen tone of her mother's voice and the touch of warmth it gave her to know they would worry, that they'd never stop caring, and sure, there would be times they'd cross the line between caring and interfering, but that was what family meant, and you took the good with the irritating. "I can't believe I'm about to say this, but it would even be nice if you called me Sunny again. I kind of miss it."

Annie laughed softly. "Well then, Sunny, let's go find out what kind of punishment the federal government has in store for your father and me."

"Nothing if I have anything to say about it." She'd gone to a lot of trouble to get them as much leniency as she could, working with the prosecutor to help close the jail-cell door on Morris Greenblatt in the hope her efforts would gain her parents some consideration. But she wasn't going to say as much and get their hopes up, only to have them destroyed. She knew how that felt.

AS SOON AS THEY WALKED IN THE DOOR, THE FEDeral prosecutor, Johnson DeWitt, drew her aside. Tall, handsome, distinguished, and a very fit late thirties, Rae guessed, he'd been a rock to her over the past weeks, both in giving her a task that allowed her to feel like she was helping her parents, and keeping her informed so the waiting was easier. He'd also made it clear he wouldn't mind providing more of a distraction than work, but he hadn't pushed when Rae kept their relationship strictly business.

And if he stood a bit too close, well, it was flattering, if not a little depressing that she couldn't muster up some sort of nonprofessional interest in such a man. But then, Connor Larkin was a hard act to follow.

"I wanted to thank you again for your help in deciphering Morris Greenblatt's finances," Johnson said. "We would never have gotten the case put together so fast without you."

"I'd been through the records already, that made it easier for me."

"And easier for the forensic accountants. They said you have a real knack for this kind of work."

"I'm just grateful I was allowed to be involved."

"You sort of insisted," he said, but with a smile. "You refused to turn over the files you'd copied unless you could be a part of the investigation into the ring's finances."

"It helped having something useful to do. And you could have made it harder for me, so thank you." Even though the FBI had met her terms, it would have been problematic for DeWitt's case to rely on her assessment of Greenblatt's finances since she had such a personal stake in making him out to be the bad guy. But the FBI's forensic accountants had verified all her findings, and they were the ones who'd testified against Greenblatt and the rest of the conspirators.

Conn appeared a few feet behind DeWitt, and her system took a punch that turned her muscles to jelly and fuzzed her mind, if only for a second or two before irritation put some iron back into her spine. It had been months, but her love for him only seemed to get stronger. His feelings for her, however, seemed to be . . . less intense. He met her eyes, shifted his gaze to the lawyer, then looked away as if they were nothing more than complete strangers.

"Rae? Did you hear me?"

She took a minute to replay the prosecutor's words, thankful when she didn't have to ask him to repeat himself. "Yes, I heard you."

"I hope you'll give it some real consideration."

"I will, thank you."

Her eyes shifted over DeWitt's shoulder again, and this time he turned around as well, and saw Conn lurking down the hall.

"You know, he went to bat for your parents."

"I expected as much. He said he would, and he's a man who keeps his word."

"Yes, well . . ." Johnson looked around at Conn again. "I hope to hear from you soon."

"How about right now?" she said, making a split-second decision. It felt right, though, and she was learning to go with her gut once in a while, not hold back so much.

"Is that a yes?"

"It's a yes."

"Wonderful." His phone rang, he checked the display, and said, "I'll give you a call with the details," turning away to take the call—and leaving her face-to-face with Conn.

He stood there a second, as surprised as she was, and then he pulled his cop face on, his eyes going as flat as his expression. "Big day," he said, shooting a look at her parents. "Greenblatt and his friend at the Bureau of Engraving and Printing have already been sent to jail, along with Lockner and Cornelius. Joe, Kemp, and Harry are being sentenced later this week."

"I heard," she said. "I'm up to speed."

Within hours of their short flight and frigid splash-down, Conn had turned Morris and the plates over to the Secret Service. They'd dispatched agents to pick up the other conspirators and to set a guard on Lockner's hospital room. And they'd arrested her parents. It had been the worst moment of her life, watching them get handcuffed and taken away. Conn had made sure it was done discreetly, but there wasn't enough discretion in the world to erase that picture from her brain.

She'd gone off to change, determined to do whatever it took to bail them out, but the agents had knocked on the door of her parents' Airstream before she was finished.

She'd given her statement—abridged—told them about the files she'd copied onto her work computer, and promised to turn them over if it would help her parents. Not that she'd had a choice.

"They're getting probation," Conn said.

Rae realized she'd been staring at her parents. It wouldn't have taken much for Conn to guess her thoughts.

"The clerk told me," he added.

The very pretty, young clerk who sighed and mooned every time Conn showed up in the courtroom—at least all the times Rae had been there.

"I guess it's all okay then—the arrest, the interrogation, the imprisonment."

"You're determined to see this in the least positive light."

"Isn't that what happened?"

"It's what had to happen."

"Well then." She turned to go tell her parents, looking instead at the hand he rested on her arm, then up into his face.

The cop was gone, and it wasn't slacker calm on his face, either. There was intensity there, raw emotion she couldn't bear to see with her own emotions so raw.

"I'd like to go tell my parents they aren't going to federal prison."

"They already know."

Her eyes flew to his, and she could see the chagrin there, the understanding that he hadn't even left her that much.

"I told them while you were talking to DeWitt," he said, looking uncertain. It was another emotion she'd never seen on his face before.

"He was thanking me for my help in deciphering Greenblatt's books and finding the money."

"Which you did in exchange for leniency for your parents."

"I helped you for nothing." She started to walk away, turned back. "You already know all this, Conn. You've been following the case closer than I have, so why are you asking me . . ." And then it hit her. "You want to know if I accepted a position with the FBI."

"Did you?"

"Why do you want to know? The FBI is a big agency. It's not like we'll ever run into each other."

"What if I want to run into you?"

"Between missions?" She shook her head. "You said it yourself: I'm not that kind of woman."

"What if I wasn't doing fieldwork anymore?"

She snorted softly, amused at the idea of Conn giving up his lifestyle. But she crossed her arms, too, a defensive gesture that wasn't lost on her. She still wasn't over him; she didn't dare add a layer of hope to a solid base of un-requited love. And yet she couldn't help herself. "What if you just say what you have to say, Conn?"

"I'm giving up fieldwork."

That stopped her for a second, but only a second. "Not trying to make up for past sins anymore?"

"I'm staying on as a handler," he said, and the hope she'd been unable to prevent jumped up another notch. "I won't say I've come to terms with what happened, Rae, I probably never will, completely. But even if I forgave myself, this is what I do, and who I am. I like knowing I'm making a difference."

"Why tell me? I mean, I'm glad for your sake, but what do I have to do with it?"

"I love you."

He said it so simply, so sincerely she had to believe him. And the hope in her heart blossomed into love so deep and so strong that what she'd felt before paled by comparison. Music played, angels sang, the sun came out, and all the anger and hurt, the weeks of battling her own heart, disap-peared because he loved her. There had to be something wrong with that, but she just didn't give a damn. Common sense would no doubt sap the glow out of being loved at some future point, decisions would have to be made, and they'd need to be tempered with caution, but she was giv-ing this moment everything she had.

"Took you long enough," she said, taking a step closer.

"If we weren't in the hallway outside the federal court-room where my parents are being sentenced—"

"The hell with where we are." He gathered her into his arms and kissed her, just long enough to make her want more before he pulled away and rested his forehead against hers. "If we weren't in the hallway outside the federal courtroom where your parents are being sentenced . . ." he said. "Although I don't think it's going to take long."

Rae glanced toward the closed doors, surprised to see the hallway was empty. She'd been so focused on Conn she hadn't realized everyone had gone in.

"So what are you doing later on?"

"Well," Rae said, "I think I'll be seeing my parents off. I imagine they'll want to get to Colorado Springs and their winter camp."

"That works for me."

"After that I have to pack."

"Pack?"

"And put my house up for sale—since I took the job Mr. DeWitt offered me about a half hour ago."

"So, you're going to be working at the FBI?"

"Forensic accountant."

"Convenient."

She turned serious. "I didn't do it to be close to you, Conn."

"I know, but it's pretty damn convenient, so I'm hoping you'll want to anyway—be close to me, I mean."

"Possible," she said, grinning as she headed toward the courtroom.

Conn got there first and put a hand on the door. "I said something to you a couple minutes ago. You didn't recip-rocate."

"If we're keeping score, you were behind. And since it took you several months to catch up, consider it pay-back."

He started to pull the door open; she stopped him this time. "You know, Madame Zaretsky's prediction came true. She said you weren't long for this life. I'm glad it only turned out to be a job change."

"Yeah? How glad?"

She slipped her hand into his, gave him a sidelong glance that came along with a little bit of a smirk. "Ask me that question again tonight."

Penny McCall lives in Michigan with her husband, three children, and two dogs, whose lives of leisure she envies, but would never be able to pull off. Her children and husband have come to accept her strange preoccupation with imaginary people. The dogs don't worry about it, as long as they're fed occasionally and allowed to nap on whatever piece of furniture strikes their fancy. Come to think of it, that pretty much goes for the husband, too. Visit her website at www.pennymccall.net.